Visions & Lies

STARGLEN CITY

AE MCKENNA

STRIKETHROUGH PUBLICATIONS

Published by ~~Strikethrough~~ Publications

www.aemckenna.com

ISBN 13—979-8-9908870-3-9

Edited by Lori Diederich

Cover art by Miblart

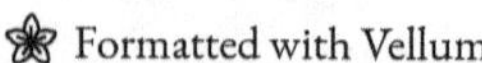 Formatted with Vellum

For Buddy. You will always have a place between Mint and Thai Basil, even when you sneeze in my face and try to push your nose into my mouth while I'm still asleep.

Always for Ben—I love the way you twerk

VISIONS & LIES

A STARGLEN NOVEL

AE MCKENNA

Author's Note

Canada and its people are awesome. While it is mentioned that there was a war between the United States and Canada in the 70s, it's merely world building. It is my hope that there will not be a war in real life between our countries.

Chapter One

The dense, brooding darkness sealed me in the room, the stale odor crowding me like I'd stepped into a warren of dust bunnies instead of my client's home. The terse *tick tick tick* of a clock swelled as it marked off time. I couldn't see anything except for the halo of light behind the heavy curtains shrouding the large bay window. My client Renee made a soft, dissatisfied noise, as if she hadn't expected this to happen when she'd closed the door. Again. I believed her absentmindedness was a symptom of her larger distress. Once my sight adjusted to her living room, I moved toward the coffee table, stepping around the wing-backed chair.

"Light the candles while I set up, please." I set my over-sized bag on the sideboard.

"I should've had them ready for you. We know the drill, don't we Sergeant Buttons?" Renee said, flitting around the room.

She certainly hadn't called *me* Sergeant Buttons. It was her way of calling her familiar to quick cast the fire spell. Every caster had a familiar, and I'd asked her to use her familiar less when we did readings so it wouldn't clog up the spirit realm with unnecessary white noise. From the corner of my eye, a flame erupted at the end of Renee's pale finger. She moved around the furniture-crowded living room, setting each wick alight.

Born on July 28th, Rene was a Leo and her casting element was fire. I knew this because I read crystal tarot for her. One of our ley abilities was determined by our zodiac signs, but which ones we received—alchemy, casting, or enchanting—was entirely random. However, if a child was born on a solstice, that child was practically guaranteed to have all three ley abilities, making them ACE.

Although mother nature is a fickle bitch and sometimes that switch in our DNA that allowed people to manipulate ley energy never flipped, leaving them Muted. Even in Starglen with one of the largest nexus of ley nodes in the country, touching magic was out of reach.

"Oh, your check's on the plate," Renee said absently.

My name on the check had caught my attention the moment she mentioned it, so I tucked it in my bag. Then I removed the redwood crystal grid plate I used for crystal tarot readings, my tarot deck, and finally a reddish-brown acacia box that rattled as I set it on the coffee table. The crystals and tiny bells attached to the sash around my waist tinkled with my every movement. The royal purple silk crepe skirt almost had a will of its own with how it swished around my hips and ankles.

"Would you like anything before we begin?" Renee asked.

The candles in the room gave off light almost as bright as LEDs, probably a condition she'd added to the flame since blackout curtains covered the windows in the middle of the day. Despite how bright the lighting was, the room still felt dreary thanks to the brown carpet and the dark, heavy furniture standing against the walls. Renee, with her white skin and baby pink tracksuit, was the only blip of color in the room. I turned toward her, my response nearly past my lips.

"Oh!" Her hands plopped to her hips, and she shook her brunette head. "Willamina, your makeup always makes me jealous. I wish you'd tell me what brand you use. When I try to make my eyes look like yours, I look like a raccoon!" She laughed, nerves wringing her voice and tightening her smile. She was stalling; I'd shared my makeup routine with her several times.

I tilted my head. "What's bothering you, Renee?"

"It's just that our last reading didn't answer my questions, and I'm getting to the point of not knowing what to do? My mother's still in hospice. It's getting tight around here." She gestured at the living room, as if that was what she meant. "I love her, I really do. But is there an end in sight to this?"

"Of course there is." I approached her and scooped up her clammy hands. "Death comes for us all, but I've explained to you that the readings you're asking for do not have me directly in contact with the spirits."

Her fingers clenched around mine. "But can't you, just this once, cut me a discount? I've been paying for your readings for a better part of a year, and I think I've been a rather good client."

"You have." I smiled to lessen the blow of what I needed to say next. "It's just that gentle possessions require a hazard payment because they can be dangerous, you know?" They were called "gentle possessions" because whoever came up with that term didn't know their head from their ass.

"I *don't* know!" she cried, ripping her hands free as she turned toward the coffee table. "Your answers to my specific questions are always vague. Was my mother even ready for hospice? It's been six months! The nursing home said it's helping to ease her pain, but she's playing bingo!"

I frowned and returned to the sidebar. "How often?" My

grandmother, who was enjoying her late 80s, played bingo almost every other night at the community center in downtown Starglen. She'd get rambunctious if something ticked her off—or tickled her feathers.

"Twice a week, I think." Renee slumped onto the loveseat, her gaze landing heavily on my profile as if the weight of her stare alone could change my mind about directly contacting a spirit without hazard pay.

I removed my headdress and veil from my bag. Both were made from silk, and the enchantments carefully attached to them made the pieces heavy—especially the many small chlorite crystals carefully sewn into the lining of the headdress. I'd found over the years that clients liked to watch me prepare for readings. Apparently, it soothed their suspicions that what they were getting was the real deal. Scraping my red hair back from my forehead, I peeked at Renee. Honestly, I was surprised her mother was still alive if she'd entered hospice care that long ago. When Renee began asking how long until her mother died, I'd thought she was being a gold digger. A leech. Someone who only cared about the money.

Now, I realized she was at her wits' end, and I wondered if it was . . . morally wrong of me to continue accepting her requests for readings. We all needed money for something. And that bolt of sea island cotton at Wildest Seams, the local fabric store, called my name whenever I was within a three-mile radius. By now, I had visitation rights with the store. However, Renee was a grown-ass adult who could make up her own mind. It wasn't for me to decide how she spent her money and whether she made responsible choices.

I secured the headdress over my hair. The flat aquamarine crystal lay heavy on the crown of my head as I centered it so the beaded fringe didn't swing into my eyes. Then I hooked the veil to it, pulling it across my nose, mouth, and chin, securing it to the other side and brushing the white phantom quartz near my ear. My fingers followed the long, powder blue celestine pendulum enchantment, ensuring it covered the chakra in my throat. This ritual I had when dressing activated all the enchantments on my costume, ensuring my third eye was open, my ears attuned to the spirit realm, and that all communication revealed the truth.

She squeaked. "Every time you do that, I can't get over all the ley energy that appears around you. It's like you're swimming in it."

Of course it looked like that. I lifted my brows. "Your mother plays bingo that often?"

Renee sighed, shaking her head. As if she couldn't believe this was the thing to focus on. "Yes."

"Have you seen her at bingo?" I opened the wooden case. The dazzling candlelight glinted over the faceted and smooth crystals within. The collection of tumbled or raw crystals was deliberately gathered for the crystals' natural claircognizance abilities. I turned the case toward her and gestured as if they were the most delectable offering of chocolates. Then I set up the grid plate in the center of the coffee table. There were many types of these plates available, but mine had belonged to my mother. Made from redwood, it was possibly older than my grandmother and engraved with multiple grid layouts for these stones.

Sitting across from Renee, I began shuffling my tarot deck. The cards were a prop for me. My deck wasn't infused with ley energy like most enchanters did. I relied solely on crystals, but the deck encouraged people to loosen up. Maybe it was the relaxing sound of cards sliding against one another, like the effervesce of waves against a shore.

"She called the numbers the last time I visited while a game was going on. She got into an argument with one of the residents." Renee grabbed crystals at random. "How on *earth* do you get anything with these rocks? There's no ley energy in them."

"They've been purified in salt water and charged in the sun and the moonlight, enhancing their innate abilities." I'd explained this to her countless times, and she willfully forgot it every time. I've long suspected Renee might be a ley purist, and that was fine so long as she didn't interfere with my reading.

I placed the crystals on the grid, and something just clicked perfectly with them. I couldn't explain how or why, but I knew this was the correct order and the perfect stones.

"What will it take to get you to agree to contacting the spirits for me?" she asked, her desperation wringing her voice into a whine.

Hazard pay. And maybe a touch less guilt.

I flipped a card and closed my eyes. In an explosion of pale blue glitter, my third eye revealed the crystal grid in front of me from the stones she'd selected and what they had picked up from our conversation while I shuffled the prop deck. Renee gasped again, but she thankfully remained quiet. I could only imagine what I looked like to her now.

The grid lit into perfect clarity behind the backs of my lids. I followed the sequined motes of light with my mind's eye, watching its lazy contortions. The stone for the past faded into nothing.

"The past has no impact on the present anymore," I whispered slowly, the enchantment sitting on the crown of my head growing warm. Or I was imagining it. I could never tell.

Keeping my eyes closed, I flipped another card. The sparkling blue-violet ribbon slipped and glided over the grid until it shifted to the stone resting on the present placement. It turned brown. I frowned, racking my brain for a plausible reason. Brown wasn't necessarily bad; it could mean the earth or it could mean a malignancy. I pursed my lips. Sometimes, looking at the next stone allowed me to piece together what was before me.

With that thought in mind, I flipped the last card. The stippled glitter flared, cascading into a strange mélange of brown and green. It reminded me of greed. I exhaled slowly and touched my fingertip on the present stone once more. It flared brown.

"There's something staining your mother—"

"Oh no." Renee's voice pitched higher. "I doubted her and—"

"Your mother never lied about her illness. We've gone over this. She's been truthful with you. But someone close to her has not been honest with her." I touched the stone representing the future and the glittery ribbon split off into two pathways. One was lined with a dark green-brown glow that made me believe it would lead Renee to financial ruin. The other color faded back to its natural periwinkle luminescence —almost as if hinting there was something that could give back what had been taken from Renee and her mother.

"What?" Renee asked. "What do you see, Willamina?"

"You're correct about being swindled." Heat flashed up my back and my seat became uncomfortable. The band of green and brown flared while the lighter path faded. "You're running out of time to correct this before it costs you too much." I opened my eyes and met Renee's aghast stare. "I'd launch an investigation into the hospice care and the administration for the nursing home immediately. Also . . ." *Oof. This was going to hurt.* "I think it's time we end our partnership."

She drew back sharply. "What?"

I shuttered my gaze once more, seeing the difference my words made. The dark path had lost some of its impending doom, and the lighter path seemed more solid. I focused on the aquamarine enchantment on the top of my head, hoping it'd reveal more, but it never did.

"Yes," I said. "This is the right path for you going forward."

I swallowed the sour taste in my mouth. Renee was having money troubles. Though I thought she could solve some of it by selling a handful of the furniture in her home, like the tall grandfather clock, I had no clue how much she could get for any of it. To my discerning eye, it was all somewhat dated but well made. So I would lose Renee as a client going forward, but it wouldn't hurt me—not financially. Or at least not in the immediate future. I gathered the tarot cards, hardly paying attention to what was flipped, and returned them to the pouch.

"I'm confused," Renee said. "What does stopping our appointments have to do with my mother? You said something was staining her, and now you want me to stop using you? What was it? Will she psychically hurt you? Is it your safety?"

"Renee." My tone was sharper than I'd used with her before. "You're having money troubles."

Her wounded expression did all the talking for her.

"I'm not . . ." I groped for the right word, pulling this and that before rejecting it for something she'd accept. "I'm not essential for her health or for you to make the right decision. Not anymore. I think it's time you get a lawyer. Someone who can help you with your mother. Maybe move her out of that nursing home?"

"But you . . . Have you been lying to me about everything this whole time?" Renee asked.

I froze, a coil in the cushion persistently poking my right butt cheek. "I've interpreted what the stones and tarot show me when we have sessions as best I can."

Her brow wrinkling, she nodded. "Ley energy doesn't lie."

No. It never did, did it?

Her eyes widened. "It's the hospice nurse? She's lying about how sick my mother is, isn't she?"

I licked my lips behind the veil, the soft fabric brushing against them. "I think it's something to investigate, but I can't see any more and it's definitely above my abilities, Renee."

"So you don't think you can help me anymore?"

"No. Not with this." I packed up my stones, then reached across and laid my hand over hers. "My services are only adding to your burdens now."

She half-smiled. "Then I don't suppose you'll give back that check?"

"No, sorry."

She chuckled half-heartedly and patted my hand. "Well, I just didn't expect this outcome at all today."

I stood. "Me either, and I'm psychic."

She laughed, and I finished packing up my things.

"Sergeant Buttons, it's too bright in here," Renee whispered.

I glanced up in time to witness all the candles go out in a wink, the sooty smoke hanging in the air like an omen.

But then I was blinded twice, once by the candles extinguishing, and second by Renee opening her curtains to let the early afternoon sun blaze through her large windows. While I removed my veil and headdress, I blinked my vision back into working order. Carefully folding them and deactivating every charm, I studied Renee.

She stood by the window, rubbing her brow and frowning. "My nephew might know someone who can help. He's interning at a firm right now."

I nodded. "That sounds like a good place to start." A peek at the clock had me edging toward the door. This session had gone on longer than normal thanks to her distraction from the real problem at hand today. I needed to get back home and make sure my grandmother was behaving.

"Oh, Willamina, would you wait a couple days before you cash that check?" Renee flashed an embarrassed smile.

"Sure." I made a note to update my website that I would no longer accept checks. This wasn't the first time a client had some kind of issue with their bank, and honestly, I was worth the cash or the transfer on the same day. "Take care, Renee. And let me know if anything comes from the investigation."

"I will, thank you."

I stepped outside into the bright sun and hurried to my maroon Malibu parked at the curb. Once settled in the driver's seat the powdery scent of sweet peas enveloped me and I pulled out my journal and quickly jotted down today's session and the outcome in shorthand. I'd given Renee all the info she needed, but sometimes I got extra insights, like what might be around the corner for them in the next week. I rarely gave this information because it could change as quickly as a bird flying across the sky.

I thumbed back a few pages to my previous entry with Renee and skimmed over the slashes and swoops, checking if anything I'd seen last had been important. I hadn't, not this time. I quickly leafed through the pages, reading the slashes and swoops all in shorthand, and smirked. Sometimes I was perfectly accurate.

Chapter Two

Declan laughed at the punchline, and I joined in like I'd paid attention to the exchange. The tinny music from the band in the next room played over the speakers in auction room one. Or whatever it was. I glanced over the shoulder of . . . I forgot who we were schmoozing, and now that I think on it, I wasn't certain we were.

There was a stand-up bar in the hallway right outside, and this Manhattan was a watered-down mess thanks to several things, mainly bad whiskey.

"I'll be right back," I whispered to Declan.

He nodded and continued the conversation. I ambled toward the hallway. My brother Guy had insisted I attend the black-tie charity event for the Familiar Care and Animal Rescue League instead of donating a sum of money, or some packages like the ones people were now bidding silently on. Said it was important for Slater Technologies' image. Which made me laugh. *I* wasn't the man for that job. Especially after that unfortunate offhand comment I'd given about Muted people more than likely being responsible for the fiasco in the Nettles.

Look, I had nothing against the Muted, not personally. They could still consume potions and use charms, they simply couldn't see ley energy or manipulate the ley lines around them without the aid of an enchantment or a potion. Time and again, when charms or potions went awry, Guy bitched about the Muted being the reason and it simply popped out of my mouth. Right into that reporter's recording. No amount of effort in attempting to walk that comment back had worked.

Once out of the auction hall, the noise decreased to a soft hum and the air smelled cleaner. The woman behind the bar flashed a smile as I approached. I'd say bar loosely. Really, it was just a mobile counter with a black cloth and a few upscaled coolers full of beer. The stuff you'd find at a tailgating party in a parking lot of some stadium. Then I saw the taps.

"I'll have a Starglen Raspberry Beret," I said, retrieving my money clip from my inside pocket. "Twenty ounces."

"Right away," she said.

I turned away from her as she poured my fruit sour. Like a Guinness, it needed a minute between pulls to settle. At least it should. The bartender set my drink down, the red-purple foam sliding down the glass to pool at the bottom. That was exactly why it needed to be poured like a Guinness.

She smiled. "Fifteen dollars, please."

I didn't react to the price, not really. Alcohol at these events always cost more than anywhere else. Maybe this was why Guy wanted me here. My brother knew I'd shell out for the expensive alcohol all night. "Can I get a napkin?"

A smirk tilted her lips to the side. "Sure." She jotted something down before handing it over.

It was her name and number. "Thanks, April."

I grabbed my beer and turned away, then cleaned the glass up with the napkin, the ink blurring before I tossed the stained thing in the trash. I meandered into the auction hall and paused at some of the lots. There were baskets full of toys geared toward cats and dogs. One had enchanted balls that would lead your pet on a merry chase, which I thought was nice. I'd had a dog once. Well, Guy had a dog that was starved for playtime. I was pretty sure it was being trained as my niece's familiar, but I assumed it didn't work out as the dog wasn't around anymore and it certainly wasn't Alexa's familiar now.

"I thought you said you'd be back." Declan placed a hand on the small of my back and whispered into my ear.

I glanced at him and shrugged. "I was checking out the stuff here. Guy said I should bid tonight."

"So pet toys?" His dark brows lifted, and he half chuckled and smirked at the same time. When he'd first done that in response to something I'd said, I thought it was kind of charming on him, in a mean, arrogant sort of way. But tonight, I simply couldn't be bothered to have an opinion.

"Well, this is an animal rescue event, so yeah, there'll be pet toys." I rolled my eyes and meandered down the aisle. And this guy was a doctor.

Declan grabbed my hand and looped it through his arm. I swallowed a sigh. Now wasn't the time, so I scanned the large room for a distraction. Instead, I saw cutouts of animals and their stories, a few people on the fringes of the room with animals in their strollers and people petting them, and Guy Slater giving me a dirty look. My brother dearest could fuck right off.

I finally took a sip of my beer and smacked my lips. It was tart and sweet, and the bright raspberry flavor smacked me right in the mouth. The Raspberry Beret might be my favorite of the Starglen Brewery sour line.

"Oh look," Declan said, stopping in front of a basket. "We could finally take that picnic up in the mountains I was telling you about."

I don't fuck around with picnics in the mountains. "Are you sure you were talking to me?"

His head tilted as he took in the picnic basket with the blanket and some dinner plates and glasses. "You have a point."

We weren't exclusive; we'd barely started hanging out, so this mishap of his wasn't a big deal. If it didn't happen all the time. Was he trying to show me he was in high demand and a suitable partner? Like with his possessiveness? I pulled my arm from his and opened the app to read the basket details.

"Oh, it's going for eighty bucks if you want to bid on it," I said, then spotted the next lot. It was a cabinet *Pac-Man* machine, and I did bid on that.

Declan's phone went off, and I knew before he even looked that he was going to leave. He unlocked it, and his entire demeanor changed. Gone was the easygoing yet weirdly dominant act, quickly replaced by excitement. "The ER needs me."

"Okay." I stepped back from him. What else was I supposed to say? Have a good night? Take it easy?

"There was a four-car collision with a logging truck." He shrugged, lifting his head from his phone finally and scanning the hall. He smirked and nodded. "You won't be alone for long. I'll call you."

And as he walked away, I turned to see whom he'd nodded at. Cheyanne smiled at me, and I thought about it. I really did. She was never one for misplaced displays of affection or the act of making plans just for the sake of showing they knew what a good time was. She knew. We knew together.

I sipped my beer, feeling somewhat lighter now that Declan had left. I didn't know why I'd followed through with the invitation with him. He was handsome, and I enjoyed the way he looked without a shirt on, but I didn't like him. That was probably why he was being aggressive with me. Which, in hindsight, was hysterical. I'd been called stubborn and dominant, but with him, I was a pushover. No. I was blank.

He'd bored me.

Tediousness had been a problem for me for some time now. Even here, alone with a great beer and the opportunity to pet some doggos and cats, I wasn't feeling it. Some time ago, and I wasn't sure when, I'd become impossibly bored with everything, constantly spacing out and letting my mind blank.

I almost crashed into Julian Christensen. Luckily, I didn't lose a drop of beer. But his scotch took a hit.

"Slob," he hissed.

"It was your drink," I muttered, stepping around him.

"You should watch where you're going, or is the big bad wolf too busy looking for a replacement?"

Julian followed me, keeping his tone casual and his body language "relaxed." I didn't believe he was relaxed for a moment. Not after that "big bad wolf" jab. It'd been an accident the first time I'd blown him over in private school. I'm an air caster; the nickname stuck.

"I saw your date leave," Julian said. "They always seem to make a quick exit. Nothing new for you."

"Oh, were you scavenging for more of my seconds, Junior? You'd think one would be enough."

His face turned red. "Don't think too highly of yourself, Slater."

I leaned closer to him, lowering my voice. "I think you like being second to me. That's where you always ended up in school, and look at you now."

Guy caught my attention and motioned me over. I couldn't have planned a better exit myself. Until I saw Luther Christensen was with my brother; he also happened to be

Julian's father. So instead of leaving the bastard choking on my words, we walked toward them together.

This was my ill fate for the night: schmoozing. Unfortunately, the Christensens and Slaters were more than simply social rivals, we were business rivals too. However, some of that had eased a bit when Luther won a seat on the city council, and now he was running for mayor of Starglen, so of course Guy wanted to butter up the old bastard and get on better terms with him.

While Slater Technologies dealt with munitions for the front lines in Canada—like charm grenades, flash bombs, and some larger weapons. The Christensen company, Ley Technica, did as well, but they were more into protective gear. At least until recently. Guy had tried for a couple years now to get a bid with the US military on our armor and protective gear. The quality hadn't been an issue, but the price was. Until a few days ago.

"Oh, Guy, I heard about your military contract," some rich old lady said. She wore a wine-colored dress and tons of glittery silver around her wrinkly white neck. "The stock market's been exciting since that."

Julian and Luther's expressions flared with identical scowls. Yeah, they were definitely related.

A blink later, Luther was back in his couldn't be bothered demeanor, clutching an unlit cigar between his thumb and index finger. "Oh, so you're the bastards who undercut me, eh?" He barked out a laugh.

"I hadn't thought of you still in the game, what with you campaigning now," Guy said.

"Your underbid was so low, I didn't want to risk my business by winning the contract. I guess you get what you pay for, isn't that right, Guy?" Luther sneered, but covered it up by sticking the cigar in his mouth. "It's like the ley baton all over again."

Shots fired. While the Christensens snickered, I could feel everyone holding their breath, waiting for my brother's response to that jab. It was still a sore spot for both companies.

Guy forced a closed-lipped smile. "Well, we didn't want to be greedy with protection gear, thinking of our men and women on the front lines."

"It's not like it's the 70s again," a rich old White man said. "Niagara is secure."

Back in the early 70s, the US and Canada had a discussion about the largest nexus of ley lines in that area. It lasted seven years, the last two being hostile, but eventually it was declared half US territory and half Canadian. So the area remained patrolled on both sides. Honestly, it was probably for the best. Half the nexus shifted onto the land on both sides, and no one wanted to give up an inch of territory because we all knew it wouldn't have ever stopped there if either country had a toehold.

"Yes," I said. "Thank goodness for the United Nations."

"And how!" The pink blush on the old White lady's cheeks stood out more as she lifted a hand to the old White man—who kind of reminded me of my father: absent—and pointed at Luther. "Dear, this man says that when he's mayor, there'll be tax cuts . . ."

I tuned them out, drifting to the table. My phone buzzed and I pulled it out, noticing that someone had outbid me on *Pac-Man*. Not for long. I set my max bid on the app and tucked my phone away.

"When you said you were bringing a date, Hendrick, I'd expected you to bring a respectable date." Guy edged me farther from the campaigning talk and the Christensens. For good measure. I yearned to beat the shit out of Julian on a good day, and today wasn't that great.

I cocked my head to the side and feigned confusion. "Declan's a doctor." And a douchebag. "He's saving lives right now. I don't know how much more respectable that can get."

Guy's eyes narrowed. "You know what I mean."

I did. Guy wasn't comfortable with my sexuality, and I wasn't comfortable pandering to his needs with my happiness, not anymore. Unfortunately, it was a generational issue, him being twenty years my senior and sometimes thinking he needed to be a father figure to me. I'd tried dissuading him from that, but then he'd pull shit like this, and there we were. Me, without a date at a charity event, and him berating me for bringing the wrong gender with me. I glanced over his shoulder and caught Luther and Julian mean-mugging us while having a hushed, private conversation. That also wasn't unusual. Julian and I had attended the same school, even dated the same girl once. When *my* relationship with her ended, she hadn't hidden away, but when *she* ended things with *Julian*, she left the country. Telling, if you ask me.

"I don't want to have this conversation with you," I said.

"I don't enjoy it either, but—"

"Guy." I passed him my empty glass. "You're determined to have it, and I'm not. You asked me for my best behavior here, and I've given it. And now I'm going to go above and beyond and leave."

Guy stopped me. "By leaving, you aren't keeping your end of the bargain."

"What bargain? You asked me to come and play nice. I've done that, and I've made bids. I don't want to stay here and get into a loud argument with you over why I brought a man as my date. So I'm going to leave and you're going to pick up my *Pac-Man* game when the auction is over."

Guy scowled. "Why would I be your pack mule?"

"Because you're being a dick." I grinned, clapped his shoulder, and strode out.

THE LIGHTS BLINKED ON AS I STEPPED INTO THE temperature-controlled lab. It was as quiet as a church in here, and it was my church. Passing bays of windows overlooking standing desks, enchanting and alchemy tables, I stepped inside my smaller lab. I slung my suit jacket on the hook and grabbed my lab coat, shrugging it on. The knots in my shoulders loosened as I tugged off my tie and hung it on the hook. Formulas for quick casting and enchantments together covered the walls.

Hey, El Diablo, I called to the spirit realm. *Wanna hang out, buddy?*

I didn't call out loud for him, especially when we were alone, a habit I'd kept from my time in the Air Force. The veil to the spirit realm parted, and my familiar, a giant ley-energy-blue raccoon, stepped through. Sigils filled with concentric circles and runes covered his massive body. The more spell workings I memorized, the bigger the familiar was, and El Diablo was no slouch. He was as large as a black bear. He shuffled over to me and nudged my hip. I pulled a packet of peanuts from my desk and opened them. El Diablo couldn't eat them anymore, but he really liked having them. It was, after all, how I'd gained his trust. Then I fed him some of my ley energy every day for the rest of his natural life, bonding him to me. When he'd passed, he'd left behind a spirit stone, a forever companion kept in my pocket.

I stepped behind my standing desk and turned on the light box to illuminate the thin paper I traced spell workings on. Slater Technologies had been founded in my father's younger days when a skirmish on the Canadian border wouldn't have caused a blink, not with World War II raging on in Europe and the Nazis intent on eradicating the Jewish and Muted communities.

Unfortunately, war was good for business, and being a Slater, it was my business as well. If I hadn't been groomed for this lab, this very desk I stood over, I wondered what I would've done with my life. I'd rarely considered it before, but as of late, something hadn't felt right.

Not to mention that my last breakthrough on the delayed flash bomb wasn't innovative. Someone else had come out with one right before my debut. The competition was ruthless, and for a while, that spurred me on—to be the first, the best, the It Thing in munitions. And I was, for a while.

But now, I was tired of it. In a few years, I'd look forty in the face, and I guess I just thought I'd be happier with what I was doing by now. I had a job that allowed me to mix my casting and enchanting abilities, which I enjoyed. Money wasn't an issue, not for a few years with some substantial investments, but I could always have more. Men and women seemed to like me, so I was never long without someone next to me. My penthouse overlooked downtown Starglen, and it came with a gym membership. I had everything I needed.

And yet I was bored.

El Diablo's spirit paw floated through the bag of peanuts and back to his mouth, as if crunching on one. He silently chittered at me and reached for more nuts, happy in his simple life as a familiar. Maybe simple should be a goal for me.

Well, fuck me, if I only had a few years before I hit forty, I should figure this shit out.

I grabbed a clean sheet of paper and began making a list of the things that didn't bore me and the things that did. What bothered me the most was that I put my career in the bored column. Right under dating. I frowned. Well, I wasn't entirely bored with my job. I got a kick out of creating new charms and spell workings. But I wasn't sure if what I made was my calling any longer.

Chapter Three

I stood off to the side as the doctor chatted with my grandmother. Mimzy had a mulish set to her mouth whenever she wasn't smiling, and she tried to smile often with the doctor.

"I'm only saying reducing the amount of red meat and alcohol will get those numbers down, Erma," Dr. O'Neil said, passing a prescription to me. "Okay, I'll see you in a month." Her cat-shaped brown eyes met mine. "Nice seeing you again, Billie."

Mimzy flapped the paper. "Thanks, Doc. Be good."

When we stepped out of the office and into the drab, gloomy day, I could feel my spirits deflate. I'm just gonna say it. Gloomy days bummed me out, and Starglen had a lot. Today was no exception. We walked in silence to the car, my heels clipping along the way in time with the thuds of Mimzy's orthopedics. Mimzy held her hand out to me, palm up.

I gave her a low-five and raised my hand. "Up high."

She rolled her eyes. It wasn't hard to miss thanks to her

ginormous bright blue glasses that magnified her brown eyes to the point she reminded me of those sad animals with enormous eyes paintings. She wiggled her fingers. "Gimme the car keys."

I laughed. "Your license is no good, Mimzy."

She cupped her hand around her mouth, leaning in to me as a twinkle glinted in her magnified peepers. "I won't tell if you don't."

I playfully swatted her. "Maybe after the grocery store."

We climbed into the Malibu and buckled up. Her sweet pea and baby powder perfume immediately overpowered the cabin. Probably because she'd worn it for years and the car upholstery held onto it. I swear I could smell it when I was alone.

I turned on the car. "I need to make a stop at Wildest Seams before we hit up Robertsons and refill that prescription."

She laughed a little. "Sure, sure, Chipmunk. I've got all day."

I'll be straight—I have many names, and so do the people in my family. We've got formal names, nicknames, and the names we always call each other. I give my clients my full name. When my mother was pregnant with me, she'd believed she was going to have a boy. She'd named me William after my father but called me Billie when she spoke to me in the womb. She'd passed during childbirth, and my father—who was just as dead—named me Willamina. Mimzy called me Billie because that was what my mother called me, and I wouldn't ask my grandmother to go against her daughter. To be honest, I've never really liked either, but what am I gonna do? Nothing.

I headed toward the shopping district. She turned the radio to the oldies station, which wasn't her music anymore, and grumped about bingo.

"Flo and Ro brought their damned trolls again," she muttered, twisting open a strawberry candy she'd pulled from her purse.

I held my hand out for one, as was customary. "Wait, which trolls?"

She slapped a candy in my palm. Don't ask me what they were called. I'd never known my entire life, and I was convinced it was a government secret. "The ones with the gems in their tummies."

"So not their grandkids." I tugged the candy from the wrapper with my teeth into my mouth.

Mimzy cackled. "Right. Those darn trolls have enchantments. I saw them." She wagged a long, gnarled finger at me. "They've got dementia if they think I can't see an enchantment from a mile away."

"Not without those coke bottles on your face." I crunched open the candy, probing the strawberry gel in the center. "Why not go to a different bingo night?"

"What?" Mimzy twisted her tiny, wiry body in the seat to gape owlishly at me. "And let those broads have *Benny Rodriguez?* The good caller?" She shook her head so vehemently, her tight and short cloud of blue-tinted curls shivered with indignation. "Never."

"How about switching tables from Flo and Ro?" I pulled into a spot and turned the car off.

We unbuckled and headed into the fabric store. Mimzy looked around but stayed close as I headed toward the thread.

"You know, it should be them who leave the front row. Flo and Ro. Bah. Sounds like a dumb team name for some Florida buttholes."

A bolt of off-white lace caught my attention. It was tightly crafted. As I reached up and rubbed it between my fingers, I thought of the charms I'd sew into the lining. This was sturdier, made exactly for that . . . I stepped back, scanning the price. It was on sale.

Mimzy's voice turned into white noise as once more I inspected the bolt of lace. I didn't need the entire bolt. A few yards, maybe five, would do me just fine. I could dye it to match my costume easily enough, and thanks to Renee yesterday, I had the funds for this extravagance. Well, I would tomorrow when she'd promised the check wouldn't bounce, but today I could afford it, and tomorrow's deposit would supplement what I spent today . . .

I sighed and clutched the strap to my purse as I led Mimzy to the thread aisle. That kind of thinking had gotten me into all this trouble. My impulsiveness in fabric stores. Don't get me started on clothes. I *loved* fashion. I loved seeing the newest and sexiest designs out there, and I found I have excellent taste because the price tag matched it.

But this kind of thinking landed me in hot water. I'd had more debt than I could pay off. I'd lost my apartment, lost my car, and I had to sell my purses and shoes. And a few bolts of fabric. I still thought about that hunter green silk chiffon. But that was seven years ago. I wasn't the same Willamina I was then that I am now. I'd become debt free, and now I worked on rebuilding my credit. I did everything I could to not carry over a balance to the next month. My psychic business, The Ethereal Eye, had helped get me out of that hole a lot faster than if I hadn't done it.

Living with Mimzy came with the condition that I take her where ever she wanted, her appointments and what have you. Now I cared for her, because she'd cared for me when others couldn't.

I bought my one spool of thread and then, at the grocery store, bought the ingredients for today's dinner, also filling the prescription. Mimzy landed on the lazy boy and turned on her game shows. I had a little time before I needed to get dinner ready and retreated into my room.

I'd shoved my double bed in the corner, currently covered in the outfits I'd rejected for the day. I went about hanging them back up. I had an unfinished sewing project on the mannequin standing next to an old travel trunk I stored my psychic costumes in. On my desk sat my little sewing machine, which I set the spool on, and then turned to the stacks of crystal journals lined up chronologically against the wall. Nudging some loose crystals out of the way, I tugged one of the later journals out and opened it.

My mother's handwriting greeted me. She had this habit of writing in cursive, then switching to shorthand and back to cursive. It'd taken me years to become comfortable reading the journals without the old shorthand workbooks Mimzy had given me. Shorthand was a relic now, thanks to computers, but back in my grandma's day, it was the easiest way to memo without getting behind. It was still being taught in high school when my mother was a teen, and she used it for journaling. So I learned it to be closer to her.

My phone rang with an unknown caller, and I answered. "Hello?"

"Yes, ah, is this Willamina from the Ethereal Eye—the psychic?" a woman asked.

I closed the journal and grabbed my planner. "Yes, it is I." People expected such talk from me. I drew the line at fake accents, mostly because I could never remember which one I'd originally used with them. It got complicated. Then suddenly I'm in people's court for fraud. Well, that'd never happened, but someone once implied they'd threaten me with that. "I've been waiting for your call."

"Oh, I'm sure you have." She tittered. "My name's Suzana Bruce. And I wanted to know what your spirit package entailed."

I leaned back in my chair and closed my eyes. "I've installed a significant hazard pay for gentle possessions from a spirit, Madam Bruce. But not before I investigate the manner in which the spirit has departed from this mortal coil."

"Oh, of course. And please—call me Suzana." She drew in an audible breath. "I'm not even sure if the spirit package is what I need . . . I don't think your palm reading is either."

I sat forward, my gaze blindly straying to the journals, wondering what made picking a service so difficult. "What're you looking for?"

A door clicked, and sounds I hadn't noticed suddenly disappeared. "Closure." Her breath hitched. "My daughter has gone no contact with me, and I want to know if she's okay."

I frowned, deflating slightly. "You want me to spy on her?"

Suzanna sighed, tears choking the noise, and her voice remained quiet. "Kendra and I used to be best friends until her fiancé came along, and I complained about how her behavior had changed—"

"I'm not comfortable doing this if it goes against your daughter's wishes," I said as firmly as I dared. I knew she was troubled, and I didn't want to upset her further, but I also didn't want my actions to worsen their relationship.

"I just need to know if she's alive," Suzana said. "That's all."

It was hard to know if she was playing me or not. As a psychic, I had responsibilities, or at least, *I* made sure I did. There were thousands of con artists out there seeking to make a buck off someone's grief and pain, and I swore I wouldn't make anyone's life worse with my side hustle. I already had enough on my plate to work through; I didn't need to add bad karma.

I checked my planner. Mimzy had bingo tomorrow—the only plans she kept in her head—and that meant I had three hours of free time.

"I'm free for a consultation tomorrow evening." I plucked a pencil from the desk and jotted down her name. "Give me the address and I'll visit you around . . . say five?"

"Oh." Suzana sniffled and collected herself. "Okay, but six-thirty would be better. Here's my address."

I copied it down and repeated it back to her, confirming the time she asked for. If she was being truthful with me, I could find out for her if her daughter was alive or not. People deserved to know that sort of thing.

I SLICED THROUGH THE ONION QUICKLY, THE BLADE of my knife knocking on the cutting board when Trixie, my cousin, breezed in with her youngest in tow. Shawn stopped in the living room, and Mimzy gave up the TV for him.

Our home didn't have an open plan, but it had high ceilings and the wall between the kitchen and living room didn't go all the way up. Mimzy's tchotchkes lined it, from pictures of her daughters to grandkids, and now great grandkids, with sea turtles and otter figurines between them. It could be worse, like clowns.

"Hey, Trix!" I glanced up to smile at her and resumed chopping. "Where's Candi?"

"She's covering the shop for me," Trixie said, taking a seat at the counter. "Bolognese tonight?"

"Damn right." Mimzy turned on the tiny television in the corner and switched it to *Jeopardy!*. Then she cracked open a bottle of wine. "Do you and the messes need leftovers, Beebee?"

Like I said, so many names for one person. Trixie was short for Beatrice, and Mimzy had thought of her as a busy bee since she was a child. The messes were her kids, and I believed that was self-explanatory.

"Shawn and I will eat here, but I'll take some for Candi and Brandon." Trixie spotted my headdress left on the table and jabbed a thumb at it. "Hey, I've got some charms to recharge tomorrow. Do you want me to take that too?"

I dumped the diced onion into a bowl. "Oh, that'd be great. I'll transfer the money to you after dinner." And if I'd bought that lace, I wouldn't have been able to pay Trixie the fee to recharge my charms. Self-control was great. Even if I didn't have that lace now. Besides, I really wanted a steamer closet, anyway.

Mimzy poured some wine into a measuring cup, then split the bottle between her and me, she taking the heavier pour.

"Mimzy!" Trixie snatched the glass from her. "The doctor said to cut back."

Mimzy lifted a brow at me, her glasses magnifying the glare like a laser beam. "Tattle tale."

She grabbed another wine glass and sat at the island next to Trixie, pouring half into the glass and pushing it at her.

I started on the celery, dicing up a few ribs and chucking them into the same bowl as the onions.

"I'm just saying that if you're told to cut back, you should cut back." Trixie took a sip of wine. "Maybe save one glass as a nightcap or—"

"Don't question me if I should drink or not," Mimzy said, her tone taking on an extra prickly texture. "I'm eighty-eight, girl. I've buried my husband, my two daughters, and raised a grandchild like there was nothin' wrong with her. I can tell well enough if I want a drink while she's cooking."

"Gram-cracker!" Trixie snapped. "Not nice."

I didn't wince; I didn't have to. Trixie did it for me. Just like a big sister, she always had my back when Mimzy said something hurtful. Honestly, she'd gotten much better over the last decade or so. I didn't even take the slips of the tongue personally anymore.

"Sorry, Chipmunk." Mimzy lifted her glass.

I tapped my wine glass against hers. "You know, one day I'll make this with ground turkey."

Her eyes widened as big as an owl's. "You wouldn't dare!"

I grinned at Trixie and shrugged, starting on chopping the carrots.

"Oh, hey." Trixie leaned closer. "Candi's applying for a work release from school to earn extra money. Would you be okay cutting your shift to three hours on Wednesdays?"

Trixie was the owner and baker of TrixieCakes, and I worked five hours three days a week for her. It was all I could do with taking care of Mimzy. She had a lot of appointments and did not give a flying fuck about schedules. That was my job. It would suck, but it wouldn't hurt me.

"Sure. I can do that if Candi cleans up for me."

Trixie frowned. "She's not as good as you."

"Practice makes perfect."

Mimzy drained her glass and swapped it with Trixie's. "It builds character, cleaning does. When I was her age, I worked in a soda shop and these jackasses would blow bubbles to over-flow their malts. I got so mad at them one day I threw a wet rag in their laps." She took a gulp. "Billie, don't think I didn't notice you not buying that lace today. I'm proud of you."

Then she turned up the volume on the news regarding the new contract between Slater Technologies and the govern-ment, and the strange tornado incident in the Nettles. A caption flashed on the screen that caught my attention, blaming the destruction on a Muted. It said something like a Muted played with power they could never understand. People like the Slaters were obtuse gatekeepers.

Shaking my head, I peered at Mimzy, who was doing everything she could to keep her humongous peepers glued to the TV. It was always like that, ever since I could remember. Mimzy never praised, and if she did, she didn't want it to be commented on. She used to leave the room. Her favorite now was to turn up the volume on things as if her hearing aids didn't work.

Trixie caught my eye and smiled. I shrugged and began sautéing the vegetables.

Sometimes, I wished that just once, something exciting would shake up the routine.

Chapter Four

It wasn't so much a noise, but more of a suction of air when I opened the door to Icing, the small patisserie my best friend and his partner owned in the Flower Market. The scent of vanilla hit me first, making me think of waffle cones even though I knew Dane would never. Then came the cinnamon with an undercurrent of rich chocolate.

My mouth watered before I was two steps inside the pristine white and gray lobby.

There were no customers, but I knew it'd been a busy morning for them despite the spotless dining area. The coffee machine had signs of use, but more importantly, the crumbs in the pastry case let me jealously know what had already been bought.

"Rex!" Dane called as he came from the back. His chef's coat was spotless, and his short dark hair was tidy. He had the classic Irish complexion: pale.

I waved at him distractedly, searching for my post workout reward before heading into the lab. The croissants stuffed with vanilla and chocolate cream were always a hit, so were the tiny Neapolitan cakes. Or at least I believed that was what they were. I only guessed the pink cakes were strawberry. Dane, if anything, was predictable. And disciplined. And my favorite baker. Everything was fresh and decadent.

I lifted my head, looking past him to the large window to the back. Eric, a buff Black man, stood before a marble slab. His familiar, a betta fish in sparkling periwinkle, floated around him as if it swam on the astral currents of the spirit realm. The fish was as large as one of the bistro tables in the dining area.

On the marble slab in front of him, Eric worked a thin spread of chocolate with one of those bench scraper things in each hand, doing some scooping and scraping motion. Which, since I knew Eric well, would make some of the smoothest, delicate chocolate concoctions. He was a fire caster, and since his familiar was out, I assumed he was tempering chocolate or something. I don't bake; I wouldn't know.

"How was the workout?" Dane asked.

"Oh, you know. The usual." I leaned against the counter. It was no secret I went to the gym before here. Before I moved into my penthouse, I'd had a membership at the gym two stores down, and it became a tradition when Dane'd first opened Icing. And when my new building offered a gym, I declined because it wasn't on the way here and I didn't want to give up my daily treat.

"How was the pet thing?" Dane opened one case and, using tongs, refilled the Danishes.

"I won a *Pac-Man* game."

"Nice!"

"Guy has it."

He closed the case and snorted. "Don't you have to pick that up yourself?" He grabbed a paper cup and approached the coffee machine.

"I left early but gave him my bid number after I won."

Dane placed the coffee before me and shook his head. "So, what was the lecture about this time?"

I knew without checking it was black coffee. "The usual. Okay, I'm going to have that peanut butter stuffed cupcake thing with the hazelnuts and—is that caramel?"

Dane's dark brows slammed together. "It's not a fuckin' cupcake, dude."

I blinked innocently at him, my smothered laughter tickling my ribs. "Oh. But it's a cake, right? Stuffed with yumminess, but single serving?"

"Of course it is. You know what it is, Rex. Read the sign."

"The sign says 'peanut butter mousse mirror cake with crunchy hazelnut and caramel drizzle.' But it eats like a cupcake," I said.

The door from the back opened, and Eric stepped through with a tray of gâteau. "Is that mean man claiming your delightful petit fours are cupcakes again, baby?"

Dane closed his eyes, breathed in through his nose, and exhaled through his mouth. "Yes."

Oooh, he'd clenched his teeth for that.

I bit back a smile and nodded at Eric. "Hey, I'm just calling it like it is."

Eric carefully set the cakes out in the case, the chef's coat straining around his massive arms. It amazed me still that with all the chocolate these two worked with, their chef's coats remained pristine white. Maybe they substituted messy coats with clean spares.

"Stop riling him up, Rex." Eric's twinkling brown eyes said otherwise. "He's a bear to deal with later."

"Well, maybe if you hadn't left me for my best friend, I'd stop." I picked up the coffee and inhaled the rich and robust scent before taking a sip. Hot, acidic, with a touch of fruit on the end.

Eric snorted, waving off my comment.

"Okay, but I clearly remember you ditching him here with me." Dane moved to the case and grabbed the confection I asked for. "I think that's more of a you problem than an us problem."

I took the cake, my mouth watering yet again. "Mmhmm. Hey, does this cupcake make me look fat?"

"Oh, fuck off, you twat." Dane laughed and chucked a towel at me.

I settled my bill and glanced at the clock. I still had time before I was needed at the lab—and I could get there before Christopher and eat this thing with no shame over the noises I made. It was a good thing I enjoyed working out, because I enjoyed desserts just as much.

"How's the wedding planning coming along?" I asked, snatching a box from the top of the case near the register.

Eric passed me some napkins. "We're at a standstill right now."

"Only because he's making it complicated," Dane said lightly.

"Excuse me if I don't want you working on our wedding day," Eric replied politely.

I lifted a brow. "This still?"

"What is so wrong with me wanting to make our wedding cake?" Dane leaned on the counter, the muscle ticking at his jaw. "We'll get exactly what we want, and we know what we'll be getting too."

"Because then you'll take over everything else, like you always do." Eric placed a hand on his shoulder, tilted his head, and looked into Dane's eyes. "I want you to be relaxed and enjoy our day."

"How can I relax when the cake's wrong?" Dane scoffed, shaking his head.

Eric tossed his hands in the air, muttering something, and glared at me.

I lifted my hands to show I was harmless. "I didn't do anything."

"You called that petit four a cupcake," Dane muttered.

"I *always* call it a cupcake, dude."

"It's a sore spot today," Eric said.

His shoulders grew rigid. "Don't."

Eric retrieved his phone from his pocket and opened it.

Dane shook his head. "I can't watch this again." He shoved through the door to the back, and a moment later he was at the marble table, cleaning it vigorously.

I lifted my brows and faced Eric. "What's going on with him?"

Eric pursed his lips, fiddling with his phone. "It seems we're in a TikTok war with a local shop."

"What?" I took Eric's phone and tapped the video.

It was Dane, making one of his baller chocolate sculptures. This time it was an octopus hugging a treasure chest. I knew he'd filled everything with something decadent and sinfully delicious. Before the video was over, it cut to a woman with unfortunate braces and heavy makeup that didn't quite match her messy brown bun. Her eyes sparkled with mischief.

"*Ohmigod.* I would feel *so* guilty eating something so awesome." She smirked. "So why not come to TrixieCakes instead and get one of our *amazing* dragon cupcakes?"

Then there was a dark chocolate cupcake with a blue dragon made with frosting spouting flames. She cut it in half to show a beige filling that could be caramel or milk chocolate. Maybe even peanut butter.

Dane slammed through the door again and stabbed the air with his finger. "Those are fucking trite! Cupcakes?!" He made a strangled noise and stormed into the back room once more.

I blinked, slowly passing the phone over to Eric.

"It's not the first video, but it *is* the first one that's really pissed him off." Eric shrugged. "He memorized how long the video lasted from playing it for an hour last night."

"There are more?" I asked.

"Yeah, but they were harmless." He waved the phone. "This is harmless, but . . . I don't know. He's worked so hard to be the best, you know?"

"Yeah, and he is. You both are. Icing is amazing!"

I never call this shop by its full name; no one did unless marketing became involved. The sign behind the counter spelled "Icing" in flashy letters with soft blue backlighting, and underneath it in small caps was "by Dane." Pretentious? Maybe. But he was so proud of himself when he opened two years ago, and no one could take that from him.

"This chick can't be serious. That cupcake is nothing like what goes on here," I said.

"Yeah, but TrixieCakes is fairly established . . . I used to go there a lot before I met him, is all. They're good. Not Dane good, but they're good."

"Do you think he's gonna do anything about it?" I asked.

"What can he do?" Eric tucked his phone away. "If he responds, then he's going to look like a bully. That never goes over well on the internet."

The door opened, and a White woman entered, eyeing the cases. I glanced at the time again and straightened. I had to go.

I lifted the box. "Well, tell him I said thanks for the cake, but tell him I used the proper name for it this time."

Eric chuckled and waved. "Will do, man. See ya later."

As I headed for the door, I tucked an earbud in my ear since I listened to podcasts on my walk to work and I didn't want to be that person who blasted everything from his phone's speakers. Guy was like that. I stepped out of the way to let a couple more people inside the shop, then hit the pavement.

The podcast was typical. I was more interested in the diminished rate of ley crystals being imported from Asia as of late. They were claiming there was a shortage hiking the price up. I believed the shortage came from the lack of enchanters purging their ley energy into empty vessels.

Ley crystals are a natural formation from a large amount of raw ley energy, and don't form without human intervention. Something about the process allowed the crystals to become malleable with heat, allowing for all kinds of manipulation—like threading it into armor for protection against ley attacks. Enchanters were the only practitioners able to do this. It had to do with the mechanics of how we enchanted an object. We stood at the enchanting table, pierced our palms with ley spikes to drain our bodies' natural ley energy to create the enchantment. Then the table would pull from the closest ley line to replenish what it took.

However, making ley crystals impacted the replenishing rate of the energy back into a body. This significantly slowed replenishment, leaving many unable to practice for a week or more. Something to do with the absence of an enchantment and the body not being open to renewal.

And while Slater Technologies didn't have an issue paying the prices, there were some grumblings going on in acquisitions over how much we used.

To be honest, I'd make ley crystals all the time if it didn't mean I couldn't enchant or cast for the better part of the week after. I'd use them in every build instead of only for protection gear we were supplying to the military.

Ten minutes later, I walked into the building hosting my lab as the podcast turned to local news. Shit was getting real in the Nettles since that incident with the Fornaro family went down. I didn't know the details. When it first happened several months ago, I was in the final stages of creating The

Dome—an enchantment with a spell working to cause mass destruction in a marked-off area. Imagine a snow globe forming over a concentrated area, but instead of snow, there were tornadoes, and the dome kept the tornadoes from escaping.

Back then, the last test happened in a quarry twenty miles out of town, and the device had caused serious structural damage to the building. It'd even caused a stray rope tornado. Now, as I know it, the building was quickly erected just for the tests, so maybe it wasn't as structurally sound—I doubted it. Besides, tornadoes were a serious source of destruction, and I'd worked tirelessly to keep it contained within the dome to minimize collateral damage.

Lately, the destruction in the Nettles reminded me of The Dome before I perfected the spell working. What really bothered me about that was the military also contracted that weapon. So how were they going off in the Nettles? And to be clear, tornadoes were not common in northern California. The chances that this device was mine were high.

When I'd been asked about what I thought could've happened, I'd stupidly said, "Probably some uneducated Muted playing with power they fundamentally cannot understand." That quote spread faster than any other gossip about me. Like it was the common cold. I shouldn't have answered, but the reporter had caught me on a first date, and I'd wanted to impress her back when dating still excited me. Lots of mistakes were made that night.

I nodded to the receptionist as I walked past them and into my lab and then my *tiny* office. I sat at my desk and placed my pastry box on the list I made last night and opened it. The light reflected off the glaze on the side before I popped the whole thing into my mouth.

I moaned, closing my eyes and savoring every burst of

flavor as I chewed as slowly as possible. All worry about the concerning coincidences of The Dome appearing in the Nettles and that stupid thing I'd said about the Muted melted from my brain like chocolate on a tongue.

Chapter Five

The Bruces' home was in Old Town, a stately Victorian house with a large bay window and old oak floors. Built-in shelves overflowed with books that seemed to be flea market finds, and countless pictures of Suzana, her husband, and a young blonde woman with green eyes covered every available surface.

Suzana smiled grimly at me, clutching her hands in front of her stomach. The light reflected off the thin infinity knot bracelet on her left wrist. It caught my attention because I recognized something beautiful when I saw it.

"I've always wanted one of your readings, but there's just never been time in my schedule," Suzana was saying. "Or *you* don't have time when I do. You're quite popular."

I smiled. "Well, I can commune with the spirits easily. It's a gift. What is it you're looking for? My tarot and crystal readings might—"

"I was thinking of a séance." Suzana's eyes darted to her husband, who stood in the doorway leading deeper into the house like a guard waiting to clothesline me.

"Of course." I nodded and glanced around the room.

"Now, if your daughter isn't dead, I won't be able to contact her."

The man snorted. "Of course not. Then should we assume she's still alive now?"

"Martin." Suzana flashed me a fragile smile. "Sorry, he's a skeptic."

Let me say it amused me greatly when someone said they were skeptical of communicating with the dead when half of us had familiars. What else did they think they were? "Understandable." I approached one shelf and ignored Martin stiffening as I gestured to the picture of Suzana and the young blonde hugging each other with huge grins for the camera. "Is this your daughter?"

"Yes, that's Kendra." Suzana stopped next to me and stared at the picture. Her fingers played with the infinity knot bracelet. "I haven't spoken to her for six years. I know I should accept what the police in Cyprus said, but I can't."

I faced her. "What was that?"

"That she was lost at sea." Suzana pulled her focus from all the pictures of Kendra and met my gaze. "There's just no definitive answer. I can accept she doesn't want to talk to me if she's alive, but I need to know. I need to know if she's still on this earth."

I clasped her hand to let her know she wasn't alone. "I have an opening for a séance on Friday night." Mimzy had the big bingo game then, and Fridays were my day off from everything else. "The best room for this would be the one she used for herself, or a place she was drawn to. A kitchen maybe?"

"We bought this house after Kendra last moved out," Martin said in a low voice.

Suzana gasped, covering her mouth. "Oh no. Does it mean we can't contact her now?"

I patted her shoulder. "It doesn't mean that. What's ideal for me is a place she lived, where her spirit energy has stacked up a lot, and people who loved her. Who were the people most important to her? If we don't have access to a place, the people will be a good enough connection."

"Oh!" Suzana glanced at Martin. "We can arrange that. I . . . I have people to call. Oh! Do you need a payment now or after?"

Martin cleared his throat, left his guard in the hallway, and prowled toward the door. "I'm sure she does."

I nodded, not appreciating his meaning, but he also wasn't wrong. "It's $375 for a one-hour séance that includes up to ten people. I require 25% now. PayPal or Venmo, either will do."

"Of course." Suzana had her phone out and a moment later, I had a buzz on mine. She smiled at me, a smile broken and fragile, like crepe paper. "I'll call you to let you know if we'll be meeting here or elsewhere. Thank you for coming, Willamina."

"I'll walk you out," Martin said, opening the door.

Really, I didn't need his help. I gave my goodbyes to Suzana and preceded Martin out the door and down the walk-way. His hurried footsteps alerted me he was behind me right before he grabbed the crook of my elbow to stop me.

I turned and yanked my arm free. "Please don't touch me without consent."

He sneered. "I need you to say Kendra's crossed over. That she's gone and you can't reach her. I need you to tell my wife our daughter is dead so she'll stop spending money on this shit. I'll send you a nice bonus for the favor. She needs peace."

"I'll have no problems telling your wife your daughter has passed over if that is the knowledge I gain from the spirits."

He rolled his eyes, then jabbed a finger at me. Oh no. We wouldn't do this, not now, and not on Friday either.

"Listen, Mr. Bruce. I know she's in pain. I know your anger's a symptom of your pain, but you will not bully me.

Have a good night." I turned and walked to my car without further incident.

He shouldn't worry about this too much. If Kendra was as close with her mother as Suzana claimed and hadn't contacted them in six years, Kendra was most likely no longer alive.

THE REDDISH-BROWN BAR TOP SHONE UNDER THE pot lights at a fancy lounge not too far from the Bruces. The meeting had gone quick despite Martin. The ambiance here was dark and soft, all masculine, with dark tall-backed booths and a couple armchairs in front of a dark fireplace. Had I walked into a gentlemen's club by mistake?

Then again, I would probably be an exception to the rule. Not to brag, but I was attractive on my bad days, and today was not one of those days. I'd worn my best taupe palazzo slacks, gorgeous black heels that gave me an extra three inches, and I'd pinned my hair off to one side, letting it slide over my only green silk blouse. I looked fucking amazing.

"What can I get for you?" the bartender asked, looking me over. His eyes stopped before meeting mine.

"French gimlet if you have St. Germain," I answered. "With vodka."

I found gin muddied the lime and elderflower too much, and the flavor was far better with vodka.

He nodded, tearing his gaze from my cleavage, and plucked the bottles from the shelf behind him. I propped my elbow on the counter, and leaned my jaw on the back of my knuckles, and was watching the man pour the liquor when someone sat near me.

"Be with you in a moment," the bartender said, hardly sparing the person a glance.

"Take your time." He had a deep voice, but what made me

sneak a peek was that he sounded like he meant it. Not to be polite, like nearly everyone, but like he had all the time in the world.

I peered at him from the corner of my eyes. He wore a Henley with the sleeves rolled up, showing off his forearms. Dark jeans, slightly faded; the style looked good on him. Henleys were extra popular now, thanks to all the romance books. I stopped studying his clothes and found him watching me with piercing blue eyes.

"Do you like what you see?" he asked, a smirk playing on his lips set within a perfectly manicured beard—which was a shade darker than his wavy brown hair.

I grinned and shrugged, unable to help myself. "Eh." The bartender placed my drink before me, and I smiled at him. "Thanks."

"Do you want to start a tab?" he asked.

"I've got this one," the man sitting one stool away from me said. "And I'll take a Manhattan—Starglen single barrel. Two cherries."

"Oh, no, you don't have to do that," I said.

He waved me off. "Perhaps you'll buy me a drink after this."

"Depends. Are you going to keep drinking expensive whiskey?" I asked.

He chuckled. It sounded nice, a little raspy, as if feathering pages in a book. "Depends if you keep insulting me."

I shifted in my seat to face him, my fingers straddling the stem to my martini glass. "I didn't insult you."

"You shrugged and said 'eh.'" A thick dark brow lifted. A lock of hair above that eye was gray. "Especially since you looked at me like that. Like you were undressing me."

I snorted. "Please. I was looking at your clothes." I took a sip of the gimlet. It was clear, indicating they'd used filtered lime juice. It was bright, and the elderflower added a nice subtle floral note. "Who told you to wear Henleys? A Mrs. Henley?"

"Are you asking if I'm married?" The laughter singing in his deep voice delighted me.

"It doesn't matter to me if you're married."

His eyes widened, and he turned a bit toward me, placing a hand on his thigh. "Ma'am. I'm many things, but I am not a —" He frowned. "I'm a reformed cheater."

"Wow." I crossed my legs and swirled my finger in the air at him. "That's quite the statement. How many times did that happen?"

The bartender placed a rocks glass in front of him with two cherries sitting on a block of ice in caramel-colored liquid. The cheater shifted in his seat and dug out a money clip, sliding over a black credit card to start a tab. It struck me now that he seemed familiar. My attention trailed to the lock of gray hair at his hairline. Where had I seen him before? Couldn't be at bingo unless he also had an elderly relative he dropped off or picked up at the community center.

"Let's keep the distant past where it is," he said, meeting my eyes. "I'm Rex."

"Willamina, but everyone calls me—" I didn't want this man, whom I'd never see again, to call me Billie. Not tonight.

"Let me guess," he drawled, picking up his glass and popping a cherry in his mouth. "Everyone calls you Mina?" He scrunched his face. "Too typical."

"Mina?" I laughed. "God, no. Why do you think anyone would call me that?"

"You look like a Mina now that I know your name."

"How's that?"

"Gorgeous red hair." His gaze traveled over my body—I tried not to squirm. "You're a smoke show, aren't you?"

"I don't . . ." I liked the attention, but I also didn't enjoy being arrogant. "Willa. Call me Willa."

He grinned, lighting up his face. While I wasn't attracted to him, I could tell he was handsome, and his clothes fit him perfectly. He was what most women would call hot. Me? I didn't know him, so he really was "eh" to me. But I liked his smile. It was honest.

"I like that," he said.

"Not that it matters," I replied before sipping from my drink.

"You know, if you're nice to me, I'll buy you another of those. But if you keep being mean . . ."

"Are you one of those people who thinks their approval for something completely out of their control is necessary?" I asked softly.

"Are you one of those people who needs to be snotty when someone's being nice to them?"

"What if I came here to pout and mull over things without anyone I know demanding I smile and be happy?" There was a little more sting to my words than I'd intended.

He cocked a brow again, drawing my eye back to the silver lock of hair. Then he toasted me with his Manhattan. "I came here to brood and have someone else make my drinks. And these cherries."

"So can we pretend that we've already flirted and you've decided you're not in the mood anyway, because whatever you're brooding over is too much?" I asked.

Rex rolled his shoulders before closing the gap and taking the stool next to mine. "You know, I've found the best way to get over my brooding is pleasant company."

"And a beautiful woman?"

"You said it, not me." His knee knocked into my ankle. "And maybe conversation with me will make you less of a prickly princess."

I snorted.

"See? It's already working."

"I'm sorry." I toyed with the glass stem some more and peeked at him. "I never intended to be rude. It's just sometimes pretending to be someone else in situations like this is . . . annoying."

"What would you be pretending to be with me, Willa?" His voice sounded as smooth as satin sheets.

"Being interested in you. I'm sorry," I rushed on. "It's not that you aren't handsome, it's just that there's no chemistry and—"

"Really? You find me handsome?"

"Eh."

We both laughed, thank god. If he hadn't, I really would've felt like an ass and would've bought him a bottle of mid-shelf whiskey to make it up to him.

"What do you find attractive in a man, then?" He lifted his glass, then paused. "Or woman. I'm not going to put you in a box."

"Oh, well." I blinked rapidly, staring off into the distance. "Someone who's true to their word, who'll stand by the people he cares for. A sense of humor. Someone who won't run off when things aren't going the way he wanted."

"So not a child."

I smiled. "No, not a child."

"Those are good qualities."

"I'd like to think so. What about you?"

He rubbed his chin. "Loyalty's important."

"Says the reformed cheater," I murmured.

He tapped my shoe. "Hey, don't judge until you have the entire story. What's important is I didn't like it, okay?"

"Okay." I laid my hand near his. I didn't want to comfort or assure him I believed him, but to let him know I'd drop it. I'd never see him again, so no big deal. "What else?"

"I like it when they can match me"—he tapped his temple —"or at least put in the work to match me, but that's more of a work thing. I'm not here to brood anymore. You know, it boils down to your partner being honest, showing up, and putting in the same amount of work into the relationship as I do."

"Hell yeah," I said.

"And redheads." He flashed a wolfish smile. "I've got a weak spot for redheaded women."

I laughed and leaned in, lowering my voice. "It's fake."

He studied me, his eyes roving over my face, my mouth, my brows, and then on my hair. "Liar. You've got the complexion typical of redheads."

"I didn't want you to think I was excited I met a feature of yours," I murmured. "Didn't want you to try to get me back to your place."

He stared into his Manhattan, which was gone now, and fished out the last cherry. I signaled the bartender to make us another round and retrieved my wallet from my purse slung on the back of the stool.

"Am I poking a wound?" I asked. "I don't mean to be rude. I just don't want you to waste your time."

"Maybe you just have a too-high opinion of yourself, princess," he said.

I'd expect a statement like that to be muttered, but it was as smooth and playful as before. I narrowed my eyes. I don't think I enjoyed being called a princess. "I'm too good for everyone. I'm choosy for who I settle for."

He laughed. "That's a good philosophy, Willa."

I enjoyed being called Willa and smiled to myself. It held none of the expectancy and weight of Billie. Our drinks arrived, and the empties were cleared away, and my two twenties taken along with them.

"But there's always room for chemistry," he softly added. "Eh."

He faced me, a smile on his mouth. It did good things for

him. If I were anyone else, I'd probably be in his lap talking him up.

"I bet there's chemistry between us." He sipped his drink, watching me.

I hummed in the back of my throat. "Even if I possess all the attributes *you* find attractive, there's nothing happening if there's no chemistry for me." And, you know, some kind of emotional bond, but there was no way I'd say that to a stranger, no matter how charming he was.

He leaned in, gripping the back of my stool, his face a hand-width away from mine. His faint woodsy cologne entered the conversation. "One kiss is all I need to know if there's any chemistry here."

I blinked, my stomach taking a sour turn. "No PDA, thanks."

"Of course." He glanced around, and his eyes lighted on the dark hallway leading to the restrooms. "Tell you what, I'll go to the bathroom—washing my hands, I promise—and maybe you'll go too and we'll bump into each other."

"I won't be going inside the men's room," I said, a little surprised.

He flashed his even teeth. "Just a shadowy corner."

"And if I think you're being creepy?"

His piercing gaze bored into mine, and I didn't feel a damned thing. "Then don't follow me, Willa. Jeez."

He slid off his stool and walked toward the hallway. He had broad shoulders that seemed like they could carry a lot of weight. Nothing about him was an accident. I imagined he worked extremely hard to appear so self-assured from behind. Probably a gym rat. When he disappeared, I wondered if he really would pin me against a wall and kiss me if I showed up in the hallway. It wouldn't be that bad, would it?

"One sober-me-up, please," I said, slapping another twenty on the counter.

I drank the light blue potion, and any silly notions of not being who I knew I was vanished. Hooking my purse onto my shoulder, I slid off my stool and strode out the door.

No matter how fun it'd been talking to Rex, I didn't want to fall into the disappointment at what kissing him would lead me to.

I'd forced myself too many times to stand inside a box with too many people to ever ask myself to do that again. And I knew exactly what that kiss would reveal. There really was no point in lying to myself.

Chapter Six

From the large windows in the solarium of the main house, I stared out across the lawn at the carriage house, my hands stuffed in my pockets and fingers curled around my spirit stone. Potted plants and trees filled the room, surrounding the rattan loveseat and chair in a cozy jungle that made the room smell fresh. I'd never felt so trapped in recent memory. I hadn't lived in the carriage house for a handful of years now, not since my promotion to lead the lab. It should've been empty, but movement behind the small windows snagged my attention every time.

I don't want to be here.

"You're still here." Guy's sharp voice came from behind me.

"Of course I am." I pinched the bridge of my nose. "You're holding my *Pac-Man* game hostage."

When I'd declined Suzana Bruce's invitation to the séance, Guy called and informed me, in no uncertain terms, that I wouldn't get my game if I didn't show up. I hadn't even been able to play it yet.

"Clearly you should be here, considering your absolute

shit taste in women." Guy stopped beside me and glared out the window. "Another one of your messes, and it's still in my home."

I wouldn't even go into the semantics that the carriage house technically wasn't inside his home but a renovated building that I'd lived in after returning from the Air Force. Soon after that, I met and fell in love with Kendra Bruce. We'd lived in the carriage house, for the last few years of our relationship—before she blew it all up and left me, then disappeared—making it the best location for the séance the Bruces had access to. Apparently.

"So we let this medium do her thing," Guy said in low tones. "She'll say whatever she'll say about Kendra and her woo-woo whatever. And then . . ." He glared at me. "It better be fucking over, Hendrick."

I pulled my hands from my pockets and lifted them. "It was over when she left me, Guy."

He faced me, prodding a finger into my chest. "I don't want any more bullshit from you. Now's your chance to come clean."

I brushed his hand away. "There's nothing to come clean about."

The door opened, and the maid stepped aside, allowing Suzana and Martin Bruce into the solarium. Followed by Julian Christensen. The room grew fuzzy around the edges as I ground my teeth. This motherfucker . . . Seeing him again at the FCARL charity event had reminded me how much I hated him. How much I just wanted to smash my fist in his face over and over again until I couldn't recognize him. So I'd called him "Junior," and now we were back to where we were six years ago.

I'd known he'd be here thanks to Guy's warning, but seeing him with the Bruces reignited old anger and poked at old wounds that'd healed as best as they could.

He stood a couple inches shorter than me, and he still sported patchy stubble on his cheeks, which was funny to me. Still unable to grow a decent beard. I bet if his father were here, he'd linger in the old man's shadow. But I knew what Kendra had seen in him to leave me.

Money. Power. A different social class.

Once she realized the Slater empire would go to Guy's children before me, Kendra was done. Based on the expression on Suzana's face, like she'd stepped in dog shit, she'd encouraged Kendra to move on to greener pastures.

Julian glared at me, and I narrowed my eyes. We were both air casters, but I knew I could knock him on his ass before he could blink—something we'd tested countless of times while we were at Fulton Prep. I might've leaned into the big, bad wolf persona a little too much then, but it'd worked.

"Martin, Suzana." Guy nodded, most of the frost melting off him. "Julian. Is this everyone, or did you find her childhood friends?"

"This is it," Martin said.

Suzana worried the bracelet on her wrist, identical to the one Kendra always wore. "They couldn't make it, not tonight, and the medium could only do tonight, so . . ."

The porch lights for the carriage house flicked on, the sign that the medium was ready.

"Let's get this over with." Guy opened the door that would take us to the paver stone path to the carriage house. "Ladies first."

Julian bumped his shoulder against mine, but he was the one who missed a step as he tripped over the threshold. Loser. Guy and I strolled side-by-side behind everyone in the dewy night air toward the carriage house, my shoulders growing tighter with each step.

At the door, the medium waited with a sack. She was tall, her hair hidden by a headdress that rested on her shoulders.

Backlit by the carriage house, I couldn't see much of the . . . costume. But it was purple and it fitted her well, the lacy sleeves coming to points on the backs of her hands. A sash, also adorned with crystals and tiny bells, cinched her waist, accentuating her hourglass figure. A long flowy skirt brushed the paver stones at her feet. She glittered under the light thanks to the many enchantments she had sewn into her headdress and veil. Amber eyes, lined heavily in dark makeup, widened when they fell on me. A tickle of familiarity hit me, but I couldn't place what struck a chord with me. She looked exactly like a late-night infomercial psychic.

"Your phones must be turned off and set here," she said. "You'll get them when the séance is over."

Everyone surrendered their phone, but Guy hesitated. "You know, I didn't know her well. Maybe I shouldn't participate."

"My relationship with Kendra was a bit . . . contentious." I wondered if that'd also get me out of sitting in the same room with Julian in the house I'd shared with the woman he'd stolen from me. I was over Kendra. Honestly. That wound had closed, scabbed, and healed in the six years since she left me. But Julian would always be a rival, and I'd always want to get him where it hurt the most. Likewise for him, and I didn't want him to see me in there during this.

The medium tilted her head, her eyes narrowing slightly. "Sometimes a rival is a better draw for spirits than a loved one. Electronics, please."

We both dropped our phones in the sack and stepped inside the carriage house.

It hadn't changed since I'd moved out. We stepped into the main living and dining area. Gauzy cloths and clutter linked to Kendra littered the old table. Pictures, candles, crystals—those weren't Kendra's—a mound of dirt—she was an earth caster—and a duck stuffed animal.

The medium dropped a crystal wand at the door, sealing a grid. Ley energy leaked off every crystal on the floor, blocking the bedroom, kitchen, and bathroom off from the room. When she turned, the enchantments on her costume faintly glowed with ley energy. She was ready to get this party started and wasn't messing around.

"Sit, please," she said.

Did I recognize her voice from somewhere? Maybe I'd inadvertently seen some of her infomercials late at night while trying in vain to fall asleep. I glanced at Guy, wondering if he'd seen them too, as insomnia was something we shared, but he appeared bored and checked out. Anyway, I watched where Julian sat so I wouldn't have to sit next to him, which placed me between Guy and Suzana and directly across the table from the medium.

A wooden grid plate sat in the middle of the table, and the medium leaned over and placed a box before Suzana, opening it up. Inside were several crystals, none of them giving off a ley signature. I frowned but kept my comments to myself.

"When picking the crystals, think of your daughter," the medium instructed. "Use your strongest memories."

Suzana took her time, rifling through the stones and picking them. They were raw stones, some dull with stripes, others strikingly pretty with crystal formations. None of them had a lick of magic. Yet when the medium placed them on the grid plate, a puff of ley energy followed each one. When the final stone locked into place, the ley energy hovered like a screen over the table.

"Spirits, hear me," the medium said, her voice steady and confident. "A family desperate for answers seeks your endless knowledge."

The charms on her veil and headdress winked on with pale blue energy, swirling around the medium's head. Her eyes, which were focused on Suzana, closed.

Suzana gasped softly, and Julian peered at the medium, his brow furrowing. I waited. No practitioner just ignored ley energy like this. At least, not in my experience.

"Let's link hands," the medium said. "Suzana, ask your questions."

I loosely grasped Guy's hand, as well as Suzana's—which gripped mine like a lifeline. The tips of her nails dug into my skin.

"I'm looking for my daughter, Kendra Bruce?" Suzana swallowed. "Have you seen her? Last I knew, she was in Cyprus."

Kendra loved to travel. She'd take quick weekend trips to any place that struck her fancy. Sometimes I went along with her; other times she was cheating on me. I didn't go with her for the last couple years of our relationship—work had me too busy and too tired. Cyprus had turned out to be Kendra's favorite weeklong adventure, and she tried to go once a year or more. The ley energy didn't change, not surprising. However, the medium's eyes remained closed.

The medium drew in a slow, deep breath. "Kendra Bruce, if you're near, give us a signal."

Julian smirked and knocked on the table. Still the same jackass.

"Kendra Bruce, your fiancé is looking for closure and knocks his intent," the medium said. "He's quite the disruptive one, isn't he?"

This time, the ley energy swirled in quick swoops of periwinkle and robin's egg, surrounding the medium in a halo. This had become more intense than I'd expected.

"Suzana," she whispered, "ask your questions."

Suzana trembled next to me, and I squeezed her hand. For support? No, I wanted to leave; I wanted a drink. And if it helped to get this over sooner rather than later, I'd give her support.

"I-Is she here?" Suzana asked. "Is my daughter dead? Do you see her?"

The medium's eyes clenched tight, and her head jerked a bit. The enchantments on her headdress, especially the ones resting on the crown of her head, at her ears, and dangling in front of her throat practically glowed neon. The ley energy swirled with mine, brushing against me. I'd yet to see it so thick in a room like this. And the medium wasn't even looking at it.

"Yes, I'm sorry. She's here," the medium whispered. Her breathing changed, fluttering the veil covering the lower half of her face.

Martin let out a relieved breath, briefly meeting my gaze. I guessed finally knowing instead of always wondering was a good thing. The state of California had declared Kendra dead, but well, it didn't surprise me Suzana hadn't. Her daughter was her best friend, and Kendra had adored her mother.

"What happened, baby girl?" Suzana asked, a tear slipping down her cheek.

The medium made a face, which was hard to read thanks to the veil. Her enchantments continued glowing. She flinched, nearly tearing her hands from Martin and Julian. Her breath became ragged. "I can't breathe."

I wasn't sure if it was the medium speaking, or . . . what.

"Was it an accident, baby? Did you fall into the ocean?" Suzana prodded, then shot me a scorching look. "Or murder?"

Jesus Christ, woman. Accuse much?

"I can't breathe." The medium's breath turned shallow, and when she exhaled, the veil barely fluttered. "It's so dark. I can't breathe!"

Everywhere inside my chest clenched, particularly the space around my heart. I didn't want to know this. I hadn't ever wanted Kendra to suffer, not like this. And that she had . . . I swallowed and averted my eyes, unable to bear watching the medium either fake drowning or relive Kendra's final moments. God, I hoped she was faking it.

"Enough," Guy said. He could've directed that to the Bruces or the medium. It wasn't clear.

I lifted my gaze to see the unhinged ley energy twist around the medium, her eyes remaining tightly screwed shut while she panted for breath.

I turned to Suzana and whispered, "Ask a different question."

"What happened to you, Kendra?" Suzana wailed, completely ignoring me.

"I can't breathe." The enchantments on her costume faded rapidly in brightness, and the medium drew a long breath. She opened her now bloodshot eyes, her shoulders heaving. "I only have enough energy for one more question tonight."

"Is your spirit stone still in Cyprus?" Martin asked. "We want to have that of yours."

The ley halo whirling around her head flared, her eyes rolled backward, and she tipped her face to the ceiling. A snarl of ley energy rippled across her face before it completely extinguished. Nothing but the filmy screen from the raw stones on the wooden grid plate remained.

Silence filled the carriage house. Julian squinted at the medium before his attention darted between me and Guy. My heart thudded heavily against my ribcage as we waited for her to answer the question. Right as I believed she wouldn't answer, she released a rush of air from her lips, the veil quivering against her mouth.

"Kendra's spirit stone is here."

Chapter Seven

"You're a liar and a con man," Guy Slater snarled.

My eyes flew open, my heart still racing and my lungs painfully tingling from the echo of the spirit—Kendra—when she came to answer. It'd been so quick, her arrival, that for a moment, I'd thought I'd imagined it . . . Like when the determined Rex from last night walked along the path toward me. I peered at him for the first time since I opened my eyes and he seemed . . . Like he didn't want to be here.

That was the case with nearly everyone aside from Julian Christensen and Suzana. Holy shit, what had the Bruces gotten me into? No one in this room liked each other much, aside from the Bruces.

"Hold on a moment." Rex wrenched his grip from Suzana and leaned on the table, his piercing blue gaze on mine. "Did she—Kendra's spirit—tell you her familiar was here?"

I placed a hand at the base of my throat, taking in a deep breath so I wouldn't sound like I'd run out. "Her spirit spoke little." Aside from repeating she couldn't breathe and showing me flashes of water. I shuddered.

"The last time my fiancée contacted me," Julian said, a sneer curling his upper lip, "she was in Cyprus." He glanced at me. "That's in Greece."

What a mansplaining asshole. I *really* wanted to correct him that the territory was in a dispute with Greece after a coup from the Turkish military, but I wasn't here to give a history lesson to a moron. Google wasn't hard to use, and I'd totally availed myself of it after having a discussion with Suzana when advising her what to bring tonight. I'd known it was a favorite vacation spot of her daughter's.

"Well, if her familiar's here, then she must've returned to the states." Suzana swiveled in her seat and gripped Martin's hands. "Why wouldn't she see us? Did she reach out to you and make you promise not to tell me?"

Martin sighed softly, as if he didn't know how to ease her distress and it also upset him. "No, Sooz, she hasn't reached out to me since she left."

"This is ridiculous." Guy shoved back from the table, a couple of crystals toppling over from the force. "There's no reason for her to come around here anymore. She knew better."

My brows lifted, and I couldn't help but look at Rex. How did he know Guy Slater?

"What do you mean by that, Guy?" Rex asked softly, his expression going from blank to suspicious in an instance.

"Because you were no longer living here, Hendrick." He lifted his chin and turned toward the Bruces. "Kendra hadn't left anything here, so there was no reason to come here."

"Clearly she left her spirit stone here if she said so when we asked." Julian reached for my hand. "Let's ask her. I'm sure she's still hanging around."

I pulled my hand away and clasped them together in my lap. I didn't like the vibe Julian gave off. Smug and malicious.

Then I glanced at Martin, remembering what he said to me, and frowned. I wouldn't add more to that.

I closed my eyes, searching for any residuals of Kendra's spirit and the echoes of memories she had within this carriage house. I got the sensation that there were many spirits here, ghosts of memories, mostly broken and . . . and gone. "She's not here anymore."

"Okay, well, we can easily solve this." Julian grinned. "We call her familiar."

Guy threw his hands up in the air and muttered something under his breath.

"Quackie Chan!" Suzana called out. "Are you here?"

Quackie Chan?! That explained the stuffed duck Suzana had given me. I sucked my cheeks into my mouth and gently bit down, hoping my amusement wouldn't show. There were sharp inhalations and a muttered curse.

"Oh, Quackie Chan," Suzana said, a sob breaking her voice.

I didn't need to look for it. The familiar had shown itself. I read the room and realized the biggest threat was no longer the possibility of a hostile possession. It was the living now. I hadn't needed magic for that. Guy attempted to kill me with a look. I leaned slightly back from the stare. Julian focused on Suzana, then slowly shifted his attention to Rex and smirked, but it went mostly unnoticed.

Rex rapidly blinked and closed his mouth, tearing his gaze from the Bruces, and sent a bewildered expression to Guy. "What the hell is Kendra's familiar doing here?"

It was a good question. The Slater estate was in a rich neighborhood in what people would call the sticks. About ten or fifteen miles out of Starglen, situated in the country with the nearest neighbor a quarter of a mile away. Spirit stones had a radius of twenty-five miles, so there was a possibility it was somewhere within that reach, but where? And how?

"That's a good question, Hendrick." Guy's complexion turned flinty. "Why *is* it here?"

Oh fuck. *Rex* was Hendrick Slater? Now I understood why he'd seemed familiar the other night. I'd read about him in the tabloids while I waited for Mimzy's appointments to conclude. He was one of Starglen's most eligible bachelors with a reputation of being a playboy. I sincerely hoped he hadn't recognized me.

"Willamina," Suzana said, destroying almost all chances that my identity would remain unknown, "you said Kendra told you the spirit stone was here. Ask her where exactly."

"Oh, come on." Guy stood and loomed over the table. "This is ridiculous."

Suzana clenched her jaw along with her fists. "If Kendra said it was here, it's here."

"It doesn't have to be here." I gently pressed my palms together. "Sometimes spirits can be confused, and Kendra was . . ." Drowning for air. "Distressed. She very well could've meant only that her spirit stone was here on this plane."

Suzana gestured, taking in the entire table with a sweep of her hand. "Then how do you explain Quackie Chan? Kendra wouldn't go far without him. So she was here when she died." She turned to Martin, covering her mouth. "My baby's dead."

Martin made soothing sounds and pulled her into his arms, rubbing her back as she sobbed. He gazed helplessly at me from over her head. "Where's our daughter's stone? We'd just like it back. Can you find it with your magic?"

Julian's mouth thinned into a grim line, but something told me all of this delighted him. Perhaps it was boredom, always having to be on his best behavior as the son to the next possible mayor of Starglen. "Yes, Ms. Dade, you can find the spirit stone, can't you? Especially if it's here."

"Which it isn't," Guy snapped.

"You're protesting too much." Julian stood.

Rex pinched the bridge of his nose. "It's ridiculous if it's here. Kendra made it perfectly clear there was never anything here for her."

I had no idea where it could be, though I'd gotten a creepy vibe when the maid walked me around from the front door through part of the grounds and to the carriage house. Like how dare I ring the front bell? But on the way here, there was a . . . menagerie of stones, most likely a fancy type of garden, as it was a little wild. But it'd given me the creeps.

"In that stone statue area," I said. "The garden. It has a heavy spirit residue."

Guy's face turned mottled, and he stormed to a window. Rex pushed back from the table and stood. He and Julian watched each other, like a pair of lions sizing one another up for the best way to kill the other the fastest.

"Then let's go there." Suzana had collected herself, but her face remained tearstained. "Let's collect her stone, and we'll be on our way."

Martin nodded. "That's a good idea."

"No, I don't think so," Guy said. "I've placated this silly notion long enough. You've got your answers about your daughter. That's all I'm willing to do for you."

When I'd met Guy Slater's eyes, chilly skeletal fingertips walked up my spine and flooded my chest with ice. My fingers moved on their own, wringing the tied ends of the sash between my hands. Those flashes of water, of feeling submerged while fighting to breathe, ricocheted through my memory one more time. My throat tightened, and part of me wished I had something better to clutch to make me feel safe. Like a knife.

"Come on." Rex joined him at the window. "I don't think the spirit stone's here either, so it can't hurt to look for it. And then the Bruces and Junior here can leave. Right?"

Julian bristled beside me. "For the last and final time, Slater, don't call—"

"Very well." Guy shoved his hands into his pockets and speared me with a double-edged glare. "Do you have a way of finding lost spirit stones?"

Maybe I should pack up and be ready for a quick exit. I also didn't believe I should mention that locating spirit stones was an entirely different service with a fee of its own. I didn't have to check my costume's enchantments to know they didn't have enough juice to help locate the stone. However . . .

"I don't have anything as powerful as the new tech in finding spirit stones," I said.

Suzana gasped in dismay. "Surely your method's just as good."

"I'm sure Willa—*Willamina*—can figure it out and won't leave you hanging, Suzana," Rex said.

Crap on a stick, he remembers who I am. I shouldn't have been surprised he'd recognized me, especially when she'd used my name in front of him.

"No, of course not. This isn't an inappropriate request at all." I stood and hefted my box of crystals on the table and opened it. I slid out the compartment housing my pendulum crystals and tucked it on the lid, then selected one that was three tones in color—umbra, lavender, and seafoam—and loosely grasped the chain in my fingers. "It acts as a dowsing rod."

But my pendulum didn't move. Not even a smidge. I studied everyone, reading their expressions. *Please don't tell me I didn't have this recharged before I packed it up last.* Suzana's gaze remained trained on my crystal, but a small wrinkle appeared between her brows. That could mean anything. Martin wouldn't glance in my direction; I knew he believed this was a waste of time. Rex frowned, his right hand slipping into the deep pockets of his jeans. Julian also seemed perplexed.

However, Guy smirked. That echo, the memory of Kendra's spirit gasping for breath, hit me one more time, and I sucked in deep, reminding my lungs that they could breathe.

"Is that the right charm?" Suzana asked.

"Of course it's the right one," Rex snapped. "Look at it closely."

"I'm not an enchanter, Hendrick," she said acidly.

I cleared my throat and ran my fingers over the charm twice, once to deactivate it, and again to activate—kind of like a ley energy power cycle. Nothing.

"Maybe there's interference in this room . . ." Julian said, rubbing his forehead as his attention flicked toward the crystals lining the perimeter of the carriage house.

"Okay, there's one more option." I couldn't believe I was suggesting this, especially after I promised myself I'd never let it happen again, but people were desperate. I was desperate for this to be over. "I can call her spirit inside me to guide me to it, but I'll need to cleanse the area first . . ."

I trailed off from the waves of hostility barraging me from Guy.

Rex shook his head. "That's dangerous."

"Well," Julian drawled, "we're all here with her. Some of us are ACEs, so she won't be without support."

I furrowed my brow, glad that my veil hid most of my expression. Call me crazy, but I didn't think I could depend on these people for protection from spirits if a malevolent one decided my meat sack looked cozy.

"Absolutely not," Guy said. "There will be no gentle possessions. This séance is over."

And you know what? I was relieved.

Chapter Eight

Suzana rounded on me, her face mottled and tears filling her eyes. "Please, Hendrick," she said, pressing her fists between her breasts. "I need to know."

It spun me back to years ago. She'd almost worn the same expression, and we were in the same spot, but instead of everyone here, it was only me, Kendra, and Suzana. I could still perfectly recall the incredulity in her voice. *"Here? You're a Slater. Why are you making her live here? In a carriage house?"*

Kendra had objected too, now that I thought on it, but then she realized if she ever needed anything, she could go into the main house whenever she pleased. She'd been okay with our arrangements. What else could we do with me fresh from the military and still in the reserves, hoping to get a job at my father's company?

Suzana's clammy hand jerked me from the past. "If you ever loved my daughter, you'll let us look for the spirit stone."

Quackie Chan still waddled the floor close to Martin. The duck was bright blue, and Kendra'd said he'd been so white he'd been alive, he'd almost had a blue glow to him. Now he was about the size of a baby hippo, his spirit body covered in an array of sparkling spell workings I couldn't read since I wasn't an earth caster. Because familiars were grimoires of quick casting for casters, they grew in size every time they learned a new spell working, which took the caster a year and day to memorize. It was always worth it to have your familiar memorize a spell working because sometimes one simply did not have the time to sketch out the spell working with chalk.

And why had Quackie Chan been able to come when he'd been called upon, here of all places? I studied Guy, recognizing his stance. He wasn't willing to budge, but this shouldn't hurt anything. And if Kendra had somehow left her stone near the property, then surely everyone would want it back in the right hands. Spirit stones were sacred artifacts to casters; Guy understood that.

"I don't see an issue with looking a little closer for the stone." I shifted and peered at Willa and the pendulum charm hanging uselessly from her fingers. "As long as you think it's worth it?"

"Of course it's worth it, Slater," Julian snapped. "Finding my fiancée's spirit stone is the sole purpose of this meeting."

"Here?" Guy asked. "You've been looking long?"

"I only want closure." He cupped Willa's shoulder. "You can find it, right?"

"Of course," she said, her eyes flicking around the room, landing on every stone that had sealed this grid off. "Leaving this room could unblock the chakras—"

Guy crossed his arms and bowed his head, exhaling so loudly that everyone turned and stared at him. He shrugged. "I don't think this is a good idea."

"I don't see the harm for you," Martin said, finally tearing his gaze away from Quackie Chan. "Our daughter died, and her familiar was precious to her. It's the closest thing we'll ever have to a living memorial to her."

Suzana latched on to Willa's arm and dragged her out and through the door.

"Hey!" Willa spun and broke the grip once she stepped over the threshold. "Don't touch me like that."

"You have to help." Suzana grabbed her again and tugged. "You must know where the stone is. You can find it."

We piled out of the carriage house, Martin hurrying after them. Julian shot me an expression I didn't understand before he followed. And Guy . . . His lips pressed so tightly together, they resembled a white slash. I hadn't seen him this rigid since my nephew briefly dropped out of college.

This evening was officially bizarre, and I wasn't sure how to proceed yet. So I hurried after them.

". . . never discussed this in our meeting about the séance." Willa's tone implied she was trying to be professional.

"It's a séance, Willamina," Suzana said. "What did you expect to happen?"

Willa blinked her amber eyes at her over the veil and took a step away from the other woman, just out of reach, and then at Martin. "I expected to answer the question regarding the fate of your daughter. Which I have. This . . ." She gestured wildly around her. "This isn't normal."

I snorted. If a psychic medium found this display at one of her séances strange, then she was in for a real treat if she kept dealing with the Bruces and even Julian.

"We'll pay an extra fee." Martin wrapped his arm around his wife. "Really, we want to find our daughter's spirit stone."

Julian plunged his hands in his pockets and scanned the grounds. Not too far from here, Guy had landscaped the garden around the skinny stream at the edges of the property some years ago to add in tall grasses and large, flowering bushes to expand the small pet cemetery. Some trees were close to full maturity. Since then, a few sparkles of ley bugs had taken residence, and they were active now, pale blue globes blinking in and out as they moved from plant to plant. Here and there, one could make out a small headstone, some ranging back to the 18th century when the main house had been built.

But instead of Willa heading directly toward the pet cemetery, she shifted, her attention drifting toward the small stream at the edge of the cemetery. That area was always bad for pests. It was even a little marsh-like, especially during the rainy season. Mosquitos loved it. I never understood why he'd approved the landscaping design.

She held her spirt-stone-seeking pendulum out and the charm barely moved with gravity. I slipped my hand in my pocket one more time, folding my fingers around my spirit stone. Why wasn't she picking up on the one in my pocket? Julian and Guy must have had theirs on their person too. And by merely glancing at the charm, I also knew that it was charged. Perhaps she'd used just any charm to get this over with? Wasn't that what Dane'd said about palm readers? They'd say and do anything to keep the cash flowing in their direction?

Was Willa truly a con man? Sure, she'd left me high and dry at the bar last night, but she hadn't been into me, so I couldn't hold that against her. But this? I would.

Willa took a reluctant step toward the stream and lifted a hand, pointing in that direction. "There."

Suzana froze, and Martin took a step closer to it. He turned back to Willa, a wrinkle between his brows. "You're certain?"

"Yes." Willa folded the charm in her palm, her eyes tracking over something I didn't see. "It's here."

"Okay." Guy laughed. "That's enough."

Julian frowned, edging closer to the stream, as if searching for the stone right there. "You're certain, Willamina? The stone's here?"

"I said that's enough." The finality in Guy's tone had the

hair raising on the back of my neck. "I'm afraid I must ask all of you to leave."

"I'm sorry," Willa murmured to Suzana, "I have to stop. I have nothing left tonight."

Suzana fisted her blouse, as if she could clutch her heart, her chin trembling. But honestly? I was glad this was over, and that Willa signaled she was done too, because how long would she let this sham continue?

"I'll help you pack up." I dislodged Willa from Suzana and turned her toward the carriage house. I didn't let my grip on her linger.

She nodded at me, plucked at the fabric of her dress to lift the hem, and hurried back to the house. Behind us, Julian and Martin ganged up on Guy, demanding to know why he'd refused to let them search for the spirit stone further.

I opened the door for her and leaned down. "What the hell do you think you're doing, Willa?"

She eyed me as she walked by and shook her head. "I'm here to help the Bruces gain closure on their daughter's death." She hefted the wooden box on the table and opened it, displaying many small compartments filled with crystals. "Suzana didn't tell me she'd call on a familiar."

I collected the few crystals on the floor by the door and handed them to her. "That really fucked with your scam, didn't it? You didn't come prepared for that."

"Excuse me?" Her tone had gone from guarded to ice princess in an instant.

"You and your parlor tricks. Although, I should say, it was fun watching you." I dropped the crystals into empty compartments.

Willa froze in collecting stones on the other side of the room, her headdress falling askew, and her large amber eyes latched on mine. A strand of red hair slipped from its pins, sliding against her skin like a bloody gash against her ivory cheek. "What're you implying, Rex?"

I retrieved my spirit stone and showed her. "Your trick about the spirit stone. I had mine on me this whole time and not once did your pretty crystals pick it up."

She halted in collecting her crystals, and the dowsing pendulum appeared in her hands again, as if summoned. Lifting it by the chain, she stepped to me, and again, it didn't point at the stone in my palm. Yet periwinkle ley energy glowed from within her enchantment.

"Why isn't it working, princess?" I asked.

"I don't know." She thrust the charm into my hands. "Figure it out, since you're so clever."

I turned the crystal over in my hands, inspecting it. The charm didn't have a full charge. It'd been used before tonight, but that shouldn't have kept it from detecting El Diablo's stone, especially this close to it. And the enchantment was a seeking one, the kind that'd be able to point out where a spirit stone was hidden, or buried.

"It's charged, though," I said.

She took it from me. "I know. I used it a few weeks ago to find a misplaced spirit stone."

I lifted my brows. "Was it on the estate of a wealthy family?"

"No." She made a quick order of clearing away her crystals. "In the freezer next to some cookie dough."

Before I could ask for more information, the door burst open and Guy barged in, the room suddenly feeling distinctly frigid.

He took one look at Willa, and his lips peeled back from his teeth. "Who do you work for?" he snarled.

She glanced at him while she tucked her box into a bag and folded her headdress. "The Bruces are the ones who consulted me."

"And who do you spy for?" Guy rounded the table to get close to her.

Willa stepped back and peered at me around Guy before shaking her head. "It's just the Bruces, Mr. Slater. They're the client."

"Who else, Ms. Dade? Who put you up to this?" Guy closed the distance between them, backing her up against the table. "Which company are you spying on me for? How much did they pay you for this?"

Willa braced her hand on the table behind her, but she didn't shrink away. They were practically nose-to-nose. "I've already told you, Mr. Slater. The Bruces are my clients. They paid me for a séance, and I am not a spy."

Guy leaned in, lifting a finger. I hated he was acting this way, that he was threatening another person when he couldn't interrogate them into giving what he wanted.

"That's enough." I gripped him by the shoulder and dragged him back a few steps. Then I stepped between them, giving her my back. "She's answered your questions. Back off."

Guy grew silent, his intent stare focused on me. Willa shifted away from me, snatching the grid plate off the table and shoving it in her bag. She hurriedly scanned the room once more before hoisting the bag on her shoulder. "I'm going now." She gave me a tight-lipped smile. "Be well with this, Rex."

Whatever that meant. I shrugged and nodded. "Yeah. Same to you."

Then she left.

Guy spun me around, and his finger was in my face, brushing the tip of my nose. "Did you murder her?"

My stomach knotted sharply. "Excuse me?"

"Did you kill Kendra for leaving you?" he repeated, this time his finger bumping my nose.

I smacked his hand away and pushed him back a few steps.

"No. I did not murder her." I flexed my fingers, aching to do more than shove him. I understood why I was always the scapegoat. Alvin, our father, had had an affair, and I was the glaring reminder of everything that could go wrong. If there was a problem, I was the cause. It'd never really stopped, but it had lessened to some degree. But accusing me of murder? That was insulting.

Guy shoved his hands through his short, salt and peppered hair, ruffling it. "Then why the fuck was her damned familiar here?"

I narrowed my eyes, thinking back to the last few times I'd seen Kendra before she left me for Julian. I tried to remember any interactions she had with Guy, how they'd behaved together, but it wasn't revealing. I needed to ask. "Did you have an affair with her, Guy?"

The tension coiling in his stance disappeared so quickly, it was a miracle he remained standing. His brows squished together. "What?"

"With Kendra. I mean, she wasn't always faithful, but I assumed my brother would be off-limits. But was she off-limits to you?" I swallowed, my heart hammering against my chest as I replayed our time living here together. Again, I didn't see anything off, but she'd had full access to the main house. "Did Lynne catch you and you had to 'take care' of Kendra?"

"Are you even listening to yourself, Hendrick?" Guy's lost expression broke as he scoffed. "I'd never cheat on Lynne. That's not how our relationship works." He sat at the table and rubbed his forehead. "What a shitshow. Who *was* that psychic?"

"You know who she is. Just an enchanter making a buck off people's grief." I wondered if I should mention that the charm had the proper enchantment and ask him why it didn't work here, but I thought better of it. Guy was in a state. I didn't understand it, and I didn't know how to get him to confide in me, anyway. "Why did you ask if she was a spy?"

"Oh, you know . . ." He swirled his hand in the air. "I've suspected some corporate espionage. I just . . ."

That was news to me. "For how long?"

Guy scoffed and stood from the table. "Slater Technologies has always been a target since before Dad retired. If you're certain she's only here to make money off the Bruces, then we need to make sure none of it splashes back on us."

My head spun. "What the fuck are you talking about?"

"She's found a cash cow, Hendrick. She'll milk it for everything it's worth. I do *not* want her to think we're easy targets." Guy's gaze swept over me. "So you're going to dig into her past. I want to know everything about her: when she was born, where her talents lie, what she does during the day, and who she fucks at night. I want the dirt on her so I can be ready when she comes for us."

I laughed. "Are you serious? Why me?"

"Because she called you Rex. You two clearly know each other."

"We don't know each other at all. We met last night."

"Did you sleep with her yet?" Guy asked.

I glared, refusing to answer that. "I don't have time for this. I have new flash bombs to create, and I'm working on a throw away charm that'll keep an area airtight." I thought about the previous tests and rubbed my chin. "It peters out within ninety minutes, but if I can get it to stay active until it's switched off, this would secure crime scenes better. Then we can—"

"No." Guy shook his head. "No, this needs to be done first. We need to get ahead of this ASAP. Now find out everything she knows, and then tell me what she doesn't know."

I sighed, staring at him. "Really?"

"Yes." He strode to the door and opened it, then glared

back at me. "And it's best if you don't fuck her. You never know how these things will shake out."

I hid my hands inside my pockets and averted my face. So many comebacks rolled through my head. Like maybe he should be the one worried about how this shook out since he was the CEO of the family company, but I kept my mouth shut. Peace was a fragile thing in the Slater family. A lot of the responsibility rested on my shoulders to keep it.

Fine. I'd solve this mystery. I'd save face for the company. He was lucky I didn't want his job, because I'd take it from him just for this.

Chapter Nine

I leaned against the pale green counter next to the cash register in TrixieCakes, watching my niece film Trixie decorating the second batch of dragon cupcakes, since the morning batch had finally sold out. They were a popular cake, most likely thanks to Candi doing these videos of them all the time. I stood off-centered from the register, because it was the best place to be downwind of vanilla, cinnamon, and nutmeg.

"Okay, I'm done." Candi walked away to one of the little pink tables where her things were hanging out and sat in a yellow chair.

Next to her, my nephew Shawn played with a flexible dragon. When he wiggled its head, the whole body moved like a serpent.

"That's pretty cool," I said, glancing at the clock. My shift would be over soon. "Goes great with the cupcakes, huh?"

Candi's head popped up, and her eyes widen when she spotted the dragon. "Let me use that."

"No." Shawn curled the toy up on itself.

"Shawn, come on." Candi rose from her seat and stood next to him, her phone in hand. "It's perfect for my videos."

He hunkered over the table, blocking the toy from his sister. "No. It's mine, and I don't want it in your stupid videos, Candice."

"Stop being a dick," Candi snapped and reached around him. "You know this is perfect, so let me use it."

"Hey!" Trixie set the tray of dragon cakes she was filling aside and stepped around the counter. "Don't call your brother that. Shawn, let Candi use your toy for a video."

"Fine." Shawn's arms snapped around his chest, and he shoved his chair back. "Let Candi get whatever she wants."

Trixie didn't even react. The kids baited each other, then one of them would pull Trixie into their arguments. It'd gotten significantly worse when Shawn became a tween. Go figure. These kids were great when they weren't bickering.

Trixie picked up the dragon and smiled a little. "That's cool." She wagged the shimmery pink tail. "Where'd you get this?"

"One of my friends from school. She let me have it because I liked it so much," Shawn quickly said, pulling out his phone and unlocking it. That was his signal he was checking out.

Trixie handed the toy to Candi. "Give it back when you're done."

"Duh. It's just a toy." Candi rolled her eyes and then jogged to the counter and grabbed one of the cupcakes. "This is mine, okay?"

Candi used to try to return the prop cupcakes back into the case, but Trixie said no and made her pay for it. Now she did it on her own. I had fifteen more minutes left on my shift, and I really wanted to go home. After the terrible séance last night and the nightmares of drowning, I needed some downtime.

Candi made quick work of the dragon curling up on itself,

then she did that thing with her phone where she smashed it into the toy then pulled back. Setting it aside, she replaced the dragon with a cupcake, the lizard made from frosting curled around a faceted gelled candy, which also resembled an egg, and resumed filming.

The bell over the door jingled, and Rex walked in.

I blinked, not believing my eyes. He wore a lifeguard T-shirt with faded red letters; the sleeves were tight on his biceps, and he'd tucked part of the hem into the waistband of his faded jeans. A devastating appearance for anyone who had a pulse. Except for me, of course. His hair was stylishly messy, and his beard seemed to be recently trimmed. Shawn glanced up, and his attention glued onto Rex's arms. Rex filled the entire space of the lobby by only taking a single step inside. When he spotted me, his brows hopped an inch, nearly bumping his lone lock of gray hair.

He recovered from his surprise, taking in the pastel green-pink-yellow decor of the bakery, the big sign behind me, and then nearly drooled over the sweets on display. But instead of approaching the bakery case, he came to me instead.

"Willa." His voice held a teasing tilt, and his blue eyes twinkled. "Don't you make enough money causing mayhem with your séances?"

Oh, he wanted to play. How adorable. I struck a Vanna White pose, gesturing to the glass case. "I also spread cheer with cupcakes." I gifted him my best smile. "It helps keep my chakras balanced."

"Do you make these?" he asked.

I shook my head. "Nah, I just hawk 'em. I do sometimes help with the cookies."

Rex perked, his piercing gaze finding their prey in the form of a giant peanut butter cup-shaped cookies. Trixie leaned over, her brow raised as she rubbernecked between me and Rex. He ignored us, of course. He only had eyes for cookies and cakes, especially the ones with peanut butter.

Candi hopped up from her seat and stepped behind the counter, her phone held out to Trixie. Rex rubbed his chin, stroking his beard as he debated between the peanut butter cup or the peanut butter fudge. What a dilemma he had, because I could attest both were fantastic.

"Why're you tagging Icing again?" Trixie asked, passing the phone back to Candi.

"It's just a challenge," she answered.

Rex straightened, his attention darting between Candi, Trixie, and the phone. Apparently, he'd made his choice and now he wanted to eavesdrop. It was time to get him out of here before Candi noticed him. Evidently, Rex wasn't attractive enough to steal the sixteen-year-old girl's attention from her phone.

Then Candi spotted him. Her eyes widened and her lips parted, revealing the pink rubber bands in her braces. I'd clearly thought too soon. She tripped over her feet, her face turned bright red, and she sat, keeping her head down. Poor kid. Rex hadn't noticed any of that.

I opened a takeaway box and grabbed two of the giant peanut butter cup cookies, one PB and fudge cookie, a standard oatmeal and cranberry cookie, and the shark cake—a yellow cake with a bright blue frosting shark lurching out of the cupcake with one of the gelled jewels in the middle of its mouth.

I closed the box and rang up the contents. "That'll be $31.34."

Chuckling, he approached the register. "I didn't ask for these."

I grinned and opened the box one more time to let him see inside. "But your eyes did."

He gripped the counter, his blue gaze capturing mine while he slowly leaned in. "No means no, Willa."

His voice sounded like whiskey, and his cologne, while faint, had a cedar note to it. And it was all completely lost on me.

"Very well." I closed the lid and lifted the box from the counter.

Rex quickly pulled out his phone, and it chimed to signal that the payment was sent. I faced the counter again, doing everything I could to keep my expression blank.

"What's done is done," he said. "Let's call it a . . . peace offering."

I slowly lifted a brow. "I didn't know peace needed to be brokered."

Candi stepped behind the counter, her cheeks still pink but nowhere near as red as before. She tied the apron strings behind her. "It's my shift now," she mumbled. Spotting the receipt, she handed it to Rex and giggled. "Enjoy."

Perfect timing! I smiled at Candi and stepped into the back room. I swore I could feel the weight of his gaze on my back the entire time, even through the doors. I quickly hung up my apron and grabbed my purse. When I stepped into the dining area again, Rex waited by the door, the box of goodies in his hand. I wished this place had a back door.

"Bye, Trix!" I raised my voice, waving at them. "Bye, kids."

Shawn ignored me, but Candi called out, and so did Trixie, who gave me a knowing look. I brushed past Rex and stepped out into the late afternoon on Main Street. The sky was a perfect robin's egg blue, and the clouds were huge, fluffy things—something you'd only see in cartoons. The mountains in the distance, for once, were clear. It was a perfect day. Almost.

I spun around and faced him. "Why are you following me?"

Rex lifted the box. "I wanted to chat over cookies."

"You could've asked, you know." I headed across the street to a small green area with a bench and a little free library.

"Well, you've got a bad habit of leaving me hanging," he said, sitting on the bench.

"Oh, the peace offering's for you because I didn't want to make out with you in a hallway at a random bar." I scoffed, ducking my head, and peered inside the free library. People had stuffed it with memoirs, Starglen locals, religious reads, and the stray Nora Roberts or that woman who wrote *Outlander*.

"No." He laughed. It was nice, not forced, not held on for too long, and just a tad deeper than his normal talking voice. "But now it is, a little."

I sat next to him, the box from TrixieCakes between us. "Then what's it mostly about?"

He watched me like a predator, and I sensed a trap.

"It's about the séance," he said.

I frowned. The trap was the séance. I was still angry with Suzana over how it'd turned out. She knew it was only a séance. I should've taken Martin's offer and said Kendra had crossed over and there was nothing I could do to get her to come back. Now her mother was blowing up my texts and my email, begging me to do more.

I opened the box, smiling at the blended aroma of vanilla, sugar, and chocolate wafting from it. I carefully removed the shark cake and placed it in Rex's hands. "Eat the jewel first before you take a bite of the cupcake."

"Okay." He popped it into his mouth, chewed and swallowed. "It reminds me of those fruit snacks in grade school. No flavor though."

I smiled and nodded at the treat. "Take a bite."

He shot me a confused expression before he bit into the yellow cake. His eyes popped wide and he covered his mouth and chewed before releasing a happy sigh. "Oh wow. I haven't tasted raspberry like this in cakes for a long time."

He took another bite, groaning and savoring the flavor. I smirked to myself, scanning the street. Down the block, I watched a couple step inside Sweetie Pies, an artisanal candy store. I wondered if they sold the strawberry candy Mimzy kept at the bottom of her purse.

"Shit. These're good." Rex had finished half the cupcake.

"Think of a different flavor, and take another bite," I said.

He tilted his head, peered at the cake, then bit in. Once more, his blue eyes went large, and he swallowed. "Whiskey!"

I laughed. "Really? You wanted to taste whiskey when you bit into that cupcake?"

He leaned slightly toward me. "I was thinking about your eyes."

I did everything in my power not to roll them at him, even if it was a flattering thing to say. I knew his type. "Are you trying to fetishize me?"

"No." The tips of his ears grew pink. "I was trying to be charming."

"It didn't work." But his ears had done the legwork. Blushing Rex was adorable.

He pinched the bridge of his nose. "I need a drink."

"Have another bite of your cupcake."

He grinned and laughed, and I gave in, chuckling with him.

"How did you know to find me at TrixieCakes?" I asked when he finished the cupcake.

He seemed reluctant, almost shy, when he glanced at me. "I was actually there for a different reason. I also don't think the guys at Icing realized they're taking part in a challenge."

Ah. I nodded slowly. Rex must know them, and based on his clothes and . . . well, *who* he was, it didn't surprise me he got his treats from a pastry shop in the Flower Market.

"Candi can be a little dramatic." I lifted my face to the sky and shook my head. "Sorry, she's always dramatic."

"She's a teen." Rex shifted on the bench and closed off his remaining treats, the cardboard lid flap sliding against the sides of the box. "Have you seen her videos?"

I hummed in the back of my throat, wondering where this line of questioning was leading me. "I watch her make them." I leaned closer to him, and he mirrored my movements. "Can you keep a secret?"

"I'll carry it to my grave." His voice was so solemn I believed him.

I placed a hand on his shoulder and moved so close I could feel the heat of his body on my lips. He shivered.

"I hid both their accounts a long time ago." I sat back and crossed my legs. "Candi posted too much when her mom let her start those accounts, and it just dominated my feed."

He laughed, shifting to prop an elbow on the back of the bench and facing me. "I get it." His free hand inched forward, tapping the box thoughtfully. "One more thing . . . I'm not sure how to ask this."

I peered at the time on my phone. "Then just ask. I've got to pick up my grandma and take her to her appointments."

"Okay. How much of the séance was made up and you just knowing things beforehand?"

What the fuck did that mean? Since I refused to ask, I put on a show. I smiled, making sure it tilted to one side, lowered my lashes, and peeked at him from the corner of my eye. "I shan't divulge my secrets to a nonbeliever."

"Right." He smirked right back at me. "Is it because my brother called you a fraud?"

I blinked. "Guy Slater's your brother?"

He rocked his hand back and forth. "Half-brother, but I'm not here to split hairs on that. What made you say the spirit stone was next to the pet cemetery?"

Pins and needles flooded my hands, as if they tried to shoot from my fingertips. I sure as shit wouldn't say I'd *guessed.* Not after the whole pendulum debacle, and my charms had been depleted of ley energy. Plus, that area had a bad vibe, so it felt natural to select it. I should've kept my mouth shut.

When in doubt, double down. "I listened to Kendra's spirit."

"That doesn't hold for me." He scowled some, ruining the fun back and forth we were finally having again. "Or for my brother."

I shrugged. "Maybe you should ask him why the spirit stone was there and then follow up with where Kendra is."

His eyes narrowed. "Are you accusing him of something?"

"I see a lot of things during séances, Mr. Slater." I stood and faced him. "No secret is safe when you're dead."

He stood, and when I went without heels, he was maybe five inches taller than me, give or take.

"You know . . ." I should've shut up, but I couldn't resist one last taunt. One last comment to stick with him. "Your brother's behaving mighty suspicious for someone who's innocent of any lies or . . . more."

I gave him a three-fingered trill of a wave and walked down the footpath. Truth be told, what I saw—those flashes of dark, murky waters, and the sensation of losing every breath I had left in me—had terrified me.

Chapter Ten

I slashed through the formula and shoved the paper away. Part of me wanted to crumple it into a ball and toss it across the room, but I knew I'd want to reference the errors later. Sitting back in my miniscule office, I pressed the heels of my palms to my eyes and took a second to reset.

Every time I attempted to create the air vacuum, the spell working to keep it in a secure area broke, letting in air. It shouldn't be an issue, but that pocket of air came in like a Tasmanian devil, destroying everything. This would destroy the evidence if used at a crime scene.

Since the séance, the past week had been frustrating. I'd avoided Guy as much as I could. That meant he still had my *Pac-Man* game. I hadn't gotten the chance to talk with Willa about it again either. The one time I thought about going into TrixieCakes, it was the young girl and some other employee behind the counter. So I went to Icing instead to get the sugar fix I'd been denied.

I sipped my coffee and grimaced. It'd gone cold, and a glance out the small window in my office showed me the warmer was still on in the communal coffee area. Which was a joke. It was only me and Christopher, and the coffee area was the odd counter by the coat tree that was beside an outlet. I tucked my chair into the desk—because otherwise I wouldn't be able to open the door—and stepped out.

Christopher was at the alchemy table in the adjacent lab, his mouth gaping open as he stared at the wall, a potion sitting on a ledge for the table dimly emanating a ley-energy-blue light. The channels of the five-point star on the alchemy table glowed aquamarine, underlighting his face. I knew, not from experience, that his body was currently distilling the ley energy from a nearby line to create the potion. We called this state White Out, and nothing would reach him until the table was done activating the potion.

I poured my coffee and leaned against the counter, staring at the TV on the wall. It was currently showing local news about mass casualties at Sutter's Mill in the Nettles. While I was sure it wasn't one of *my* enchantments that caused the problem, it'd had the same effect. Destructive winds centered on the power source.

"Madness." I sipped my coffee and winced. It was almost too hot.

I suppose what bothered me was that I made weapons. Sure, someone had to do it, and it was me, and I knew these were being used in a way that wasn't harming civilians. Slater Technologies had a contract with the military, and I provided the charms, grenade enchantments, and other munitions they'd need with enchantments that worked in tandem with spell workings. My ideas weren't revolutionary, but it sucked to see something similar to what I'd made used in the wild. I wished, not for the first time, that I could figure out a way to prevent civilians from using them. What if a kid got their hands on one?

It hadn't helped that they kept flashing my quote after these things either. *"The unfortunate incident in the Nettles could easily be explained by uneducated Muted playing with power they fundamentally don't understand. —Hendrick Slater via Starglen Gazette."*

That was from a couple years ago, before I stopped giving reporters my time. I knew better now to simply refuse to comment and move on.

SLTK, the ticker symbol for our company, flashed on the display, and the reporter on screen switched to the camera focused on them. "In a shocking deal, Slay-Tech outbids Ley Technica on a massive overhaul of protective gear for the troops."

I grimaced. The awful nickname for our company stemmed from the ticker symbol, and people preferred to pronounce the acronym instead of the company name. It hadn't helped that for the longest time we'd only dealt in weapons. The rebranding wasn't taking, at least not now.

My phone buzzed in my pocket and I answered it without screening, my second mistake of the day. "This is Slater."

"Hendrick," Guy's voice hissed across the line. "I'm going to ask you one more time, and this is your absolute last chance to come clean."

I tensed and clenched my jaw.

"Did you kill Kendra Bruce?" Guy sounded fed up with me too, like some kind of overworked parent.

I threw my hand out. "No," I barked. "Jesus Christ, Guy. How many times do I need to say I didn't hurt anyone for you to believe me?"

"Suzana went to the police after the séance," he continued. "She told them what happened that night, and take a guess who just left my office. So, are you sure you had nothing to do with her disappearance?"

Pain throbbed behind my brow, and I pinched the bridge of my nose. "One hundred percent."

"Did you dig into this Willamina Dade woman yet? What did you find out?"

I found out she had a close-knit family and a wicked sense of humor. "No. I didn't find anything useful about the séance."

"Nothing? Not how she does her work, if she does research on the subjects or—"

A blonde White woman in a blazer knocked on the doorjamb and stepped in, hovering by the threshold. She'd clipped a badge to her hip and sported a weapon on the other. Her demeanor, her expression broadcasted she was a no-nonsense type of person and wouldn't put up with anyone's shit. When her hard eyes locked with mine, my scalp itched, and I couldn't shake the sensation of bugs crawling through my hair.

"I'll call you back." I ended the call and approached the woman. "Can I help you?"

"Hendrick Slater?" she asked.

I nodded.

"Hi." She held her hand out. "I'm Detective Johnston with SPD. I was here to speak with Guy Slater and saw you were in today as well."

I shook her hand. "How can I help you?"

"Oh, well, looks like we have a little case of wrongful death and a stolen spirit stone," Johnston said. "I understand you and Kendra Bruce dated. For how long?"

I glanced to the lab and watched Christopher break out of the White Out before meeting the detective's stare. "We dated for eight years."

"Mhm." She pulled out a notebook and pen, referencing what she had down. "How'd that end?"

"I think you know."

"Well, I've heard from the Bruces, then your brother." She gestured at me. "Think it's about time I get it from you."

I sighed, aggravated. I hated to relive this, and it was all I could do since the séance. "We weren't getting along at the time of the split. Kendra and I had a . . . contentious relationship, especially at the end. Then she became engaged to Julian Christensen and left me."

Johnston's brows lifted slightly. "In that order?" She waved the pen around. "She gets engaged to Christensen and then leaves you?"

"Yes." I set my coffee cup on the counter behind me. "In that exact order."

"And you didn't see that coming?"

"Not exactly that, no." I shook my head. "I've got six years of hindsight on me now. Back then, I wanted to work it out, get married, all that. Now, I see we never would've worked."

She made a note. "Why's that?"

"Because whenever she cheated on me, I cheated on her, and then she'd cheat on me for it." At some point, it'd stopped hurting, and it almost became a game. That time in my past had left a greasy feeling on my skin, and I didn't like it, but it had hurt. And it drove me to never fully trust people, to never get into a relationship again. As soon as anything got serious, I bailed.

"Hmm." Johnston regarded me. "What about her finances? The Bruces said she was a big travel junkie."

"Yeah, she'd scrimp and save and as soon as she had enough money for a ticket, she'd go someplace for the weekend," I answered.

"Did you go with her often?" she asked.

"In the beginning, whenever I could, but I couldn't take off from work like she did. And I didn't have the extra funds, since my landlord was ruthless in his rent."

"Wasn't your brother your landlord at this time?"

I smirked. "Yes."

"Did you and Kendra share joint bank accounts?"

"I guess I dodged a bullet on that one." I scratched my cheek, sifting through the past. "We never got engaged, so I didn't see a point to combine finances. I wasn't as well off then as I am now."

"Do you think that's why she abruptly left you for Julian Christensen?" Johnston asked.

"More than likely." I flashed her a smile, all clenched teeth.

Johnston glanced around the lab, then she checked me out, her gaze lingering on my lab coat before jotting something else in her notebook. "Alright. Thank you for your time, Mr. Slater. I'll follow up with you if I have further questions." She handed me a business card. "But if you remember anything else, give me a call."

I took the card, and she left. The funny thing about that analogy of the rearview mirror was small because the past was behind you? I couldn't tear my gaze from the mirror, and it felt like my past was in front of me all over again, tricking me into dwelling over all the mistakes I'd made.

"What did the police want?" Christopher asked, all wide-eyed and innocent.

He'd always been a little naïve since he'd transferred to my lab a few years ago. At first, it was a little cute. But eventually I simply wondered what rock he was living under and if I should move it for him. But he did good work, so I didn't let it get to me.

"Just some questions about my ex," I answered. "Did the potion go well?"

"Yeah." He waved a pH strip at me. "More antidotes for that order."

I nodded. "Good. I'm going to knock off early today. Hit the gym."

"Yeah, work off that stress, dude." Christopher glanced at the TV, then approached his standing desk. "I can close the lab for you."

See? Good work, and that's all I expected from him.

By the time I'd pulled open the door to Icing, the unsteadiness in my legs and arms from my workout had vanished. So had the stress from the unexpected interview about Kendra. I also felt better about the vacuum spell working. While lifting, a lot of the fog obscuring my brain had parted, allowing me to think more clearly. I'd set goals on how to work through the sigils to locate the weakness. Once I found that, I was confident I'd be able to fix the issue. And now, the smell of confectionaries washed over me like I'd stepped into an ultra-expensive spa, and I knew I'd be in better spirits by the time I left.

Compared to TrixieCakes' colorful decorations, Icing was modern, industrial, and cold. The display cases were on the light side, having gone through the whole day of customers coming and taking treats before I got the chance.

"Rex!" Eric called from behind the counter.

I grinned and sauntered up. Dane had his phone out and wore his pissed face. He didn't acknowledge me.

"What's wrong?" I asked.

Eric sighed. He didn't look happy either. This was bad. "TrixieCakes tagged us again."

"Cupcakes," Dane seethed, barely glancing up at me. "They're comparing my chocolate sculptures to cupcakes! I'm no Amaury Guichon, I get it. But I put real confections in them. They aren't just boring blocks of chocolate—*How is chocolate boring?*" Dane tossed a towel on the counter and gestured to the back. "It's shaped like an Emmy because it's going to the afterparty. There's hazelnut chocolate mousse with a coffee ripple inside. A fucking block of chocolate?!"

My brows rose to my hairline. I'd never seen him this upset. "Dude."

Eric placed a hand on Dane's arm. "Sweetheart, calm down."

Dane wordlessly yelled and slammed into the back room.

Eric winced. "Oops."

"What the fuck was that?" I asked.

"He's stressed."

"You told him to calm down."

Another wince, and he turned toward the door. "I'll be back."

I was alone. With nothing better to do, I gazed at the treats, wondering if they had anything with a whiskey flavor. It'd been an accident with the shark cupcake, but I'd liked it. I settled on a maple leaf, which was really maple nougat surrounded by cashews, pistachios, and roasted peanuts, drizzled in dark chocolate when Eric and Dane came out of the back room.

"Sorry about that," Dane said.

"You got anything with whiskey?" I asked, not wanting to bring up the video, but also kinda did, but they hadn't known I'd gone to TrixieCakes.

Eric laughed. "No."

But Dane paused, his eyes narrowing on me. "Is this your chicken and waffles with a Manhattan deal?"

I grinned. "Kinda." I pointed at the maple leaf.

"Okay." Some of the fire went out of him. "I'll think about it." He grabbed a small plate and tongs.

"Will you also think about checking out the cake shops I gave you?" Eric asked.

He frowned, opening the case but not getting the cake. He turned to Eric. "What?"

"I gave you a list of bakeries for wedding cakes, babe. Last week."

"You did?" Dane shook his head. "Really?"

I tapped the glass. "Maple leaf."

"Sorry." Dane served it up and passed it to me.

I inhaled the complex aromas of dark chocolate with the caramel notes. My mouth watered.

"So you didn't look at any of the cakes?" Eric said, his voice losing its friendly tone. "You just . . . What did you do?"

"I have Icing to run. I need to find someone to cover for us while we're in Mallorca. Honestly, wouldn't it be easier—"

"No." Eric lifted a finger. "Don't think I can't hear you listening to those videos, ignoring everything else. We're getting married in six months, and we don't have a caterer, Dane! *Six. Months.*"

"I'll do it," Dane said. "It's not a big deal, and we can get what we want."

"What videos?" I asked.

Eric released a frustrated breath. "TrixieCakes."

"Really? That much?" I asked.

"They keep tagging me!" Dane said. "You know what? I'm gonna fight fire with fire. I still have the video on making the chocolate Emmy. I can do a reply." He cleared his throat and lifted his phone to his face.

Eric pushed his hand up higher. "The shadows were giving you a double chin."

"You know, this Emmy, which is filled with hazelnut mousse and a coffee drizzle—"

"Don't," I said. I gazed longingly at the treat and set my plate on the counter. I'd eat it soon. "The person behind the videos is a teenager."

"Oh." Eric frowned and glanced at his fiancé. "Those filters make her look like she's an adult."

"This makes so much more sense," Dane said. "I'm gonna send her a message and ask her to stop."

"Because that goes well with teenagers," Eric said. "But whatever makes you feel good, baby."

Dane mumbled under his breath but it seemed, for the moment, I was free to enjoy my post workout treat. I lifted the chocolate and nut treat to my mouth and bit in. The chocolate melted on my tongue while the nougat coated it in silky, spicy tones of maple and sugar. I smiled, wondering if this would go good with a Manhattan.

"How've you been, Rex?" Dane asked out of the blue. He tucked his phone in his pocket. "Get your *Pac-Man* game from Guy?"

I snorted. "That fucker's holding on to it until I give him all the dirt on the woman who led the séance."

Dane rolled his eyes. "Just tell him she made everything up and be done with it. That's what psychics do, anyway. I don't see why he's wasting your time."

"Right?" I said, but this was a little different; a little odder.

"Not every palm reader's a con artist," Eric said.

"I love your insistence on seeing the good in everyone, babe, but you're wrong here." Dane ran a hand down Eric's arm. "Ask my mom."

For years, a palm reader swindled his mother, wiping out most of her savings until Dane stepped in. Instead of retirement, she worked part-time as a greeter at one of those big superstores. I didn't feel the need to defend palm readers and psychics either, no matter how gorgeous Willa was.

"I think the séance went as expected, even with Julian knocking on the table. She knew what it was," I said.

"Well, yeah." Dane wiped down the counter. "They watch for body language and micro expressions to lead their marks on a merry chase with their bank account."

Eric folded his arms on the register and rested his chin on them. "Knocking probably wasn't her gimmick, anyway."

"You know . . . The whole time, she had her eyes closed." I

picked a cashew from the treat and popped it into my mouth. "She didn't pay any attention to the ley energy in that room. It was a little spooky with her. It's hard to believe there wasn't something really there. And then the whole mess with Kendra's spirit stone."

"Her familiar appeared?" Eric asked.

I nodded. "At the carriage house."

Dane frowned. "One of the Bruces, or maybe Julian had it."

I shrugged. "That's certainly possible. My money's on Julian. Her parents were shocked. Couldn't fake that. But . . ." I rubbed my mouth. "She wasn't able to detect my spirit stone, and her enchantment for that was charged."

"I'd just stay away from that whole mess." Eric made a face. "It's not something you want to get involved with."

"Yeah." Dane laughed. "You don't need a psychic to tell you that."

Chapter Eleven

I added the shrimp shells to the Ziploc bag that had some already and chucked it into the freezer. The strange digital noises coming from the table had me glancing over. Shawn was playing some pocket game. Candi sat next to him, scrolling through an app, and the blue light underlit her face. Trixie stood near the water cooler, having a quiet phone conversation with her husband. While I'd had my back turned, Mimzy had topped off my white wine. If I wasn't careful, she'd get me drunk.

Trixie said goodbye to Brandon and tucked her phone into her back pocket. She approached a stool at the island and sat. "Where'd you get that, Shawn?"

I moved back to the counter and began dicing an onion. The pungent odor made my eyes sting, and I blinked back tears. "Isn't that one of those virtual pets?"

"Yeah," Shawn replied, zombie-like.

Candi stood and headed to the bathroom, her nose pressed into her phone. When she closed the door, it only took a moment for her to start talking. Trixie caught my eye and rolled hers. I smiled slightly.

"Did one of your friends give that to you?" Trixie asked, shifting on the stool to stare at Shawn.

Mimzy sidled close to me, her baby powder and sweet pea perfume briefly overpowering the onion, and poked at the ingredients. "Is that enough garlic?"

"It's three cloves," I said.

"When they say three cloves, they really mean four." She shuffled to the pantry and broke another one off the head of garlic.

"I'm trying to do your bingo friends a favor, Mimzy," I said, taking the clove and peeling it anyway.

"Who needs friends when I have my grandkids and the messes?" Mimzy laughed and took a gulp of wine.

"Shawn!" Trixie said, using her mom voice. "Who gave that to you? Was it the girl with the dragon?"

Shawn scowled, looking up from the gadget. "No. I bought it with my own money. *God*."

"Watch your tone when you speak to your mother, young man," Mimzy grumbled, her coke-bottle glasses only emphasizing her scowl. "The oil's hot, Chipmunk."

"You're backseat cooking, Mimzy." I held my hand over the pan; she was right. I tossed the onions in, and they sizzled. I mixed them in the oil and butter mixture and set the spoon aside.

Trixie settled more at the counter, sipping from her glass. I noticed Mimzy didn't keep refilling her drink. The last time she pulled that, Trixie and the kids stayed overnight because Brandon couldn't get back into Starglen from a job he'd taken before she'd passed out.

"So you were saying about that séance?" Trixie asked.

"Oh." I stirred the pan. The savory aroma of cooking onions in butter was heavenly already. "She called again, asking me more questions about what I'd seen during the séance and the spirit stone."

"What else is there to know?" Mimzy asked. "She got her answers when that ghost tried to get you. Though I feel for the mother. You're not meant to outlive your kids."

I nodded a little. "Kendra only gave me sensations. I wasn't in any danger."

Mimzy made a noise in the back of her throat and tuned in to the little TV. It was *Jeopardy!* time, but she had subtitles on so we could talk. I wasn't worried she'd miss anything. She could probably read the captions from across the street with her glasses.

I glanced at Trixie. "I think she's gearing up to ask me to call on Kendra's spirit directly."

"Why's that?" she asked, her brows furrowing.

"She really wants the spirit stone." I sighed and propped a hand on my hip. "I don't know what to do about this. I want to help them, and the money will help me. But people only call them gentle possessions because whoever named them didn't know their own head from their ass."

"What is *Game of Thrones*," Mimzy said. "Stir the onions."

"I don't like this," Trixie said. "It's too dangerous. Even with all your protections, what if she doesn't want to leave?"

I swirled the onions, tapping the spoon on the side of the pan. "She might not."

"I doubt you could trust anyone there to help you with ousting her spirit." Trixie grumbled.

"Yeah." Mimzy turned, setting her wine down. "I don't care how much they pay you—don't do it without Trixie."

We both blinked at her, and I met my cousin's eyes. "I don't know—"

Frigid water dripped on my head, right on my part. I squealed as goosebumps scattered across my entire body and peered at the ceiling. Where was the leak? I didn't see a crack or even gathering moisture.

Everything sounded muffled.

Another drop splattered on my forehead, two drops, then a trickle. Ice creeped beneath my skin as the light shifted and darkened, eerie shadowy scenes playing across the walls, cast by floating entities that living eyes were never meant to see. The water's frosted fingers dug into my nerves as streams of it sluiced over my body and chilled me to the bone.

A hissing murmur slipped into my mind. *"Tell me what you know, and this won't hurt."*

My chest grew tight with tingles. My heart raced.

The stream grew into a river, and a swell of water crashed over me, plunging me into the deep, brown-green darkness of an ocean. My lungs seized, and my heart pounded so hard it echoed in my ears as currents swept my feet out from beneath me. I tumbled within the deathly cold embrace.

"What are you after?" a wet, sibilant voice asked—distorted as if I were underwater.

Nimble currents gripped my arms, and I struggled against its grasp, certain they were tugging me to a watery grave.

I don't want to drown.

I choked, the artic water sliding into my nose and mouth like a serpent, sticking its flickering forked tongue deep into my brain. Visions of my wide-eyed, bloated corpse floating near the Never Peak Cliffs played in my head. I shuddered. Something floated nearby, dark, long—a wild thought? It could be another body.

"Where did you learn all your little secrets?" the voice asked.

I sucked in a breath, but something foreign pushed the air from my lungs, crowding in my throat like a trapped scream. I kicked my feet and flailed my arms, desperately needing to break the ocean's surface.

But I stood on solid ground, and the smell of onions frying in butter slammed back into me. I sucked in a large breath of air, my eyes popping open to the kitchen. Trixie had her arms around me. The onions were a moment from burning, and Mimzy gaped at me.

My chest ached, and I panted harshly, my breaths coming in shrieking wheezes. "It's—"

Water leaked from the ceiling, dripping from the corners like liquid wraiths slithering for me. I was under a psychic attack. I broke Trixie's hold and clamped my palms on either side of my head. *Who the fuck would do this to me? Why?* I had to protect myself, but I'd never prepared for an attack. It'd been unthinkable. Heart in my throat—it was hard to breathe already—I raced out of the kitchen.

"The onions!" Mimzy called after me.

Trixie said something, but I didn't catch it.

The swelling wave thundered after me as I sprinted into my bedroom and slid across the slippery wet floor to my costume trunk. The water lapped at my feet, rising and flooding my calves. I still couldn't catch my breath.

"What other little treats would I find in that head of yours if I cracked it open?"

I shuddered and tore the headdress from within the trunk and slapped it on my head.

"I think I'd find the source of your lies." Menace slipped into the murky waters. *"And I'll take your magic as a price."*

My fingers tripped over the enchantments as I activated them, the water reaching to my chest. The charms sewn into my headdress warmed one by one until the protection against psychic attack activated, but the heat did nothing for the watery chill that gripped me.

The soaking bubble around me popped. The illusion of water disappeared, and I sank to the dry floor, placing my back against the trunk. I couldn't catch my breath, and I rested my hand on my chest, trying to calm all my organs.

Mimzy and Trixie appeared in my doorway.

"What's going on?" Mimzy demanded. "Did one of your charms go haywire? That was a *lot* of ley energy coming from you. For a second, I thought—"

"Holy shit, Billie." Trixie crouched next to me. "You look awful."

"Someone attacked me," I wheezed, adjusting the headdress so it sat fully on my head. Never had I'd ever been so glad that I'd taken all those weeks to sew all that chlorite into the headdress. It was heavy, but it protected me.

"What happened?" Mimzy demanded, stepping fully into my room, her once easygoing attitude now on high alert. "Let's get you in the kitchen. Beebee'll make you a margarita and things'll be fine."

"Not everything is solved with alcohol, Gram-cracker," Trixie said, but she still pulled me to my feet. "Though tequila might help put some color back in your face. You look scared to death."

I followed them back into the kitchen, shaking. "Someone attacked me. They asked about what secrets I knew."

Shawn gaped at me, his toy forgotten in his hands.

Candi wrenched open the bathroom door. "You guys are really loud and ruined my video!"

"Shut up, Candice." Shawn's gigantic eyes exaggerated his pale face as he scanned the kitchen and dining room. "Something happened to Aunt Billie."

"Oh, my god, what?" Candi sank into a chair.

I ignored them and rubbed my upper arms in hopes of tricking my body into thinking it was warm.

"Do you think it's because of that séance?" Trixie asked?

"Oh, that makes sense," Mimzy lifted the pan and tsked. The onions were burnt.

I wasn't *that* surprised by her cavalier attitude right now. I'd learned over the decades spent with her that when something scared her, she acted like everything rolled right off her.

"How does that make any sense?" Trixie snapped, wrapping an arm around my shoulders.

"Who else would want to hurt her?" Mimzy scraped the onions into the trash and went to the sink. "Those families are too big to not have skeletons in a closet thanks to a dead girl." She pointed a sponge at me as she waited for the tap to get hot. "You need to set up a protection grid so they don't get you while you're sleeping."

Trixie nodded. "I'll help."

"I've got the crystals for it ready, thanks." I gulped the wine in my glass. "Do you know of any practitioner who can talk through this kind of attack?"

"They talked to you?" Trixie's eyes widened, and she sat next to me.

"Yeah." I swallowed, trying to get that dry, sticky feeling out of my throat. "They asked me about the secrets in my head and said they'd drain all my magic out of me if I didn't."

"Jesus." Mimzy dried the pan and set it back on the stove. "You stay away from them. You hear?"

Then she grabbed a cleaver, and I knew I needed to rescue all of us because she planned to cook. Which was sweet, but Mimzy, for how large her glasses were, had lost her touch for cooking. At the moment, she was the bigger threat.

I stood and gently took the cleaver from her, then grabbed another onion from the pantry. At least this hadn't happened when I was cooking the shrimp. Mimzy would've found who did it and taken care of it herself.

Aside from the worrying looks Trixie sent me, and the endless chatter about a dance trend Candi was trying to perfect, I was stunned. Shawn and Mimzy played dominoes, and all I could do was replay what the voice had said right before I'd activated the psychic protection enchantment.

I knew it was a threat to stop helping with this whole Kendra business, especially because Suzana was insistent that I help. Which meant someone at that séance last week had killed Kendra Bruce, and they weren't against killing me to keep their secret. I was done. This wasn't a gig that was worth doing—not after these threats. And I'd tell the Bruces that the next time they contacted me.

"I'll take your magic as a price."

The joke was on whoever was behind my attack. They'd never steal any magic from me, and I'd never have to worry about them trying.

Being Muted had a perk after all.

Chapter Twelve

I hadn't encountered such reluctance to meet for food and drinks since I asked for a lunch meeting with Guy to talk about my path in the company. But Willa always outdid everyone, it seemed, especially when I took a chance that the number listed on her website was her personal number and sent a text.

Then nothing. All the text showed was delivered, but there was no response. Maybe she had two phones, and this was one she only checked during business hours. Boundaries were great, and I respected them, but I honestly needed to talk to her. My friends needed me to talk to her. Dane was driving Eric up the wall, and it was usually the other way around.

Ten minutes later, no response. It occurred to me I didn't know her at all. I just knew what she'd shown me, which was a well put together woman who used her enchanting abilities to bring people closure. Well, in my case, a pain in the ass, but she'd looked good while she did it.

> It's about the social media war between Icing and TrixieCakes

HOT PSYCHIC

> There's a war?!

It'd taken her no time at all to respond that time. That told me two things: TrixieCakes was a priority for her, and she didn't like me. Well, the latter might be a stretch; she might like me fine, but it wasn't me that made her text back in less than thirty seconds.

> Yep. I'll tell you all about it over dinner. You in?

HOT PSYCHIC

> Sure.

It'd taken her a few minutes to respond that time. As I started asking where I could pick her up, I saw she was typing again. So I waited.

HOT PSYCHIC

> Meet me at Guadalajara at 6. This is not a date.

Seemed I was right about her not liking me all along. That made things a little easier now that I knew where she stood.

I HADN'T BEEN TO THIS MEXICAN RESTAURANT YET. There were so many Mexican places in Starglen, it was easy to go to the ones you liked and ignore the rest. It surprised me to find a line, but tons of empty tables and booths. This place was bigger on the inside than it looked. A tall redhead with a sleek ponytail ahead of me grabbed my attention, and I stepped around the few people to tap her shoulder.

Willa turned, a pinched yet polite expression on her face quickly morphing into an amiable smile that met her amber eyes. "Oh, hi, Rex. How're you?"

I smiled at her, my gaze following the soft lines of her body. She wore a dark green V-neck cotton shirt that drew my attention to the deep shadow of cleavage, her trim waist, and jeans that hugged her curvy hips. A classic hourglass figure. I placed my hand on the small of her back as we advanced in line, licking my lips. I was a little stunned by how her casual attire knocked me upside the head. Usually, formal wear did this to me. Seeing a man or woman dressed to the nines did things for me. You know, maybe I needed to shake up the typical partners to snap myself out of the boredom that'd been dogging me for months now. Willa could be that change of pace.

"You look great," I said, not bothering to hide checking her out once more. The shirt was my new favorite.

"Thanks." Her smile remained neutral. "Whoever you hired as your stylist has a good eye. You look nice."

I'd chosen another Henley, this one blue, because I knew she'd approve. I also wore my best faded jeans because my ass looked amazing in them—I put in a lot of work to make it look this good at the gym. Not to mention I'd also groomed my beard to make it look neat, and the beard oil I used smelled like a cedar hope chest, which *I* liked.

I mock-scoffed in outrage. "I dress myself, princess. Are you impressed?"

Her amber eyes twinkled and she shrugged. "Eh."

I chuckled, and her grin brightened the entire restaurant.

It didn't take long to seat us, and once we were settled in a booth, salsa, chips, and water were placed on the table along with the menus. I glanced around. There were colorful murals of candy skulls with cacti and agave plants painted all over the walls. By the bar, TVs tuned to ESPN hung above the counter.

Willa set her menu aside without opening it and sipped her water.

"Do you come here often?" I asked, scanning the selection.

"Yes. Best chorizo nachos around." She flashed me a smile. "Mimzy likes their pollo and rice."

"Who's Mimzy?"

"My grandmother."

The server took our orders, and she sat back. She seemed pleased with herself, and I couldn't help but grin back. *Damn, she's sexy.*

"Thanks for meeting me here," she said. "I really needed a pick-me-up, and those nachos and margaritas are my *favorite.*"

"Now I kinda wish I'd gotten a margarita." I ate some of the salsa. It was pretty good.

She helped herself to some chips and salsa. "What's your go-to?"

"Oh." I grinned. "Brew & Chew in the Flower Market has the best chicken and waffles. They don't fry the chicken to shit, so it's still moist. I like to eat it with a Manhattan. In fact, I think it's a crime if you don't."

"I never would've guessed waffles go well with a Manhattan."

"It's more like the maple syrup. Plus, waffles don't soak up whiskey like chicken does."

Our drinks came. The margarita was nearly as big as her head with lime and orange wheels floating along the bowl. I squeezed juice from a chunk of lime into my Modelo Negra and pushed the wedge inside the beer.

"What's your sign, anyway? I'm an Aquarius." She wrapped her heart-shaped lips around the straw, lifting her amber gaze to mine.

My dick joined the conversation, but I politely shut him down.

"Oh, I'm a Libra and a disappointment." I winked to let her know it didn't upset me to say that.

She laughed lightly. "What do you mean by that?"

"There's a lot to unpack with that, but since we're getting to know each other, I'll say that I missed Mabon solstice by a couple of days."

"Oh." She smiled and slowly pushed her drink aside, spilling a little. "Me too. I missed Imbolc by a day. I only work with crystals as well, bigger disappointment. At least you have two ley abilities."

"Your parents were . . . petty about that?" I asked. "Because my father was for a while."

She shook her head. "My mother died during childbirth, and my father's just as dead." She gave me a serene smile that didn't smooth over that loaded comment in the least.

"I'm sorry."

"Oh, it's fine." She waved it off. "I dealt with that trauma a long time ago. Mimzy raised me, and now I'm looking after her."

It didn't make it any less uncomfortable for me. I picked at the gold foil around the neck of my beer. "So to move on to a different subject . . . where'd you go to school?"

"Starglen East High." She took a careful drink from the fishbowl. "You?"

Oh, okay. I hadn't meant high school, but may as well. "I went to Fulton Prep until I was sixteen, then transferred to Maincastle."

"Oh, right. I almost forgot you were a rich boy. I've heard of Fulton. An all-boys private school, but what's Maincastle?"

"Military school. I played soccer."

"Oh." She grinned and leaned in, folding her arms beneath her breasts. "Were you a bad boy?"

"Do you like bad boys, princess?" I asked, leaning closer and lowering my voice to a purr.

"I'm going to tell you something." She bit her plump lower lip and shrugged. "Just so you can stop wasting your time."

I smiled patiently, because whenever someone said that, it meant they'd assumed something about me, and I knew what Willa would say. She was in a relationship. *Or* she wasn't interested in forever, but one night would be fun. And I could do a night. That'd be all I needed to get her out of my system. "What's that?"

She wagged her fingers between us. "I need a strong emotional bond before I can even be in a relationship, let alone to want to get physical with someone."

I leaned back from the table, blinking. That wasn't at all what I'd expected. I stared at her, processing. Our food came, knocking me out of my stunned silence. A server placed three tacos in a holder before me. Then a small plate with refried beans, cheese, and pico de gallo was set beside it. The chopped marinated steak piled with cilantro and topped with a pickled radish made my mouth water. I distributed the lettuce and pico over the tacos, then dripped a healthy amount of the house hot sauce on them. The carne asada tacos smelled amazing. And her nachos did too.

I hadn't experienced rejection recently. Kendra had been my last. Could I even call this a rejection, though? I'd been bored with dating, and Guy warned me not to get caught up with her, and he was probably right. This situation with the

Bruces was already messy, and now the police were involved. It was probably for the best I didn't take Willa for a ride.

Besides, she needed an emotional bond for romance and intimacy, and I didn't want to get that deep with someone just to become bored a couple weeks later.

After a few bites, which wow, their cilantro was fresh and fantastic with the taco—thank goodness I didn't have that terrible genetic problem that made cilantro taste like soap. I didn't know who could live like that. I took a drink to wash it down. She shoved a whole damn tortilla chip in her mouth loaded with crumbled chorizo, jalapeno, and cheese.

I wiped my chin, making sure my beard was clear of cilantro. "So back to you coming out to me as demisexual . . ."

She blinked at me.

"That's why you left me hanging at the bar the other week?" I finished.

"I wouldn't say I'm demisexual," she said, her gaze roving over her plate.

"Why's that? You said you need feelings to have an attraction toward another person. That's basically that."

"Well . . . I don't know." She shrugged, her brows wrinkling as she sipped from the margarita. "I haven't come out to anyone like that, or even told anyone . . ."

I hated seeing her this uncomfortable with something about herself. I knew how it felt, once upon a time.

I reached across the table and laid my palm over her hand. "Hey, just because you haven't told anyone about your orientation doesn't mean it's not true. I don't tell people I'm bi, and it doesn't make me less bi. So thanks for telling me. I thought you hated me."

Her eyes widened while I spoke, and a soft smile touched her lips. "I don't hate you yet."

"'Yet,' she says." I laughed and lifted another taco.

"Actually, you might after we talk about why I asked you to meet here on our definitely not a date."

"Why? What's going on?" she asked while she tugged another loaded chip free and pushed it into her mouth. Queso dotted the corners of her lips, and she licked them clean.

My dick still liked it, and that was okay. He wasn't in control of me.

"It's about the social media war going on between Icing and TrixieCakes." I took a bite, then quickly another. These tacos were amazing. And now that I no longer felt obligated to get her into bed, I didn't care what I looked like while I ate.

"Oh no—a war? Really? Isn't that a little extreme?" Willa paused, her fishbowl halfway to her mouth. "Do you know the people at Icing?"

"Yeah. My best friends run it. And Dane sent her a private message asking her to stop roasting him, and she mocked him in a video over it."

She winced. "Jesus."

"Look, I wouldn't bring it up, let them take care of it and figure it out, but it's interfering with the wedding planning, and Dane's upset." I took a drink.

"No, it's okay. Trixie would want to know about this . . ." She frowned. "I'll talk with Candi about it first before Trixie, if that's fine?"

I smiled, glad to hear all of this. I didn't even need to ask for her to do it. "Yeah, that's great. Thanks, Willa."

The smile slipped from her eyes, and she toyed with the last of her nachos. "Is there something more I need to know about the Bruces?"

I froze, a strange feeling of dread settling on my shoulders. Even though this night wasn't going as I'd imagined it, it had been nice and stress free up to now. "What about them?"

"Well, earlier, when I first consulted with Suzana, Martin asked me to lie and say their daughter had crossed over. Then, after that . . ." She shuddered and wiggled her shoulders as if shaking something off. "She messages me every day, begging me to do another séance to find the spirit stone."

It didn't surprise me that Martin had tried that. He'd asked me to forgive Kendra and her wild ways and let her settle down—which led us into a downright long and terrible relationship. "What do you know about the Bruces?"

"Just that they love their daughter and want closure." She took a long drink. "Whatever else that's going on, it's dangerous and I don't want a part in it."

My spine tensed. Now, she could mean séances were dangerous. There was a vast difference between a gentle possession and a hostile one. "Will you give me more information about that?"

She grimaced and shook her head. "It's not . . . that big of a deal."

"Hey, I need to know the nature of the danger," I said.

"Last night, I was attacked psychically." She tilted her head and showed off a hair clip that I'd paid little attention to. It was a butterfly, and I could see it was an enchantment. "I stopped it, but the person asked about the spirit stone."

I frowned, completely surprised that had happened to her. The spirit stone shouldn't have been that big of a problem. But while the familiar had shown up when Suzana called for it, I believed it was probably at the edge of town somewhere. "Can you tell me anything else?"

"Well, it was a little similar to the séance and the impressions her spirit gave me. Like I was drowning, and that's exactly what was happening last night. Just more extreme. It looked like I was in an ocean or something and I couldn't breathe. When I realized I was being attacked, I stopped it."

"Of course. Anyone with your education would be able to," I said. Enchanters learned protection early, and they honed their skills in college.

And I couldn't help but think of Guy. Born on Samhain —a point of pride for Alvin—Guy was an ACE, which meant he was also a water caster. And angry about the spirit stone and this whole debacle. Would he threaten Willa psychically? It wasn't out of his wheelhouse.

"You know, and don't take this the wrong way, but I think it might be best if you let the police do their work," I said.

She laughed. "No kidding. I told Suzana last night I wouldn't help any further with this. I mean, it's a cold case." She bit her lip. "And I was attacked over it."

The server took that moment to come by and clear our plates. I also ordered flan and another round of drinks. Willa's phone rang. She grimaced and flashed the screen at me. Suzana Bruce.

"I'm gonna ignore—"

"Wait. Put it on speaker."

"No, that's rude." She accepted the call. "Hi, Suzana."

I left my side of the booth and scootched in close to her, my arm resting on the back of the booth behind her. Willa lifted a brow but surprised me by shifting the phone to my side so I could listen in.

". . . stone's all we have left of our daughter," Suzana was saying. "I wish you'd reconsider."

"I understand you're still grieving, especially after the séance, Mrs. Bruce," Willa murmured, "but I already explained to you why I won't be helping any further with this. It's dangerous. I'm letting the police handle this, and you should too."

Our drinks and my dessert arrived, although there were two spoons. I hadn't intended to share, and set one off to the side.

"I don't understand how it's dangerous. Spirits can't hurt you," Suzana continued. "Please summon my daughter so we can recover her familiar's spirit stone. When we call to Quackie

Chan, he doesn't reveal himself, even when we go to our old house!"

I met Willa's eyes and rolled mine, shaking my head.

"I won't even get into a debate with you over possessions," Willa said, "but if you remember, I already explained it wasn't a spirit, Mrs. Bruce. It was a person with access to enchantments. They threatened me."

"And you protected yourself!"

"Yes, but—"

"Think of it like this, Willamina. When you summon Kendra's spirit, not only will we discover how she died, but we'll be able to collect her familiar's spirit stone. Then there won't be any danger for you. Mystery solved!"

This would kill a lot of birds with one stone. I'd be able to assess Guy for attacking Willa. We wouldn't find the spirit stone on Slater property anyway, and the Bruces would get an answer. Guy was an asshole, but I couldn't wrap my head around him murdering Kendra, especially since water casting was particularly common for ACE practitioners. I motioned for Willa to take a moment.

"Hang on," Willa said, frowning, and placed the call on mute. "What?"

"I think you should accept," I said.

She laughed. "We just agreed to let the police do this."

"Yeah, but Suzana has a point," I said. "Plus, getting things like this will allow the police to move more quickly."

"I don't know . . ." She shook her head; she wasn't going to agree.

"I promise nothing will happen to you. Suzana, Martin, even Julian will make sure nothing goes wrong, but you can definitely count on me to protect you."

Willa studied me, her eyes darting to the flan. I placed the other spoon back on the plate, letting her know I'd share now.

She pursed her heart-shaped mouth into a line and picked up the phone again.

"I'll do it," she said.

"Oh, thank god," Suzana exclaimed. "I'm so glad you've come to your senses. My daughter was my best friend, and I need to know what happened to her."

"I have a couple of conditions," Willa said, taking the spoon closest to her. "Hazard pay is to be paid in advance, and I'm bringing my own insurance that if the possession isn't gentle, it gets rejected."

Suzana easily agreed and said she'd text with the details before ending the call.

I slid my spoon through the flan and caramel sauce. "Insurance? I can definitely help with your terms."

"No offense, but I'd rather have Trixie there." Willa scooped up some flan and popped it into her mouth and groaned. "Wow, this is great. Mimzy never wants desserts."

I nodded, indulging in the sweet egg custard and the rich, toasty caramel sauce.

She set her spoon aside. "Can I ask you a question?"

"Sure." I scraped up the last of the sauce.

"Why're you insistent on this now?" She shifted to face me, our thighs brushing together.

"Oh, Guy's holding my *Pac-Man* game ransom until this is all sorted out."

She laughed and nodded. "Okay. That makes sense." She grinned. "I think I'll be in good hands with you and Trixie there, so long as you didn't murder Kendra."

Chapter Thirteen

Trixie followed me around the perimeter of the carriage house, primarily in the main room, passing me crystals from my redwood box. I set the protection grids to keep malevolent spirits from entering the sacred space of the séance and planning a possession. She chatted about Shawn—something about money, and possibly more unacceptable behavior—but I couldn't concentrate on what she'd said.

I worried this would go wrong.

I checked my phone. I saw that Rex'd read my message—my tenth confirmation of his arrival today—but he hadn't replied. Not this time. I trusted Trixie to have my back, but the more people here to help, the better my odds that Kendra's spirit wouldn't decide to keep my body. I'd heard there was a special ward in hospitals for people with a spirit who hijacked a body, but I've never actually seen it. Still, the thought terrified me.

The door opened, and Suzana, Martin, and Guy stepped inside. The pungent malodor of cigarette smoke preceded Guy and overtook the room. Trixie waved the air in front of her nose. Then Rex stepped in. Our eyes immediately connected, and he nodded. I hated the relief I felt, but his assurance at Guadalajara had been the only reason I'd agreed to this gentle possession. And, you know, Suzana had paid the hazard fee.

Someone knocked on the door before opening it, and Julian stepped in. He grinned when he saw us setting up the perimeter. "Am I early?"

Suzana welcomed him with a hug. "Just in time."

Julian's expression brightened when his attention landed on me. I'd yet to put on the rest of my costume, and the way his eyes traveled over my body gave me the heebie-jeebies.

"Let's get this moving on, shall we?" Guy tapped the watch face circling his wrist. "I have a video meeting with a client in Australia later this evening."

I locked the last stone in place at the door. I glanced at Trixie, and she nodded, her eyes tracking an invisible—to me —show. Without looking at anyone else, I returned to my bag and retrieved my headdress. I worked my fingers over every charm, activating them. Mimzy and Trixie had gone over it earlier, ensuring that the charms were charged and the enchantment on each stone was the right one. Otherwise, I would never have my body back.

It'd only been in the last five years or so that they really started to support me in using charms and enchantments for gentle possessions. I had to prove over and over that I under-stood having a spirit in my body meant I was not myself and I could become lost in finally touching and manipulating magic. Being Muted, I lacked the intuition everyone else had when it came to manipulating ley energy. I certainly never got the education for it, as no school would ever accept me. And of course, other people in the Muted community had tried and unfortunately proved that people without magic weren't to be trusted with it. The great earthquake that tore a gorge wide open in the flatlands of Nebraska forty years ago proved that point horrifically. Hundreds of people had died, and the crack had expanded for years until a prodigy earth caster stepped in to stabilize it. The area still suffered minor aftershocks to this day.

Once I had my headdress and veil clipped together and in place, I pulled out a chair and settled into it. "Let's all sit and join hands."

Julian and Rex reached for the same one. Rex growled softly under his breath.

"No need to get all huffy, little wolf." Julian tugged on it, his lips splitting into a shark-like smile. "I think we should keep the same order from the last time. You know, so the spirits will find everything as it was."

"The spirits will know regardless of where you choose to sit, Mr. Christensen," I said.

"Yeah, Junior." Rex made himself bigger by squaring his shoulders. "Sit somewhere else."

Trixie slipped on glasses. The frames didn't have lenses, but the crystals in them were enchanted. This was so she could see spirits. She took up a position behind me. Everyone settled around the table once more, Julian scowling as he took Suzana's hand in his, and Guy's with his other.

I hummed in the back of my throat. The aquamarine charm at the crown of my head steadily grew warmer, and I closed my eyes. As the chakra atop my head opened, the glittery blue magic swirled thick in the room, the pale ethereal fog rolling as if there were obstacles disrupting its flow.

"Kendra Bruce." My voice came out breathy. The ley energy shifted. "I'm sorry to disturb your rest once more, Kendra Bruce, but we need you one more time. I invite only you to speak with me."

The enchantments framing the seams of my headdress and veil grew warmer. From behind my closed lids, the magic morphed, revealing the spirits waiting within the eddies of the ley ocean. They were of all different shapes, some humanoid, others hunched and crouched. Thanks to the protection and the parameters of the enchantments within the carriage house, they couldn't approach.

Except for one.

I couldn't see much of the spirit's features, other than the most prominent ones were lined in sparkling blue. She had eyes, a nose, mouth, shoulders, breasts, and legs. She settled over me like a suffocating mantle stretching from the spirit realm. My heart raced in my chest, and I swallowed.

"Kendra . . ." I sighed, my voice soft and almost as if the soundtrack to us was off a millisecond as my words didn't line up right with the shape my lips took. "Your parents miss you."

"Oh, baby," Suzana sobbed. "Are you here?"

"Mommy," I said, the voice track to my body sounding just a little different, like a stranger. "Mommy, I'm sorry."

Suzana covered her mouth. "Oh baby! I miss you."

My eyes opened against my will, and I saw magic within the world—a perk of being a spirit host. Kendra's spirit had a small amount of control over me, like it was her voice that came from my throat instead of mine. From an urge from Kendra, I let go of Rex's hand. But I slipped it back in, adjusting our palms with no resistance.

My father—Martin—his face scrunched, his shoulders hitching. Suzana glanced at him and tightened her grip on his hand before returning her attention to me. Or was it Kendra?

"What happened to you?" she asked.

I fell into the water, feeling swaddled and empty. I stilled. I sucked in a sliver of air. "I can't breathe."

I closed my lids against the images, but Kendra occupied half of my brain, and all I saw was the darkness with darker, gloomier shadows around me.

A hand squeezed my shoulder, and the image disappeared. My eyes popped open again.

"Don't ask about how it happened, not yet. Ask about the stone," Trixie said.

"The spirit stone." Suzana blinked rapidly. "Do you know where Quackie Chan's spirit stone is?"

The veil parted like a curtain, and a beautiful, huge duck, resplendent in sigils and runes across its body, waddled into the room and straight to Kendra. To me. Martin finally sobbed out loud. More magic absorbed into us, and like strings for a puppet, I felt Kendra's ley energy attach to my arms and legs. She tore our hand from Rex's, jerked the seat back, and stumbled to our feet.

"Shit," Trixie muttered.

I wanted to turn around, but Kendra wouldn't allow it. In fact, I no longer had control of my body. I whimpered in my brain.

"Don't be dramatic," Kendra said, her voice like an echo. *"You invited me in."*

We stumbled and half-glided to the door. Trixie kept close to our heels, thank goodness. Chairs scraped on the hardwood floor as everyone hurried to stand. Kendra kept walking into the door. When it didn't open, we'd back up and walk to it again, as if she had forgotten the concept of turning the knob and instead wanted to walk through walls.

It didn't help that on the edges of our vision, the ley energy washed against us like an ocean and my lungs pinched with every inhalation.

The door opened, and someone gripped our shoulders and guided us outside. My lungs stopped. I coughed and spat, finally sucking in a dry draft of air, which stuck in my throat, and I coughed.

"How close is the spirit stone?" I gasped, stumbling when I gained the brief control over my limbs.

But the control bar for my puppet strings jerked with a scintillating twist of ley energy. It was so beautiful. I never knew how to compare it, and my gentle possessions before had shown me glimpses of what a practitioner saw as normal. It was extraordinary. I finally belonged.

"It's near," Kendra said, her voice startlingly not mine. And it'd come right before my lips moved with the words.

I wrenched on the shiny periwinkle strands, attempting to move toward the pet cemetery. But Kendra jerked us away and to the stream nearby. "I can't breathe," we said.

"We need to stop this," Trixie announced.

"No!" Suzana said.

"We're close," Martin said.

Quackie Chan stepped back into the spirit realm, but we could see him from beyond the veil. All kinds of familiars idled there. A giant raccoon, a hawk, a crazy-big bull frog that sat on the petals of a lotus, its throat inflating with a *brrrp*. It was perfect, almost like they were alive. Or maybe it was because I was dead?

I shook my head, dislodging Kendra's thoughts from my personal conscious. *I* was not dead; she was.

Julian stopped on my other side. "I've never seen anything like this before."

"Don't go to many of these, Junior?" Rex asked softly.

"Fuck off, mongrel," he replied.

I turned in a circle, the ley energy so deep inside me as it suffused my limbs. All my enchantments had grown hot as we wobbled and toddled toward the spot I'd shown to everyone nearly two weeks ago.

"Quackie Chan! Momma needs some love!" Kendra's voice called from my mouth.

"There he is!" Kendra said.

Quackie Chan appeared once more, quickly waddling to us and head-butting our stomach. We bent slightly and rubbed his head. Kendra's thoughts bloomed with love as we dropped to our knees in the dew-stained grass and embraced the duck. I felt his downy soft head and his stiff wings, so completely solid you'd think he were alive.

"Are you a good little duckie?" we asked, sucking in breath between each word. "Show me your stone."

Quackie Chan waddled toward the stream and faded into the spirit realm. A soft ping of bright blue light on the other side of the stream bed, and then nothing. Martin spun, his wounded gaze landing on Rex and Guy.

Suzana approached us, her arms out.

"You agreed to no touching." Trixie firmly pushed her arms down. Then she retrieved a bundle of azalea leaves and a lighter. "This is edging from gentle to hostile. Ask your questions 'cause I'm ending this."

Suzana nodded. "Kendra, baby? What happened to you? How did you die?"

"I'm scared." We gasped.

Kendra turned us, tilting like an out of balanced spinning top. We wobbled away from Trixie, coughing and clutching at our throat.

"I can't breathe!"

"This is over." Trixie lit the leaves and began tossing the smoke at us. "Kendra Bruce, your time is over. Leave this host peacefully or never be called for again!"

Kendra let out a strangled scream that abruptly cut off. The ley energy that wafted amid the world poured into my nose and mouth. I stumbled and teetered, trying to get to Rex. He'd help, he'd promised.

Rex hurried forward as my knees gave out, his arms catching me. I gasped and struggled for air, fright and anger fighting within my heart as Kendra struggled to keep her sticky spirit fingers hooked into my mortal body.

Rex laid me gently on the damp grass. Then Trixie's head appeared in my vision next to his, followed by Julian, Guy, Suzana, and Martin.

"You." We sucked in a breath. "You killed me."

The tangible ley energy finally broke from me. I sucked in one last breath, one that sounded like it'd never stopped, and my eyes rolled back into my head.

I SAT ON THE BENCH OUTSIDE THE HAIR SALON while Mimzy got her hair tinted. My body remained physically drained from the gentle possession last night. When I'd come to, I was sitting in the front seat of my car, and Trixie had parked in the driveway next to her van.

My head ached; my body felt abused—a side effect from the possession. I swore to never agree to be another spirit host again.

Mortal flesh was not meant to host something from the spirit realm.

I logged into my website on my phone and removed all mention of gentle possessions from my site. Hazard pay wasn't enough for the lingering effects of Kendra Bruce's death. My throat was sore, and when I breathed deeply, there was a sharp pain that lasted a millisecond, but it was there. My lungs—no, my body—didn't enjoy drowning, and Kendra hadn't stopped thinking about her death.

You ever wonder if spirits themselves were haunted? They were—by their own violent deaths

"You killed me."

Shuddering, I leaned fully against the bench and tipped my face to the partly cloudy sky and breathed in—right before that painful pinch in my lungs—and held it. I loved sunny weather. I didn't care if there were clouds in the sky. The warmth from the sun relaxed me, and I dared to close my eyes.

Instead of murky green-brown waters with questionable *objects* floating unanchored within, I thought of the steamer closet I coveted and the way it'd erase the worry of eating red sauces in nice clothes.

"You look like you're having the best daydream anyone could have," a deep voice said.

Then a shadow fell upon me, and I cracked my eyes open. A man stood in front of me, backlit by the sun. I held my breath, squinting. I couldn't make out his features, but the width of his shoulders gave me a guess. I pushed to my feet. Sure enough, it was Rex, and while he'd watched over me last night, I didn't appreciate having some man loom over me. I stared down the street, trying to see what would've drawn a man like Rex Slater to this part of Starglen.

"What're you doing here?" I asked.

He smiled, his gaze dipping over my body before meeting mine. He jerked his chin at a nondescript office building a block over. "I had a meeting with a supplier. I noticed you when I was walking to my car."

I arched a brow. "You noticed me?" I checked the time and glanced into the salon window. The hairdresser was giving Mimzy the final touches.

"Your hair, actually." He flashed a grin. "You really can't miss it."

Whatever charm his sweet tooth had gained him over the past few days was wearing off. Rex hadn't hidden his interest in me. And when I explained to him it wouldn't happen, I'd expected all communication to cease. He still texted me random things. At lunch today, it was a picture of a protein dessert bar saying he wished it was the giant peanut butter cookie instead.

"Yeah, well." I shrugged. "It happens."

He softly laughed. "I'm sure it does. How're you feeling?"

I scrutinized him, wondering where this line of questioning was going. Was he genuinely curious, or building up goodwill until he could get me into bed? I didn't know, and frankly, I wasn't sure if I cared. I brushed my hair back, touching the enchanted hairpin to make sure it was still there. "I'm still a little tense."

He nodded. "Me too. I haven't seen anything quite like that before."

"Really?" I tilted my head to the side, regarding him. His suit jacket fit him well. I could tell it was custom-tailored to him, as it didn't strain around his biceps and shoulders. "Not even when you were in the military?"

"Oh no. I was in a lab or behind a desk through my entire career in the Air Force." He tucked his hands in his pockets. "Last night was downright spooky, Willa."

"You're telling me."

I sucked my lower lip into my mouth, observing him. What I saw before me didn't mesh with what I'd learned and what I'd assumed. Rex was quite fit. I'd believed, when I learned of his military career, that it stemmed from him being on the front lines or doing secret covert stuff, and he'd kept the workout regimen. But if he was creating enchantments or spell workings all day . . .

I peered at him. "So you enjoy working out a lot?"

His piercing blue eyes twinkled as he pushed his fingers through his dark hair, the gray lock falling on his forehead. "Are you checking me out, Willa Dade?"

"No." I flicked my hand at his jacket. "I noticed earlier that your clothes are tailored to fit you because your arms are big. I assumed you worked out to . . ." I shrugged. *Why was I saying this out loud?*

He laughed. "It's really obvious if you think about it."

I crinkled my nose. "You just like working out, is that it?"

"No. Dessert is my favorite food."

I laughed. The door opened and Mimzy stepped out, her white sneakers bright against her royal blue velour tracksuit. This time her tint was something like a blue or a purple.

Blurple? She clipped sunglasses to her overlarge frames and stepped aside me. I could hear the squint as she blatantly checked out Rex.

"Who're you?" Mimzy asked.

He held out a hand. "Rex Slater. Are you Mimzy?"

"I'm Erma to you." She shook his hand, and with her free one, tipped her sunglasses down and assessed him with her rheumy eyes. "Are you Billie's friend?"

"Hmm." He peeked at me, then returned to Mimzy. "It's complicated. I don't think she likes me that much, but . . ."

"Oh please." I plopped my hands on my hips. "This man will be anyone's friend for a cupcake."

Rex gasped. "I can't believe she said that."

"Oh, that was nothing," Mimzy said.

"She isn't exactly wrong." Rex gave her a conspiratorial wink. "I could be easily convinced to follow anyone home with a cupcake."

"Oh yeah? Were you warned about taking free candy?" she asked.

He laughed. "All the time. Especially after I tried to get in someone's car for candy."

Mimzy choked on startled laughter.

"You did not!" I said, not believing him for a moment.

"I would've if my mother hadn't grabbed me." He shrugged and faced my grandma. "It was nice to finally meet you, Erma."

"Oh, sure! Nice to meet you too." Mimzy turned to me, unclipped her sunglasses so I could see exactly how wide her eyes were, *and* to convey whatever hidden message she tried to give me.

Rex squeezed my shoulder. "I hope you feel better soon." His attention trailed to the pin in my hair. "If anything happens, call me immediately. Okay?"

I blinked, not expecting the whiplash from him being playful to dead serious. "Okay. Thanks."

"Take care, Willa." He nodded at Grandma. "You too, Erma."

We both watched him head toward the corner.

"He's got a nice set of trouser hams." Mimzy tried to rearrange my kidneys and liver by jabbing her elbow in my side. "What're you doing?"

I stepped away, rubbing my side and realizing she'd been talking about Rex's butt. "Huh?"

Mimzy sped-walked after Rex. "Hey! Wait, young man."

Rex turned, raising a brow. I briefly covered my face, then followed her.

"You look like skin and bones," Mimzy said. "Have you eaten?"

He does not.

"Oh, not yet." He glanced at his phone. "I still need to get back to the office—"

"*Pfft.* Fuck schedules, that's what I always say." Mimzy waved his statement off. "Besides, it's almost five! Come with us. Billie's making meatloaf"—she mimicked a chef's kiss—"and you'll be sorry to miss it."

"Oh, leave him alone, Mimzy." I looped my hand through her arm, trying to pull her away so we could leave. "I'm sure Mr. Slater has better plans for dinner."

"But we have fresh baklava," Mimzy said.

Keen interest flashed on his face, something I hadn't seen since he'd sat next to me as a stranger in the bar. "Wait, really?"

Mimzy waggled her brows at me and tried to dislodge my appendix.

I sucked in a breath, my lungs pinched. "Yes. Trixie's practicing, so it's not—"

"I'd love to try it." He faced me. "And your meatloaf."

I shook my head. "Oh, no, it's not—"

"It'll be nice. We haven't had company that wasn't related to us for dinner in ages." Mimzy jabbed me again. "Isn't that right, Chipmunk?"

Rex grinned.

I grimaced. "Yes, but—"

"Good." Mimzy clipped her sunglasses on. "It's settled. Follow us."

Oh, he could try. I flashed him a smile that said "this is a lovely idea" while my eyes shouted "get lost, buck-o." I didn't want him to know where I lived; I didn't want him to eat the food I made. And maybe, only a little, I didn't want to share the baklava with him.

I spun Mimzy around and hurried her to the car, glancing over my shoulder to catch Rex watching us get into the Malibu. Hah. If he didn't hurry, he'd lose us. Poor him. I cranked the engine and buckled up. Mimzy didn't. She clutched her purse and watched Rex cross the street.

"Buckle up, buttercup." I revved the engine.

"You gotta wait for him and be nice."

Fuck that noise. I pulled onto the street and zipped down through the alley so I wouldn't drive past the exit to the parking garage. Someone honked at me as I quickly turned onto Market Street.

"What're you doing?" Mimzy hastily buckled her seatbelt. "You'll get pulled over!"

It'd be worth it if Rex couldn't follow us. "What were you thinking? Inviting him to dinner without asking if I was okay with it?"

"He's a good-looking fella," she said. "Why wouldn't you be okay with it?"

"Because I don't want him to think I'm interested."

"Oh jeez!" She threw her hands in the air. "You hate men. I get it. I'm not asking you to marry him."

I once tried to explain to Mimzy that attraction didn't

happen for me until I knew them, and sometimes not even then. She'd thought it meant I didn't like men and didn't want to date. Sometimes, she got it in her head to play matchmaker with me.

"I don't hate men. I like them just fine." I glanced in my rearview mirror and didn't see anyone intentionally following me. I relaxed some. *Sucker*.

"You don't date. Are you sure you're not a lesbian? You know I'm okay with that."

I laughed a little. "Yes, Grandma. I'm sure I'm not a lesbian."

"Then what's the problem?"

"I don't know him!"

"Well, it's good he's coming for dinner. Then you can get to know him." She chuckled. "If I were fifty years younger, I'd get to know him too. Get my hands on some of that ham."

"Mimzy!" I laughed.

We made it home in record time, and Mimzy shared the gossip on the hair dye debacle with Flo and Ro as I pulled into the driveway and parked. As we approached the front door, a car pulled up to the curb.

I turned and blinked as Rex crossed the street, locking his car with a key fob. Mimzy waved and headed inside. I waited, a strained smile on my face.

"Were you trying to lose me?" he asked as he stopped next to me.

"I'm surprised you could follow me at all," I said.

"I know a race when I see one." He smirked. "Thanks for inviting me over."

"I didn't." I opened the door for him. "But you're welcome all the same."

Luckily, I'd prepped the meatloaf and had it resting in a loaf pan in the fridge, and all we had to do was preheat the oven and make the sides. And the whole time I peeled and chopped the potatoes, Mimzy flirted with Rex, asking about his family, his Air Force career, and even chatted about the tornado in the Nettles. She also attempted to get us drunk off red wine. She'd even told him to call her Mimzy, that's how cozy they got.

The meatloaf looked nice with a side of mashed potatoes and peas. I wasn't a fan of peas, not the kind Mimzy wanted— a call back to her era. They were more beige than green, but it was what she liked. Rex didn't take any, I noticed, but he had three slices of the meatloaf on his plate next to a pile of mashed potatoes.

The water creeped up on me. I'd smelled the dampness, but this was Starglen; it always smelled damp. And then a dribble of dirty water slipped into my mouth and, with a mind of its own, tried to go into my lungs. I gasped sharply.

A wave hurtled into the room, upsetting the dinner table and washing away the meal. The crashing surf tossed the baklava onto the wall. I blinked hard, seeing the room was still in order. No water. I was being attacked again psychically, meaning my hairpin had run out of juice. Or it wasn't strong enough.

"Water—"

I was submerged. Surrounded by the brackish water and bodies. My lungs screamed for air. I could still feel the solidness of the chair beneath me. I gargled, trying to spit up water, and I couldn't breathe.

I tipped over. I heard distant shouting. The hardwood floor under my hands and knees connected me briefly to reality. I sucked in air like I had a straw, only for more water to slide into my stomach. I dragged myself forward. Mimzy screamed something. Strong arms lifted me.

In the wash of water over my eyes, Rex stared at me, his lips moving. I couldn't hear what he'd said. I just pointed to my room. He shouldered his way into my sanctuary and dropped me on my feet. I stumbled and sealed the protective grid with a wand made from chlorite, and I could breathe again.

Another flash of water, another threat blasted through my mind. I cried out, and ripped my headdress from the mannequin head and threw it on, activating the protective charms on them.

"Are you okay?" Rex asked, but it sounded like we were underwater.

"No, I . . ."

He gently steered me to my bed and helped me lie down. "Is it another attack like you described?"

"Yes." My lungs ached. It hurt to breathe, and they felt bruised.

"Take all the time you need. I'll wait with you."

Minutes went by, maybe hours. I knew only darkness and fear.

When I finally felt safe enough, I opened my eyes and pushed some of the fabric away. Rex was looking at one of the crystal journals, and when he saw me watching him, he set it aside.

"How're you feeling?" he quietly asked.

"Better. Is Mimzy okay?" I asked.

"Yes. She let me know she sealed the grids in the house." He lifted a plate with a lone piece of baklava on it. "These are amazing."

"Did I fall asleep?" I asked, but it hadn't felt like it.

"Yes." He stood and placed the plate on my bedside table. "Are you going to be all right?"

I sat up and took the headdress off. Nothing happened. My hand tremored as I pushed back strands of hair. "Yes, I think so."

He frowned. "I wish I could stay, but I have things I need

to see to." His brows met above his nose. "But you say the word and I'll cancel."

I blinked. I hadn't expected this from him, especially after he'd gotten his bribe to have dinner with us. "I appreciate the thought, but I'll be fine."

"Okay. I'll check in with you later." He pressed a quick kiss to my forehead and headed to the door. He turned, his hand on the knob. "If anything changes, call me."

I mutely nodded.

"Good night, princess." Then he left.

I rubbed my forehead where his lips had briefly touched and frowned. What was that about? More importantly, why was I still being attacked?

I gathered it had to do with a murderer present at the séance last night.

Chapter Fourteen

Perry burst out of Guy's home office, his fake-tanned face contorted in a scowl. When he spotted me, he paused, flicked a glare back at the closed door, and snorted. "Good luck with him. He's being a dick more than usual."

My nephew was not the favorite child, and he knew it; we all knew it. Guy and I came from a day when having ACE children was the priority. They were skilled in every line of ley energy and would be an asset to the family regardless of what solstice they were born on. Perry and I had greatly disappointed our fathers. I won't go into detail about *how* disappointed Alvin was, seeing as not only was I a bastard, I wasn't an ACE bastard.

"So no chance of me getting my *Pac-Man* game, I take it." I'd make myself a drink before I talked with Guy if he was going to be like this.

Perry laughed. "No. Dad plays it all the time."

I plucked a globe of ice from the wet bar freezer and dropped it into a rocks glass, then added some regular ice to the bottom half of a shaker. "Does he really?"

"Yeah. Pissed Mom off quite a bit the other day when they were late for a party." Perry set a glass with an ice ball in it next to mine. "Make me one, too, will you?"

I lifted a brow. Perry usually liked rum and cokes, but if he was willing to step into the whiskey world, far be it from me to deny him. I grasped the Starglen Brewery single barrel whiskey, removed the cork lid, and poured a few shots into the shaker, followed by sweet vermouth, and a few dashes of bitters. Then I stirred the mixture.

"How've you been?" I asked as I topped each Manhattan with a cherry and passed him one. "Any new headway with the job?"

"Yeah, I have the job, but it's intern level, and he won't up my allowance." Perry took a gulp, and the ice ball booped him on the nose for his efforts.

I liked Perry; I connected with him more than I had with Guy, because of a lot of things, but mostly that we both got the rotten end of the stick. I also respected that Perry had decided not to work at Slater Technologies, to make a name for himself on his own.

However, and this is where I thought Guy might be right, Perry still lived at home. I didn't know his finances, but I had it on good authority that he wasn't being responsible with his money. Neither was his sister, but that was because she was the favorite child. Alexa had recently graduated from the Kennedy-Irwin Institute for casting, and she was currently deciding on the next university to continue her education.

Instead of giving him advice for his money—I learned that lesson years ago—I sipped from my glass. The ice ball barely moved. "Eh, your dad's being weird about a lot of things right now. Give him some time. I'm sure he'll see how little you make as an intern soon enough."

"Yeah. Thanks, Rex." Perry took another sip and shook his

head, looking at the glass. "This isn't that bad. The cherry's good though."

Guy opened the door to his office, and when he saw me, his bland expression froze. "I've been waiting for you, Hendrick."

I clapped Perry on the back. "I'll talk with you later." Then I strolled into Guy's office, one hand in my pocket, my fingers curled around my spirit stone while I held onto my glass in the other. "Ah, my *Pac-Man* game."

It stood in front of the built-in bookshelves, plugged in and scrolling high scores, which were all my brother's name.

"I didn't see a reason not to give it a spin while I waited for you to do your part with the whole Kendra Bruce mess." Guy stood in front of it and pressed a button. "Tell me what you've learned about Willamina Dade."

I stared into my drink, slowly swirling it to trap the cherry on one side. When I "agreed" to look into Willa for him, I hadn't known about any of this bullshit that was happening. The attacks against her bothered me to a degree I didn't like, especially because they were water-based attacks. So whoever was doing this was at least an enchanter and a water caster. I watched Guy navigate the yellow man around the screen. He fit the criteria, and he was far too interested in this.

"She seems legit as far as the séances go. She lives with her grandmother and takes care of her. She also works part time at a bakery on Main Street," I said.

Guy snorted. "So she's in it for the money."

"Well, it *is* how she's earning money." I did my level-best to keep that from sounding like a question, because really. How was it strange that she was using her gifts to make money? I did. Everyone at Slater Technologies did.

"I mean, she's a con artist." Guy glanced at me. "What else did you learn? Who're her other clients? Does she have other ley abilities?"

I took a sip of my drink, savoring the warm spices the whiskey left on my tongue. I had suspicions about her ley abilities. She never acknowledged familiars. Then again, whenever I'd seen her around a familiar, she'd been in the thrall of a gentle possession or dealing with misbehaving guests at a séance. I kept that thought to myself and switched gears.

"Someone's attacking her." I studied him, watching for any signs of guilt or schadenfreude. I wouldn't put any of that past him.

"Oh?" He didn't look at me, his focus intent on the screen.

"At least twice that I know of. Threatening to drown her."

There was a knock at the door before it opened—before I could get any kind of read on Guy about the attacks. I glanced over.

The butler stood to the side and cleared his throat. "Sir, a detective is here for you."

The arcade game made the noise of Pac-Man dying, and Guy took a measured step away from it. The muscle in his jaw bunched as he faced them. "How can I help you?"

Johnston stepped forward and handed him a folded paper. "We have a warrant to search the pet cemetery on your property."

I didn't have to be a mind reader or an expert in body language to know Guy was livid. The ley energy around him snapped taut, ready to be drawn upon the moment he wanted it. He unfolded the warrant and read it.

"I see." He moved to the door. "Follow me."

I hastily finished the last of my drink and fished out the cherry. Setting the glass on the side bar, I popped it in my mouth and followed my brother and the detective outside. The garden lights emitted a soft glow, and the ley bugs were out in full force. Guy led us past the carriage house and to the pet cemetery. I looked at the spot where Willa had indicated

Quackie Chan's spirit stone was, wondering if there was anything there. Guy took them into the middle of the cemetery, far from the stream.

"It's a coincidence Kendra Bruce's familiar can be called upon here," Guy said. "I'm sure the stone's somewhere in town. Twenty-five miles is quite a bit of distance."

Johnston nodded, pulling out a scanner. She activated the spirit attunement enchantment by pulling on a trigger. It reminded me of a speed gun. "We're just covering all our bases, Mr. Slater. That the familiar can be called here is a big one."

"And if someone in town had a connection with my familiar, they'd be able to call it even if my spirit stone is here with me." Guy slipped the warrant into his back pocket and folded his arms.

Johnston's brows furrowed as she glanced from the reading on the scanner to Guy and back. She wandered along the small markers for pets, some centuries old. The scanner gave nothing away. I studied Guy as she walked through all the vegetation and bushes and even when she came to the stream. He didn't break a sweat, didn't seem nervous, just upset at this inconvenience.

Again, I wondered if something more had gone on between him and Kendra. At first, I'd rejected the idea of an affair, seeing as Guy and Lynne's prenup covered everything, but what if it wasn't an affair? What if Kendra saw Guy do something, and that was what had him so upset over this whole Kendra Bruce debacle with Willa?

Johnston deactivated the scanner and tucked it away. "Nothing's coming up on the scanner for a spirit stone here."

Guy nodded. "Not surprising." He started back toward the main house. "You can leave by the side gate there."

As we parted ways with the detective, I rubbed the edge of my spirit stone, feeling the ley energy resting beneath my fingertips. Twice now, my spirit stone hadn't been picked up by any means of locating a spirit stone. But it was new technology, maybe five years old, so perhaps it still had some kinks.

I HAD A MESSAGE WAITING FOR ME WHEN I OPENED my locker at the gym.

HOT PSYCHIC

> What do you think of a peanut butter cookie with a raspberry thumbprint?

I think I'd do anything for that cookie, including THAT

HOT PSYCHIC

> THAT would be a guinea pig

Somehow I never imagined Meatloaf having a guinea pig encounter, but now I understand why he put limits on what he'd do for love

HOT PSYCHIC

> LMAO

> No. Just no

What else am I supposed to think, princess?

HOT PSYCHIC

> That you'd be my guinea pig and eat this cookie, you ridiculous man

You never have to ask if I'll eat a cookie

Texts like that with Willa went on for days. She sent

me pictures of brownies, cupcakes, and cookies, telling me about the flavors. Apparently, Willa had a lot to do with the cookies at TrixieCakes, and she was testing out new types and different methods. Then she'd text me pictures of the food she made with Mimzy. I sent her pictures of my drinks. I wasn't much of a cook, but I could make my favorites, and perhaps entice her with gimlets.

I'd just finished testing out a new spell working for the vacuum seal on an area when my phone went off again.

Christopher looked over at me. "Dating someone new?"

I laughed. "God, no."

But I didn't know how to explain the disappointment when I saw it was Eric texting me, and not Willa.

ERIC ABRAHAM

You gotta talk to your girl about the TikToks

My good mood dribbled to a halt. I'd never followed up with her about her niece. I didn't feel it was necessary, and of course, she hadn't proved that she was the type of person who needed reminders.

What's going on now?

ERIC ABRAHAM

They just haven't stopped. He's being a major dick and I slept at my dad's last night

I gasped softly, my eyes widening.

Is everything ok with you two?

ERIC ABRAHAM

I think Dane's more troubled by our wedding than he's letting on and using this as an excuse to not plan catering

This floored me. I pulled the stool close and sat down, staring at the message until my screen locked. Dane and Eric were a sure thing the moment those two got together. They were perfect, and they made each other better. And best of all, I'd never felt like a third wheel around them when I definitely could have.

> How will taking care of those videos make this better?

There was a pause of him typing for a while.

ERIC ABRAHAM

> Then he won't have any distractions so when I finally get him alone and ask him if he wants to go through with the wedding he won't have this as an excuse

> Ok. I'll talk to her. Maybe even Trixie

ERIC ABRAHAM

> Ty

Then, as if Willa knew I was going to reach out to her, she texted me a picture of a bowl full of tan batter.

> What's that?

HOT PSYCHIC

> Possibly your new favorite cookie. Ready to be a guinea pig?

> Definitely. I need to talk to you too. When do you get off work?

HOT PSYCHIC

> 4. Perfect time for you to stop by TrixieCakes. See you then?

> See you then, princess

THIS FUCKING GUY

Get to the estate. Now. 911

I glowered, the muscles pinching in my shoulders as I stood from the desk, pocketing my phone. "Christopher, I have an emergency. Will you close up for me when you leave?"

Christopher blinked and nodded quickly. "Sure thing."

I didn't bother responding to Guy. He was one of those people who assumed you were jumping to do exactly what he said when he demanded it. I hung my lab coat up and grabbed my jacket, tugging it on as I hurried to the parking garage. Many possibilities ran through my head. Perry was hurt. Perry was in trouble. Maybe something to do with Slater Technologies, but in the past, all major discussions regarding the company happened here in the building, or in Alvin's house on the coast.

Fifteen minutes later, I pulled into the circular drive of the estate, behind a crime scene van. Or, at least, I thought it was that. I hurried around the side of the house toward the carriage house, where a team of people were sweeping the area. Guy was off to the side, a cigarette between his fingers. When he saw me, he gestured sharply for me to come to him.

"What's going on?" I asked.

"They got another warrant for an invasive search." Guy drew off the cigarette and exhaled through his nose. "This is ridiculous. I never should've agreed to let that mockery of a séance happen here."

"You're not hiding anything." I leaned against the side of the house, surprised to see techs grabbing shovels and digging. "There's no harm, and once they realize this is a lost cause, they'll move on."

Guy made a disgruntled noise in the back of his throat, staring pensively at the cemetery.

It didn't take long, maybe five minutes, when there was a

startled shout from the techs. Then more followed and they swarmed everywhere, digging more and expanding their search. Guy sighed and lit another cigarette from the end of the first one.

Detective Johnston slowly wandered up to us, dropping a spirit stone into an evidence bag. Guy and I straightened immediately, his eyes darting to mine, then to the detective.

"Mr. Slater," she said slowly, "do you have anything you want to say about Kendra Bruce's spirit stone buried on your property?"

Behind her, Quackie Chan waddled around and then stepped through the veil into the spirit realm. I gaped, my mind spinning back to the gentle possession, and Kendra/Willa's out of breath accusation of murder. Surely Kendra's spirit was having a flashback. Right?

Guy rounded on me, jabbing a finger in my face. "What the fuck did you do?"

I smacked his hand aside. "I had nothing to do with her spirit stone or anything else."

"Then why the fuck is it here?" Guy scraped his fingers through his hair. "I can't believe you'd jeopardize us like this."

"Hey!" I clenched my fists. I was done with this, and if he accused me one more time of murdering my ex, I'd rearrange his face. Not in front of the police, of course. I wasn't an idiot. "I did not, in any way, separate Kendra from her spirit stone. You need to stop placing that particular blame on me, Guy, and tell us why it's here."

"I don't know how her spirit stone ended up buried on my property," Guy said. "No clue. Maybe that psychic planted it here with the help of an earth caster."

I frowned. That seemed like a stretch to me.

Johnston folded the bag over on itself and gestured behind me. "Do you have any idea about those?"

Guy's complexion lost a shade or two as we followed the detective back toward the cemetery.

"I mean, this is a pet cemetery. Spirit stones aren't uncommon there," I said.

I tried to catch Guy's eye, but he wouldn't look at me. He just hot-boxed his cigarette. We turned the bend of an over-sized bush to find a team of men and women digging up broken spirit stones.

My mouth fell open briefly before I snapped it shut. I'd never known a spirit stone could break. What happened to the familiar if its stone broke like this? Every single one was split in two, the spiritual runes on them empty. No sign of ley energy upon them. I reached inside my pocket and palmed my stone, feeling my familiar's energy.

"We're going to have to call an animal welfare consultant here," Johnston said, scowling at us.

A broken spirit stone meant one thing: the familiar was gone for good. Suddenly, I believed Quackie Chan's stone being found here hadn't been the source of Guy's worry this entire time.

But how did it end up here, whole and unmarked, amongst a mass grave of broken spirit stones?

Chapter Fifteen

The three-tiered wedding cake smelled divine. Like little vanilla angels dusting the air with marzipan and love. It made me yearn, just a little, for a hint of that in my future. I doubted any time soon. I gathered the cake drum—a far sturdier base for tiered cakes like this—and set it beside the table as I helped Trixie move the cake on top of it. In the front, it was a classic, white-frosted cake. Red crystals filled a slice cut into the back of the cake. A classic geode cake, however, those crystals were the same ones that were in our cupcakes, sure to charm the guest to taste their favorite flavor.

"This thing is huge," I said.

"I know, but this is what the mother of the bride asked for." Trixie grabbed the cake box and glanced over her shoulder. "I measured the van, but . . ."

I studied the box as we moved the cake inside it. "Will it fit through the door?"

"Yeah, but it's so heavy. I'm going to use the rolling counter. I wish this shop had a deliveries door."

"Okay. I'll get the doors for you." I hurried ahead of her

and held open the double swing doors while she pushed the cart out with the large box on it.

"I'll get the van." Trixie left the cart near the front doors and ran around to the rear parking to get the van.

While I waited, Rex stepped inside, dressed like he'd just come from a fashion shoot, wearing a two-piece suit, jacket unbuttoned and shirt open at the neck. His tailor was excellent at their job. Seeing him made me want to smile, but I bit that back. The more I got to know him, the more I had these strange impulses to smile at him or send him a text hoping he'd laugh.

Yet when he smiled, it transformed his entire face from a grumpy bearded man overworked from a job he didn't like to the playful person with more than one sweet tooth. This time, I didn't resist grinning back.

"Hey," he said. "How're you doing?"

"Eh." I shrugged. "It's a busy day."

Trixie stepped in beside him, and the light came on over her head. "Would you help me load this cake into the van, Hendrick?"

He studied the box on the rolling cart. "Sure, but only if you call me Rex from now on."

"I'll call you the Prince of Funk if it'll get you to help me instead of Billie." Trixie secured the doors to stay open.

"Hey!" I said, plopping my hands on my hips.

"Sorry, babe. Your upper arm strength's lacking, and I don't want the cake to tip into the box." Trixie rolled the cake outside.

I couldn't be mad. She was right, and that cake was a beast. While I waited for them to load the cake in the van, I gathered the cookies I wanted Rex to try. Then I fixed my hair. I frowned as I finger-combed it, wondering why I felt the need to do that. It was only Rex Slater trying my cookies. I threw it back into its original ponytail.

Rex came back inside as the van pulled away from the curb, fixing it so the doors to the front could fall close. "She really likes Prince."

I laughed and nodded. "If it weren't for Candi, that's the only music she'd play in this shop."

"What did I just help load?" He approached the table where I had the cookies and plates set out with two glasses of ice water.

"A wedding cake. Here." I fished my phone out from my apron and unlocked it, going to my last photo and showing it to him.

He stepped beside me, his arm against mine as he stared at the picture. His cologne, while subtle and smelling like he worked in a sawmill, washed away the scent of vanilla hanging the air temporarily. I flicked to the other picture, showing off the geode side.

"Wow, that's a really great-looking cake," he said. "Are those the gems that taste like whiskey?"

"Only to you." I laughed, glancing up at him.

His eyes met mine, and something tickled my gut. I shied away. He knew I wasn't interested, but I also didn't want to signal that had changed. Something told me he'd jump all over that if it went unchecked.

Rex stepped away from me and tapped the pink table with cookies and water. "You said something about cookies and me being a pig."

"You are not a pig!" I sat in one of the yellow chairs and gestured for him to join me. "You need to be honest. Don't worry about hurting my feelings."

I nudged the peanut butter and raspberry thumbprint to him. I was especially curious about this one. I thought it might be a little too crumbly, but the jam should counteract it.

He picked it up and examined it, then held it under his nose like he was a cookie sommelier. "It smells great."

"That's good." I bit my lip, watching him and trying not to grin at how serious he was being with this business of taste testing. It was adorable.

He bit into it and chewed. He set the remaining cookie on the plate and flicked crumbs off his fingers. His brows screwed together as he took a drink of water.

"Well?" I asked, leaning forward. "What'd you think?"

"It's a little dry."

"Oh." I knew that might be an issue, but I'd hoped it wouldn't bother him. I *might've* had him in mind when I decided on the flavors.

"The flavors are great, but I prefer the jam in my cookies not to have seeds." He shot me an apologetic look.

"Oh." I whipped my phone out and jotted down his notes. Not that I'd forget them. "That's good feedback. I didn't even think of the seeds."

He relaxed and ate the rest of the cookie. "What're you going to do with the rest?"

"Oh, I'm going to give them to Mimzy to take with her to bingo tonight." I peeked at him and the crestfallen expression on his face as he stared at the crumbs on the plate. "You look like someone kicked your dog."

"I just wanted another, that's all." He flashed me a wicked grin. "I'd do anything for peanut butter and raspberries. That right there." He mimed his head exploding. "I can't resist."

I stepped behind the counter and snagged a couple more from the box I'd set aside earlier and wrapped them in a napkin. I placed them in front of him as I sat down. "You sure are eating a lot of cookies that aren't perfect."

"Ah." He lifted one up and examined it. "The flavors are perfect. Do you think they just need to be baked for less time to soften them up?"

"Probably. I'll run the recipe by Trixie for her opinion."

"Ah." He winced slightly. "Speaking of, I need to talk to

her about Candi and her videos. It's really causing a problem for Dane."

I frowned. "I'm sorry to hear that."

The bell above the door chimed and, thinking it was Candi coming in to relieve me, I turned with a smile. "Hey, over here!"

But it was Suzana Bruce. She halted halfway across the floor when she spotted me and Rex sitting at a table, clutching notebooks in her arms. He scooted his chair closer to mine to make room for her at the table. Slowly, Suzana sat, her eyes darting between us and the cookies on the plate.

"I hadn't realized you two were . . . friendly," she said, and a sourness that didn't belong in a cupcake shop twanged on her last word.

"It's a small world and an even smaller town, Suzana," Rex said.

I folded my hands on the table. "Is there something I can help you with?"

With one last glance at Rex, Suzana took in a deep breath and placed the stack of notebooks on the table. "A few days after the gentle possession, we got a past due notice in the mail from a storage company Kendra used a credit card on. Turns out it finally expired."

I leaned back, amazed. First, what was Kendra's credit score that she had a card with over a three-year expiration date? Second, the timing was something else. Was I being played by the Bruces, and maybe by Rex as an extension? I frowned, peering between them both.

"I thought you'd moved after Kendra disappeared when I'd asked if she had a room in your home," I said.

"No, we moved before she disappeared," she said. "She was living with Hendrick at the time."

Rex nodded. "Kendra was good with money, sure, but paying for a storage locker years after her death is a stretch."

Suzana shrugged. "I don't know what else to say, Hendrick. The notice came, we went to the storage place, and they let us empty it." She pushed the stack toward me.

I didn't reach for them. "What do you expect me to do with these?"

"Willa's done everything she can to help you," Rex said. "I think you're taking this too far."

Suzana scowled at him. "They gave us back the spirit stone today, but they won't look into this. There's no body, you see." Her face pinched and she rapidly blinked back tears. "And without a body, there isn't a crime to investigate. Maybe there's something in those journals that'll give you a clue where she is."

I tilted my head, my brows drawing together. "Did you read the journals?"

"I can't read the code she wrote in," Suzana said.

Code? Interesting. Against better judgment, I flipped open the notebook on top. Swoops, slashes, and oddly formed letters covered the page. Shorthand. Chills ran up and down my arms. Rex leaned over, his knee brushing mine, and peered at the pages.

"I can't read these," I lied.

"You don't have to." She shrugged and flicked her hands in the air, as if it were obvious. "You're a medium. You can read the energy off them and help me find my daughter. She doesn't deserve to be an unsolved mystery."

"No one deserves that," Rex murmured.

I nodded. "Still, though. I'm really sorry, but I won't call on her spirit again. Or any spirit. Let the police work on this."

I pushed the journals back to her, and she pushed a thick envelope to me. I could smell the cash from where I sat.

"Just do what you feel's safe, Willamina." Suzana stood. "You're the last person my daughter can count on. I'll be in touch."

Suzana left, and I gaped after her, then at Rex. I couldn't believe that I was being dragged into all of this still. I wasn't qualified for this. I should return Suzana's money, along with the journals, and firmly tell her to never contact me again.

"You okay?" Rex asked.

I blinked at him. "Of course. Why wouldn't I be?"

"You seem shaken."

"This entire ordeal with the Bruces and your brother have really taken a lot out of me spiritually. Of course I'm shaken."

He hummed in the back of his throat.

"If I'm honest, no possession has ever been gentle." I crossed my arms. "And I really don't want to be involved in this." My eyes drifted to the fat envelope on the table and thoughts of a steamer closet danced through my head.

"Maybe I can help. I might know someone who can decipher whatever code this is written in." He reached for the journals.

I slapped my hand on the top. "No." I smiled to lessen the harshness of my voice. "Thank you. Suzana placed her trust in me, and I'm not about to break it by giving away her daughter's journals."

His piercing blue eyes studied me for a long moment. "Are you sure?"

"Yeah." I nodded. "I'm sure."

He stood and gathered his cookies. "Okay, but if you need anything or want me to be your guinea pig again, don't hesitate to text." He smiled at me, and I could not only see it in his eyes, but feel it in my chest. "It was good seeing you again, princess."

"Get out of here," I said, laughing a little.

Alone in the shop, waiting for Candi to arrive, I frowned at the notebooks and the envelope of cash. Sure, I could do a lot with the money, but visions of buying a steamer closet didn't sit right with an unsettled spirit roaming the ether halls of the dead. I could give everyone—the Bruces, Julian, Kendra, and even Rex—the closure they all needed to leave this pain behind.

I opened a journal and flicked through pages of familiar loops and swoops. The listed names concerned me.

"You killed me."

Ever since that first séance, I had a feeling that Guy Slater was hiding more than he was letting on. And I feared these journals might reveal all his dirty secrets.

I just hoped it didn't place me in a watery grave next to Kendra.

Chapter Sixteen

I placed the bowl of tapioca pudding on the kitchen table before Mimzy and glanced at the TV. I wasn't sure what channel this was, but it wasn't her regular game shows or soap operas. A man in a fleece jacket and a woman in overalls trudged through a redwood forest. He was saying something to the camera about only foraging what you needed, and the woman smiled at him as if he made the world turn.

I muted the volume and sat across from her. "Can I talk to you about something, Mimzy?"

The scowl that'd taken over her wrinkly features faded, and she picked up her spoon. "Sure thing, Chipmunk."

I placed one of Kendra's journals on the table. "Suzana Bruce approached me again to help her."

Mimzy's brows pulled together as she carefully scraped the top of her pudding onto the spoon. "The same woman who paid you for the séance earlier?"

"Yes."

"And now you're being attacked—" She abandoned her spoon and patted down her eggplant purple tracksuit. She shoved her hand into a pocket and came back out, placing a charm on the table. "Here. I made this for you. It's not much, but I was at the library with Trixie anyway."

I reached past the charm and grasped her hands, flipping them over. I knew what I'd see there, but the faint red marks on her palms still made my heart sink. "Mimzy, you can't keep doing that. The doctor said enchanting was putting too much strain on you."

She flipped our grip and patted my hand. "Nothing's too much when you're in danger. This is the only way I can help you."

I kicked myself for not being more careful with how I described things to her. Or that she had to see the psychic attacks at all, but I hated keeping things from her too. "You should've had Trixie do it."

She retrieved her spoon. "She was doing all those gems for the wedding cake. She didn't have enough juice." She licked the pudding off the spoon and smiled at me. "What did you want to talk about, Chipmunk?"

I took the enchantment in my hand. It was a gold scalloped shell pendant, and I had a chain I could slip it on. Lifting my eyes to Mimzy, I studied her. She continued to skim the top off the pudding, to make it last, she'd say, and chased it with a vanilla Ensure as her snack between lunch and dinner. Her eyes seemed dimmer than I remembered, and the blue veins on the backs of her hands stood out like rigid rivers of a long life spent.

And it'd been a long road. When my mother's sperm donor realized his solstice daughter was Muted, Erma Dade stepped up. She'd made significant changes to her lifestyle and her beliefs to raise me. I loved her the most.

Oh, we'd had tons of hurdles—she being a ley purist, and me being me. Personality wise, we were too much alike and butted heads on many things. We'd had a contentious relationship until my mid-teens when I discovered my mother's journals and she helped me learn how to read shorthand. Then she began making charms for me as I asked. I think teaching me and watching me learn helped her see that while I couldn't create magic, I could still use it effectively.

I opened the journal and pushed it in front of her. "Do you recognize any of this?"

Mimzy barely glanced at it. "Sure, that's shorthand. You know how to read that."

"Yeah." I pulled it back. What I *could* read sounded like a log of hotel guests. I supposed Kendra was in hospitality because she kept a record of who she checked in and whether they'd paid their bills. I flipped to a different section and showed her. "But what about this? It reminds me of short-hand, but I can't make it out."

"Huh." Mimzy set her spoon down and pulled the journal closer to her. She adjusted her huge coke-bottle glasses and blinked at the slashes and scratches on the paper. "I can't read that. What's it say?"

"I don't know." Sighing, I retrieved the journal. "I was hoping you'd know."

"You're still going to keep helping them?" This time, she scooped up a good dollop of the pudding and popped it into her mouth. "You told Trixie you wouldn't anymore."

I propped my elbow on the table and rested my head in my hand. "I don't know what more I can do for them. And someone wants me to stop."

"A water caster." She jabbed a crooked finger at the jour-nal. "I wonder if you'll find him in that book."

"It might be a woman doing this."

Mimzy snorted. "Maybe, but the only woman who knows what you're doing is her mother, and I don't see her inter-fering with finding the truth." Her spoon scraped against the side of the bowl. "I think you should help where you can.

Decipher those journals for them. The sooner that's done, the sooner it's over."

"You do?"

"Of course."

"But what about you?" I asked. "You have appointments and—"

She waved me off. "There's always a way, and this is temporary. You focus on this now." Then she waggled her brows. "And you get to spend time with Rex. Oh, he's a good-looking guy. If I were fifty years younger . . ."

"Mimzy!"

"You need to date more."

I closed my eyes. "I don't want to date."

"Give me more great-grandkids. You're thirty-five—past your prime, but you can probably get pregnant if you hurry. That clock's got to be ticking like crazy. When I was your age, I'd already had your mom and your aunt." Mimzy sipped her Ensure. "Rex has good genes."

"Okay, first of all, being thirty-five doesn't mean I'm past my prime to have children." I hurried on to cut her off. "And I don't even want kids."

"Oh, my heart." She clutched her chest. "You break it with your words."

"Okay, Gram-cracker."

"At least go on dates with him." She grinned at me, her magnified eyes twinkling. "He likes you."

"Until he realizes I'm Muted." And a waste of space in Starglen. A waste in general. And playing with power I "couldn't fundamentally understand." Or whatever that quote was on the news. I hadn't checked whether it'd been Rex or Guy who'd said that; I didn't want to lose a . . . friend. Were we friends? I thought we were on the verge of it, but he also didn't hide his interest.

"So what? Just go on a few dates with him. Have some fun."

"He seems nice, but we're not compatible."

She scowled, her lower lip jutting out. "You never give anyone a chance. That's why you're still single."

I took a calming breath. Mimzy came from that older generation where she didn't think a woman could feel fulfilled being single and childless. I wouldn't mind finding a partner, but so far it was always heartbreaking in the end. My Muted status was always a deal-breaker. His family would make sure of it.

I tapped my fingers on the journals. "You're sure you're fine with me doing this?"

Mimzy smiled and patted my hand. "Of course. I'm proud of you, Chipmunk. This is a good thing you're doing."

I left Mimzy to her show and went to my bedroom. I thought about what she'd said as I opened my jewelry box and hunted for a chain for the pendant she'd made. Ever since I told Rex I wasn't into casual sex, he'd backed off. Mostly. Sometimes his body language said other things, but he'd stopped the overly sexual overtures toward me and simply was just Rex. And I liked how easy that'd been.

After clasping on the necklace, I patted the shell at my neck, then plucked my phone from my back pocket.

Do you have time to meet?

REX GUINEA PIG

I've got some free time in an hour. Is everything ok?

Yes. I want your opinion on something and it's easier if you see it

REX GUINEA PIG

I'll be your guinea pig anytime. Can you
meet me at the Sipping Lounge in 45 min?

THE SIPPING LOUNGE WAS AN UPSCALE BAR, RIGHT outside the Flower Market. It was so close, I actually parked in the free gravel lot inside the Flower Market instead of at the curb and paying a meter. I spotted him the moment I stepped inside the darkened cocktail bar. A White woman with honey blonde hair sat with him. But the more I studied them, I could tell she was attempting to sit with him and he wasn't being welcoming. He looked up and grinned. She followed his gaze, and when it landed on me, her nostrils flared.

"Hey there, princess." He stood and kissed my cheek. "You kept me waiting."

My brain stuttered as his beard tickled my cheek for the tiniest moment his lips were against my skin. I smiled at him. *He's probably doing that to get this woman to leave.*

The woman touched his arm. "It was nice meeting you, Hendrick." She took her drink and left.

"Ooo. 'Hendrick.'" I hung my purse on the side of the chair and sat. "Does she know you?"

He chuckled. "Not in the least. What do you want to drink? Margarita?"

"Oh, here?" It was a classy place, white floors and counters and tables with black leather seating and accents. "A French gimlet's more suited."

Once he'd ordered my drink and placed it in front of me, I pulled out a journal.

"You don't want small talk?" Rex laughed, lifting his rocks glass.

I'd bet my last dollar he'd ordered a Manhattan.

"Very well. When do you think you'll be diagnosed as diabetic?" I asked sweetly.

He laughed. "I'll have you know my gym's aware of my sweet tooth." His eyes swept over me, hooded and glittering. "You got any cookies on you?"

Mimzy's words about giving him a chance slipped through my head. While I knew simply deciding that changed nothing, I also couldn't help but wonder if my heart kicked my ribs just a touch harder when he gazed at me like that. Maybe my brain was playing tricks on me.

I turned and rummaged in my purse.

"Oh, she does." He sounded absolutely thrilled.

But all I had was one of Mimzy's strawberry candies, so I grabbed that and placed it on the table. The delight dropped off his face in a nanosecond. When he didn't take it, I nudged the candy to him. "It's all I've got, sorry. I should've known better."

He picked up the candy by the wrapper twist with two fingers as if he wasn't sure what it was and pursed his lips. "Oh, princess, no. I might be a whore for cupcakes, but I don't eat just any candy. You're going to have to do better than this."

I laughed. "I'll make it up to you."

He dropped the candy in his pocket. I lifted a brow at him so he knew he hadn't gotten away with taking the candy he'd rejected so snobbishly.

He winked. "How've you been? Sorry I haven't been able to talk or come by more. This entire business with Guy and the broken stones is demanding a lot of my free time."

"I'm okay. How're you feeling about the stones?"

He sipped his drink and shook his head. "I'm at a loss for words. He won't tell me anything about it, at least not yet. He's having a lot of meetings with Alvin, so I don't envy him."

"Alvin?"

"Our father."

I nodded. I never referred to my mother's sperm donor as dad either. I didn't need to ask why Rex did too. Our answers would be similar.

"It was all over the news yesterday. Mimzy's been following it." I sipped my gimlet and sighed. It was delicate and exactly what I wanted.

"I'm not surprised. I think everyone's following it." He gestured at the journal. "Isn't that one of the journals Suzana gave you? I thought you couldn't read it."

Heat flushed my face as I opened it. "I lied. Well, partly."

He leaned a little closer and lifted a brow. "I'm shocked and scandalized that Willamina Dade would lie."

"No you're not," I said.

"What do you mean by partly?"

I shook my head. "Some of it's in a code I don't recognize. Kendra was quite clever."

He made a noncommittal noise. "What'd you find?"

"She kept a list of guests and their payments, whether they were on time or past due. Which I thought was odd. Wouldn't the hotel she worked for keep those? Why would she need them?"

At Rex's confused expression, I tilted the journal to him. "See, this is Nicholas Turner, listed as paid, but unhappy with the bill. And Oscar Mendez is past due."

"I don't understand what you're talking about," he said, his voice not as confident as it had been in the past. "What hotel is this for?"

"I thought you'd know since you dated her."

His brows bunched together as he stared at the light and heavy strokes of a pen on the page. "Kendra was a paralegal. She didn't have a second job. This might be for that instead."

I blinked back down at the page, my fingers brushing over

the handwriting from a dead woman. "Wouldn't she call them clients?"

"I don't know," he mumbled.

"And . . . There's more. I think she cheated on you while you two were together," I whispered.

The door opened, blasting the dim atmosphere with bright light, and Julian stepped in and spotted me. My smile fell, which was surprising as I hadn't realized I'd been feeling upbeat, even with the nasty topics written inside the notebook. Rex flipped the journal closed as Julian came to our table.

"Well, Willamina, what an absolute surprise to find you here," he said. "Hendrick."

"Junior," Rex said, his voice sounding chirpier than it had a moment ago.

Julian's fingers flexed, then he grabbed a chair and dragged it over to our table, the legs squeaking loudly against the tiled floor. He positioned himself next to me, so close I could feel his body heat. I shifted away.

"So, what're we chatting about?" Julian's fake smile took over his face. His eyes dipped to the journal before they flicked between me and Rex. "Is that the mongrel's diary? Let me guess: 'Dear Diary, my brother's a big jerk and broke people's spirit stones.' How close am I?"

"Not at all close." I reached up and grasped the shell pendant, swishing it along the chain as I replayed my interactions with Julian. *What had I done to make him think I'd welcome whatever* this *was?*

"Well, it's better than whining about not having daddy's approval, right, *Junior?*" Rex's lips implied his was smiling, but all the teeth made it seem otherwise. "But this is one of Kendra's journals."

Hate flashed across Julian's expression, and I wasn't sure if it was because of Rex or that Kendra was mentioned. Julian reached for my gimlet, but I was quicker. I grasped the stem of the coupe glass and slid it far from him.

Unbothered, he draped his arm across the back of my chair. "Is it the journal detailing all the times Hendrick cheated on her?"

Grimacing, I curled my shoulders in and leaned forward, darting a glance at Rex. "Would she keep such a record?"

All the playfulness, real and fake, slipped off Rex's features like melted icing. His piercing gaze met mine. "Yeah, she cheated on me. It was off and on, and whenever I found out, I retaliated in kind." It seemed like he wanted to say more, but Julian was sitting at our table.

"I never had the problem." Julian's fingers trailed along the back of my shoulder blade. "I could give Kendra what she needed—what she wanted. Maybe that's why Hendrick killed her."

I shook my shoulders and scooted farther away, only keeping one cheek on the chair. "Please don't touch me."

"I didn't kill her," Rex replied, silky soft. Then he met my eyes. "Whether or not I cheated, my feelings for Kendra were real and I wouldn't hurt her."

Julian grabbed a lock of my hair. "Isn't that what someone would say if they had killed their ex for cheating?"

What a dick. I gathered my hair and tossed it over the opposite shoulder. Grasping my gimlet, I rose from my chair and stepped away from Julian. Rex didn't move, but he stared at the hand remaining on my chair. I took a gulp of my drink, the brightness unable to wash away the sourness Julian brought to the table. He'd promptly landed on my shit list, and I was done giving him the benefit of the doubt. Or being a game piece. Though that last one might take me a little longer to execute than simply inserting distance between us.

"I'm more of the taking it out on the other party kind of

guy, and, hey! You're still breathing," Rex said. "I might change my mind, though."

My heart pounded as I glanced between the men. "Knock it off. This isn't helping or funny."

"Sorry. Junior never knows when to keep his hands to himself, princess." The tendons in his neck flexed, and his jaw moved slightly. His phone buzzed, and he read the screen. "Looks like I have to leave."

I didn't want to be alone with Julian, so I gathered the journal and stuffed it in my purse. "I do too."

"Ah, right when the party was getting interesting. Too bad." Julian leaned back, clasping his hands across his lap. "I guess meetings are important right now. This is the end times for Slay-Tech. You might want to reevaluate the dogs you let into your bed, Willamina."

I licked my lips. "Who I get into my bed with is none of your concern, Mr. Christensen, and I'd thank you to not give me your opinions."

Rex paid the tab, and I followed him out into the bright day. His expression was thunderous, and I feared the storm that would come if it broke.

I placed a hand on his shoulder to slow him down. "Are you okay?"

He shrugged my hand off and spun. "Yes. I'll be fine."

"He was pushing your buttons. Just ignore him," I said.

He clasped my hands and smiled at me, tight and forced. False. "I know." His warm fingers curled around mine. "I know. But do me a favor? Don't encourage him."

"I wasn't."

That same smile. "Sure. I know."

"Rex, even if I wasn't . . ." I rolled my wrist in the air. It still felt strange to say I was demisexual out loud. "He wouldn't make it to the list of people I'm interested in. He's disingenuous. And he makes my skin crawl."

His rigid shoulders lost some of their tension and he shook his head. "Sorry, you didn't deserve any of that."

"I know."

He flashed me a real smile. "I'm sorry, princess. Can you forgive me?"

I squinted at him. "Just this once."

"I'll make it up to you, promise." He pressed a soft kiss to my forehead. "I'll text you later."

I watched him go and rubbed the spot he'd kissed. I'd have to remind him we wouldn't be dating either, even if *he* might've made the list of men I'd be interested in.

Chapter Seventeen

A few days later, and after lunch, I stepped into Icing, scanning the tables. A Hispanic woman sat at a far table, a plate full of petit fours beside an open laptop and a steaming cup of coffee. Another customer stood at the counter, grabbing a couple of pastry boxes stacked atop one another and held together with string.

Through the window into the back room, I saw Dane focused on rolling out large sheets of dough. Eric spotted me and grinned before thanking the woman at the counter. She turned, her eyes sweeping over me twice before she left the shop.

"Hey, Rex." Eric squirted some hand sanitizer in his hands and rubbed it in. "How was the workout?"

"Nice." I stopped at the counter and examined the case. "Got a late start, but I got it done."

This entire issue with the broken spirit stones had really upset everything at Slater Technologies. Alvin had even come into the office, and it'd been a good nine months since the last time he'd showed up. While retired, he still had a seat on the board and, well, it was his name on the damned building, as he loved to remind us.

Guy had come clean to us a few years ago about a project he'd deemed "unattainable and unethical" after a few months of investing all his time and money into it. Back then, I didn't care, and our father had approved of Guy's shrewdness to back away from something as soon as he saw the issue. We never knew what the project was.

Now we knew Guy had discovered a way to quick cast without a familiar appearing.

In everyday practice, like when Eric tempered chocolate, you'd see his familiar floating near him, helping his quick cast. In active combat, our troops gave away their intent when their familiars suddenly appeared. That allowed some combatants to prepare a shield with their own quick casting or with an enchantment.

Guy'd discovered, apparently by accident, that spirit stones could be used for quick casting without calling the familiar to the mortal coil. It had something to do with etching the spell working directly onto the spirit stone. It had two major drawbacks: only one spell could be carved onto the spirit stone. And the moment it was cast, the spirit stone broke, making it incapable of calling the familiar ever again.

It was just as vile as animal abuse.

When Guy tried and couldn't find a way around this, he'd ended the program and buried the broken stones on the estate, incidentally near Kendra's intact spirit stone. And, in his shame and need to protect the company, he'd placed blockers on the property to keep people from finding any spirit stones buried there.

That explained why Willa's charm hadn't worked and the need to allow a gentle possession to find it.

I really hoped this was the end, at least with Guy's involvement with Kendra's disappearance. I also suspected it'd clear up any psychic attacks against Willa now that the cat was out of the bag about his dirty little secret. It was everywhere. It was trending on social media, all news outlets, and to whoever knew who I was.

And now, there were talks about Guy taking a leave of absence from CEO and who would temporarily fill in. Many on the board had expected I'd jump at the chance. Part of me wanted to. But in the short time I'd fill in, I wouldn't be able to make the changes I felt the company needed, and the money, while a nice boost to my portfolio, wouldn't last. I wouldn't be able to make any substantial changes to my lifestyle, not that it was dire.

But money and success bought happiness, and the more I had, the more I'd fit in. And I knew that for the lie it was, I really did, but it was always the lie that stuck with me. To be accepted into the fold as a real Slater, I needed to be filthy rich. I needed to prove myself to my family and their circle of friends. It was exhausting.

"What'll make your day better?" Eric asked, gesturing at the display case. "Dane's on a truffle kick."

The door opened, and I glanced over my shoulder. Willa and Trixie cautiously stepped inside.

"Oh, shit," I whispered.

"What?" Eric whispered back.

"The short woman's *the* Trixie from TrixieCakes," I murmured quickly. I plastered a smile on my face and waved. "Willa, Trixie! I didn't know you'd be here."

Trixie examined the entire shop until she saw Dane. She approached the window. "Is that butter?"

Eric approached her, his eyes darting between us before he held his hand out. "I'm Eric Abraham, the chocolatier here."

She shook his hand. "Trixie Morton. I'm afraid I owe you and Mr. McKee an apology for the next few months."

I stepped close to Willa. She smiled at me, though the

display case snagged her attention. I couldn't be upset over that.

"These all look amazing." Then she leaned in and said in a much lower voice, "I told Trixie what was happening."

I nodded, realization hitting. We both fell silent as everyone watched Dane roll the layers of dough and butter into a giant croissant and load it onto a sheet tray. He walked out to the far back.

"Well." Eric clapped his hands together and rubbed them. "I think we need some sugar, hmm?" Using tongs, he grabbed a few truffles, placed them upon a plate, and set them out. "Here, try these and—"

"Honey, I'm going to need some—Oh." Dane stopped short just inside the door, blinking at the three of us.

Trixie, who had quickly snatched up a white chocolate truffle, paused with it halfway to her mouth. She flushed and passed it to her other hand. "Mr. McKee, I owe you an apology." She stretched out her arm for a handshake.

Dane shook her hand. He wore his "WTF is going on?" smile and tilted his head. "I'm sure that's not the case."

"I'm Trixie Morton and I own TrixieCakes."

He grew still. "Oh." Implication sat heavily on that word. Willa patted Trixie's shoulder.

"It's only now come to my attention how my daughter's been running the shop's social media accounts. I'm so sorry. I didn't know she was trying to start a war with your shop. Even after you sent her a message asking her to stop, she persisted." Trixie almost smashed the truffle between her hands, but she halted in time and clenched her free fist. "I'm so sorry. I've fired her from my social marketing, and she's also been grounded, and my god. How much did that croissant weigh?"

Dane blinked. "You fired your daughter?"

"Of course." Trixie's chin lifted. "Maybe when she's more mature we'll revisit it, but uh . . . Not for some time." She popped the truffle into her mouth and groaned. "Lemon cream? Oh, this is divine. It practically melts as soon as it touches my tongue."

"How're you?" Willa asked softly, pulling me in with her voice.

"I refuse to complain." I placed a hand on her elbow and steered her from our friends, who were now talking about chocolate grades or something similar.

"Did you make any progress with the journals yet?" I asked.

"Some. It's slow-going." She flashed me a wry smile. "To be honest, this drama with her kids has kinda stolen the show for the past few days."

"Oh no, Shawn too?" I couldn't remember if she'd mentioned anything about the boy or not.

"Well, after Candi's online trolling, Trixie's wondering if maybe Shawn's bullying his classmates." She frowned, leaning closer to me. "He's got money he can't explain how he got. Of course he has answers, like finding it on the sidewalk or his friends are giving it to him, but she's suspicious now. She's looking for solutions online."

Ley energy began gathering inside the shop. At first, I'd ignored it because she and everyone else were. It wasn't odd for this to happen, especially if Eric or Dane were calling forward their familiars. But they weren't. And soon, the lone customer peered at the ley energy, as well as Trixie, Dane, and Eric.

Then it swelled and crashed against Willa in a blink. Her eyes glazed over, and her mouth opened and closed like a fish out of water.

"Willa!" I gripped her arms, shaking her.

Her nails bit into my skin as she tried to breathe in. She sounded like someone trying to suck air through a tiny straw already clogged with something else. Spotting the charm in her hair, which wasn't fully charged, I brushed my fingers against it to activate it.

Her lips had turned white.

"Billie!" Trixie cried, racing over and slapping Willa on the back. "Billie!"

"Breathe, damn it," I said.

The ley energy rebounded off Willa, but her stare remained unfocused, and she struggled to take in the air or let it out. The woman at the table hurriedly packed up her laptop and left, frantically glancing backward the whole time. The ley energy scrambled around Willa. I even felt a cold lick of something running up my leg, for the briefest of moments, but it was gone before I could see what it'd been.

"Should I call the paramedics?" Dane asked.

"No!" Willa said, her voice hoarse like she'd been screaming this whole time. "No, I"—she wheezed—"can breathe."

I pulled her closer, wrapping an arm around her waist. She leaned into me, trying to catch her breath, and it made me furious. I could see Trixie was just as upset while she crowded Willa, rubbing her back. The ley energy was evaporating, though some of it still clung to Willa like cobwebs.

She turned, taking a step away from me, and flashed a smile. It did nothing to hide how pale she was. "You two must be Dane and Eric. I've heard so much—" She gasped, bracing herself against the counter. "I can't catch my breath."

"God damn it, Willa," I growled. "That's enough."

Dane's brows shot into his hairline, and Trixie glared at me.

"I've got a crystal that'll work better than this charm." I slung her arm around my waist and braced her against me. I started toward the door, then thought better and met Trixie's stare. "It's a protection charm back in my apartment. I'll make sure she gets home safely after she's got it. Unless you'd like to follow me there?"

Dane and Eric shared a look, both smirking slightly.

"I'm"—Willa panted—"fine."

"Like hell you are," Trixie said. "Will you be okay with him?"

Willa nodded. "But I don't need—"

"Oh, save your martyrdom for later." Trixie rolled her eyes. "Let him help you. I have to get back to the shop, but I'll call you in ten to see how you're doing." She jabbed a finger at me. "I've got my eye on you."

I knew she was being protective, so I didn't make a fuss. I simply swept Willa out of Icing and hurried along the pathways toward the parking garage where I'd left my car. Once I got her in the front seat and her seatbelt on, she leaned forward and placed her head between her knees, taking in deep breaths. The ley energy had disappeared, but she still couldn't quite take in air.

I gripped the steering wheel with white knuckles the entire way to my building's garage. Questions raced through my head as I bundled her into the elevator and punched in the code for my place. Was this Guy attacking her? I've suspected but never confirmed. And if it was, why would he continue after his secret had been revealed? Spite and revenge, I supposed. It made my blood boil.

The elevator dinged, and the doors whispered open to the front entrance of my apartment. I took the purse from her and hung it on the coat tree and guided her to a leather armchair.

"Sit tight," I said. "I'll be right back."

I hurried into the back of the penthouse, to my primary bedroom and my walk-in closet. The lights flickered on as I entered, illuminating a mostly full closet, an island of drawers, shoe racks, a steamer closet, and a full-length mirror. Next to that, my tie rack sat atop the safe. After punching in the code,

I opened it and tugged out the shelf for my rare crystals and selected one perfect for what Willa needed. It was one I'd created while stationed in Niagara when things were getting a little dicey with the Canadians again. Long story short, a civilian hadn't realized they'd crossed the border, and we hung on to them longer than Canada appreciated.

I returned to the living room to find Willa on her feet and staring out the window. The ley energy shrouding her had vanished, which was completely normal.

She turned when she heard me. "Your front door's an elevator."

I handed her the ley crystal. "That'll work much better against these psychic attacks than your barrette."

Her eyes widened, and she still looked like death warmed over. "Is this a ley crystal?"

"Yep." I needed something in my hands. "How about a drink?"

I moved to the wet bar, suddenly uncomfortable. I didn't invite men or women back to my place. It was too awkward. Plus, after one dude figured out the code to my floor, it felt safer to go back to theirs. Not bringing Willa here hadn't even crossed my mind, and now she was gawking.

"Rex, no." Willa trailed after me. "I can't accept this."

"I don't have any citrus on hand," I said, hoping to distract her from the expensive and personal crystal I'd casually dropped into her palm. "So no gimlets for you, but I think a negroni might be nice."

"This is too much."

I glanced at her over my shoulder. She held the crystal out to me. I shook my head and selected two rocks glasses, opened the cabinet that'd hidden the mini fridge, and grabbed ice from the freezer. "You're right. A Manhattan will calm your nerves better and it goes down a lot smoother. You still sound hoarse."

"Hendrick."

I stiffened, my heart crashing down to my stomach right as the ice clinked in a glass. This had to be the first time she'd ever called me that, and I knew I wouldn't like anything she had to say. I faced her and forced an easygoing smile on my face. "Willamina."

She sucked her lip into her mouth, and for the first time since she put the brakes on a hookup, a surge of lust roared through me. I wanted to suck that lip in my mouth, to taste her, to hear her moan. *Calm down,* I said to my dick.

She held out the ley crystal once more. "I really can't accept this."

"Why not? It's the best protection you can have against these psychic attacks."

"It's rare and expensive."

I stared at her, her wide and imploring amber eyes, the color finally coming back to her ivory skin, her red hair tumbling across her shoulders to curl against her fabulous breasts. And I realized, in that moment, the ley crystal was not, in fact, the rarest item in this room.

It was her.

It blindsided me. She'd lured me into a false sense of security, thinking nothing would happen between us, and I simply . . . ignored all the warning signs. The natural little kisses on her forehead, which I played off as something close friends would do. Texting her, chatting with her. Honestly, it'd been too easy to become friends with her once the challenge of trying to get her into bed was taken away. I hadn't even noticed she was weaving some kind of spell around me while she hadn't done the same for her.

Oh no, no, Rex. This was all you.

Willa had made it clear where she stood, that she wasn't interested. There'd be no relationship outside of friendship for us. I'd accepted it easily. I knew the terms, and now, suddenly, I was sweet on her? What the fuck was that nonsense?

I cleared my throat and returned to making the drinks. "Life's just as rare. Borrow it until this mess is over. I won't have a problem taking it back, trust me." I laughed, entirely at myself. I wouldn't take it back.

I heard her step away from me, and I quietly released the breath I'd held on to. When I finished making the drinks and turned back, she'd swapped out the charm in her barrette with the ley crystal. It didn't fit the setting entirely, but it'd do for now.

I handed her the drink. "We should talk about finding her body."

Her eyes widened and jerked to mine as if sucker punched. "But wasn't she in Cyprus when she disappeared? My enchantments can't handle scrying an entire country. Even Starglen is too big for that."

She had a point. I'd noticed all the stones she used were common ones. The crystals needed to scry an entire country were expensive. I stepped away and wandered toward the large window and stared across the sprawling city of Starglen. "I checked Kendra's Instagram. Some of her posts were duplicates from one of her earlier trips. And then she made the one saying she was taking a hiatus from social media." I sipped my drink, not daring to peek at Willa when she stopped beside me. "With her spirit stone being found here, I don't think she ever went to Cyprus."

"Well, if her death wasn't an accident, then wouldn't the killer have taken the stone?" She angled her body toward me. "She still could've been in Cyprus when that happened."

"In your scenario, Guy's implicated in her death."

She winced. "I didn't mean it was him."

"Was it water again today?" I whispered. "Did you think you were drowning?"

She nodded.

"Yeah, I figured." I shook my head and took a large swallow of my drink. I'd decide how to deal with Guy later. "So, it turns out I can't track the IP address her posts were made from. That'd require a warrant. And the location was turned off for them, so no help there either."

"Then what do we do?"

"Well, right now I'm working on the theory she never left the country, so I'm thinking you do your thing with the crystals and a map and scry for her body." I eyed her purse. "You know, section by section. I don't have any enchantments prepared for this though. Do you have what you'd need for that?"

"I do." She flashed me a grin. "I even have a journal of hers too. I only need a map."

"I can get one right now." I set my drink on a coaster. "Don't let anyone up."

She quickly got to work while I ran downstairs to the corner shop and got a map of Starglen that was sold for tourists. When I'd returned, Willa had set up by clearing the coffee table and had several pendulum dowsing rods laid out before her.

She smiled when I stepped off the elevator. I spread the map before her.

"Ready?" she asked.

I motioned at the ley crystal in her hair. "Just to be safe, activate that."

She nodded absently, brushing it. Then she set up a search grid with the crystals she had. A triangular apophyllite, amethyst wands, and rough golden beryl. A seer stone, which was domed and rough around the edges—clear quartz, I thought, but could've been wrong. Each touch of her fingers sent a puff of ley energy from the stones as she placed them around the map. Then, when she was ready, she picked up the dowsing charm made from amethyst and held it over the map.

"I'm searching for Kendra Bruce's body. Let the stones guide me to her," Willa said.

Her eyes closed right as the ley energy sifted into the room. I held my breath, watching it. Here, in my penthouse, I had the means for a counterattack, and I was ready. Still, it baffled me she wouldn't watch the magic, and that tiny suspicion I had earlier about her magic grew—I didn't understand it.

Sparkling magic nudged the crystal, and Willa relaxed her hold. A moment later, the tip of the charm touched down on a quay in a commercial district where many businesses had warehouses. On the other side of the Crystal Lake Marina were seasonal residential lots.

Willa opened her eyes. "Well. I was hoping this would be inconclusive."

"Yeah." I rubbed my beard. "Me too."

"I'm going to call the detective." Willa stood and moved toward the hall.

I had to assume the police already had done this, but Kendra's death was also a cold case. And there was no body. Frankly, I didn't know what the police procedure would be for a confirmed death without a body and everyone, including me until recently, believed she'd been in Cyprus at the time of her death.

Fuck. I stared at the map and the pendulum charm. One of those residential cabins belonged to my brother. My chest grew tight and hot. I shouldn't be reeling from shock. I clenched my teeth and took in a measured breath. Guy had Kendra's spirit stone. He'd had an entire mass grave of broken spirit stones. The more this unfolded, the more it seemed like he'd done something to her. And now he was targeting Willa to keep his secrets.

"I can't get Detective Johnston on the phone," Willa said, returning to the living room.

"Of course not." I sighed. "I'm going to suggest something reckless, and you can absolutely refuse, okay?"

"Oh? What do you suggest?"

"I say we search for her body."

"You're nuts." Willa laughed. "Clearly, whoever's behind this doesn't want her to be found."

"And you'll still be under attack until she's found, Willa. If not for Kendra, then at least let's look for you."

She stared at me. I couldn't read her expression; I wasn't that good with body language. And, let's be honest, I was a little distracted from realizing I actually had feelings for her that weren't backed up by lust and boredom. She remained quiet.

"Think of it this way," I said. "This'll bring Suzana and Martin all the closure they need about her death."

"Kendra's spirit needs it," she murmured after a moment. "And Julian. Him too."

"Yeah." I nodded. Because he was *real* broken up about it, wasn't he? I didn't share my thoughts, not yet, that I believed Julian had only pursued Kendra because she'd been my girlfriend. "So what do you say? We get together tomorrow. Rent a boat while you scan for her?"

Her gaze drifted to the map and the amethyst still on the spot of open water. After a pause, she nodded. "I think you're right. The sooner we find her, the sooner the police can find her murderer and whoever's attacking me."

Chapter Eighteen

I fiddled with the shell pendant around my neck and scowled at the sky. It'd rained last night, leaving behind murky trails of dirty clouds, and a darker, gloomier sky crowded in the distance, hiding the mountains in a shroud of melancholy. The water smelled earthier, more damp, with an underlying fishy whiff riding along on the light breeze. As if it knew who I was and what had been attacking me lately. Not even the seagulls cried out like woo girls. Like they understood we'd find a dead woman today. I felt it like a stain on my soul.

I knew I was being dramatic; I had no magic, and I didn't have premonitions. However, I imagined this was what it'd be like.

A car pulled into the parking lot at the Crystal Lake Marina, and a moment later, Rex got out. My lips twitched into a smile at the sight of him, dressed in all black. I wondered if I should've as well, but it wasn't as if we were trying to be covert. I wore my workout clothes: dark green leggings, sneakers, and a blue tank top under a black, off the shoulder T-shirt. I'd even pulled my hair into a ponytail. As he approached, my attention drifted to his rolled-up sleeves and exposed forearms.

I pulled out the amethyst pendulum charm and tucked my phone into the side pocket, then waved. "Morning."

"Mornin', princess." He brought me into a side hug and pressed a kiss to the top of my hair, which was much easier since I wasn't wearing heels.

Warmth suffused me from the head down. When he'd first started calling me "princess," it'd annoyed me, and I was certain that'd been his goal. Now, it felt completely different. He didn't have that snarky expression, and his eyes seemed warm whenever they met mine as he said it.

"You okay?" he asked. "Did you have another attack?"

I absently touched the ley crystal that I'd clipped into my hair, careful not to activate the charm. "No. I'm fine, but . . ." I shrugged and glanced to the overcast sky. "It's been gloomy so much lately, and it's kinda bumming me out."

"Need a little sunshine this morning?" he asked.

I chuckled. "Well, it'd certainly improve my mood."

"Your wish is my command, princess. Don't move."

He retrieved a piece of chalk from his pocket and crouched at my feet. I took a step back, uncertain of what he planned to do.

He peered at me, the skin crinkling at the corners of his eyes. "It makes things easier for me if you don't move."

"What're you doing?"

"Getting you some sunshine."

He began drafting out a circle, and then drew another circle, with strange markings I couldn't read. They weren't blurry or smudged, just in the language of magic and his element. One that would've been mine if my fate had been different. Rex carefully moved so he wouldn't smudge the lines of the spell working as he drew around us.

I felt oddly formidable with a powerful man crouched at my feet. Rex even curled his fingers around my ankle to steady himself as he sketched, and that touch sent a current of electricity straight to my belly.

Oh boy. I might like him.

I knew I enjoyed watching his forearms twitch as he drew sigils, runes, and concentric circles, something I hadn't ever noted before. Then he stood, his chest barely brushing mine. That lock of gray hair fell onto his forehead.

Then the wind came.

The wind lashed around our bodies, ruffling our clothes and whipping my hair around. I squeaked. It grew in force, as if we were in the eye of the storm. It spun around us, churning, and the clouds parted. Light spilled around us in a spotlight of sunshine, highlighting us. Highlighting him.

My heart skipped a beat.

I laughed, lifting my face to the sky, basking in the warmth of it despite the cool gusts of wind blowing around us. I let my lids fall closed and soaked in the warmth and the light. And when I opened my eyes, Rex was gazing at me. I smiled, taking in his handsome features, as if he'd just unlocked an achievement that allowed me to finally see who he really was.

He'd given me the sun.

"If this were any other situation, I'd kiss you right now, Willa," he said, his voice all grumbly and deep.

If there ever was a moment, this was it. All I had to do was take it. Butterflies crowded my chest, their wings fluttering. I swallowed. "Okay," I whispered, taking a small step closer to him.

His brows hopped an inch as he intently searched my face. Each time his gaze dipped to my mouth, my heart sped a touch faster.

"May I kiss you?" he asked, his words barely heard over the wind.

I nodded. "Yes."

He leaned in and pressed a soft kiss to my lips. "Another?"

But his mouth rubbed against mine as he spoke, causing my lips to tingle before his lips brushed against mine, a little longer this time. I pressed my fingers against his hard chest.

"One more," I murmured. "Just to be sure."

I leaned up on my toes and caught his lips with mine, and our mouths danced together. I had experienced many kisses, both at the right and at the wrong time. The sun shone on us like a clear, bright day, but it was like lightning struck me. Every nerve in my body shouted *Rex Rex Rex* as he infiltrated my final barriers and stole within the confines of my most sacred space. My heart thudded heavily inside my chest, then raced when he pulled me closer. This was the right moment.

His soft beard tickled my cheek as he deepened the kiss with a flick of his tongue across the seam of my lips. I opened my mouth, and he explored it, sending fissures of pleasure through my body. He tasted like peanut butter with a hint of coffee, and he smelled like a forest trapped in a spa. My knees quivered. My hands slid up his chest and spanned his wide shoulders. I wanted more, to explore this new sensation, to get to know him on a deeper level, so I nipped his lip. His guttural groan sent a bolt of heat straight to the apex of my thighs, and I knew I was in trouble.

I liked Rex Slater. Like, *liked* liked him, and I didn't know when it'd happened. I wanted to press myself against him and map the ins and outs of his body.

The wind died down, and the clouds choked off the sun once more, but the magic of him remained. Our kiss naturally broke, and we stared at each other. He flashed a smile I'd seen hundreds of times before, but this time, it made me downright giddy.

"Willa," he gravely said, "I want to do that again, but . . ."

I lifted the hand that I'd wrapped a dowsing pendulum charm around. "We have a body to find."

"Exactly." He drew his hands back, his fingers brushing the underside of my arms.

I peered at the now cracked and worn spell working, the chalk faded as if it'd been mostly washed away in the rain. "That was amazing." I grinned at him. "Thank you."

"Anything for you, princess." He nodded toward the rental building. "Let's get a canoe."

They only had a two-person kayak. With both of us in life preservers—I had to go a size up to accommodate my boobs, the hateful things—we each carried an end of the kayak with paddles toward the launcher. We'd paid for two hours, and I hoped it wouldn't take that long to either find her body or conclude she wasn't here.

We launched into the water. Rex sat behind me. I dipped my paddle in, and when I went to move it to the other side, our paddles knocked against each other.

I glanced at him over my shoulder, a nervous laugh on my lips. "We need to paddle in tandem."

"Oh no. Put yours inside by your legs." He winked. "This is princess kayaking. You use your charm to guide us."

"Princess kayaking. I like it." I slid the paddle in beside my legs and unwound the amethyst charm from my wrist and activated it.

Last night, after I returned home from his penthouse, I'd set everything up for the enchantment. Thankfully, Trixie had rented an enchanting table from the library and finished the charm while Mimzy played bingo. The plumb bob charm of variegated colors tipped forward on the chain. I needed to tell him the truth about my ley abilities, that I was Muted.

"Straight ahead," I said instead.

"Aye, aye, captain," Rex replied.

I bit my lip, even though he couldn't see me grin. As we glided through foggy waters, I reminded myself not to get attached to him—though that would be difficult since I already was. But once Rex discovered I was Muted, it'd be the end of our relationship. We wouldn't be friends, let alone lovers. Ironic, since I'd resisted liking him when I believed he'd only wanted me in his bed. A shame. After that kiss, I imagined we'd have phenomenal sex together. But when I eventually told him my secret, he'd break my heart, and I'd never see him again.

I was pathetic. I had almost everything, a fantastic personality and a bangin' body, according to an old boyfriend. But because I was Muted and I wouldn't get physical with someone unless I'd developed an emotional attachment to them first, everything that was going in my favor was wasted on me. No magic, no sex drive—which wasn't actually true. I simply didn't engage in casual sex, but when I liked someone, if I fell in love, I enjoyed intimacy more and more. It was only when I lost the emotional bond that I no longer felt the urge.

But I was getting ahead of myself. I was sitting in this kayak and searching for his dead ex, and I was wondering how my Muted status would affect our relationship. Hysterical. Because there'd never be one. I didn't have magic, and he was a prominent figure in Starglen. I definitely couldn't kiss him again if I wanted to remain mostly unscathed after this was over.

The crystal swung on the chain. "Head left."

"That's called port," he called back.

"Head port?" I glanced at him as he angled us to the left. "What's right then?"

"Starboard."

We floated along, the kelp brushing along the underside of the kayak, as if some creature floating beneath us had dragged their fingers along the bottom of our craft. The fog grew denser, and strange noises drifted to us from across the water. My skin prickled, and I'd wished I'd worn a long-sleeved shirt.

After an hour of dipping in and out of inlets and floodwaters, we floated in waters surrounded by business and residential properties. Most of the businesses used the water to cool generators—I assumed—while the cabins' owners probably did a lot of fishing. Or sitting on docks in Adirondack chairs thinking about fishing. You know, rich people.

The charm swung on the chain once more, guiding us toward an inflow that was surrounded by tall river grass, eucalyptus trees, and not a building in sight. The waterway had to be at least a quarter mile wide. The charm spun.

"Stop," I said, a little too loud. The fog bounced my voice back to me.

"Here?" Rex sounded dubious.

"I think so. Is it shallow?" I asked.

I turned in time to see him plunge his paddle all the way into the water and pull it out. "I can't touch the bottom."

"So what do we do?" I asked. "I don't have a way of getting to her if she's here."

"Yeah, that falls to me. Let's get off the water."

He maneuvered the kayak to the riverbed and instructed me to hang on to a tree root that broke the surface. Then he heaved himself out, causing the boat to rock perilously. I squeaked when I nearly capsized.

"Hang on." He gripped my end of the kayak and pulled me and the boat partly onto the riverbank. "Give me your hand."

I placed mine in his, and he helped me out of the kayak, then pulled it farther onto the land. I unbuckled my life vest and took in a full breath. Rex shucked his entirely.

He clapped his hands together and rubbed them. A smile I'd yet to see tilted his lips, one of nostalgia and wonderful memories. Then he reached out and touched nothing. *Oh. I think he's calling his familiar.* Which was odd. Most casters called them out loud by their names and made sweet comments to them. Not that I could ever see the familiars, but Rex never said a name.

He peeked at me, wearing a sheepish grin. "El Diablo was already a big guy when he passed."

I plastered an understanding smile on my face and followed his gaze to nothing. "Oh, really. He's impressive."

"Yeah, we've learned a lot of spell workings together, but this one's from a long time ago." His fingers wiggled in the air, as if ruffling fur or cheeks. Or I don't know, wings? "Glad I didn't have him forget it."

The wind picked up, like it had when he'd parted the clouds. It ripped at his shirt and hair, through my clothes, and made the water reeds bow before us. I hugged myself, rubbing my arms as I suppressed a shudder. And the water parted.

A wrapped body lay in the mud. I stumbled back a few steps, covering my mouth and trying not to scream. My heart slammed against my ribcage. I hadn't quite believed that we'd find her. But I'd trusted my ingredients as much as I trusted Trixie at the enchanting table, which meant with every fiber of my being.

The color drained from Rex's face, and he ripped a smooth stone from his pocket and tossed it. A dome appeared over the body. The wind died down, and the water collected around the dome, preserving the area. We'd found Kendra Bruce's watery grave.

WE WERE WELL PAST THE TWO HOUR TURN IN FOR the kayak. Police had arrived by car, taking the service roads to this area. Rex's lighthearted mood had disappeared the moment the mud-caked shape appeared, and he kept staring out into the distance, as if the fog didn't exist, and he was studying something. I didn't know what. He'd gone silent on me.

The techs at the scene performed a similar spell to Rex's earlier and then lifted the body from the water. After pulling it open and seeing a somewhat . . . fleshy skeleton, I shuddered and turned away. I didn't want to see any of this, especially as I was certain this was Kendra Bruce.

Detective Johnston approached us. "Mr. Slater, Ms. Dade, what drew you out here?"

"We wanted to search for Kendra's body," Rex said, his voice as flat as his eyes.

I nodded.

Johnston jotted something in her notes. "I see. Does this have anything to do with the message you left me yesterday, Ms. Dade?"

"Yes," I answered quickly. "Everything."

And I went down the reasons for the Bruces contacting me, the spirit stone, and the psychic attacks against me, explaining that was the driving point.

"I see. Well, I'll be in contact with both of you if I have further questions," Johnston said. "In the meantime, I'll have Officer Rossi drive you both back to the marina."

We rode back in silence. For all the time it took Rex to paddle us to that area, it was only a fifteen-minute drive to the marina. He didn't say a word, but his phone started blew up with texts a few minutes into the drive. He responded quickly to each one, his phone chiming almost the instant he sent anything. A call came in, but he rejected it, sending out more texts.

"Is everything okay?" I asked.

"No." He never looked away from his phone.

"Are *you* okay?" I asked.

The car pulled up into the lot and stopped. The officer let us out of the back. Before I could ask him questions, Rex approached the front window and talked with the clerk, probably about the kayak still at the crime scene. I waited by his car, suspecting he'd leave without saying goodbye to me. Or telling me what was wrong. Which was silly. I knew what was wrong, but this felt . . . different. Bigger. Like a secret as huge as being Muted.

He warily approached me and stopped an arm's length from me. "I've got a work emergency."

He wouldn't meet my eyes. Should I accept what he said and let him go, or should I press? This didn't feel right.

I bit the inside of my cheek, taking a second. "Are you okay? I mean, I know they just pulled a body out of the—"

"A body that's more than likely my ex-girlfriend." He pushed his fingers through his wavy, dark hair, that gray lock falling forward once more. "No, I'm not okay, and I need to speak with Guy about this."

A chill clenched my middle. "Oh no. He doesn't have property here, does he?"

He barked out a mirthless laugh. "He warned me you were a fake psychic, but here you are, knowing exactly what's going on."

I flinched. I *was* a fake psychic.

His demeanor softened, and he closed the distance between us. "Sorry, princess, I didn't mean to be a dick. There's just a lot going on right now about this, and I need . . ." His gaze drifted to the ley crystal in my hair and back to mine. "I need you to stay safe while I'm gone. I'll call you tonight."

"Okay." I nodded, my insides doing strange things between freezing and melting. I didn't know how to act or what to say.

He leaned in and pressed his lips briefly to the corner of my mouth. Then he was gone.

If only the memory of what it was like to be kissed by Rex Slater had left with him.

Chapter Nineteen

"Mr. Slater had to leave for an important meeting with Mr. Slater," Molly, Guy's personal assistant, said. She gave me a stiff smile, her eyes hardly meeting mine.

A couple years ago, I'd stopped fucking her in the bathroom next to her office. Back then, the lifestyle hadn't bored me like it did now. And since I refused to talk about it or even explain why I'd cut it off, she'd began giving me the cold shoulder. It was her right, and I wouldn't pretend not to understand why she was miffed with me.

"Do you know when he'll return?" I asked.

"Unfortunately, reading the minds of Slater men has never been a talent of mine." She tidied the pens on her desk and straightened a legal pad.

I lifted a brow, waiting.

She sighed. "I cleared his schedule for the day."

"Thanks." I left and headed back toward the elevator and stabbed my finger at the call button.

While I was certain that our father had summoned Guy after I'd been summoned to the office, my brother could've sent me a text to let me know he wouldn't be available for whatever he needed to speak to me about. Did he know yet about the body? How quickly would they identify that person? I was about 80% certain we'd found Kendra's body this morning, but what if it wasn't?

We had property all along Crystal Lake. Most of it resided in a Slater trust for the family, but I knew one cabin was explicitly Guy's. If I'd realized yesterday when Willa had scried for the body where it'd eventually take us, I wouldn't have suggested we search for it. Some skeletons were better left alone, and I was . . . dreading finding out why there was one there.

The doors to the elevator opened to my floor, and I strode down the hallway of temperature-controlled labs toward my office. Many enchanters and casters were working on bulk orders for charms and parts to charms to meet the distribution of our many contracts.

When I stepped into my small lab, Christopher was leaving my office with a sheaf of tracing paper in his hands.

"Oh, Hendrick," he said, closing the door behind him. "I didn't think you'd be in today."

"Guy wants a meeting today," I answered. "What're you working on?"

"I ran out of tracing paper and had to get it from supplies, so I figured I should make sure you were stocked as well." Christopher moved over to his standing desk. "I'm still working on the intricacies of the spell for the incendiary spark. It isn't as big as the request indicates, and the blast area seems too small."

"You're still working on the bomb?" I frowned and glanced at the spell working. The runes and symbols within the concentric circles were blurry and out of focus— completely normal when I looked at fire spell workings. "I thought you had that finished a couple weeks ago."

His mouth pursed, and he shrugged one shoulder. "They want a bigger boom."

I'd have to read the order again. It seemed ridiculous, but the government was the government, and they liked their big booms.

"Well, good luck with that." I waved it off and headed toward my office. "I don't know how long I'll be in today, so if I'm suddenly not here, you know why."

I stepped inside my office. It was small, and there was a small stack of tracing paper on my desk. I slid it onto its shelf, which was empty; I never let it get that low. I guessed Christopher had been borrowing from here so he wouldn't have to go to supplies. I'd told him plenty of times there's no point in procrastinating and to get the damned paper when he'd run out, but that fell on deaf ears. It irritated me. I found it inefficient, but not good enough of a reason to transfer him out to the production floor.

Yet when I stared down at the blank paper, I didn't see sigils or symbols. I saw Willa's face when I'd used that simple spell working to part the clouds, something I'd learned in Fulton as a boy. It was like she'd seen magic for the first time, and it was me. I'd known that I'd developed feelings for her already, but she'd looked at me as if seeing me for the first time. Somewhere along the way, things had shifted between us.

Which was ridiculous. Ever since Kendra, I was never in relationships that were based on soft feelings and emotions. I couldn't trust anyone with my inner self, my worries, or my happiness; I'd never wanted to try. Sex had been enough for me, and my title as a playboy was well-earned. When Willa'd explained she wasn't attracted to people without an emotional bond, it took all the pressure off to get her in my bed. I'd stopped. It'd actually been easy to take a step back and simply take her word for it.

And somewhere along the way, I'd fallen for her and felt at

ease with sharing things about myself with her. Now, I needed to make sure I didn't fall from grace.

I WALKED DOWN THE HALL TOWARD GUY'S HOME office the next evening, angry and impatient. Things were popping off on the news about the violence in the Nettles and where the weapons were originating from. Four people had died when Sutter's Mill collapsed, and it was because someone had gotten their hands on a Slater Technologies charm for tornadoes.

And all I got was radio silence from Guy until an hour ago.

I should've let him wait, like he'd made me after he demanded I come in to the office. I could've stayed with Willa, ensuring she was safe. Instead, I texted to let her know I had nothing new to tell her. Neither did she, but she continued to make progress on the journals.

Neither of us brought up the kiss. I wondered if she couldn't stop thinking about it like I couldn't. I'd even hopped on Reddit to see how other demisexuals felt about kissing—I know, I'm that guy, but I couldn't ask Willa without revealing all my cards. But based on what I'd read, Willa hadn't recoiled or *seemed* grossed out by the kiss, so . . . Maybe she liked it?

I laughed at myself. Never had I ever been this insecure about a person.

I knocked on the door and stepped inside, not bothering to wait for Guy to call me in. He stood at the window, hands in his pockets, legs braced, and stared.

He glanced over his shoulder, then turned to fully face me. "It's about time. I've been waiting on you."

I scoffed. "I've been waiting for you since yesterday. You weren't even there when you called me in."

"Father wanted to talk." Guy grasped a glass and downed two-thirds of it in one gulp.

No one denied Alvin Slater a meeting. Even if you were in the middle of a crisis, you dropped everything to speak with the man.

"How's Father?" I asked, as was expected of me.

"Alive. New nurse. Paints a lot now." Guy leaned against the desk. "Let's get down to why I called you here. You're going to need to know a lot of this informa—"

"Were you fucking Kendra?" I asked.

All the sound and air were sucked out of the room. His eyes grew as large as dinner plates, his jaw hanging open.

Then he chuckled, shaking his head. "We don't have time for that bullshit, Hendrick."

"Fuck you, we don't," I said, surprised that my voice sounded considerably colder. "You've been cagey ever since the séance—"

"Because the Bruces hired a con artist to squeeze me for money." Guy spread his hands as if revealing a grand scheme, the ice clinking in the rocks glass.

"That doesn't explain why the spirit stone was found on the estate, Guy," I said.

"Fine." Guy set the glass down with a thud. "You want the truth? I'll give it to you. No, I never did anything with your girlfriend, but not for lack of opportunity."

Ice formed in the middle of my chest at the look of glee on his face.

"She came on to me whenever she could, offered herself up to me on a silver platter."

"You're lying." But was he? There had to've been an unspoken rule about her cheating on me with family, just like I wouldn't go after her friends.

Guy shrugged and waved a hand. "She was always in the main house, sneaking around. Probably looking to climb another rung on the social ladder by being my mistress, which —" He laughed. "Hysterical, you know? It was the only reason she was with you in the first place."

"No, that's not true."

"It all really started when Father declared you'd never be more than a floor supervisor at the office. When she realized you had no claim to the Slater empire, she went for a bigger fish: Me."

I clenched my fists, remembering that night for completely different reasons. Sure, Alvin had emasculated me and promised me nothing but the same treatment as the other people Slater Technologies employed, but that had never been why Kendra had been with me—I'd assumed so, anyway.

"You were never her type," I said. A lame counterargument, but denial was a big thing in the Slater family.

"Possibly, but did it really matter to a gold digger like her?" He laughed. "It's probably exactly why she got engaged to Julian first, *then* dumped your ass. And be careful, little brother. Willamina Dade is no different than Kendra was. She's just prettier to look at."

"That isn't how Willa operates."

He laughed harder. "Is that what she says for pillow talk? I warned you not to fuck her."

"I'm not sleeping with her," I said through clenched teeth. Then stretched my jaw.

"Sure. At any rate, you should stop now." Guy shifted and grabbed an accordion folder. "Because of the spirit stones and now the body found near my fishing cabin, Father has advised me to take a sabbatical."

A headache bloomed gently behind my eye and I rubbed my brow, as if that'd stop the pain. I was beginning to understand his really shitty behavior right now. Being summoned by

Alvin and basically getting fired had to've been a giant blow to Guy's world. CEO wasn't simply a job to him; it was his identity.

"And to show that Slater Technologies retains its solid foundations, *you* will be taking over as CEO until I'm able to return to office once this all blows over. The military will want to renegotiate the contract we just landed. Do whatever it takes to *not* lose it." He shoved the folder in my hands. "There's also the tiny issue of corporate espionage that you need to figure out."

"What?" I'd never heard of this. Then again, it'd also been above my paygrade. "Since when?"

"Oh, it's been happening for decades." Guy grabbed his glass and brought it to his mouth. When he realized it was empty, he smacked it back down. "Funny enough, I'd thought it was Kendra for a while and tried to catch her in the act. But it continued after she left you, so I ruled her out."

"Jesus fucking Christ."

Guy approached his dry bar and poured us each two fingers of whiskey, handing over the glass. "You've heard about the shit happening in the Nettles?"

"Yes. I read the story about how it was one of ours." I sipped the drink.

"That weapon was strictly for military use. Your job's to find out who's leaking our spell workings or equipment to those 'gangsters' in the Nettles." Guy waved a hand and strolled back to his desk. "If you do a good job, once I'm back in the office, I'll talk to Father about promoting you to something else, like COO or something."

Stunned, I wasn't sure what to say, and the first thing that popped out of my mouth was, "But I prefer building."

"Too fucking bad, Hendrick," Guy said, exasperated. "This is happening until I can return. If you don't like it, pray that body truly wasn't Kendra's, because that will only delay me."

There was a soft tap at the door and the butler opened the door. Detective Johnston pushed past him into the room.

She squared her shoulders, commanding all the attention in the room. "Mr. Slater, I need to discuss with you about Kendra Bruce's body being found on your property."

The detective's words became muffled, and all I could see was the image of Kendra's wrapped body soaked in mud. This was only just the beginning. I knew I wouldn't escape suspicion. Hell, Guy'd probably point the finger at me. I didn't know how our family and company would recover from this.

"I don't own the water, detective," Guy said.

"Regardless, Mr. Slater, she was found there, and we need to discuss her murder downtown. You can come with me as you are, or I can escort you out in cuffs." Johnston touched the cuffs on her belt. "The choice is yours."

Guy lifted his hands in surrender. "I'll come with you." He pinned me with a glare. "You need to fix this."

They left the room together.

"*Fuck!*" I massaged my eye as I retrieved my phone.

> I just got confirmation that was Kendra in the water

PRINCESS HOT PSYCHIC

> It's all over the news

> Guy's #1 suspect. I don't believe it

PRINCESS HOT PSYCHIC

> Of course not. He's your brother

> He's an asshole and broke spirit stones, but I don't believe he's a murderer

I left out that I'd assumed it was my brother who'd been attacking her. Now I wasn't entirely sure.

> How are the journals coming along?

PRINCESS HOT PSYCHIC

Slow, but I think I'm onto something with the code she wrote in

> Good. I don't want to urge you to go faster, but if you can, I'd appreciate it

She gave me a thumbs up. I began and deleted many texts, most of them sloppy with feelings about her, Guy, and Kendra. All that stuff was for face-to-face. Because if Guy really had murdered my ex-girlfriend, I'd need more than a hug emoji back.

Chapter Twenty

I sat at the kitchen island, the tart smell of tomato sauce, savory garlic, and wine still enveloping me from dinner, earlier. Mimzy sat in her armchair in the living room, watching reruns of *The Andy Griffith Show* with her after dinner pudding and waiting to be taken to bingo without me so I could focus on Kendra's journals and the notebook I transcribed them into.

I flexed my hand, not used to writing with a pen this much, and frowned at the journal. As far as I knew, there was one kind of shorthand out there, which was called Gregg Standard. It was a collection of swoops, lines, and half-formed letters and words. Basically, the phonetic version of writing. But there were pages and pages, sometimes paragraphs, between what I could read and something that *looked* like shorthand. But I couldn't decipher any of it, and anything I thought I decoded didn't make a lick of sense.

The backdoor opened, and Trixie shouldered her way in. I breathed a sigh of relief and set the pen aside, glad to have a break.

"Hey, Trix. How's things?" I tipped the wine bottle to my glass and topped myself off.

"Well, my kids are bullies." She came by my stool and pulled me into a side hug. "How did I raise bullies?"

I returned the hug. "So Shawn confirmed . . . ?"

"That little shit has been bullying kids for their lunch money. And if they don't have any, he takes something from them—like that pink dragon." She clenched her fists. "I *knew* it was fucking weird he went with pink. But I thought—hey, I raised him to know that pink is just a color and not a sign of gender or sexuality."

"Jesus. What're you gonna do?" I asked.

"Well, I've talked with Ms. Duffy, the principal, and she's going to find out exactly how far his bullying reached and what he's done. He'll pay back through her. I had him give back the toys he took, and he has a two-week in-school suspension."

Mimzy shut the TV off and came into the kitchen, setting her pudding bowl in the sink.

"Does he seem remorseful?" I grasped her hands and squeezed them.

I couldn't guess how awful Trixie felt about her kids being bullies, especially when her classmates bullied her in high school. Because Trixie was a stripper's name. First Candi—who occasionally complained about her name being a stripper's name—and now Shawn.

"I think he's more upset at being caught right now." She rolled her eyes.

"Who?" Mimzy asked, nudging her enormous glasses back up her nose. "What's wrong?"

"I'll tell you in the car, Mimzy," Trixie said. Then she met my gaze and sighed. "I think I need to ask Brandon to cut back his hours. Maybe not take jobs as far away, so he can be home and be a good role model, you know?"

Brandon worked as an electrician and he was constantly on the move, being one of two electricians in Humboldt County that actually was worth the after-hours service fee. He also traveled to farms out in the boonies because many electricians in Starglen stayed in Starglen.

"Maybe?" I wasn't sure if that was why Shawn was acting out or not. He'd had a growth spurt over the summer, therefore he was taller than most kids his age. And he was also a caster. He could simply be having a power trip.

"Oh, did you hear?" Trixie asked.

Mimzy glanced at her wrist unironically; she wore a watch. She cleared her throat.

"Hear what?" I asked.

"People are calling for the government to cancel the contract they have with Slay-Tech because of their misconduct with their weapons," Trixie said. "Whatever's happening in the Nettles isn't sanctioned. And well, that whole gross business with the broken spirit stones."

I grimaced. "Well . . ." I didn't know what to say or what I thought. I assumed she told me this because she knew I'd caught some feelings for Rex.

And that we'd kissed.

"We gotta go." Mimzy moved to the door. "If I'm late, Flo and Ro'll get the good table, and the caller tonight is"—her brows bounced up and down—"Benny Rodriguez."

We chuckled, and Trixie gave me another side hug. "I'll text you later."

Then they left.

I scowled at the journals. My hand cramped simply by thinking about writing out more of whatever this shorthand was. I picked up my phone instead.

> How are you holding up?

I didn't expect Rex to respond anytime soon. I knew the issue with Guy becoming a suspect in Kendra's death had derailed everything for him. He'd said something about filling in for his brother, but I'd never gotten more out of him. And I'd been afraid to ask.

Would it be pushy to pester him? We'd only kissed. It wasn't a big deal to him. But it was to me. Kissing wasn't sex, no, but it was intimate. Mouths, breath, and tongues mingling —you know what? It was sex with your mouth. I didn't kiss just anyone, and I'd *wanted* him to kiss me. Damn, when I finally had feelings of desire for someone, I didn't want to waste it. Sure, there were plenty of fish in the sea and all, but when *I* found someone I wanted to swim with, it was rare.

REX GUINEA PIG

Better now that you texted me

My heart fluttered and I smiled.

Flattery will get you places now, be careful

I inserted the sweating emoji because I'm a classy bitch.

REX GUINEA PIG

In that case, my beautiful princess, meet for drinks tomorrow night?

I bit my lip. Was I ready for "drinks" and whatever happened after that? Was he alluding to sex or merely drinks? I shook my head. I wasn't ready. We'd only kissed.

He'd only given me the sun.

REX GUINEA PIG

I'll only be free for an hour at most, so I was thinking the bar we first met. Is that ok?

> Maybe this time I'll make out with you in the hallway. 7 ok?

REX GUINEA PIG

> Perfect. Give me a 15 min grace period please?

I'D GIVEN HIM TWENTY, AND I WASN'T SORRY THAT I had. He hurried in, and the look of relief on his face made me smile. It'd been the right choice. He wore a two-piece suit, his collar unbuttoned and his tie loosened.

He placed a hot hand on my back and pressed a lingering kiss to the crown of my head. "I'm so glad you waited. Hey, is this Manhattan for me?"

"Yeah, but it's been sitting there for ten minutes." I lifted my half-drunk gimlet to him.

He clinked his glass against mine, a smile lighting his beautiful blue eyes. "Ooo, two cherries. I feel special."

"Nothing but the best for the new CEO." I finished my gimlet.

"Interim CEO." Rex ate one cherry immediately. "I signed a contract promising I wouldn't glue my ass to the chair."

I laughed. "Really? They made you sign a contract?"

"It was Alvin's idea." He took the stool beside me and swiveled to face me, his knees bumping into mine. "He wanted to come back and fill the position, but he's too old and the board wasn't going to approve that."

"How old is your father?" I lifted my hand to get the bartender's attention.

"Ninety-one." My expression must've said something because he chuckled. "My mother's sixty, and before you ask, she loves me but never wanted to get in the way of my father or she'd lose her monthly stipend."

I almost said something, but the bartender came to me. I smiled at him. "A French 75, please."

"Fancy," Rex murmured when the man grabbed the champagne.

"You keep calling me princess, I may as well drink like one." I winked.

A French 75 was basically an ultra-gimlet, but with more champagne than gin.

I gripped the lapel of his suit to get a feel of the fabric used. It was nice, I had no complaints. "You should wear three-piece suits."

He chuckled, the sound lifting my spirits more than my drink. "Oh, you like cravats and all that?"

"It'd be a vest, you silly man." I sipped my drink. "That way, you'd still look smart and like a million dollars when you take the jacket off and roll up your sleeves."

He grinned. I smiled back, basking in this glow that he'd somehow imbued me with. "Do you like it when I roll up my sleeves?"

I did what I could to control most of my smile, but I could tell I'd failed. "You have nice forearms."

Rex stood and took his jacket off. Then he unbuttoned his cuffs.

I laughed and shook my head. "Stop. You don't have to do that."

"Oh, but I think I do." He rolled his sleeves up past his elbows, revealing his toned forearms.

They had freckles and a faint sprinkle of dark hair. I wondered if that could be said for his chest. Heat flared in my face, and I quickly sipped my cool drink, slightly surprised by my thoughts.

"And what if I said I liked your butt?" I grinned. "Would you wear chaps?"

"Nah, I'd twerk."

He'd said it with such a straight face I burst out laughing. "Twerk? Do you even know how?"

He grinned, his piercing eyes warm and full of mirth. "Of course. I might be a bastard, princess, but I'm an efficient bastard. Twerking'll get you all the ass without the chaps."

We giggled together, and honestly, I'd never thought him more handsome than now. Then something over my shoulder caught his attention and drained the humor right out of him like a sink hole.

"What is it?" I asked, placing my hand on his knee.

"The weapons in the Nettles." He covered my hand and curled his fingers around mine. "I wish it hadn't been one of ours."

"How do you know?"

"Maker marks on the remnants." He sipped his drink, which was amazingly still mostly full. "I've been charged with employing necessary means in finding out how civilians are getting their hands on weapons that only the military's supposed to have access to."

For a moment, I could see the weight of this resting on his shoulders like an albatross hung by his father and brother. While his shoulders were broad, it wasn't ever his fault. I didn't think I'd be able to tread the waters Rex'd found himself in.

"Do you at least have leads?" I asked.

"So far, none of the marks have been mine, thank fuck." He shuddered. "And now I'm constantly being called about Kendra's death, because everyone knows who we were together." He sent me an apologetic smile. "They all want to know why it was Guy who killed her and not me, and honestly, I can't answer that."

I didn't quite understand why he shot me that look. People had pasts, and within those pasts were relationships. He had them; even I had them. It was fine—normal, even.

"Did they say yet how she died?" I asked.

"No, but we can all guess, can't we?"

I didn't even have to think about it. Kendra was always out of breath when her spirit came to me in séances, and especially during the not-so-gentle possession. The attacks against me always involved water, and I'd seen water when she'd visited. I knew she'd drowned, but they hadn't yet confirmed it.

"Yeah," I whispered. "Drowning's frightening."

His fingers tightened on my hand. "Are you certain it was drowning?"

I blinked. "What do you mean?"

"Well . . ." He sipped his drink, his gaze taking on a faraway cast one gets when recalling something from their past. His blue eyes turned troubled. "I had a drill instructor who was a real asshole. Someone called her sir, and she couldn't take it. It was all about copy paper anyway, and when he called her sir, she stole the very breath from his lungs. It was like torture. She'd only let him have enough air to stay conscious."

"Was she a water caster?" I asked, appalled.

"No," he said, a little surprised. "She's an air caster."

"Well, every time Kendra showed me how she couldn't breathe, we were in water." I reached into my large purse and retrieved the notebook I transcribed Kendra's into. "By the way, speaking of, I have a suspect."

"Guy?"

"No. Oscar Mendez." I opened the notebook and showed him what she'd written about him. During the gentle possession, Kendra had accused someone at the carriage house of killing her, but she'd also continued to relive her death, which that statement could've been uttered to someone not there. And what I could read of her journals suggested that was likely. "I think Kendra was blackmailing people. There are a lot of payments notated, but everything is written in code I don't understand."

He whistled low, his eyes sweeping over the pages I had opened before him. "That's an interesting theory."

I floundered. He didn't believe me? He didn't seem like he had any better ideas. "I'm pretty sure that's what's happening, but I still need to decode this. Honestly, this is quite the puzzle."

He nodded. "Keep me updated on this."

"There's also a strange inconsistency about Julian in her journals," I said.

"What do you mean?"

"Well, I think he's mentioned in parts in a code I've still yet not deciphered, but his name's pretty clear. But after that, it's in the normal Gregg Standard." I shrugged. "It was probably a mistake on her part."

He rubbed his chin, smoothing his beard. "Was I mentioned?"

I rolled my lips into my mouth and shook my head. "Not yet, so far."

I couldn't read his expression; his beard hid a lot without ever intending to. I drained the last of my drink and was about to order another when he moved.

He glanced at his watch and cursed. "I have to go soon, but this was good work, Willa. Thank you."

I smiled. "I wish you didn't have to leave so soon."

"Wanna make out in the hallway by the bathrooms?" he asked, a twinkle in his eye.

I chuckled and jerked my head in that direction. "Go ahead. I won't leave this time."

And this time, his kisses made my toes curl and an ache

appear in my belly so low, I almost thought it was outside my body. His heady kisses were more intoxicating than the drinks we had, and I was sad to see him go, even if he did a little twerk while he left.

Chapter Twenty-One

I stepped out of the conference room from the zoom interview with four news sources wanting information about the broken spirit stones and how it could affect the contract Slater Technologies had with the government. Then in devolved into some snide remarks about psychics and Willa's character, which I had no patience for. The whole interview had been a waste of time.

My phone buzzed inside the pocket of my navy-blue three-piece suit.

Guy's text annoyed me because why the fuck did he always call when he clearly knew how to text? I slipped my phone inside my inner pocket and ignored him—this was probably why he always called.

I stepped inside my temporary office and paused at Molly's desk. "Hold my calls for an hour, would you?"

She paused in typing. "Of course, Mr. Slater."

I entered my office and sat behind my desk. The screen

woke up, and I got to work on looking for disparities in employees. I couldn't believe Guy planted that task on my shoulders. It worried me he knew something more than he was letting on. Like this would be my new position. Sure, becoming CEO of Slater Technologies had been a dream of mine when I was young and naïve. Working with family added that extra layer of bullshit stress no one needed.

As I scrolled through my email, searching for new mail from the government, my cell buzzed against my ribs. There wasn't anything new, and it made me worried. I'd never been in on the ins and outs of how this CEO of a company thing worked. My father had made it clear I'd never inherit the company—in front of Kendra, no less—and I'd stopped pretending that it could happen one day. Building and creating new charms was where I thrived, anyway.

A soft tinkle, sounding like a distant wind chime, went off from my inside pocket. I plucked the phone out and unlocked it.

PRINCESS HOT PSYCHIC

I've been out here for a half hour. I won't be able to stay much longer if all you're gonna do is make me wait

"What?" I texted the same question to her.

PRINCESS HOT PSYCHIC

Your PA said you were busy and invited me to wait

I stood and opened the door, and sure enough, Willa sat in one of the armchairs, her phone in her hand. Molly continued typing something up in an email.

She startled when she heard me. "Oh, Mr. Slater! You can call me on the extension. You don't need to come out here if you wanted to talk."

I lifted a brow at her as I stepped past her desk and approached Willa. "Sorry you had to wait. I had no idea you'd arrived for our meeting."

Willa smiled and, fuck me, it was like there was color in the world again.

"It's no problem." She stood, her red hair draping over her shoulder, looking like fire against her flowy beige top and matching skirt. In heels, she was about two inches shorter than me. "Are you ready for me now?"

No. I didn't believe I'd ever be ready for someone like Willa. I smiled and shifted, holding my arm out so she'd precede me into my office. Then I frowned at Molly while I stepped inside the room and closed the door behind me.

"Sorry, I didn't know you were here," I said, walking up to her.

"I had a feeling when she didn't alert you I was here, but I gave her the benefit of the doubt." Her eyes raked over me, and her full lips tipped at the corners. "I was right about the three-piece suit."

"You look amazing." I dipped my head and brushed my lips against hers.

A soft flush touched her cheeks, and she stepped back. "Thank you, so do you."

It hit me: I'd missed her. The past few days without seeing her had been busy, and we'd definitely talked quite a bit throughout the day, like I did with Dane and Eric. But seeing her right now, catching a whiff of her clean scent, hit differently. I knew I'd developed feelings for her over the past few weeks; I just hadn't had any idea how big they were.

Should I be happy about this or wary? Past experience showed me I wasn't good at relationships, but then again, Kendra wasn't either. It was tricky to navigate feelings and emotions without ever discussing the future of the relationship. Kendra had been like this, and she'd always expected me to figure it out on my own with her. Perhaps that was why she'd always cheated on me—I hadn't been able to give her what she needed.

Willa had given me a tip on how she operated, and if she hadn't had feelings, I don't believe she would've let me kiss her that day in the marina. But she'd stepped away from me merely a moment ago. I didn't want to ask about it, preferring to seem cool and nonchalant about what she meant to me. But if I continued to be aloof, if I didn't convey I felt something with her, then why would she open to me further? If we could have a future, one where we both had trust and happiness, then I wanted that. I loosened my tie and swallowed. It came as no surprise I had a difficult time with giving others my trust.

"Are you okay?" Willa asked, her head tilting, the ley crystal clipping half her hair back dazzled with caught light.

"I'm pretty stressed right now, honestly." I sat in one chair that faced the desk. "How're you?"

"Not as stressed as you." She sat beside me and slung one pale, shapely leg over her knee. I wanted to lick it. From her bag, she retrieved two notebooks. One was Kendra's journal. "I might be able to take one thing off your list that's stressing you out."

I sat forward. "What did you find?"

She opened the journal and pointed to a series of slashes and letters, some bolder than the other. "This is the code that she wrote in that I couldn't figure out for the longest time."

"What is it?"

She opened the other notebook, one I'd seen in her room when she'd been taking shelter from a psychic attack. "This is shorthand, specifically Gregg shorthand, which is standard in America. It's basically shorthand with phonetic spelling to how the word sounds."

I nodded to show I was following along.

"And *this*"—she grinned, pointing at Kendra's journal—

"is written in Pittman shorthand, which is mostly used in the UK." She chuckled. "Oh, I was tearing my hair out over that, and I finally just googled it. 'Cause I could see something like shorthand and it really made sense to be that, but I couldn't figure it out."

"So you googled it?" I asked, smiling at her enthusiasm.

"Yeah! I downloaded a translator for it and wrote out a few entries." Willa pulled a third notebook from her purse, which was impressive as it hadn't appeared like it could hold that many. She handed it to me. "From what I can tell, she'd have sex with them and then ask for money to keep quiet—" she sucked in a breath, glancing at me. She began pulling the notebook from me. "Sorry, I didn't think about how to say that to you."

I tugged on the notebook, not letting her take it back. "It's fine. I know who she was. So—if I understand this, she was having sex with these guys and then blackmailing them? Why?"

"Oh. They're all married." She pointed at the table I'd copied over. "See this? Most of these fellows are paid in full, but Oscar Mendez never paid her."

"Oh, then she told his spouse?"

"*Or* she threatened to tell his spouse, and he killed Kendra to keep his secret."

"So all those notebooks detail her affair with Mendez?" I asked.

Her silence emanated bad news. She flipped back to the page in the notebook she'd translated to show a list of names. "It's everyone, as far as I can tell."

"Oh. All these men?" I lowered my head and rubbed my neck. I couldn't hold her gaze any longer. *What did this say about me?*

"I'm afraid so." Willa grimaced.

The list of names made me feel . . . like a fool. I mean, I

knew she cheated. It was our thing—our *toxic* thing—but I'd never kept a journal about it. Nor did I demand money in return.

I pinched the bridge of my nose. "That explains all the weekend trips and why she always had money."

Willa placed a hand on my forearm and squeezed. "People lie all the time, Rex. And some people are great at it, especially if who they're lying to wants to believe the best in them. You deserved better than what she gave you."

I covered her hand with mine. "Thanks." I wanted to say more, but I didn't know what words to use. "What else did you find in the journals?"

"That she has past due . . . clients." Willa straightened from me and flipped through a couple of pages and presented the translated text to me. "Ta-da!"

I took the journal. "It's just one name."

"And a lead. She'd noted he was really angry with her when she asked for payment."

"Very suspicious, this Oscar Mendez. And you have his contact info." I glanced at her. "Did you google that, too?"

She chuckled and shook her head. "It was included. It was what clued me in that there was something important there— I mean, aside from the Pittman shorthand—that I needed to focus on figuring it out."

"What's so different between the two shorthand?" I asked, genuinely curious.

"Well, Gregg writes out how the word sounds," she explained, "and the length of the hooks designates the vowel sounds. Pittman uses shading, so the darker the strokes, the harder the sounds. And they spell out the word as it's written. I thought she might've made it up, and I worried I'd never find a way to translate."

"Good job, Willa." I smiled at her.

She returned it. "Thanks, Rex."

We smiled at each other, her gaze never leaving mine. It almost seemed like we even leaned into one another, as if she were just as drawn to me as I was to her.

She broke eye contact first. "So Oscar Mendez is past due, and I thought maybe we should talk with him. I mean, if you want."

"I think that's a great idea." I stood and walked behind my desk with the notebook.

With the phone on speaker, I punched in the number. Part of me wondered if the information was still correct, and what we'd do if it turned out that it wasn't current. Probably google him, since it'd worked so well for Willa.

"Oscar Mendez speaking," a voice said.

Willa punched the air, silently cheering.

"Oscar, this is Hendrick Slater calling," I said.

There was a sharp inhalation on the other end. "Is this regarding the application I'd submitted last year?"

Willa's brows winged up as she eyed the phone.

"No," I said, "this is about something else. I'd like to set up a meeting with you."

"But . . . It's not an interview?" Oscar asked.

"I'm afraid Slater Technologies isn't actively looking for new blood."

Silence. I exchanged glances with Willa.

"I do want to meet with you," I said again.

"Why, if it isn't for an interview?" Oscar asked.

"We have a mutual . . . acquaintance. Kendra Bruce."

"Fuck that bitch."

The call disconnected.

"Oh, the plot thickens." Willa jotted Oscar's info on a clean page, ripped it out, and handed it to me. "I bet you could commiserate with him over Kendra and get him to talk."

"She never blackmailed me," I muttered. "But yeah, maybe."

"There is something . . ." Willa placed the tops of her fingers on the journal. "There's a small . . . inconsistency? It's about Julian."

My head snapped up. "What do you mean? Is he fucking with you?" A jolt of heat lanced into my brain. I'd destroy his month.

"No. But I've been reading through what I can of her journals, and he's mentioned, especially after their engagement was announced."

"Okay, that makes sense. What's wrong with that?" I didn't want to know about this; I'd already had Kendra's explanation, and it'd cut deep. I didn't need further injury.

"She mentioned his name tied to a business in the Nettles before their engagement, maybe once or twice, but she chose to write it in the unstandardized shorthand."

"The shorthand she uses for blackmail?" I asked.

She nodded.

My brows pulled together, my focus falling on the journal. So many thoughts raced through my head over what I'd learned about Kendra's nighttime activities. Julian had never married. Therefore, blackmailing over sex didn't make that much sense to me. *Unless* she caught him doing something red-handed. I smirked, wondering what dirty secret she'd discovered. "What did it say?"

"I don't know. I need to go back and translate it." She pursed her lips and sighed. "I need to set up a meeting with Julian and ask him about that place in the Nettles."

I didn't want her to go by herself, but I also knew that if I went, she wouldn't get the information she wanted. Julian was that kind of person.

"Be careful there," I said. "I know you can take care of yourself, but be extra vigilant."

She nodded. "I will."

I hated myself a little for wanting to know, but morbid curiosity loved company. "Was I mentioned at all in the journals?"

"No," she said. "Not at all."

My brows pulled together. Not at all? Jesus. We'd lived together for years, and not once was I mentioned? I hated how clear the past was when I thought back on it.

"I haven't read them all, though," Willa said quickly.

My face must've given away my feelings. I jerked my hand, as if waving that thought out of the air. "This is great, Willa. I'm sure we'll be much closer to finding out what really happened to her. Have you been attacked at all?"

"There was something last night, but the moment I felt like I couldn't breathe, I used the crystal and it worked like a charm." She smiled as she said that last part.

"That's good. Look, I'll see what I can do about talking with Oscar Mendez and text you as soon as I get something from him."

"Okay. I know you're busy, so I'll get out of your hair."

I stepped around the desk and wrapped my arm around her shoulder, smiling at her. "Thanks for coming in. I'm sorry you had to wait." I pressed a kiss to her forehead.

She smiled over her shoulder at me as I watched her leave my office, one thought blaring in my head. Why had she let the psychic attack get that far into simulating drowning when the gathering ley energy should've tipped her off?

Chapter Twenty-Two

The doorbell rang, startling me from translating the journals at the kitchen table.

"Who's that?" Mimzy called.

"I don't know," I yelled back. "You're next to the door."

"Well." The level of exasperation in that one word was astounding. The footrest to the lazy boy cranked down. "I'm watching *Jeopardy!.*"

In all honesty, I should've answered the door for her. It wasn't a big deal. But I also wanted her to get up and walk around more. I'd noticed a significant decrease in her steps since I started this whole "Who Killed Kendra Bruce?" mystery, and Mimzy needed to give her joints a workout. And her lungs.

"Who're you?" Mimzy yelled.

I leaned forward in the chair, peering past the water cooler toward the entrance. Mimzy had the door open, but she shouted through the glass storm door. On the other side was Julian Christensen. The hair on my arms stood up. *How the fuck does he know where I live?* I stilled, as if being motionless would let me hear better—or go unnoticed should he look over Mimzy's shoulder.

"I'm Julian Christensen—Luther Christensen's son." He smiled.

"And?" Mimzy shouted back, propping both of her hands on her hips.

Julian's smile fell a smidge. I got the feeling he expected mentioning his father would get Mimzy to open the door. I'd bet my last dollar it usually did too.

"I wanted to speak with Willamina, so if I could come inside . . . ?" He reached for the door handle. You could hear the silence in this conversation—it was heavy and loaded, like a gun. "Can I come in?"

In the past, it'd annoyed me when she'd lock the storm door. We always locked the main door; why bother with the storm door? It was glass. If people wanted past it, they'd break it. Today, I was extremely relieved that Mimzy insisted on locking that door. It was a small barrier, a trifle, and I knew Julian was ACE. It wouldn't stop him—the only thing that did was probably manners.

Mimzy turned, her eyes locking with mine. "Billie? You here?" She yelled across the house as if she didn't know where I was.

Suddenly, I was fifteen again. Nikki Gilbert stood before the same door, wanting to visit. I'd had a detention the previous day because Nikki decided to become part of the popular clique. And she'd thrown me under the bus and blew up our friendship to do it. I'd reacted in the cafeteria by dumping my sloppy joe on the top mean girl's cheerleading uniform. During the game, you could see the orange stain from space. Mimzy had checked with me to see if I wanted to see Nikki, and when I shook my head, she'd sent the girl away.

I knew if I wanted it, Mimzy would send Julian away.

Something told me to activate the ley crystal clipping my

hair back. I didn't understand the feeling—Julian had been polite each time I'd met with him, and he'd never attempted to threaten me. However, I couldn't ignore that gut instinct.

I brushed the crystal and stood, stepping around the water cooler and coming to the door. "This is a surprise."

Julian smiled, flashing his white teeth. If it weren't for his spotty overgrown stubble, it would've been really nice. "Can I come in?"

Mimzy tutted and shuffled into the kitchen.

I unlocked the door and stepped outside, shutting it behind me. "My grandmother isn't doing so great today." I didn't mind lying about Mimzy, and I got the feeling she didn't want him inside, either.

Julian had his hair styled meticulously, and his button-up shirt was well-pressed. Behind him at the curb idled a black sedan, and someone sat in the driver's seat.

I gave him my attention, wanting to know how he knew where I lived, but also too nervous to find out. "What's up?"

He gave me another smile and chuckled slightly. "The meeting you asked me for?"

"Oh!" Since he'd never responded, I figured I'd have to keep asking until he caved. "Right now?" I glanced over my shoulder and into the house. I didn't see my grandma, but I assumed she lurked out of sight, probably with a big spoon to whack him with if I yelled. Or she was sneaking a vanilla Ensure.

His gaze flicked upward with a tiny shake of his head. "You requested this meeting while I was with my father. When I told him about you, he said he wanted to meet you and be present for whatever you wished to talk about."

I fiddled with the golden shell pendant around my neck and frowned. "Your father wants to meet me?" I asked slowly. "Why?"

He waved a hand dismissively. "He and Kendra got along really well."

I studied the person in the driver's seat. I'd never imagined Luther Christensen would drive for himself, but I'd been wrong before. "Is that him?"

Julian looked back and laughed. "God no. My father doesn't drive." He gestured me ahead of him. "If you don't mind, we can head straight there."

I took a step back, reaching behind me for the door handle. "I'm not ready to go out in public."

His eyes traveled over my leggings to my loose workout top to my hair. He licked his lips. "You look good, Willamina. You know that."

I let out a tiny, exasperated huff. "I'll be ready in fifteen. Wait here."

I went back into the house and locked both doors. I stepped into the kitchen to find Mimzy tossing chocolate ice cream into a blender and the malt mix on the counter.

She glanced at me. "The mayor's son, huh?"

"Luther isn't the mayor."

"Not yet." She dropped another scoop of ice cream into the blender. "What does he want?"

"I asked to talk with him yesterday, and now it's blown into this whole thing about meeting his father." I began backing up into the hallway. "No more ice cream today!"

I hurried into my room and changed out of my comfy clothes and into something that would be acceptable at a meeting with a man like Luther Christensen. A dark taupe A-line skirt with a flowy white top. I took my hair down and finger combed it, but I had a crimp, mostly on the right side, from my hair band. I clipped it back with the ley crystal and coaxed the rest to fall over my left shoulder in a wave. My winged eyeliner was still good, and all I needed to do was add a little blush and some natural lip gloss before I was ready to go. I quickly stuffed the journals into my purse.

When I stepped outside, Julian was leaning against the car, texting. Ah, so he could've contacted me and asked if it was a good time to go for a drive. He was simply inconsiderate. No surprise there.

"You look delectable," he said, his eyes raking up and down my body for the second time today as he opened the rear car door.

I suppressed a shudder. "Where are we going?"

"Downtown. My father's office." Then he hopped into the back and slid across the bench seat. He leaned toward the door and patted the seat. "Let's not make him wait longer, okay?"

I climbed in and shut the door. As I pulled on the seatbelt, the car moved from the curb. Julian smirked; he hadn't buckled up. It was illegal not to wear a seatbelt in the back seat of a moving vehicle in California, but something told me this car didn't get pulled over much. I retrieved my phone and sent a text to Rex.

> Julian showed up at my house and is taking me to meet his father.

"Why are you nervous?" Julian asked.

"Uh, well." I forced a smile and threw my hands up. "I wasn't expecting to meet with your father. At all."

"Oh, you like meeting famous people?"

"I mean, he's a big political figure. I just wasn't expecting it." I pressed my fingertips to my lips. "He's not going to ask for a donation to his campaign, is he?"

"Ha!" Julian leaned against the seat and laughed some more. "He might, you never know." He rolled his head to meet my gaze. "Politicians, am I right?"

I laughed lightly. Then we fell into silence.

GUINEA PIG REX

> Text me when you're done. I found
> Mendez's place of employment. It's in the
> same building as Christensen's office

After ten minutes, we pulled into a VIP spot in the parking garage, directly next to the elevator for Lancaster Plaza—the most recognizable building in the Starglen skyline with its diamond-shaped roof. Julian attempted to invade my personal space, but I made a show of digging through my purse and taking a sidestep to edge out of his bubble.

When the elevator opened, we stepped into a lobby on the twentieth floor. Marble tile and wood accents everywhere. A large redwood slab, nearly as wide as the car I'd arrived in, sat inside a glass container. Two women, dressed as nice as me, stood behind a reception desk and beamed at Julian as he walked by into a carpeted hallway.

We passed windowed conference rooms and offices until Julian opened one door to another reception office. This time, the woman sat behind a desk.

She glanced up, then pressed a button on the phone on her desk. "Your son has arrived with his guest," she whispered.

But Julian didn't wait to hear if his father was available; he just opened the door, ushered me inside, then closed the door behind us.

"Yeah," Luther Christensen said, smoke lazily curling toward the ceiling. "And you can count on me to make sure that the state of California sees Starglen as the shining jewel it is. Right. Right. You bet."

He dropped the receiver into the cradle, scrutinizing me up and down with dark brown eyes. He grunted. "You're the psychic?"

I nodded.

"I expected you to look like a gypsy," Luther said.

I cringed, not daring to correct his racist slur; I didn't really know who I was dealing with yet.

"She does when she performs," Julian said.

"You're dismissed, Julian."

I glanced at him, surprised, but Julian nodded and left the office, the clicking latch ricocheting in the room. I'd wanted this meeting with Julian, not his father. Why had he summoned me?

Luther kept his hard eyes on me as he rested his cigar on the crystal ashtray. "Well, take a seat."

I sat in the leather chair farthest from the smoking cigar and crossed my ankles, tucking them beneath the chair. I'd adopted Mimzy's style of clutching the straps to my purse on my lap so no one'd steal it. My palms felt as if they were on fire, and I could feel the thin layer of sweat between my skin and the straps in my fists. While Luther studied me, I looked around his office.

It was a man cave. All dark wood and leather with heavy crystal at the dry bar with top shelf spirits. There were golfing and fishing photos, in which he had a cigar clamped between his fingers in every one. Framed pictures of him at political events, and even when he met Madame President Shonda Carpenter last year.

"So you wanted to talk to my boy." Luther's roughened voice sounded like he'd smoked his entire life.

"I did, yes." I tilted my head to the side. "But here I am. With you."

"Julian gets distracted by pretty faces and bodies." He eyed my bare legs, then tried to ogle my chest.

I pulled my purse closer to my torso, knowing it'd block most of it. "What if I'd wanted to ask him on a date? Would you have still insisted on meeting me?"

He still hadn't lifted his male gaze above my neck. "I would. Especially as I know what kind of business you're in.

Palm reading? Pah!" He grabbed the cigar and had lifted it halfway to his mouth when he finally met my eyes. "Taking advantage of the gullible. My son? Yeah . . . He'd be gullible for you."

"Okay." I held my hands out, annoyed. A slight breeze flowed against them from somewhere, and it was a relief to my ultra-hot palms. I pulled out my big guns since he was being so pleasant. "Then you know Kendra was blackmailing him?"

He laughed. "She was social climbing."

"Then whatever happened at the Pioneer was the first rung?" I lifted a shoulder. "Kendra already had an in at Slater Technologies. Why would she go down that many rungs to the Nettles?"

The Pioneer used to be something similar to Lancaster Plaza during the gold rush that had made Starglen the crowning jewel it was today. Now, it was a hotel and casino, a rumored hotspot for the Fornaro family. More like a meeting place for organized crime. And it'd been notated next to Julian's name in Kendra's blackmail shorthand.

"With Hendrick Slater?" Luther guffawed. "He never would've made it to the top floor if his brother hadn't broken all those spirit stones. Kendra knew it, and she charmed my son into falling in love with her."

"Or whatever she caught him doing was enough to force an engagement."

Luther tapped a thick chunk of ash from his cigar and set it on the groove to the ashtray. "Where did you come up with that idea?"

"I have a way of knowing many things that people keep secret." I flashed my best enigmatic smile.

"Ah, yes." Luther tented his fingers, clearly comfortable in his pedantic asshole routine. "The ostensible predictions of Willamina Dade. How did you come to this conclusion?" He lifted a hand to stave off my response. "Let me guess . . . the spirits told you?"

No way would I mention the journals, so in for a penny, in for a pound. "Yes. They tell me all sorts of things because I listen."

"Then listen well to this: Julian is *not* available to the likes of you." His voice was hard edged with hate—as if he knew magic had rejected me and he would too. "Stay clear of him, and don't give him any more ideas about you in his bed."

I gaped, my mouth falling open. "Excuse me?"

"Don't act surprised I figured out your game." Luther waved a hand at me. "My campaign's more important than whatever you think you can get out of dating him, and if you try to wedge yourself in, I'll tell the entire world who you are."

"And what's that, Mr. Christensen?"

"A charlatan. A pathetic enchantress doing anything for money."

I stood. I'd known for a minute I'd wasted my time with this meeting, but I'd wanted to hear what Luther had to say about all of this. Mostly, I found he thought himself more important than anyone else.

"This was enlightening." I lifted my chin to look down my nose at him. "On many levels. This was more than I expected from your most unwelcoming meeting, Mr. Christensen."

I thought about adding more, explaining what a weasel he was and that no one in my family would vote for him, especially after this. But the less I talked with him, the less I'd shoot laser beams from my eyes and burn his flesh off. I left his office. God, I hoped he lost the election.

Julian was nowhere to be seen, not even when I walked into the lobby, and both women were there. He'd fucking ditched me. I gnashed my molars and took a deep breath through my nose. How dare he hijack me from my house, leaving me without transportation, and disappear on me while his daddy told me I wasn't good enough for him.

I scoffed, jabbing the elevator call button so hard my finger tingled. Julian wasn't good enough for *me*.

> What floor is Oscar's office? I'll go talk to him now

GUINEA PIG REX

> Not without me, you won't

I stepped inside the empty elevator and frowned at the display of buttons. "Someone save me from bossy men."

GUINEA PIG REX

> 12th floor. I'm nearly there. Wait for me

I smashed the button, then brushed my fingers against the ley crystal in my hair. I didn't want to drain it over nothing. I'd barely waited five minutes, working myself up into a tizzy, when the elevator dinged and Rex stepped off.

"Thanks for waiting." He tugged the sleeves of his suit jacket down. "You look nice."

I didn't mind Rex's gaze lingering on my legs because he wasn't sleazy about it. I liked his attention, and I knew it had everything to do with how I felt about him.

We stepped inside Linski & David stock brokerage and headed to reception. Behind her was a wall of glass, and at least two stock tickers were on each of the walls over the cubicles of men and women talking on phones. I could hear the buzz of voices from outside.

Oscar, a Hispanic man, came out after fifteen minutes. He was on the stocky side, maybe a couple inches shorter than me in my heels, with a strap of hair combed over a bald spot. His white shirt was unbuttoned at the neck, and frosting smudged his black tie. At least, I hoped it was frosting.

"Hi, I'm Oscar Mendez." He shook my hand, then Rex's. He kept his attention on Rex, knowing where the money was. "Let's get us a meeting room. Come along."

Rex and I exchanged a glance before following him down the hall and into an enclave that could barely seat four people comfortably. I opted not to sit, still unsettled by my meeting with Luther Christensen.

"So." Oscar smiled. "If you're here, you must be interested in the brokerage—"

"Kendra Bruce is why we're here," Rex said. "I'm just going to cut to the chase, and you're going to only give yes or no answers."

I'd never seen him use Big Dick Energy before, but suddenly the room was filled with it.

Oscar blinked, stunned. He frowned at me, then back to Rex. "I haven't seen or . . . met . . . with Kendra in years. What's this all about?"

"Were you being blackmailed by her?" I asked.

Oscar's tan complexion faded, and his jovial yet confused expression froze.

"That's a yes," Rex said.

Oscar stood. "If this isn't about business, then I'm going to have to end whatever this meeting is supposed to be."

"It's about business, Mr. Mendez, just not brokerage business. We have it on good authority that you and Ms. Bruce met, and then she asked you for money. Yes or no?"

Oscar threw his hands in the air, his face turning red. "Okay! Fine! I had sex with Kendra a few times. It was fun. We had *confidential* fun together. Then she said that if I don't pay her a few grand a month, she'd tell my wife about our sessions. That fucking bitch."

I studied his left hand, noting there was no wedding band there, but that meant nothing these days. "What happened next? Did you . . . act against her?"

The anger receded some, but the memory of it lingered around him. "No! I told my wife—my ex-wife."

I blinked.

Rex propped an elbow on the table. "And to get around paying the blackmail, you told your wife."

"Yeah. We have kids together. That money was supposed to go for tuition for SAU." Oscar patted his comb-over gently. "That bitch came for me again, like what now? What else did she want to take from me?"

"So you killed her."

"No!" Oscar's eyes bugged out of his face. "No, no! I gave her my phone to tell my wife. She wasn't happy, but she didn't bother me again."

"So after you told your wife about the affair . . . ?" I asked, trying to guess what happened next.

"We entered couple's counseling, and it worked out. We got through it." Oscar lifted his hand. "What split us up was her embezzlement at the grocery store she managed."

"Safeway?" I asked, unable to resist. I'd heard about this last year.

"Yeah, that's the one." Oscar sighed and gestured at the door. "Can I go back to work now?"

We didn't stop him, and the ride down the elevator was silent. As we stepped outside, I turned to him, opening my mouth, but the world turned upside down.

It was like a tornado dropped on us. The sky turned greenish-black. Gale-forced winds ripped at my clothes and hair, tugging the ley crystal nearly completely out. I clamped a hand on the charm, activating it as I rubbed my stinging scalp. Rex wrapped his body around me. From the corner of my eye, his hands jerked at nothing. Then a glittery sky-blue dome sprang around us. The wind died down, my wheezing breaths the only sound.

Fissures of dark blue splotched against the wall of the

dome. Once. Twice, three-four-five more times. The dome shattered with a pop, disintegrating into fine dust. Rex shouted something. As he shoved me behind him, he flung a hand out and a hexagon shield tinged with ley energy formed in front of us.

Rex jerked it up and down, catching projectiles, all the while keeping his body as a living shield in front of me. I couldn't see what was hitting us or who was attacking. The wind was too strong. People shouted; I screamed. Something shattered on the sidewalk and stung my leg.

People ran from us. I glanced around wildly, holding my hair down—because apparently that was what mattered at the moment. I froze, squeezing my eyes shut. Someone was attacking us—or had it been me? Then finally, with a whimper, the wind died and the sky cleared, leaving debris in its wake.

Sirens kicked up in the distance, making my already speeding heart trip over itself and beat faster. I couldn't catch my breath.

"Willa." Rex gripped my shoulders and shook me lightly. "Willa!"

I trembled, lifting my gaze to his, and finally sucked in enough air to feel like I could breathe on my own.

"Why didn't you protect yourself?" he demanded. "Didn't you see the ley energy form around you?"

I froze. Everything inside me turned to ice, and I knew this was it. This was the end of whatever was going on between us. I shook my head. "It was so . . . sudden."

His brows slammed together. "It's because you're Muted, isn't it?"

Chapter Twenty-Three

There was a line at Icing. I glanced at my watch and glared. My entire schedule was off now that I was filling in for Guy. I worked later, I slept less, and I started my workout later. Because when I woke up, I had piles of emails and messages marked urgent that I needed to get through before I could even get my ass out of bed.

I hadn't realized how well I'd balanced my work and my life until the scales suddenly tipped heavily toward work.

It also hadn't helped that I'd had irrefutable proof that Willa was Muted and a liar. And I hadn't been the only one. After some news sources did a segment on the broken spirit stones and how they were found on Guy's property, some man claiming to be Willa's father, of all people, contacted me and confirmed she was Muted.

She'd told me he was dead.

I hadn't engaged with him; I didn't have the headspace to have that conversation. But for fuck's sake . . . No wonder so many people called mediums or psychics con artists. Look at her. She lied about being an enchanter. She did all that work with crystals, even the ones that weren't charmed, and she . . .

She'd found Kendra's body.

"Wow."

I jerked my head up, realizing that the woman in front of me had already left with her order and Dane was waiting on me for mine.

I glanced behind my shoulder. Seeing two more people, I stepped aside, and waved them forward. "I don't know what I want yet. Go ahead."

Dane shot me a look before he helped the next customer. I approached the cases, sighing. I'd never say this right now, but I wanted a big ass peanut butter cookie, and that was not an option here.

"Come, Bubbles!" Eric shouted.

Dane laughed under his breath. "Come bubbles."

I cracked a smile as the large betta fish swam through the veil and Eric quick cast a spell working as he made a chocolate. My attention drifted toward the rapidly dwindling chocolate truffles and petit fours. And the lies of Willamina Dade.

"Peanut butter or raspberry?" Dane asked.

I jerked. "What?"

"What're you craving?"

"Oh, peanut butter." I rubbed my beard and then shrugged. "You know what? It's been a fucking week. Both. I want both."

Eric stepped into the front of the shop, grinning. The morning rush had ended, and while there were a couple of people at the small tables, the counter was for me and my two best friends. Who seemed really relaxed and happy. I hadn't seen them like this for a hot minute.

"What's new, guys?" I asked.

"Trixie came through." Dane opened a box and rapidly clicked the tongs three times. "There haven't been any videos, and she's been all over our page hyping us up."

"Yeah, it's been real nice." Eric grinned at his fiancé.

"I think Trixie's still figuring out social media. I told her to get a stand like ours." Dane plucked two dark chocolate petit fours from a tray with the tongs and set them carefully in the box. "So why the long face? Is Guy having a hard time adjusting to home life?"

My shoulders tightened, and I rolled them. "Of course, but mostly he's pushing me to do things sooner than I'm used to and longer than anyone should. All I do is work, and when I'm not working, I'm . . ." Was I still trying to solve my ex-girlfriend's murder? I should leave that to Julian. And Willamina.

"How's Willa, by the way?" Eric asked. "Is she still getting the short end of the stick?"

"She's Muted." It simply fell out of my mouth. I glanced around quickly, holding up a hand at their shocked faces and gaping mouths. "Shh. That wasn't my secret to tell."

Dane smirked. "I'm not surprised to hear this. She's like every other palm reader out there, taking advantage of the old and the grieving."

Eric placed a hand on his shoulder, but his attention was on me. "Have you always known this about her?"

"No!" I threw my hands in the air, then shoved them in my pockets. "I only just got confirmation. I can't believe she lied to me."

Dane's brows lifted and his mouth pursed, but he simply swapped tongs, clicked them three times, and selected two pink petit fours and placed them into the box.

"But she told you," Eric said, taking the box from Dane and folding it up.

"Not exactly." I sighed. "We were attacked the other day coming out of Lancaster Plaza, and she let it happen. Now I know it's because she can't see ley energy."

"Mmhmm." Dane gestured at the point-of-sale system. "So she didn't tell you."

"No, but she didn't deny it when I confronted her." I tapped my card against the machine and paid.

"How do you feel?" Eric asked.

"Excuse me?" I took the box from him, tempted to open it and slam the cakes.

"Okay, she kept her Muted status from you, but she clearly knows the ins and outs of enchanting, even if she can't physically do it herself. Right?"

"Yeah," I said slowly.

"You mentioned she was pretty good at it." Eric nodded. "You seemed impressed."

"I was, but she lied."

Dane frowned, glancing between us, then sighed. "I think my sensitive guy's trying to say that even though she lied about being an enchanter, she still got the job done."

"Well"—Eric smiled at Dane—"sort of. Let's be transparent. Rex caught some feelings, and I'm just trying to figure out if her Muted status matters that much in the grand scheme of things."

My head ached as I thought on it. I conjured Willa's face and a warm burr opened in my chest, soft, gentle. I hung my head, staring at the box. Did it matter that she was Muted or that she'd lied about it? I hadn't asked, so I suppose that wasn't technically lying, but come on. She knew I'd assumed she was at least an enchanter, and she never corrected me.

And this lie about her father being dead . . .

"It's more the lie than the fact she can't touch ley energy," I said. "She can definitely use enchantments and understand it . . . Ah. That's why she closes her eyes." Because she didn't need to see the ley energy, especially with spirits that weren't familiars, and humans couldn't become familiars.

"As much as I feel vindicated that palm readers are lying criminals," Dane said, "I can tell you like her."

I opened my mouth to protest, but he held up a hand.

"Shush. We've"—he waved between himself and his fiancé—"seen it already, and we've discussed it. Mostly because of TrixieCakes, but that's all settled as far as we're concerned."

"Yeah," Eric said. "We think you should talk to her about it. Ask her why she kept it from you."

"Yeah." I looked back down at the box in my hand. It'd eat me up without knowing why. "Okay."

"And you know," Dane continued, "we're always here for you, dude. Day or night."

"Thanks." I smiled at them. "So you guys make any progress on the wedding planning?"

Eric's smile froze, his eyes darting to Dane, then back to me. Dane's brows lifted.

"The venue's been booked," Eric said. The "but" hung in the air, covering the entire shop.

"What's the problem?" I asked.

"Dane still wants to do the cake *and* the catering," Eric's words rushed out of him. "And he if does all that work, do you think he's—"

"*Excuse me* for wanting the perfect food for our perfect day," Dane said.

Eric faced him and threw his arms above his head. "Fine! If you want to be stretched as thin as possible, then be my guest."

I blinked. I'd never seen Eric lose his shit in the store like this.

"Babe, shh." Dane patted the air between them. "It'll be fine. I'll oversee the menu and the preparation, but I'll have our cake baked by the day before our wedding and decorated. It'll be fresh and gorgeous—"

"And you'll have bags under your eyes when we exchange vows!"

"No, I'll sleep well the whole week." Dane shook his head.

"Okay. I want birthday cake." Eric said, his jaw turning hard. "With sprinkles in the batter. Green ones."

My chin dropped slightly.

"Really? You want *birthday cake* for our wedding? Do you want that as a sheet cake?" Dane wagged his finger. "No, it'll be a classic almond wedding—Are you *gagging*?"

Eric stuck his finger in his mouth and made retching noises. "You love birthday cake so much, I figured it'd be fine."

"It's our *wedding*," Dane said.

"Oh!" Eric waved his hands and faced me. "*Now* he gets it."

I laughed and waved at them. "Guys. Why don't you just have TrixieCakes do it?"

They both frowned and stared at each other.

"I don't know," Eric said. "She's got a lot on her plate right now."

"She's more of a cupcake gal, you know?" Dane said. "And like, we're not cupcake wedding people."

"You're such a snob." I snorted, taking a step back. "Have you checked out her catalog at all?"

My phone buzzed in my pocket and I pulled it out.

PRINCESS HOT PSYCHIC

The police are here at TrixieCakes

My heart stuttered, then raced.

PRINCESS HOT PSYCHIC

Sorry, I know you hate me, but I don't know who else to tell

"I gotta go." I headed for the door, then turned. "Ask Trixie about cakes."

I hurried out of the building and half-walked, half-jogged through the Flower Market to my parked car. I didn't know why the police were talking with Willa. Maybe it was an investigation into her because they knew she was Muted too. The police force had tons of info on people; they were probably trying to figure out exactly how Willa knew where to look, given her status. That had to be illegal though, and discriminatory. I made a note to find a lawyer that would fight for her in court.

By the time I pulled up to TrixieCakes, I had a solid plan to help if the worst-case scenario played out. An unmarked sedan idled at the curb, and I could tell by the antenna it was a cop car. I parked behind them and jumped out. The bell jingled over my head as I stepped inside TrixieCakes and immediately made eye contact with Willa.

It was a gut-punch. I'd missed her, and seeing her filled me with so much yearning that I stood there like an idiot, staring at her.

Detective Johnston looked over her shoulder at me and nodded. "Good, this makes this easy and saves me a trip. Oscar Mendez filed a complaint about you two. I don't know how many other ways I can say this: leave *innocent* citizens alone. Stop investigating this murder yourselves. Drop it. Let me do the work."

"Yeah? And what protection are you going to give Willa?" I asked, stepping deeper into the shop. "Ever since this started, she's been targeted, and no one is doing anything to help her. Why's that?"

Johnston peered at Willa. The ley crystal I'd given her glittered in her hair. Then the detective sighed. "Come by the office and file a police report, so we have it already."

"That's not going to help," I said.

Willa placed a hand on my arm, and I relaxed slightly. "It's the first step, I suppose."

I turned to her, and she dropped her hand, taking a step back. "And what happens when those psychic attacks finally catch you without any protection? Will the police report magically appear and save you?"

Johnston sighed. "It's better than nothing, especially if you find out who's doing this. We'll already have a file that this is happening—"

"So now she's supposed to find out who's attacking her?" I asked, anger boiling my blood. "Isn't that *your* job?"

"Mr. Slater, I appreciate the stress this is causing, and I sympathize you're both in a situation that doesn't look good, but there are some things that you need to do to get everything on file *if* worse comes to worst." She opened the door. "Again, I feel I need to stress to allow the police to do their work on this murder case, and both of you have a good day."

The bell jingled as the door closed behind her. I gaped at where she used to be and then turned to Willa.

"Well . . ." She bit her lower lip, then shrugged. "Sounds like Oscar Mendez isn't a suspect."

"Fuck that right now. She told you to figure out who's attacking you in one breath, then demanded you let the police do their jobs in the next." I reached for her but jerked my hands back. "Have you been okay since I saw you last?"

Her amber eyes clouded, and she glanced away. "Physically, sure. No attacks since."

I didn't know what to do. It stung she hadn't confided in me she was Muted. But I didn't know why. I could guess, but I'd already assumed she was an enchanter, and I'd been mostly wrong.

She peeked at me, and her wounded expression cramped my stomach. "How're you doing? Is the new job—"

"Why didn't you tell me you were Muted?" It tumbled from my mouth without thought. "Why did you let me think you could manipulate ley lines this whole time?"

She gaped at me, all the color draining from her face. At first, I thought I'd made a mistake, that I should've taken a long road and made vague statements and asked open-ended questions to get her to freely give me the information.

"I've read your quote about Muted," she murmured. "That we play with power we can't understand. It'd sounded like such a 'Guy thing' to say, but it was you." She pursed her lips. "You know, the Muted community is tired of being the scapegoat when things go wrong with magic. Eight out of ten times, it's usually one of you."

My stomach clenched. "I'm sorry. That's just—It was what I was told to say to the press when asked about the connection to the company. I know that's not the case with you."

"How was I supposed to know that?" She stared at her hands, then clasped them together, a sad smile touching her lips. "Everything's temporary, Rex. Everything except magic. Not many people can see past me being Muted." She shrugged. "And I just wanted to enjoy our friendship for as long as I had it."

"You were being selfish." My voice sounded harsh with emotion.

She forced a humorless laugh as she nervously fiddled with the scalloped shell hanging around her neck. "It's no one's business what I can or can't do with magic. *I'm* not hurting people."

"I meant you were being selfish with me." I stepped closer to her. "You were waiting to tell me because you liked my company." Some of the raw feeling smoothed out a bit inside my chest, healing some of the bruising there. "Is that what you mean?"

"Yes." Her eyes glittered and she shook her head back, scanning the ceiling. "I would've confessed eventually, but I finally felt like I belonged in that secret circle, and I knew if I told you the truth, you'd stop being my friend. Then I started to like you more, and it got complicated, and the more you assumed, the more I let you, and at some point, it got too big to just bring it up."

I took another step closer and hooked my finger around her palm. "You didn't think I could look past you being Muted?"

She finally met my gaze and shook her head. "No, I didn't."

I stared at her. I took in her ivory skin and her red hair that was beautiful against it, her stunning eyes and sexy mouth. Her kind soul and wicked sense of humor. I pored over her features, then stared at *my* ley crystal in her hair. She'd never be able to recharge that herself. Not once had I felt taken advantage by her; even when she'd confirmed she was Muted. I'd felt lied to, and I still had a question about her father, but that guy could've been scamming for money or something. So I asked myself: *How important is it she can manipulate ley lines?*

"Will you have dinner with me tomorrow night?" I licked my lips. "As a date."

A wrinkle appeared between her gathered brows. "You're asking me on a date?"

I nodded. "You'll have to dress up. I'm no slouch with restaurants."

"But I'm Muted," she whispered.

"I know."

"You're not asking me out to prove it doesn't matter and then never contact me again, are you?"

"Only if you suck." I frowned at her. "And I've already spent some significant time with you, so unless you reveal you're a serial killer, I don't think I'll ghost you."

She planted her free hand on her hip and tilted her head. "What do you have against serial killers?"

I laughed, and she grinned at me.

I fully grasped her hand now. "Then tomorrow night. Seven p.m.?"

"Yeah, okay. Tomorrow at seven."

"I'll pick you up at six-thirty." I smiled and kissed the back of her hand. Then I headed for the door.

"Wait, you said seven!" she called after me.

"The reservation's at seven. You'll have to get ready faster than that, princess."

Chapter Twenty-Four

I hadn't been this nervous for a date in years. I wore a flowy green dress that accentuated the girls, pulled in tight at the waist, and flared at my hips to my knees. It looked like a wraparound, but it wasn't.

I'd made this dress earlier in the year as a treat for not slipping back into old habits with my credit cards. Did the soft silk crepe fabric seem like an extravagant expense? Yes, but I'd had many interested clients, three palm readings, and a séance booked, covering the cost of the fabric.

It'd felt like I'd finally stepped out of the past.

Now, I smoothed the fabric down my hips and smiled. The dark emerald complemented my skin and my hair color. I wore the golden shell necklace, and I'd swapped the ley crystal to a different clip that matched my outfit.

The expression on Rex's face when I opened the door made it all worth it. Hunger sparked in his piercing blue gaze as it roved over me from head to toe and back up to my eyes. Then he pushed a box of tapioca pudding into my hands.

I frowned at it. "Pudding?"

"For Erma," he said.

My heart stopped, then thudded hard against my chest. I bit my lip, but it didn't stop the grin creasing my face. I set the pack on the table and turned to him. "Ready?"

On the way to the parking garage in the Flower Market—the best places were there—Rex didn't talk much. We listened to the radio, which he'd immediately switched to a classic rock station. I wondered if he thought that was my jam, or if it was his. I wondered if I should break the silence. Instead, I stared at his profile. He'd styled his hair and his beard remained neatly groomed, as always. I allowed my gaze to travel over his midnight navy suit jacket, so dark it could be mistaken for black, but the way it heightened his eyes, I knew that wasn't the case.

When we stepped out of the elevator of the parking garage and onto the stone pavers of the sidewalk, Rex held his elbow out to me. "Will you walk with me, princess?"

I laughed and tucked my hand into the crook of his elbow. "I'd be delighted to."

We walked arm in arm along the Flower Market. The smells of the restaurants and street stands filled the air. We passed flower carts, ice cream stands, and one of those roasted nut places, the people calling out to potential customers. I stared longingly at the nuts. Honey roasted cashews were divine, but also a trap.

"Did you want some?" Rex paused, pulling me closer.

I shook my head and laughed. "No way. I want to save room for this fancy dinner you're taking me to."

"Me too. Maybe afterward, if we still have room." He grinned and gently pulled me along the footpath.

He turned toward the heavy doors to Flemming's, the nicest place in all of Starglen. I'd never even eaten there, not even in my impulsive days. For one, you had to make a reservation months in advance, and I was never that prepared. I sent him a raised brow, and he winked. There was someone being seated, and Rex pressed close, his hand going to my hip while he leaned down to my ear.

"I'm really glad you came out with me tonight," he whispered, his hot breath kissing my skin and scattering tingles across my body.

I hadn't expected him to say that; I figured he'd make a comment on my appearance, as he'd said nothing, but he didn't need to. Not with how his eyes devoured me every time I caught him looking.

"Mr. Slater." The maître d' was an older gentleman in a suit and tie, a narrow mustache riding over thin lips. "I'm glad we could accommodate you and your guest tonight. Come with me."

He took us up a flight of stairs. Other guests noticed and watched; the curiosity on their faces matched what I was thinking. I hadn't realized there was an upstairs dining room.

Roses, lilies, daisies, and an assortment of wildflowers in overfilling vases stuffed the small room. Hurricane glasses with flickering candles littered the surfaces while fairy lights twinkled in the rafters, and I breathed deeply. It smelled faintly sweet, like passing a flower shop on an early summer morning. Heavy red velvet curtains flanked the open French doors to the balcony. There, outside, was a white-draped table set for two, with a small votive candle in the middle. An ice bucket with a bottle of champagne sat next to the table, the bottle already opened.

"Oh, this is lovely," I said as Rex helped me into the chair.

"Only the best for you, princess," Rex murmured and sat across from me.

"Your server will be up soon," the maître d' said. "Enjoy."

Then we were alone.

"You're gorgeous." Rex took my glass and poured. "I mean, you're always gorgeous, but right now it's hard not to stare."

I laughed lightly and took the glass. "Thank you. You're gorgeous too."

He smirked, a small chuckle rumbling from his throat. "Thanks."

"No, I really mean it, Rex. You're gorgeous."

He paused, and a smile lit his beautiful blue eyes. He reached out and squeezed my hand. "Thank you, Willa."

"Well, if this is us starting over, I need to tell you some things." I shifted in my seat, nerves mixing sourly with the semi-sweet champagne. "I didn't lie about my age."

His brows reached for his hairline.

"But I lied about the day I was born on." I grabbed the cloth napkin and smoothed it out over my lap. "It was Imbolc."

He sat back, the stem of the flute between his fingers. "Jesus. That . . . makes sense."

I twisted the napkin. "Right? Like if I said I was a solstice baby, everyone would assume I'm ACE."

"It's never a 100% guarantee children born on the solstice will be ACE."

"But it's rare, so I just made myself a day younger." I smiled slightly, my gut trembling as I rushed on—because if I didn't say this as quickly as possible, I'd never say it. "And Mimzy's a reformed ley purist. It was kinda awful. She hid my lack of abilities under the carpet for years until well into my teens. It wasn't until I asked her a question about crystals that the tensions between us began to relax."

He was quiet, almost stiff. Then his shoulders relaxed, and he nodded. "I know that your séances and palm readings are top notch readings, but how did you even get into that?"

What a compliment! A giddy feeling, just as bubbly as the champagne, poured into my chest. I sat straighter, and I dropped the napkin on my lap. "My mother."

His expression clouded. "You told me she died when you were born."

"She did," I quickly assured him. "But I found her journals, and Mimzy showed me how to translate them—they're in shorthand—and I'd read them over and over. At first, it was just to read something she wrote, to have that connection with her. But then she talked about ignoring ley energy because there's so much of it in the world that it can make you blind to the magic you're searching for."

He nodded. "And you tried it."

The server came and we ordered drinks, then answered questions about steak and dietary restrictions. Apparently Flemming's did one kind of steak, and they gave me three options: medium rare, medium, and medium well—he'd said the last one with a slight curl to his lip. We both chose medium rare, and he left.

I never once saw a menu. I frowned, wondering what else was coming.

"Okay, so I see how you got into the medium profession." Rex took a sip. "Was your family supportive?"

"Hmm." I turned my head, looking out over the Flower Market to the mountains in the distance, dark shadows against the darkening sky. "Do we want to talk about my family on our first date?"

"I want to know what makes you you," Rex said softly. "I want to know why I can't get you out of my head, Willa."

"Because you think I'm hot." I flashed a smile.

"True, but I've seen a *lot* of 'hot' people, and I don't give them much thought."

The server returned with our drinks; I'd gone for another French 75, while he'd ordered a Manhattan.

"I forgot you're a playboy." I took a sip and smiled at the brightness of the drink.

"A *reformed* playboy."

"Rex . . ." I licked my lip, not knowing how to say anything, not with my heart randomly skipping beats and butterflies living in my belly. "I'm sure it's because I'm a novelty, what with my lack of magic abilities."

"It's not." He merely smiled lazily at me, shaking his head. "It . . . sucked that you'd kept it from me. But every time I thought of you, every time I dreamed about you, I never once thought your ley abilities made you attractive."

"But I'm not a suitable partner for you."

"Says who?"

"I'm sure everyone who has a say in your life." My hands returned to the napkin in my lap, and I gripped the ends.

He watched me over the rim of his glass. There was that voice in my head, yelling that I'd never be someone's first choice to love because I had too many hang-ups. That because I was Muted, I wasn't worthy. *I* knew it was a random genetic switch that never flipped inside me. There were thousands exactly like me out there, born this way. They'd had normal lives and sometimes had magical children, and I understood it wasn't a problem for most. But with someone like Rex Slater, pedigree was a big deal to his family.

"There aren't many who have a say in my life, and even then, I can still make up my mind," he said.

"I'm sure your father and your brother have tons of say," I said.

"They *say* a lot of things," he said forcibly, "but most of it's bullshit over their disappointment in me. And before you latch on to that, let me promise you that I've historically followed my heart when it comes to partners."

I blinked at him. "Who has the most sway with you?"

"Oh, Dane and Eric, definitely. My mom a little, but she's happy if I am."

I grinned, and he smiled back. The butterflies multiplied, and I shivered slightly.

"You cold?" he asked.

"No, it's the butterflies."

He cocked his head, then reached over and grasped my hand, threading his fingers with mine. Time slowed, and I gazed into his beautiful blue eyes over the candlelight. I still couldn't believe this was happening, but in the moment, the soft, giddy connection that inexplicably drew me toward him warmly pulsed between us.

Our food arrived, and we reluctantly let go. The server set two identical plates before us, along with small side dishes, bread rolls, and another bottle of champagne, compliments of the manager.

The night continued, but thankfully he stopped asking me the deep questions about family and living as a Muted. We laughed together, talking about desserts and our favorite activities. I knew he enjoyed going to the gym; he'd mentioned it before, but he talked about building charms to help preserve crime scenes, like the bubble he'd placed in the lake.

I told him about my impulsiveness and what it'd cost me. And in the end, we were laughing more over anecdotes of his friends trying to compromise over wedding planning and Trixie trying to pick up on the new lingo her kids were using. I hadn't felt this light and carefree in a while. We were just finishing the last of the second bottle of champagne when the server returned.

"Care for dessert?" he asked. "Today, the pâtissier has prepared a Schwartzwald cake with a cherry drizzle. It pairs well with—"

"Do you have vanilla ice cream and maybe a raspberry sauce?" I asked.

Both men blinked at me. Well, the server frowned; Flemming's had a planned menu, and I was throwing a wrench in it. Rex beamed at me. It felt better than the sun breaking through clouds on a gloomy day.

"I think . . ." He glanced at Rex and then nodded. "I think it can be arranged."

When he left, I leaned across the table and whispered, "Is he afraid of you?"

"I had to pull out some big guns to get a reservation." Rex leaned forward. "They're booked solid for the rest of the year, so yeah. Maybe a little."

I stole a kiss from him, since he was this close. That tiny peck went straight to my belly. His eyes gleamed and fastened on my lips as I sat back in my chair.

He slowly leaned back. "Do you approve, princess?"

"I do." I smiled at him. "This has been amazing."

"Willa, in all seriousness," he said gravely.

Oh no. I braced myself for the worst, for the heartbreak.

"I . . . have feelings for you, and I want to see where this thing between us goes."

I hadn't thought that was what he'd say, and the uneasy nerves and sinking sensation vanished. The butterflies in my stomach were getting drunk off the champagne. I grinned. "I want to see where this goes too."

The ice cream and warm-ish raspberry sauce were a hit, and the sober-me-up potions were equally subtle. He pulled a white lily from one arrangement and tucked it behind my ear before we left the restaurant. We strolled down the paved street, me hugging his arm and resting my head against his shoulder. I'm pretty sure we'd just become boyfriend and girlfriend, and I felt like a teenager again.

When he opened the car door for me, he turned me around. He cupped my jaw and captured my lips, kissing me deeply and tasting like raspberries. I sighed into his mouth. His other arm snapped around my waist and pressed me against him, making me cling to his strong shoulders. His tongue slid and flicked against mine, stealing all the breath from my lungs in the most delicious way.

"I wish I didn't have to take you home," he murmured against my lips.

I wasn't sure how to respond, because if I said I didn't want to go home, that pretty much meant I was down for sex. And while I knew I wouldn't hate myself in the morning if we did, I wasn't quite ready. Not yet. I lifted my hand and caressed his beard, marveling at how soft it was. Then I gave in and flicked his gray lock of hair, smiling before leaning in and softly kissing him. A tiny part of me was stalling to find the right words to let him know I wanted to go home alone.

"I'm also dead on my feet, princess," he murmured, his fingers trailing up and down my arm. "I don't think I have it in me for much more."

"I can get an Uber—"

"No." He kissed me again, then nudged me into the car. "I'm taking you home."

When he sat in the driver's seat, his phone went off, and he read the text. "Wow."

"Everything okay?" I asked.

"I have some contacts—don't ask who—and they got back to me about the findings for Kendra's autopsy." He met my gaze. "Her cause of death wasn't drowning, but from ley energy."

Chapter Twenty-Five

I placed little stock in the dreams I had without a dreamstone. To me, those dreams were random images my brain filed away while I slept, nothing more than entertainment. So when I had a steamy dream about Rex and when he finished, he finished me off by stealing all the breath from me, I woke troubled.

Not because I believed Rex would do that, but because my first thoughts went to Kendra Bruce.

This shouldn't have surprised me. My night ended with slow, deep kisses from Rex, and I'd discovered Kendra's death wasn't by drowning. Just before he'd left to go home, he'd received further clarification on the autopsy: while there wasn't much of her lung tissue remaining, there was no evidence they'd been filled with water. However, her throat had the telltale signs of ley manipulation. Someone had dumped her body in the water.

I yawned and stretched, parts of my body still feeling delicious from the dream, despite the way it'd ended, and stared at the ceiling. Each time Kendra's spirit had come to me, I'd had trouble breathing. Because I saw water—which I supposed in hindsight she was showing me where she was—and the attacks against me involved water, I'd assumed she'd drowned. Hadn't Kendra's journals given a bio on each "guest" she'd seen for her blackmail scheme?

I got out of bed, pulled the covers up, tossed on a royal purple satin robe decorated with Chinese dragons, and took care of my morning routine. I also made sure I'd clipped the ley crystal in my mussed hair. With my teeth tasting like mint, I sailed out of the bathroom and down the hall to the kitchen. Because when one wore a robe like mine, sailing was the only way to move in it.

Mimzy sat at the table, a bottle of vanilla Ensure before her while she examined the box of tapioca pudding I'd left on the table. She blinked up at me through her enormous glasses. "Mornin', Chipmunk." She lifted the box. "Where'd the fancy pudding come from?"

"Rex left that for you." I passed her on the way to the coffeemaker and hit the brew button. I'd gotten it ready before my date last night.

"Oh, yes." She turned in her chair and waggled her brows. "How was the hot date?"

"Really good." It was so easy to smile. I leaned against the counter. "I told him everything."

A guarded expression slipped over the playful one. "And?"

Because Trixie was temporarily taking over my duties for Mimzy's appointments, I hadn't seen her much in the last few days. I gave her the quick rundown of how he figured out my Muted status on his own, and that he'd also been the one to ask me on the date.

"He was upset that I hadn't trusted him with it at first, but last night went really well." Heat spread in my cheeks. "We went to Flemming's in the Flower Market."

"And?"

"And what?" The coffee maker beeped, and I poured

myself a cup and doctored it with cream and sugar before sitting next to her at the table.

"Was he a butthole?" Mimzy patted the pudding box. "I'm not eating pudding that came from a butthole."

I coughed, spraying coffee on the table. "Mimzy!" I got up, laughing hysterically, and grabbed a couple of paper towels to clean up my mess. "No, he wasn't a butthole." I giggled. I couldn't wait to tell Trixie this. "Actually, it was really romantic, and we both decided to see where things go between us."

"You're dating!" She clapped her hands and clutched her chest, then stood and hugged me. "I guess being picky paid off, if you can get a hunk like that. Did you get your hands on some trouser hams? Oh! You two'll give me the most beautiful grandbabies."

I shook my head.

She gathered the box of pudding and padded to the fridge. "Dade women have beautiful children. Just look at you and BeeBee. And Candi'll be a looker once she grows out of the acne. And braces." She shoved the box onto a packed shelf and returned to the table. "And those Slater men have amazing genes."

"We're only dating." I pulled the journal I translated into from the middle of the table and opened it. "Stop planning children for me, please."

"You're thirty-five," she said. "You don't have time to wait and see."

"I doubt that's true. It's ridiculous, especially with the advances of medicine we've made in the last forty years." I flipped through a couple of pages. "Plus, I finally have my shit together. I would've been a horrible mother up to now."

"You know, it's probably a good idea to give him a test drive before you commit to children."

She'd said it so nonchalantly, I didn't quite parse what she'd meant.

She swatted my arm and winked. "Maybe a few test *rides*. You know. Make sure he's consistent."

"Oh, my god, Gram-cracker!" My face, ears, and neck all felt like they were on fire. "Please don't say anything like that in front of Rex."

Mimzy cackled and pushed out of the chair, humming as she walked to her bedroom. I wasn't *too* worried she hadn't promised. She was almost ninety; she got away with a lot, and I did too by extension.

I finally found the pages and read over the names of the people I thought might make good suspects. Their names, addresses, dates of births, and the date and time of their affairs were listed. Oscar Mendez was an Aquarius, like me, which meant he was an air caster. Running my finger down the page, I paused at the next suspect, Nicholas Turner. He was a Gemini, another air caster. I remembered something Rex had said about his time in the Air Force and a drill instructor choking an airman with air.

I can't breathe.

I shivered and sipped my coffee, letting the dots connect with little effort.

My phone rang, and Suzana Bruce's name flashed across the screen. Her call didn't surprise me. I could only assume she'd received the same information Rex had last night.

I answered the phone. "Hello?"

"Willamina? It's Suzana."

"Yes, how're you?"

"I'd like to meet for brunch today—for an update on the journals," she said.

"Yes, I can meet you. Where at?"

"Brew & Chew," she replied. "It's in the Flower Market. Are you familiar with it?"

"Yes. Is eleven good?"

"Yes. I'll see you then."

I pulled up my messages with Rex.

> I had a great time last night. Thank you for a wonderful date

GUINEA PIG REX

Me too. Save time for me later tonight?

> Definitely

> Suzana wants an update on the journals today. After I meet with her, I'm going to take them to the police

The three dots showed up and disappeared a couple times, but no texts came through. I finished my coffee and sailed back down the hallway to my room.

GUINEA PIG REX

You sure that's smart?

> Which part?

But he never replied, and I had to get dressed for the day. As I applied my makeup, I sent a quick plea to the universe. *Please don't let him turn out to be a butthole.*

BREW & CHEW WAS A CUTE BISTRO ON THE MAJOR thoroughfare of the Flower Market. I walked in from the free parking. Since it hadn't rained in a week, I didn't see the point in avoiding the mostly gravel lot. I hurried along the decorative pavers, stepping around people who'd stopped for whatever reason. Honestly, most people were unaware of their surroundings in the Flower Market.

Suzana and Martin waited for me on the bench in front of the bistro—to my dismay, with Julian. After the bullshit stunt he pulled with his father at Lancaster Plaza, he'd officially run out of my good graces. Julian approached me to give me a hug, and I stepped away, shaking my head.

I looked him up and down and tossed my shoulders back. "I didn't expect to see you here."

A flicker of anger flashed across his features before he held the door open for us. "Why wouldn't I be here? Kendra was my fiancée, and I want closure."

Suzana gave me a tight smile. "It was his idea to meet today."

"It's always been his idea," Martin mumbled as he walked past me to the hostess station.

She led us through the semi-crowded dining area filled with tables. Remembering my gut instinct when Julian showed up unannounced at my house, I took the moment to activate the ley crystal clipped in my hair. The only splashes of color were the small flower arrangements resting on the stark white tablecloths. I found Martin's comment interesting as we sat and were given menus and gave drink orders. I asked for a Manhattan, because I already knew what I'd order.

"What do you mean by that, Martin?" I asked.

"Oh, when the state officially declared her dead, I couldn't let it go." Julian leaned back in his chair and stared at me. "So Sooz and I chatted about what we could do to find out."

"And we found you." Suzana set her menu down and waved to get waitstaff attention. "Well, he gave me your—"

"I just hoped we'd find out she'd started a life in Greece." Julian rubbed a hand over his patchy beard.

Martin's mouth flattened into a thin line. "These past weeks have been . . . painful, and I hope you have something more for us. I don't know how much more I can . . ."

Silence joined the table, sucking up all the good vibes there might've been left. Suzana stared at her hands, fiddling with her gold infinity knot bracelet, and Martin stared through me, probably seeing the past. I wished there was more I could do for the Bruces, but I really was in over my head.

Our drinks arrived, and we placed our orders. Julian's eyes lit up when the server placed a strawberry daiquiri before him. I'd requested chicken and waffles because Rex raved about it and I wanted to see what the fuss was all about. Both Suzana and Martin put in for biscuits and gravy, and Julian ordered steak and eggs.

"So how's everything going?" Martin asked. "Have you made any headway on the journals we gave you?"

"Progress has been made," I said, wondering how to put this out there delicately.

"Oh good." Suzana brightened. "I knew you'd be able to find something in those journals with your psychic ability."

A nervous laugh threatened to bubble past my lips, so I cleared my throat. "Well, believe it or not, I didn't need to."

Martin snorted. "I believe it."

Suzana shushed him.

Our food arrived, which surprised me as I hadn't thought enough time had gone by. Then again, no one was in the mood for small talk, and Julian had finished more than half of his drink already. He'd ordered another. While I buttered my waffles, which were golden brown and slightly crispy against my fork, I explained what I found.

"Your daughter wrote in two different shorthands, which really threw me for a loop," I said.

"Shorthand?" Suzana's brows crinkled together. "Really?"

Martin tilted his head. "Why's that so odd?"

"Computers," Julian said, sawing into his steak—which he'd ordered well done. "They made shorthand obsolete in the 90s."

"Were you able to read what she wrote?" Martin asked.

Suzana swirled a wedge of her buttermilk biscuit in the sausage gravy, a frown on her face. Julian continued sawing into his steak, taking forever to chew the gray pieces of meat. At least he hadn't asked for ketchup. I took a moment to drizzle maple syrup on my waffle and fried chicken. This would be uncomfortable. I didn't relish the news I'd give them, and maybe I should've left it to the police. But Suzana had paid me to do this, so it was my job.

"It seems Kendra might've . . ." I gazed around the room, searching for a polite way to explain that Kendra had sex and blackmailed people for money. "She . . . put some people in compromising situations, and they paid her not to talk about it."

Suzana's fork clattered against the plate, and she gripped the edge of the table with both hands. "She would *never*."

Martin dropped his forehead into his hand and shook his head. Julian studied me, his eyes narrowing, but thankfully he was still chewing and didn't speak up.

The maple syrup and the Manhattan were perfect together, basically soulmates. But this conversation was ruining my appetite. I set my glass down and sighed. "She had quite a list of clients who—"

"Don't call these people clients!" Suzana said. "Kendra was my angel."

Martin reached under the table toward her. "Of course she was, dear, but this makes sense of why she always had that extra money."

"No, I raised her better than that."

I didn't know what to say. If I took the journals out of my purse and showed her what I'd found, I still doubted she'd believe it. I couldn't imagine what she must be feeling right now.

There was no point in beating a dead horse. So I waited for some of the shock to wear off before I moved on to the next topic. "I do have some ideas on how she died."

Julian glanced sharply at me over the rim of his glass. The

paper umbrella was too bright and cheery for this topic. When he swallowed, he smirked. "Oh yeah? What do you think?"

"Well, each time I've been in contact with her, and especially during the gentle possession, I've had trouble breathing."

They all nodded.

"And looking over the list of"—I almost said clients again but stopped myself in time—"friends she had, the ones she was really worried about were air casters."

"Really?" Julian asked. "She kept bios on the men?"

Suzana's face crumpled, and Martin scooted closer to her, whispering soothing words to her. Once again, I wished I'd taken his suggestion to at least save a mother from this kind of pain. There was nothing that could be done. I was destroying her memory of her daughter.

"Yes," I said. "All the info she'd need to get paid."

"Do you have the journals now?" Julian nudged his plate away; it was mostly cleared except he never touched the hash browns.

"Why?" I asked.

"I'd like to see them, is all."

I did my best to keep my expression bland and shifted my attention to my half-eaten lunch. Why was he more concerned about the journals than Kendra's murderer being an air caster? Was it because he suspected he'd been mentioned in them in connection to the Nettles? He was probably more worried about that and his father's campaign—and suddenly all of this made sense. Luther's popularity and the sensation of his son's estranged fiancée turning up dead hadn't tanked his polls. It'd helped, instead.

"Is there anything else you can do?" Suzana asked. "Find out who made her behave this way?"

"Suzana," Martin whispered.

"No," I said, shaking my head. "I'm sorry, but I'll be

turning the journals over to the police. They're best suited for all of this. I can't help anymore."

Martin jerked his attention to me, surprised. Then he nodded. "That's probably for the best."

It was no surprise that brunch ended shortly after that. I paid for my meal, said my goodbyes, and strolled down the paved lane toward the free parking lot. I was glad my part in this was over. And that it also meant that whoever was trying to scare me was probably done with me as well. Tonight, I'd see Rex, and then tomorrow, everything would be back to normal. I was certain Trixie would be glad to be in her shop all the time now.

The explosion startled a yelp out of me. I spun, seeing one of the flower stands swirling in a dome of clouded winds with streaks of lightning zapping through it. People screamed, running away or taking cover. The barrette in my hair grew hot.

I knew, the moment I felt the heat, that the enchantment was working. Someone was attacking me. Icy sweat coated my body. I ducked near a patio for outdoor seating, shielding my head, searching for a better place to hide while the ley crystal grew hotter—there was no way I'd drive while this was happening. The heat was getting to the point that it started to sting.

The wind solidified before me in rushes of faded blue and gray speckled with leaves and debris, forming into a giant hand. The windy fingers wrapped around my neck, and another ethereal hand slipped down my throat, as if the fingers were pulling the very breath from my lungs.

I clutched my icy throat, my thundering heartbeat thrashing in my ears

I couldn't breathe. I couldn't talk. The ley crystal had grown hot, and then it stopped. Panic overwhelmed me as black spots formed in the peripheral of my vision. I tried to turn, to look around, to see who was attacking me, but the wind continued to choke me. My lungs were closing in on themselves and I couldn't breathe. Tears blurred my vision.

I knew this was it this time.

My life didn't flash before my eyes. Nor did I think of Mimzy or Trixie and the kids. Oh, no, nothing like that. Instead, my dying brain conjured Rex.

"*Oh!*"

But the realization was too late. I sank into the black waters where the dead belonged.

Chapter Twenty-Six

I watched the explosion in the Flower Market again. Many people had filmed it, but a tourist had gotten the whole thing. Out of nowhere, the stands outside the main drag shot into the air and a blast wave hit the entire width of the street. There were casualties, but no idea who had died in the explosion. My first thought was of Willa and her brunch with the Bruces.

I pulled up our text thread.

> There was an explosion in the flower market. Did you see it?

I swapped to the text group with Dane and Eric.

> Are you two okay?

THE BOYS
ERIC ABRAHAM

> The front window has a giant crack in it, but we're ok

THE BOYS
DANE MCKEE

We're closing for the day though

Nothing from Willa, not yet. She could've already made it to the police station, or been on her way, when the explosion hit. A terrible sinking feeling shifted in my stomach as I replayed the video once more. I'd seen that kind of blast before; I'd spent many business hours working on keeping the blast area small and contained. I knew it was one of ours, a weapon made by Slater Technologies for the military, designed to keep casualties to a minimum in urban areas.

I'd read over the files that Guy gave me, but honestly, they made little sense. There were incidents in the Nettles dating back ten or so years, which would've been around the time Kendra and I were together. It didn't feel right she was the corporate spy. I'd dismissed it immediately. But when I saw that notebook of her tallying men like a source of income to float her lavish lifestyle, it wasn't hard at all to believe it. I was relieved she'd never paid for me when I'd joined her on some of those trips.

I grabbed my phone and, again, nothing from Willa. I frowned.

Were you in the flower market when the explosion went off?

My desk phone rang, and I grabbed it. "Hello?"

"Did you see the news?" Guy asked.

I deflated slightly. "The explosion in the Flower Market?"

"Yes. You need to get ahead of this. Call my contact with the police force and ask about the maker's mark on the device. There's a—"

"It's one of ours." I pinched the bridge of my nose.

"Are you sure?" Guy asked. "We don't want to take responsibility before we're certain it was one of ours."

"I'm pretty sure that's my build, Guy. But I'll still get verification before we go public."

"Have you read my notes?"

"The news clippings and your list of suspects?" I leaned back in the chair. "You listed me."

"Don't be offended, Hendrick. You'd gone off the rails for a while there. Obviously, I ruled you out or you wouldn't be sitting in my chair right now."

"Who do you even think is behind this? We're neck and neck with Ley Technica, but they've got so much to lose. I think you need to get past your cockfight with the Christensens and look at someone else who's far more desperate."

"Luther Christensen *is* desperate to have all the contracts with the government," Guy said.

"Why?"

"Don't be obtuse, Hendrick. Money."

"Yeah. Okay. I'll keep you updated on the explosion today." Then I hung up.

Money and success were the driving forces for me, and that I enjoyed building. These things made me happiest in life, but none of it guaranteed I'd have a group of people loyal to me. If Guy had believed he'd found concrete proof I was selling Slater Technologies' secrets, I'd be done. They probably would've driven me out of Starglen, preventing me from ever working in my chosen field again.

And we were blood.

Sure, half-siblings, but we were still blood. No matter how much money I had or how successful people found me, it wouldn't have saved me from being tossed to the wolves by my family.

My thoughts strayed to Willa, a mixture of concern and

longing overcoming me. I knew I was in deep with her already. She'd consumed my thoughts almost from the moment she made me buy all those cookies and shot me down, not to mention I had a weakness for redheads. I thought it was because she was playing hard to get and I loved a challenge. But it was because we'd somehow became friends in that moment, on that bench. When she'd given me a pass to simply be me.

It was ridiculous. We weren't a good match. She demanded attention wherever she went, even if she didn't want it. She was big and showy and loud, enjoying being the center of attention, while I'd rather quietly command it. She used all her energy into putting on a show, and I put mine into work: more productivity; more enthusiasm.

She still hadn't responded to me, so I broke down and called her. As if that'd make her magically use her phone.

"Hello?" a frantic voice said. "Rex? Is that you?"

Oh fuck. Who was answering her phone? *Why* was someone else answering her phone? She'd been hurt; she was in the morgue. I cleared my throat. "Yes. I'm calling Willamina Dade's phone."

"Oh, honey. Billie's been hurt. We just got home from the hospital. You should come see her. It'll cheer her up good."

"Erma?" I asked.

"I told you to call me Mimzy," Erma said. "Now get over here."

ERMA OPENED THE DOOR BEFORE I MADE IT TO THE porch. "She's in her room."

I stepped inside and paused. "How bad is it?"

"The price the ER charges for a small healing potion is astronomical," Erma said, locking the storm door. "But she's more . . ." She twisted her hands together and then rotated her arm with a grimace. "Something's not right."

I headed down the hallway with Erma behind me and knocked on the door.

Willa opened it, wearing her headdress and veil, which she steadied with a shaking hand. "Rex!"

I gripped her shoulders lightly, thoroughly inspecting her. She looked perfect, unharmed, but I knew based off that she was wearing half her costume, something had happened. "Where were you attacked?"

Her eyes grew big and glassy. "Right when the explosion happened."

"You were there?" My heart crashed against my ribcage, and a dose of adrenaline pumped into my system. My fingers flexed on her shoulders as I studied her again. "You took a healing potion? Where were you hurt? Did you see who set it off?"

"It was another psychic attack," she answered. "I was too far away from the blast to get hurt, but close enough to feel the wind."

I continued checking her over, searching for signs of cuts and scrapes or bruises, but other than a tear in her blouse, she seemed fine. "Did this happen before or after your meeting with the Bruces?"

"After. I was actually headed to the police station when it happened."

"Was it the same attack like before with all the water?" I asked.

"I think I burnt out your ley crystal," she said instead of answering my question.

"It needs recharging," Erma confirmed. "She hit her head when she passed out."

"Jesus." I crushed her to my chest, cradling the back of her head with my hand. I rocked her, assuring myself she was solid and healthy within my arms. "I'm so glad you're okay."

She wrapped her arms around me tightly. "I'm sorry about the crystal, but I think it saved my life."

"Good." I kissed the top of her head. "I don't care that you drained it. I'll make you a thousand ley crystals just to keep you safe."

Erma made a pained noise, curling her arm slightly.

"Are *you* okay, Mimzy?" I asked. All this excitement surrounding Willa lately had to be freaking her out.

"I think I went too hard on my walking weights." Erma nodded at my own arms. "You know how it is."

Then I remembered the back of my tie clip had a ley crystal in it for protection. I reluctantly pushed Willa back and unclipped it, pressing it into her hands.

"Here. Take this now. I'll recharge the other for you, and we'll get it so you have a rotation."

Willa lifted her amber eyes from the charm in her palm to mine. "Rex, I can't take this."

"You can, and you will."

Willa tucked my tie clip in her pocket and pulled off her headdress and veil, setting them aside on the travel trunk near the mannequin.

Erma wrung her hands. "I don't know what else to do. Billie needs help, and I can't protect her the way she needs it."

"I'll be fine, Mimzy," she murmured. "But I could use some coffee."

"Did either Suzana or Martin say anything out of the ordinary at brunch?" I asked as we walked down the hallway toward the kitchen.

Willa glanced at me over her shoulder. "Not at all. Why do you ask?"

"I just wish you hadn't shown them the journals so soon.

Here." I ushered Erma into a chair. "I'll make coffee. You both sit."

Erma and Willa slowly sat down, staring at me. I ignored it and headed to the coffeemaker and paused. Then Willa was at my side, smelling soft as she smiled at me.

"No, sit down and let me do this for you," I whispered.

"You're a sweetheart, Rex," she murmured back, "but you don't know where anything is."

She had me there. I got out of her way and leaned against the counter while Willa scooped out coffee grounds from an airtight container and began filling the machine.

"I'll take a small cup, Chipmunk," Erma said. "And one of those fancy puddings."

Willa's expression turned impish as she and her grandma exchanged an inside joke with merely a glance. Then her smile turned warm as she nodded me toward the fridge. "They're in there. I'll make you a cup too."

I tore open the package, retrieved a pudding, and brought it to Erma. Willa was already on top of giving her a spoon and setting down two mismatched mugs before us. So I sat at the table, feeling useless.

Erma peeled the lid off her pudding cup and licked it. "What do you have against the Bruces, Rex?"

Willa sat next to me at the table, placing an empty mug before me. The coffee machine whooshed into action and began gurgling on the counter behind us.

"What do you mean?" I asked.

"They paid me to translate Kendra's journals," Willa said. "Why shouldn't I have shown them?"

"Yeah." Erma skimmed the top of the pudding with the side of her spoon and sucked it off. "Ooo, there's nutmeg in this. This is Christmas pudding."

I ignored the pudding comment. "I think there might be a

leak with them. Every time you've met with them, something happens to you."

She tilted her head to the side. "I think they're just grieving and updating their family. Which is their right."

"It's possible that whoever they're telling is the same person who's been attacking you."

"It was different this time." Her brow wrinkled in thought. "Whoever was doing it was trying to strangle me with the air I was breathing."

"My fucking ass they'll hurt you," Erma yelled, jabbing a finger at me. "Do something."

The coffeemaker beeped, and I motioned for Willa to stay seated. As I moved to grab the coffee carafe, I wondered if a protection grid was strong enough. The ley crystal had helped her twice, and it'd barely been enough this time.

I returned to the table and filled their mugs with coffee, the rich aroma infusing the air. "You should stay with me."

"What?" Willa laughed, reaching for a covered sugar bowl on the table. "No. I'm done with this, and Trixie needs to get back to her regular schedule with the shop."

"But you need protection," I said, setting the pot aside and sitting.

"And I need to stay here and get back to my normal routine." Willa sipped her coffee and frowned at Erma. "Mimzy didn't tell Trixie she had rescheduled her appointment with Dr. O'Neil, and she missed it."

Erma rolled her eyes and blew on her mug. "Fuck schedules, that's me."

Any other time, this would've been hilarious. But Willa was ignoring her safety, and the need I had to make sure she couldn't get hurt grew increasingly more urgent.

"I'm serious, Willa," I said, reaching for her hand. "I can get you another ley crystal tonight, but I don't think you're safe here, not at all. I have security."

"I think he's right, Chipmunk." Erma rubbed Willa's shoulder. "It'd make me feel better if I knew you were safe."

"Me too." But I recognized the stubborn glint in her eye. If she didn't say we were right when she opened that pretty mouth of hers, I didn't think I should be held responsible for chucking her over my shoulder and dragging her back to my cave.

Willa covered Erma's hand. "No. It's ridiculous—What're you doing?"

I'd jerked to my feet, my chair legs rubbing loudly on the tiled floor, and strode down the hallway toward her bedroom. It smelled good in here, like soft women's things: flowers, sweet musk, and powder. I pushed past a mannequin to the closet and slid open the door. Bolts of cloth, blouses, slacks, dresses, skirts, purses, and shoes crammed the closet. On the floor, I noticed a bag and I grabbed it.

"What are you doing?" Willa asked from the door, her voice hard around the edges.

"Packing for you." I stepped back from the closet and approached the dresser, opening the top drawer. A collection of lacy bras and matching panties took me off guard. I froze. Did she have underwear that didn't make me want to peel them slowly off her? That wasn't the reason I wanted to pack for her. "Where are your sweats?"

"Hey—"

"Her workout clothes are in the bottom drawer," Erma said.

I grabbed a random bra and the matching panties and shoved them in the bag. I crouched and pulled open the bottom drawer, revealing rows of leggings and stretchy tops. I plucked a pair and tossed them in the bag as well. Then I stepped toward her cosmetics and frowned. I didn't think she needed that much, but I could sweep it all in.

"Woah!" Willa squeezed between me and her makeup. "What do you think you're doing?"

"He's packing for your dumb ass," Erma muttered, her mouth taking a sour downturn. "And for only one night, by the looks of it."

"It'd make me feel better if you stayed the night with me," I said. "I have a guestroom."

"A guestroom. What a shame," Erma muttered. "Besides, I go to bed early." She squatted and gripped a pair of heels from the floor and slowly stood up, grunting softly. "I don't see ley energy when I'm sawing logs. I can't help if you need it."

"But what about you?" Willa whispered. "What if you need me?"

Erma batted that statement out of the air. "I'll be asleep, Chipmunk. Won't need you if I'm unconscious."

She visibly softened, a long breath sighing from her in resignation. Then she turned her gorgeous eyes on me. "Just for one night."

"Play it by ear," Erma said.

I nodded.

She shooed me away from her makeup. "Fine. *I'll* pack an overnight bag."

Now that I didn't need to act like a caveman, I didn't need to pack for her. I handed her the bag and left the room, returning to my coffee. They left the door open, and I could hear every word they said. I drank my coffee, trying to ignore their conversation.

"Don't look at me like that, Mimzy," Willa said.

"Like what?" she asked.

"Like the cat who ate a canary. Oh, knock it off."

Erma cackled. "This is a great opportunity to get some good ole fashioned pelvic pinochle in."

I snorted, covering my mouth.

"I don't want to talk about this."

"Why not? Your grandfather and I tested it out a lot before we got married." Erma said. "Honestly, I think it did me a huge favor. That man could—"

"Gram-cracker! No!"

"Oh, don't be such a prude, Billie. That man wouldn't hurt a hair on your body. He loves you. Have some fun. You've earned it."

I'd been laughing at their exchange; Erma had taken me by surprise. But when she dropped the L word, I almost spilled coffee all over my lap. Me? In love?

Willa stepped back into the kitchen, wearing a green wrap-around dress and the heels Erma had grabbed. She slung the bag over one shoulder, her glorious red hair spilling over the other.

My heart thumped against my ribs. *Oh, shit.*

Chapter Twenty-Seven

All that remained of the sunset was a thin ombre line of magenta, eggplant, and midnight navy against the Starglen skyline playing peek-a-boo between soft curves of clouds with a twinkle of stars. Everything felt warm and positive. On our way to Rex's penthouse—I still couldn't get over the fact his front door was an elevator—we'd stopped at a market to pick up some shrimp, noodles, an onion, a lemon, and chilled white wine. We set up a protection grid of green phantom quartz and chlorite around the perimeter of his home before settling in for a nice dinner I insisted on making for him.

Cooking with Rex wasn't much different from cooking with Mimzy, aside from the flirting. He'd sat at the island where the countertop range was situated and drank wine with me, chatting about how much we cooked. Him, not so much, but he had a few key meals down, such as waffles. No surprise I cooked more.

Now, we sat close by one another, facing the large windows, our empty plates scattered between us. Everything about this screamed intimacy: the soft noises of the city drifting up to us, the low lighting in the room. Rex playing with the ends of my hair.

"Dinner was delicious," he said. "Thanks for cooking, but I feel like I should point out the discrepancy of the shrimp division." He slanted me a look, the gray curl falling against his forehead. "You had more than me."

I smoothed the curl back into his hair, only for it to fall forward again and grinned into his eyes. "Chef's tax."

He leaned closer, his arm wrapping around the back of my chair, and tugged it toward him. "Oh, so the fee for that meal was all the extra shrimp?"

"I gotta get paid somehow."

"I had other ideas of how I'd show my appreciation for it."

I laughed in the back of my throat, slid my hand to the nape of his neck, and kissed him softly. His quick inhale sent a rush through me. He tasted like wine and desire, instantly piquing my need for more. I leaned back and bit my lip.

His gaze darted to it, then back to mine. "That's only a small preview of how I'd planned to show my appreciation."

"Oh?"

He stood, holding his hand out to me, and I took it. He led me to the couch with our wine, setting the glasses on the coffee table and relaxing next to me on the leather cushions. A small rush swept through me, sending a tiny shiver up my spine. When he reached for me, I grasped his hand with mine and threaded my fingers through his, laughing slightly. I was nervous.

"Hey," he murmured. "I'll only go as far as you're comfortable with. All you have to do is say the word, Willa."

I lifted a brow. "Oh, you planned to go somewhere with me?"

His piercing blue eyes twinkled, and his lips twitched. "About as far as this couch, honestly." He ran a knuckle along my jawline. "I'm more than just attracted to you, if it isn't obvious. I'm happy to take things at your pace, and I know tonight feels like . . . Like I expect more. But if we just sat here, watched movies or whatever, then I'll go to sleep a lucky man. It's not . . ." He lifted his face to the rafters, clearly struggling with his words. "It's not only about—it wouldn't be just sex. For me. I didn't invite you here for that. But also, you know, I'm not against it either, but I know—"

"Rex."

Holding his breath, he met my eyes.

"I'll let you know if I get uncomfortable." Then I tugged him closer.

His lips pressed to mine, the soft hair of his beard brushing against my skin. I didn't wait for him to coax my mouth open, and I licked him. With each deepening kiss, we grew closer, our arms pulling and tugging one another tighter against our bodies. My heartbeat picked up speed as my head swam. Kissing him was intoxicating.

His fingers slid to the back of my neck and up into my hair. I murmured in the back of my throat as he wrapped my hair around his palm and gently tugged my head back, breaking our kiss. Heat flooded my chest as his lips floated down my throat, nipped my clavicle, and followed that line to my shoulder. I sighed softly at the soft caress of his mouth on my neck again, my hands roaming his broad back.

His teeth clamped on my earlobe, and I gasped at the shock of desire that shot right to the apex of my thighs. His tongue traced over the shell of my ear. My nails bit into the meat of his shoulders through his shirt. Then he sucked my earlobe into his mouth, and I purred.

"Jesus," he groaned into my ear, then bit it again.

I arched against him, then pushed him back. If I let him suck on my ear much longer, I might cum right in my panties. His lids were half-mast as he held back, watching me with unbridled desire. I shifted toward him and caught his mouth with mine. My fingers tripped over the buttons on his shirt, unbuttoning a few before I realized I hadn't asked for permission.

"Rex," I said between scorching kisses, "is this okay?"

He broke away, grabbed the back of his collar, and yanked his shirt off, baring his sculpted chest and the soft curls of dark hair tapering into a V down muscular abs and disappearing beneath the waistband of his slacks. Then he was kissing me again. My body grew a mind of its own, responding to him; demanding things from him. My fingers skimmed along his bare back before exploring the sharp planes of his chest.

He tugged my hair again, making me tilt my head back as he kissed down the throat and the entire V of my wraparound dress. His tongue dipped into my cleavage, and I squirmed. I wanted more. His hand drifted to the tie and stopped, but he continued to drop soft kisses along my exposed flesh.

Then he lifted his eyes to me. "I want to untie your dress."

"Yes," I breathed.

He untied it and slowly bared me to him. My breasts heaved within the lacy black confines of my bra, not hiding how erect my nipples were. He made a pained face, as if seeing them hurt, but I knew that wasn't the case as his gaze devoured my body, roaming from my breasts to the lacy black panties that matched the bra and then down my legs. I wished I'd kept my heels on; he would've eaten that up. And I loved how he looked at me like this, that he wanted me and appreciated my body. It made me want him more.

"Damn, you're gorgeous, princess." He cupped my breasts, his thumbs whispering over my nipples as he placed gentle kisses along the exposed flesh not covered by lace and satin. His hands smoothed over my stomach to my hips, his fingers toying with the lace before sliding to my back. I arched, and he supported me. "So damned enchanting."

He sucked on my nipple through my bra, and I moaned,

my eyes sliding shut. I hooked my leg over his and slowly slid my hands up and down his toned arms to his shoulders, then to the back of his head and curled my fingers into his hair.

His hands quested along my back as he released one breast and shifted to the other. His fingers plucked at the band of my bra, and I chuckled. With one hand, I inserted my fingers in the front of my bra and released the front closure. He peeled my bra back, crooning at the sight of my breasts before licking a peaked nipple. He sucked the bud into his mouth, and my hips lifted off the couch.

He paid homage to my breasts, not giving one little worry to the scorching knot of silky heat building between my thighs. He'd tease the band of my panties, even dipped behind and cupped my ass. I needed him to touch me, but I only moaned and gasped at the lavish attention he paid to my breasts.

"Can I take these off, Willa?" he rasped, sliding a finger under the skinny band at my waist. "I want to touch you."

"Yes," I hissed, lifting my hips again.

Using both hands, he tugged them off and dropped them somewhere on the floor. He stared at me, my dress and bra spread wide, and I thought his eyes couldn't get darker, but the lust and desire had turned them almost black.

"Touch me, Rex," I murmured, trailing my nails along the side of my breast and ribs.

He dragged a finger from my navel down, and my thighs parted. He sucked in a breath as he watched his finger glide right into my damp folds, sending an electric bolt of lust straight into my core. He slid it inside me, one quick dip, then up to my clit and back. I gasped at the pleasure. Then he lifted that same finger and sucked it into his mouth, his eyes locking with mine. I couldn't breathe, and I craved—*ached* for him to keep touching me, because if he didn't, I might take over for him.

"Delicious," he rumbled.

Holy shit.

He slid off the couch, knelt before me, hooked my legs over his shoulders, and kissed my hot core, his tongue slipping inside. I cried out, throwing my head back and gripping his hair. His thumb tapped my clit while tight, hard rosettes of pleasure continued to coil inside me. Then, right when I thought I'd plateaued and this aching pleasure of almost being there took over, he sucked my clit into his mouth and flicked his tongue over it.

I gasped sharply, then moaned low and long, my hips rolling on their own against his mouth until all those knots inside me came undone. He gave me a few long licks, sending delicious shivers through me. Honestly, I was ready for another, but I wanted to explore him just as he had me.

He kissed the inside of my thighs and then my stomach. I sat forward, cupped his face, and kissed him, tasting myself on his lips. My fingers went to the belt around his waist, and I unbuckled him, tugging the leather free.

He broke the kiss and caught my hands. "Willa—"

"I want you, Rex," I said, breathlessly. "I don't want to stop. Not yet."

He stared at me for a long moment, his mouth wet from me and his breathing hard and ragged. Then he stood, the bulge in his slacks unmistakable as he held a hand out to me. I stood, leaving my dress and bra behind. He pulled me along to his bedroom, illuminated only by the soft glow from the city. I could make out a massive king-sized bed with dark finishing touches and that about it. It smelled like cedar in here, like him.

"Lights off?" he asked.

I turned to face him. "Yeah."

He kissed me, his hands roving my back and squeezing my ass. "Birth control?"

"Yeah, I'm on it," I breathed into his ear while I unbuttoned his pants. "Is this okay?"

"God, yes. You can touch me whenever you want, princess."

He groaned when I slipped my hand into his boxers and gripped his hard, silky length in my palm, examining him by touch. He let out a puff of air as I rubbed my thumb over the hot tip. Then I pushed his slacks and boxers down.

He stepped out of them. "I got tested recently. I'm clear, but—"

"I'm clear too." Licking my lips, I dropped to my knees.

He pulled me right back up. "There's time for that later. Now's all about you."

I grinned and moved to kiss him, but he nudged me toward the bed. "Hop on."

I reclined on the mattress, pillowing my head on my arm, and caressed under the swell of my breast.

He'd gripped his dick, staring at me as he moved closer. "Roll over, princess."

I hesitated, watching him lightly stroking his hard length. He'd told me I could refuse at any time, and though I wasn't entirely sure of his intentions, I trusted him. And damn, I *wanted* him. I rolled onto my stomach. He jerked my legs until I knelt on the mattress.

Then he lowered himself and licked me from behind.

"Oh, god," I gasped. *"Yes."*

It felt wildly different from earlier, and it was hard to keep still as he brought the fire right back. He moaned against my folds, and I cried out with pleasure. Right when I thought I'd climax, he pulled back. I whimpered.

"I could eat you all night," he said huskily.

"I'm not stopping you," I breathed.

He chuckled hoarsely. "Get in the middle of the bed."

I crawled into the center of the bed, and he followed me.

Then he reached over me, his dick brushing against my bottom—moisture dripped down the inside of my thigh at the touch—and grabbed a condom from the nightstand drawer. Before I could say anything else, he tore it open and rolled it on.

"This is your last chance to stop me before I'm inside you," he whispered.

I tossed my hair and looked at him again. He held his wrapped dick, pointing it at me while his other hand braced my hip. I wiggled my ass. "I need you, Rex. I need you inside me right now."

"Ass in the air, princess."

I bent myself over the bed, my breasts pressed into the soft duvet, and I gazed at him over my shoulder.

He huffed. "So fucking beautiful."

He nudged my knees a little wider and pushed inside me. He groaned, deep and long. And when he finally filled me all the way up, I sighed.

Then his hips rocked against me. That soft and hot pleasurable pull ensnared me again as I found his rhythm and matched it. He plunged into me so deep, it nearly stole my breath. I reached down and lightly rubbed my clit as he continued with his slow and steady pace, my moans of pleasure echoing his.

Right when it was becoming unbearably hot, he shifted on the bed, pulling me up so I was sitting on him, his chest against my back and my thighs spread wide. His dick twitched inside me, and I rocked against him. I leaned my head back, my fingers drifting back to the aching bud between my legs. He kissed my neck while his hands caressed my breasts, then swept down my stomach and brushed my hand away so he could massage my clit himself.

"This is all about you." Hunger strangled his voice as he pumped into me.

I moaned, arching into his touch and grinding my ass against him. We moved together, chest to back, as he glided in and out of me and his fingers built such hot, almost painful pleasure deep inside me that when I came again, I screamed.

Then he pulled out and eased me gently onto my back, his dick jutting up proudly, and he delved inside me once more. He growled, the sound jerking my hips upward. He leaned down and captured my lips in a slow, deep, soul rending kiss as he fully seated himself. And when he opened his eyes, I grabbed his hands, knotting our fingers together. I had to hold on to him for whatever he'd do next because I was already weightless; I was already in the clouds.

"I love you, Willa," he whispered, slowly easing his weight on me, pulling his fingers from mine only to run them through my hair. "I'm so damned in love with you."

I blinked and cupped his face, my heart suddenly too big for my chest. "I love you too."

He grinned and kissed me, his lovemaking turning sweet and tender. I imagined us in the heavens, guiding the stars to our next journey. And when I felt that tightening clench once more, I cinched my legs around his waist and he drove into me, shouting my name.

We showered after that, and he finally let me explore his beautiful body with my hands and mouth. We made love once more in the shower, quick and fierce. By the time we settled under the covers in bed together, I fell asleep with him wrapped around me, my body deliciously sore and tired.

I'd never felt this safe or sated. And for the first time in my life, I felt like I was the only choice for Rex.

Chapter Twenty-Eight

I woke up to the sun streaming on my face and an empty bed. For a moment, I was scared last night hadn't happened. That Willa and I hadn't bared ourselves to one another or had the most amazing sex I'd ever had. However, there were signs of her everywhere: the rumbled bedding beside me, the comb on the bathroom counter, and the lid to the toilet was down. The big sign was when I stepped into the hallway and smelled coffee, vanilla, waffles, and bacon.

In the kitchen, Willa stood bathed in the sun, her red hair on fire and messy like she hadn't bothered to comb it when she woke up this morning. She was also wearing my blue linen robe, and the sight of her at the counter monitoring the waffle iron had me aching—for a life I hadn't believed I wanted or deserved.

She smiled when she saw me. "Rex! You didn't tell me you had a steamer closet!"

I leaned against the center island, my gaze dipping to the scrap of ivory skin the robe and shirt she wore didn't cover, down to her bare feet in my kitchen. I *liked* this turn of events.

I grinned. "I didn't know my steamer closet would be such a hit with you."

"If you had led with that at the bar when we first met, I totally would have met you in the hallway." Her amber eyes twinkled. The waffle iron beeped, and she opened it, getting a steamy facial of sweet waffles. "I hope you like your waffles golden and crispy on the outside."

I didn't have the heart to tell her I didn't eat breakfast like that. I usually had a protein shake, worked out, then had a treat from Icing. Which, when I think about it, wasn't very healthy either. However, she'd made it for me, therefore I'd eat it. When she set the last waffle on the plate—she'd made an entire stack of them—I hooked my arm around her waist and pulled her against me.

"How're you feeling?" I murmured, nuzzling her ear.

She chuckled and looped her arms around my neck. "Amazing. You?"

I caught her lips with mine, a soft kiss that packed a heavy punch, driving me from six to midnight. "Better now that I have you in my life."

She tilted her head back and rose on the tips of her toes, her body sliding against mine, her hips cradling me. I squeezed her ass and nipped along her jaw to her ear. Her nails dug into my shoulders.

"You know," she murmured in a husky voice, "I was surprised to find I didn't have whisker burn. Especially on my thighs."

I chuckled, and even though I heard her correctly, I pretended I hadn't. "Oh, that can't be comfortable. Let me see. I'll make it feel better."

"No, I said—Rex!"

I hoisted her on the counter, the mixing bowl and whisk toppling off to the floor with a clang. Willa threw her head back and laughed as I parted her legs and pushed aside the robe.

"Oh, no." I leaned down and pressed kisses to her perfect, pale thighs. "Here, I know just what to do to help with this . . ."

I licked her thigh, my hands sliding up to grab either side of her underwear and slowly began tugging. She giggled, her fingers curling in my hair. If I had to guess, she liked me going down on her as much as I loved tasting her.

Her phone chimed on the counter behind us, but we were too invested in the moment to stop. I stepped back, sliding her panties off her ankles, and dropped them to the floor. Then I skimmed my hands up her calves, tickled her knees, and smoothed my palms over her thighs.

"God, you're even more beautiful today," I said.

Her phone had been chiming a lot once it started. Willa glanced at it where it sat charging before gliding a foot against my leg. "I feel beautiful when you look at me like that."

I had her exposed. I could see the glisten on her soft pink flesh, but I merely caressed the insides of her thighs, enjoying seeing her in full light. Her breathing turned ragged the closer the soft circles I drew on her skin inched to her core. I met her gaze and licked her lips before covering her mouth completely. We both moaned, my fingers centimeters from dipping in.

Her phone rang.

We broke apart, her chest heaving as she peered again over my shoulder. "I forgot to charge it last night, and it was dead this morning."

I stepped out of the circle of her long legs and flipped her phone over. "It's Trixie. Hey, she does wedding cakes, right? Does she have any consultations open?" I was holding it out to her when the ringing stopped. "Oh, you just missed it."

Willa slipped off the counter and snatched up her panties,

stepping back into them. "She does. Is this for Dane and Eric?"

Ah, well, I'd get those back off her another time. I stepped out of her way so she could keep her phone charging and still use it. The waffle batter had made a mess, so I grabbed some paper towels. "It might just help the boys out if she can."

"I'll see if she does, but Eric and Dane need to make the appointment." She placed the phone to her ear. "Hey, Trix. What's up? Sorry, my phone died. Yeah, I'm with Rex."

I tossed the paper towels, set the bowl and whisk in the sink, and grabbed some cleaner from the cabinet.

"What?" Willa's voice sounded alarmed, shocked, and reedy high.

I frowned, glancing at her, and dropped the cleaner. Her already pale face had lost all color. Her body caved in on itself, as if her spine could no longer hold her upright. Tears welled in her eyes.

"What?" Her voice cracked, shattering the word. She clenched her eyes shut, nearly losing her balance. "No! No!"

I froze, staring at her. Then anxiety flooded my chest, and my throat constricted. I didn't know what was happening, but whatever it was, it was terrible. I gathered Willa in my arms as she began sobbing. I glanced at the elevator, the windows, the protection grid, looking for something to explain what was happening, searching for a way out of here, but she gripped my shirt, her shoulders shaking.

"When? When did it happen?" She trembled against me, a broken sob escaping her. "Oh god, no!"

I could hear Trixie crying too and all I felt was dread. I had an idea what happened, but I didn't dare say it out loud in case it made it true. I rubbed Willa's back, holding her, bracing her.

"I'll be there as soon as I can. I love you too. Bye." Then she lifted her head, her eyes rimmed red and tears overflowing. She tried to speak, but she only sobbed.

"What happened?" I asked.

"Mimzy died last night." And she bawled.

I held her tighter, my gut bottoming out while her tears soaked through my shirt and all I could do was stroke her back. I didn't even have words.

"I have to go to the house," Willa said after a few minutes. She hadn't stopped crying when she pulled from me. "I don't know what's . . ." Tears skated down her cheek, and she wiped them away, but they kept coming. "I'll call you later."

I frowned, following her to the bedroom. "I can drive you."

She gathered her toiletries and tossed them in her bag, then glanced around. "Where's my bra?"

She pushed past me into the living room. I trailed after her, stunned, worried. She gathered her clothes from the floor in front of the couch and hurried past me, still not meeting my eye. Then she pulled off my robe and buried her face in her hands, her shoulders rocking.

I gathered her close again, and we sat on the edge of the bed, Willa burying her face in my chest while I held her. My heart broke seeing her grieve like this. I wished there was something I could do to physically make her feel better, to get her to stop crying, but all I was capable of was holding her. It didn't feel like enough.

"I'm sorry," she whispered.

"*I'm* sorry." I kissed the top of her head. "You have nothing to be sorry about."

She stood and grabbed her dress and scowled. "I can't wear this." Then she crumpled it up and jammed it into the bag before ripping out jeans and a shirt, quickly changing into them.

I felt helpless watching her change into clothes while tears sporadically dripped down her cheeks. She seemed angry that it kept happening, and all I could do was hold her or say nonsensical things like "I'm sorry" and I wouldn't even dare ask if she would be okay.

"Where's the nearest bus station? You know what? I'll call an Uber." Willa slung her bag over her shoulder and strode to the kitchen where her phone was still charging.

I hurried after her and grabbed her bag. "No way. I'm taking you home."

She tugged on her bag, trying to break my grip. "It's fine."

"You're not fine."

"It doesn't matter!" she yelled. "I have to go home—I have to be there for Mimzy!"

"It *does* matter," I said calmly, but wondered if yelling might be better for her to actually hear me. "I'm not letting you be alone, not for one second. Not while you're grieving and someone attacked you yesterday. If I can't protect you from this, at least let me protect you from that."

Her face crumpled. "I don't want to be protected."

I pulled her into my arms, and she clung to me. "I know, princess," I murmured. "I can't let you be alone. I just can't."

"You have to go to work." Her voice sounded fragile, like broken glass.

"I'm the CEO right now. I can do whatever I want." I rubbed her arms, leaned back, and peered into her eyes. "And right now, I want to take you home and do whatever I can to help."

So I drove her home. She leaned against the seat and stared blankly out the windshield. I hated seeing her like this. I knew she and Mimzy were close. You could see it in how they interacted with each other. Some people who lived with their elderly parents or grandparents, did it out of obligation, but Willa and Mimzy had been friends too. There was genuine love between them, and her heart was broken right now.

When I pulled onto her street, they were wheeling a

gurney out to an ambulance. Willa became agitated and reached for the door. "Stop the car. Stop the car!"

"Hang on." I pulled up to the curb one house away.

She bounded out of the car before I'd fully stopped and raced to the gurney. The paramedics tried to block her. I finished parking and hurried toward her. Right as I reached her, Trixie bounded out of the house, and Willa pivoted, running to her. They hugged, crying together.

One paramedic paused in loading the ambulance and glanced at me. "Mrs. Morton has all the information. All she needs to do is call the mortuary."

I nodded. "Thanks."

Willa and Trixie walked into the house as the ambulance pulled away. I returned to my car, grabbed Willa's bag, and headed after them. The door was open, though the storm door wasn't. I wasn't sure if I should step inside without knocking. Last night, I felt like I was part of Willa's life, especially when she'd said she loved me back when it'd just slipped out. I'd never planned on telling her like that, and certainly not this soon. And I loved her; there was no misspeaking then. I hadn't had the chance to process my feelings yet. But now, in light of their grief, I felt like a stranger and I wasn't sure I belonged.

Shawn, Trixie's youngest kid, saw me and approached the door. "Aren't you Aunt Billie's boyfriend?"

Was I? I hoped so. "Yeah. I've got her bag."

He pushed the door open. "Okay." He'd said it like he couldn't figure out why I wasn't simply coming inside.

"When did it happen?" Willa asked.

I followed the sound of her voice to her room. She and Trixie sat on her bed, both crying.

"Overnight." Trixie dabbed her eyes with a tissue. "When I came here to take her to her doctor's appointment, I found her in bed."

I could see something break even further inside Willa. Her eyes met mine, and all I felt was the guilt coming from them. Then she covered her face once more, and Trixie wrapped an arm around her. She smiled wanly at me, but she stayed put. I set the bag down and headed to the kitchen, looking around and feeling lost.

Not much was different. There were the remnants of dinner in the sink, and the coffee pot, while half full with coffee, was cold. I set to cleaning that out and making another pot of coffee. Then I washed the dishes in the sink, but I had no clue where to put them. It was when I was opening and closing the upper cabinets that Willa and Trixie emerged into the kitchen.

Trixie gave me another tight smile. "Thank you for cleaning up, Rex. You shouldn't have, but thanks all the same."

"I didn't know what else to do," I said, then looked at Willa. "How're you feeling?"

"Awful." She frowned. "I think it might be best if you go for now. Let me and Trix work things out."

"Are you sure?" I stepped toward her. "I don't mind being here for anything you need."

She gave me a small, watery smile. "Thanks, but right now, I just want to be with my family. I'll call you later."

I really didn't want to leave. It felt wrong, but she didn't want me to stay. I wrapped her up in a tight hug and kissed her forehead. "I'll see you soon."

I stepped out into the late morning sun and climbed into my car. I stared at the house, wondering if leaving her was right. She wasn't alone. She had her family to comfort her, but it felt like I was abandoning her. And what sucked even more, I had no idea how she'd deal if I left or if I didn't. I felt like . . . It felt like her telling me to leave was the only thing she had control over, and I didn't want to take it from her.

Chapter Twenty-Nine

I woke choking for air.

It took several moments to calm my hammering heart and remember it was only a dream. I lay there, staring at my ceiling while the night still held the sky hostage. These dreams of suffocating had been tapering off over the past few days, and . . . I didn't care.

I listened for Mimzy. Sometimes, she'd get her day going super early if she'd gone to bed early. She only needed four hours of sleep to be perky, she'd said. But the house was quiet. Like a crypt.

The thing that made my eyes burn and my throat close the most these days was that I'd remember, right about now, that Mimzy had died. She was gone; she'd never return. We'd learned a few days ago her cause of death was a massive stroke. She'd died in her sleep without pain. I kept pulling up that day in my memories, searching for clues, and I'd found them. She hadn't said a word, but her arm had been bothering her.

Maybe if I hadn't been so caught up in myself, I would've noticed the early symptoms of a stroke. I would've known to take her to the ER. I wouldn't have left with Rex; I would've stayed here. She wouldn't have died alone. And now, I needed to make sure there'd be food at the gathering after her funeral tomorrow. Or was that today?

I rubbed my face, surprised to find it somewhat oily. Trying to remember the last time I showered, I decided now was as good as a time as any to get out of bed.

I stepped on a crystal. "Ouch! *Sonuvabitch!*" I kicked it across the room, the sole of my foot throbbing, and promptly stepped on another. "God damn it!"

I flicked on the light and glared at the random crystals littering the floor. The protection grid had been broken for the last week, and I was positive the charms were no longer charged—thanks to the bad dreams.

Fisting my hands, I craned my head back and released a strangled shout. It didn't help. Then I grabbed an old shoebox from the closet, tossed the pumps to the bottom of my wardrobe, plucked an amethyst from the floor, and dropped it in the box. Hubris and deceit. That was all enchanting had ever granted me. Hubris because I'd fooled everyone, even myself, that I knew what I was doing with these stones. Deceit because in the end, I was still Muted and Mimzy was still gone.

If it hadn't been for these crystals, none of this would've happened. I wouldn't have been dragged into a séance that led to me being attacked. I wouldn't have had those journals that not only made me find her body, but you guessed it: be attacked.

In fact, enchanting had gotten me into too many messes and awkward conversations that maybe it was time to pack it all in. I mean, I certainly would've been here rather than fucking Rex when Mimzy had needed me.

Instead, she'd died alone.

I gathered all the stones from my floor and tossed them into the box. Then I snatched the dreamcatchers and suncatchers from the walls and windows, not caring that they'd get tangled, and crammed them on top of the crystals. Smashing the lid on, I almost threw the box across the room. Instead, I put it on the top shelf beneath my high school yearbooks, never to see the light of day again.

Wiping my face, I strode down the hallway to the kitchen and blinked. It wasn't as early as I'd thought, since the sun was rising. And by the time my coffee finished brewing, it was bright and cheerful in the kitchen, the glint of rainbows splashing against the wall from another suncatcher.

I yanked that down and poured a cup of coffee. They were everywhere. Most of these crystals had never been imbued with ley energy, but they'd been charged in the sun or the moon or some kind of special water, and it all went back to my obsession with enchanting—an obsession that had caused me nothing but grief.

Being Muted had always . . . *Ha*. Muted the joy I thought I'd found in the world. It'd never been enough to make anyone happy—*I* had never been enough. I should've accepted that while magic was everywhere, not everyone needed to touch it and moved on with my monotone life.

Instead I'd lied to myself. I'd lied to the world. And I'd lied to Rex.

As I deposited another crystal in the middle of the table, the doorbell sounded. I turned to glare at it, suspicious. Who the fuck was here? I grabbed my coffee, took my first sip, and flinched. It was ice cold, and I realized I'd spent an hour clearing away crystals. Someone knocked on the door now.

I pulled it open to see Rex. I almost smiled. Okay, I did a little because his grin was immediate. But seeing him reminded me that I'd neglected Mimzy on her last day. That I'd made it all about me all over again when the world only cared how a person could manipulate ley energy.

I unlocked the storm door and nudged it open. "What're you doing here?"

"Why do you always ask that?" He stepped in and pressed a kiss to my forehead. "Morning, princess."

I grimaced, feeling bad that he'd placed his mouth against my oily skin. He pushed a paper bag into my hands, a grease stain forming in one of the bottom corners. It smelled delicious, and I peeked inside. I was pretty sure it was a sausage and cheese biscuit.

"I told you yesterday you don't need to come by every day," I said.

He paused at the table, staring at the pile of stones and my to-do list—that still needed to get done. I could tell by the way he tapped the table with one finger he was thinking through something. Maybe he was trying to decide if I was still worth the effort. Spoiler alert: I never was.

"It's fine," I said. "You really don't need to say anything."

He sharply turned, furrowing his brow at me. "It's not fine, Willa. I don't know why you expect me to drop off the face of the earth. I get you need space to grieve and prepare for Erma's funeral tomorrow, but to ask me to stop checking in on you? No. I will not. I'm giving you space. I'm not calling you every hour, but you can*not* expect me to stop caring."

"I know this is a lot." I waved at the stack of sympathy cards that'd come with casseroles. "And it's not like we had a lot of time to—"

He gripped my shoulders and shook me. "If you say we're not serious, I *will* get angry and insulted."

"But—"

"I know you're blaming yourself, and maybe even me a little, considering you slept over with me."

"We barely slept."

He smiled a little and enfolded me in his arms, his chin resting atop my messy hair. "I'm worried about you. You're not doing anything you normally do, and you don't even help out at TrixieCakes anymore."

"There's so much to do here still." I looped my arms around his middle and pressed my palms to his back, splaying my fingers. "And . . . I don't think I want to keep working there. Or maybe I should. I don't know what to do anymore."

"I can help, you know. And if you pull that crap about us barely being together again, I will not take you out for chorizo nachos tonight. For a week, at least."

I huffed, but it came out as a laugh. His arms were secure around me, soaking me in a warmth. I hadn't known I'd been cold a moment before. "I see you're choosing violence this morning."

"Drastic measures and all that, princess." He stepped back and motioned at the bag. "Eat that. Then take a shower, put on some clean clothes, and let me take you wherever you need to be today."

And so I did.

MIMZY HAD WANTED TO BE CREMATED, AND WHILE there was no viewing—she hadn't wanted that either—the pictures of her lacked the vibrancy she'd brought to a room. The urn was simple and final on a pedestal surrounded by flowers. The service took longer than I expected thanks to Mimzy's bingo activity. It was an ocean of geriatric attendees who murmured about what everything looked like, what was going to hell, and how many people had died already. There were plenty of speeches about the good times and a sad farewell.

I hadn't spoken at her funeral, but Trixie had. Rex sat beside me, sending concerned glances my way. It was kind of irritating. I wasn't some delicate flower; I was processing the biggest loss in my life. He didn't need to fix me. Honestly, I was trying to remember what I'd decided to do with all the flower arrangements. There were so many lilies, and Trixie couldn't take them because of their cat. Honestly, you'd think with people's inclination to make cats their familiars, florists would understand how dangerous lilies were in flower arrangements. At least they came with warnings in shops now.

"I don't think I've ever seen you glare this much," Rex murmured.

I blinked. We were at the community center that hosted the bingo games. The ball tumbler was on display with pictures of Mimzy and friends. And the troll dolls she always bitched about. Sitting across from me at the plastic table with a plastic cloth were Brandon, Shawn, and Candi. Trixie was somewhere taking care of things. Or crying because she'd mentioned she'd been putting on a brave face for the kids. Which I thought was bullshit. Kids needed to know it was okay to feel sad.

As an electrician, Brandon was hardly ever out of his work clothes, so it was odd to see him in a dress shirt and slacks. Yet somehow, I'd missed the fact my whole family had met Rex at a funeral. I peered at him sitting beside me, a plate of cookies and a shitty ham sandwich in front of him.

"I'm just thinking about what to do with all these flowers," I said, my fingers drifting up to touch the scalloped shell pendant hanging around my neck for the countless time today.

"Maybe you could get the funeral home to set them out around graves," Rex said, nudging the shitty sandwich toward me.

"Yeah, and give some to her friends." Brandon swiveled on his chair. "Those troll ladies were admiring a few."

I scowled.

"Woah!" Shawn said. "Are you trying to shoot lasers from your eyes?"

"Don't be stupid," Candi snapped.

Trixie approached the table at that moment with a plate full of fruit and frowned at me. "What happened?"

"Brandon suggested we give some flowers to the women who set up the trolls," I said.

Trixie laughed. "Mimzy hated those things, but it's a good idea."

I glared. "Really? After just saying she hated them?"

"Sweetie, why does it matter?" Trixie speared a piece of pineapple. "Mimzy bitched about the dolls, but the troll ladies were friends."

I sighed and shrugged. "Just trying to do right by her wishes."

Trixie scowled and shook her head. "We have. She didn't say anything about not giving Flo and Ro her funeral flowers. Do they have cats? We can give them those lilies over there if they don't."

Rex draped an arm over the back of my chair and rubbed my shoulder. I tensed, waiting for him to chime in, but he simply pushed the sandwich closer.

Brandon glanced between us, then stole a piece of fruit from his wife. "So how's that murder investigation going, Billie? Any new leads?"

I don't remember what I said, only that I knew for certain I would never investigate that again. It had caused too much grief. Hell, it was probably why Mimzy had that stroke. Sure, the doctors insisted a stroke wasn't uncommon, especially for someone her age. There was nothing that could've been done. But if I had been home, something could've been done. And I hadn't been home because of this murder investigation.

I counted down the minutes until everyone would shuffle off to the rest of their day. Candi had taken the car and her brother home. We stayed behind and cleaned up, wrapping up food, and donating the leftovers to the center. And some flowers.

Rex took me home, and I sat at the table in front of the pile of stones and crystals still sitting there from yesterday, wondering what the fuck I was supposed to do now with my life.

"Let's get out of the house," Rex said.

"I don't want to go anywhere," I murmured.

"Then come to my place and not go anywhere with me."

I shook my head.

"Willa, I think you need something else to occupy your brain." He sat beside me and cupped my shoulder. "What about the journals? Have you finished decoding them? We can pick—"

"For fuck's sake!" I slapped my hands on the table, rattling the crystals. "I don't want anything else to do with those fucking things, but if you want them, *fine!*"

I shoved from the table and stormed into my bedroom. The journals were in a stack on the desk, and I snatched them up. When I returned to the kitchen, Rex remained stiff in his chair, his mouth pursed tightly.

I slammed them on the table in front of him. "Take them and get them the fuck out of my house. I never want to see them again."

"Willa . . ." He lifted a hand in the air like he was warding me off. "I can't read these."

"Lucky for you, there're translating apps out there." I plopped my hands on my hips. "I'm done with this."

"I just want to help." He slowly rose from the chair, as if sudden movements from him could set me off. "I think you need to focus on something else right now, and if this isn't it, then we can find something else."

I huffed and cast my gaze to the ceiling, shaking my head. "I don't need your help, Rex."

He made a noise in the back of his throat. "What do you need, then?"

I took a beat. The air between us had become muddy with sour grief and a volatile oily mass dropping anchor and dragging against the bottom of my stomach. He didn't want that; I didn't want him to have that. I knew the moment I made the suggestion, he'd be upset, but I believed it was the best one right now.

"I think I need to be alone right now," I said.

"I think that's the last thing you need."

"I don't care what you think," I snapped, already regretting it. I winced and closed my eyes, taking a breath. "I didn't mean that."

When the silence between us stretched, I opened my eyes. He stared at me with an expression I had yet to see from him. Maybe it was pity or sympathy, but there was also betrayal lingering in his eyes.

"I'm sorry, Rex." I swallowed. "I do care what you think—a lot, actually. But I'm a real bitch right now, and I don't want to say anything else that might hurt your feelings. I don't want to say or do anything I can't take back."

He relented and nodded. A huge breath streamed from my lips. And while hot tears blurred my vision, I was so grateful he hadn't fought me further on being alone.

When he gathered the journals and headed to the door, I followed him, the relief I felt seconds ago dissolving into panic. But what was said was said, and maybe my apology wasn't as sincere as I'd thought it'd be.

At the door, he turned and pinned me with his piercing blue gaze. "Tonight, I'm going to leave you alone like you've asked, but don't even think for a minute I've given up on us." He shifted the journals to one arm and pressed a chaste kiss to my mouth.

I felt nothing. I almost began crying because if I'd felt nothing, it meant there was nothing to feel. But the kiss was over far too fast.

He leaned his forehead against mine. "I love you." And he pressed another kiss to my brow.

My heart gave a small thrum of warmth, and I smiled up at him, possibly the first real one I'd given him in weeks. "I love you too."

He kissed me once more, soft and lingering, and that bit of warmth grew to fill my entire chest.

"I'll call you tomorrow." Then he was out the door.

I turned and spent the rest of the evening finding all the crystals in the house and shoving them into boxes. After that, I deactivated my website by turning it private. It was time to face the music. I wasn't a medium. I was never meant to be one. I needed to find out who I was. All over again.

Chapter Thirty

The journals were enlightening, at least what I could read of them. I'd tried using the translator app Willa had told me about, but what I saw there and what was before me were different, it seemed. Based on Willa's translation and her thoughts, Nicholas Turner seemed like the next best suspect, and it was easy to find his current employer and address—it hadn't changed since Kendra last updated her journals.

It felt . . . I huffed, staring up at the high-rise building that was on the same side of Starglen as my penthouse. These last two weeks since Erma's death had been hard. Willa ghosted me, and when I came by the house—I texted first every time— was the only time she'd talk to me. And she'd ask me to leave all the time. She was grieving, she was depressed, and she was punishing herself.

I got the feeling she saw me as the punishment, but I didn't quite know how she came to that conclusion. Though anyone with two brain cells to rub together could guess it was guilt for being with me when Erma had passed. This really tied my hands. I wanted to be supportive and be there for her, but

I also wanted her to see me, to put in a little effort once more. But also, you know, the woman who raised her was suddenly gone, and she needed time to come to terms with it. Two weeks certainly wasn't enough.

The ghosting bothered me the most. If Willa wasn't in it with me any longer, I didn't want to be strung along. Now I was embarrassed for telling her how I felt. No matter how unexpected that confession had been, it was out there, and I had even doubled down on it.

I was frustrated. She shut me out with no warning or explanation, though I supposed a reason wasn't really needed. It was like she wanted me to forget she existed—that *we* existed. There hadn't been a sign at all that we'd make it through this yet. Perhaps I'd been fooling myself all along.

I stepped inside the building and noticed immediately the difference between my place and his. No doorman to bar my entry to the elevator—which I pressed the call button for. The lobby was nice, with a waiting area and a room with a keypad, which I assumed was for mailboxes and maybe entrance to the gym. The elevator dinged, and I stepped inside, pressing the button for the tenth floor, the second from the top.

I found Turner's apartment easy enough, and the door opened not long after I rang the bell.

"Can I do something for you?" the man said in a somewhat deep voice. A baby was fussing in the background. He looked at me, then past me into the hallway and back.

I smiled. "Nicholas Turner?"

He frowned. A dog barked and claws clicked on the wood floor, growing louder. The man glanced behind him and then stepped out, keeping the door barely open. "Yeah?"

"I'm Rex." I offered my hand, and when he took it, I continued, "I'm here to talk to you about Kendra Bruce."

He froze and stared at me once more, harder, deeper, his

brows converging over his nose and slanting angrily. He jerked his hand from my grip. "I don't know who that is."

"I beg to differ," I said. "I know you two had a standing appointment at the Eucalyptus on Pea Street."

Exactly as I expected, the moment I mentioned the pay-by-the-hour motel on the outskirts of the Nettles, Turner turned rigid and a vein bulged in his forehead.

His lips flattened, and he jabbed a finger in my face. "I don't know what you think gives you the right to come here and say vague shit like that, but you can leave."

"It doesn't seem like it was so vague."

"You know what isn't vague?" Turner pulled out his phone. "Me calling the cops right now if you don't fuck off out of my building."

I lifted my hands and backed away. While I knew this man was hostile about his arrangement with Kendra—though not hostile enough to stop it—I really didn't have any authority to demand he answer some questions about his arrangement with her.

He retreated inside his apartment and the deadbolt clacked into place.

Willa frowned at me, and the journals in my hands, from the other side of the storm door before she unlocked it, opening it. "What're you doing here?"

"Man, that seems to be the only reception I'm getting today," I said, forcing it to sound like a joke. "Can I come in?"

Her frown only deepened, but she gestured me inside. The TV had *Project Runway* playing on a low volume, and a family sized bag of Doritos with a pair of orange-stained chopsticks resting beside it sat on the coffee table next to a cup of soda. Her laptop sat open with a job search page up for seamstresses.

Willa crossed her arms and leaned against the pony wall that separated the entryway from the living room and pinched her golden shell pendant between her fingers. "So why didn't you text to say you were coming over?"

My brain spun through thoughts so quickly it made me dizzy. She wasn't happy to see me. As usual. I swallowed heavily. "Because you wouldn't have responded."

"No, I would've told you this wasn't a good time."

I stared at her. Her ivory skin was pale and slightly blotchy. I could tell she wasn't getting enough sleep. She'd left her hair in a messy braid, and she still hadn't changed out of her pajamas. Other than all the junk food, I didn't think she was eating, and I'd probably interrupted the one time she'd feed herself today. I pursed my lips at the chips; I supposed baby steps were baby steps.

I set the journals next to the chips, then sat along the arm of the sofa and pinched the bridge of my nose. "I've lost you, haven't I?"

She shifted uncomfortably on her feet, tilting her head slightly. She closed the door and flicked the lock. "Mimzy just died. I'm allowed to be moody."

"And you didn't answer my question, just like you don't answer my texts or calls. I have to come over here to get you to talk to me, Willa." I sighed and rested my hands on my thighs. "That's how I used to ghost people when I was no longer interested."

"We had sex. You got what you wanted." Her brows screwed up and her mouth took this condescending turn I'd never seen before. "Oh, am I still in your system? Do you want another go to—"

"Shut up, Willa." I clenched my fists and glared at her. "Don't you fucking dare finish that thought."

"'Cuz it'll hurt your feelings?" She sneered, or tried to, but tears welled in her eyes. "Afraid to get dumped by a Muted?"

The wind punched out of me, and it felt like my head was disconnecting from my body from how dizzy I'd become. "Is that what's happening here? Are you dumping me?"

Her chin crumpled, and she blinked rapidly. "I don't deserve you."

The way she said those words, like she couldn't breathe even thinking of saying them, that it almost hurt more saying them out loud than thinking them, stole the wind from my sails. A tear skipped down her cheek and fell to the floor.

"What makes you say that?" I whispered, afraid if I spoke at a normal level, she'd erect her walls again. But something inside me trembled—with rage or desperation. I couldn't tell.

She swiped at her cheeks and shuffled past me, sitting almost next to me on the couch. I turned to face her, aching to touch her, to comfort her, but I couldn't reach out to her. If I held her while she admitted we were done, I'd beg her to reconsider. And I wasn't sure if I was too proud or too hurt to beg.

She hugged herself. "It's just . . . When I was with you, no one else existed. I had no responsibilities, there was just you, and I loved it."

Despite the tears coating her voice, it felt so damned good to hear that. I slid off the armrest and onto the cushion beside her. "You didn't blow off work or anything for me."

"I know. I had carte blanche, but still." She swallowed and gazed blindly around the living room. "I felt like I had a place in the magical community, like a really good place, and you knew I'm Muted, but I still felt like I belonged."

"Of course you belong, princess," I murmured.

She sent me a small smile and knotted her hands together, staring at her fingers. "You don't get it."

I placed a hand over hers. "Will you help me understand?"

Her shoulders heaved with the huge breath she took. "Because I can't use or see ley energy, I don't fit in with those circles." She glanced at me. "My looks get me further than some, but in the end, most people brush me off. But the other side of that coin is that I *can* and *do* practice with enchantments, and I'm pretty damned good at it. Just look at this mess we're in now. But that also means I'm *too much* for the Muted community."

"I don't understand." I tilted my head to get a better read on her expression. "How can you be too much for them?"

"There are some Muted, those of us born this way, that believe we were cut off from the ley energy for a reason." She shrugged. "They say ley lines are finite resource, and when all the magic is used up, there'll be no going back to that world. It's up to us to learn how to live without magic so we can guide everyone into the new era of only manmade technology."

My scoff shot past my lips before I knew I was reacting. "Magic isn't just going to disappear. No one in their right mind thinks that."

"It's all out there if you look for it." She snorted. "It's bunk, if you ask me. From everything I've seen, ley energy is a renewable resource, like the sun or wind or water. There aren't ever any ley shortages."

"And because you are a medium and a psychic, you don't fit in well with the Muted community here, and because you're Muted, you feel you can never truly fit in," I said.

She nodded.

"But I knew you were Muted, and I suspected it before there was no denying it."

"You also wanted in my pants." She sent me a wry smirk.

I frowned, her earlier comments still ringing in my head. "In the beginning, yes, but when you friend-zoned me, I just went with it."

"Okay, but you were still *really* friendly with me."

"You're being an idiot on purpose, aren't you?"

She reared back, glaring. "Excuse me?"

"I was falling in love with you—what do you think was happening? Ah, don't answer that." I sighed. "I have a reputation, I get it. All I'm trying to get at is that what does all of this —the communities you don't quite fit in to—have to do with me—with us?"

She vaulted off the sofa and strode around the coffee table and threw her hands up. "Because magic distracted me from who I am! It pulled me away from Mimzy. And because I didn't have magic to protect myself against those attacks, I couldn't be here for Mimzy when she needed me the most. If I'd had magic, she wouldn't have died alone!"

I could see some of the weight lifting from her shoulders, but also that her words were too heavy for herself. She covered her face and shook her head. I rose from the sofa and gently pried her hands away so I could look into her glassy amber eyes. I wiped a tear from her cheek.

"Oh, Willa," I murmured. "You're so magical, you don't even know how not to be. Even without ley energy, you have something magic doesn't."

She closed her eyes, but it didn't stop her from weeping.

I finally gathered her into my arms, and she didn't resist; she leaned into me. Some guilt trickled in that I was taking comfort from this embrace, so I kissed the top of her head. "Despite you not being here, Erma died with a loving family. Her grandkids and great grandkids didn't avoid her, and when you were all together, you guys were happy." I ran my hands down her back. "You were a real, loving family, all of you."

Her body quaked beneath my palms. "I just wished I'd been here."

"I know." I continued to rub soothing circles on her back, gently rocking her. "And she passed away in the middle of the night, in her sleep. Even if you had been here, that wouldn't have changed."

I winced. That hadn't come out the way I was thinking it, but Willa didn't pull away. She returned my embrace and wept. We stood there, quiet, while I watched some guy make jazz hands, or was he gesturing wildly at a model on the TV?

She shifted in my arms and stretched against me, planting a soft kiss to the underside of my jaw. "Do you have to be anywhere soon?"

"Nowhere important," I said.

"Will you sit with me?" she shyly asked, peeking at me from between her damp lashes.

I kissed the tip of her nose. "Of course."

When we settled on the couch, she curled against my side. I hadn't realized how starved I was for something like this, not until I finally had it. I wrapped my arm around her shoulders, determined to keep this. I could see, as long as we both worked together and put in the same amount of effort, we'd go far together. And all it took was me being too stupid in love with a woman to walk away when she'd given me the signs. And even now, after giving me those signs, Willa held on to me as fiercely as I did her.

"Did you read the journals?" she asked after a while.

"Yeah." I let out a humorless laugh. "I went to see Nicholas Turner, but he wouldn't talk with me."

"Ooo, yeah, I remember Kendra noted he was kind of mean." She tilted her head up and peered at me. "What did you say to him?"

"I asked about his meetings at the Eucalyptus."

She gasped and laughed. "You just went there?"

"I was in a hurry." I frowned. "I was polite."

"You didn't charm him."

"I'm not you."

"Oh please, Rex. You're charming when you want to be." She sat up straighter. "It requires a little more finesse than what you did. This is probably why everything went a little crazy with Oscar Mendez." She grinned and lightly poked me. "You have no chill."

I smiled at her and shrugged. "I think these guys open up better to pretty *female* faces."

"Maybe."

"Hey," I said after a moment, "will you talk to him?"

"No." She didn't even think about it. "I'm done with all of it."

"Oh, come on, princess. One last chat with him. It'll give you practice from the next time you have to investigate something like this."

She snuggled into me, nuzzling her cheek against my chest. "Nope. I deactivated my site and boxed up all my charms and crystals. This shit became too much, and I promised myself a long time ago I'd quit if it did. So I quit."

I stilled, a little stunned at hearing this. I understood that right now, this whole mess was dangerous, but Willa excelled in the psychic medium area of enchanting. I would've sworn it'd been a passion of hers; exactly like it had been her mother's.

"Besides," she continued, "now that I'm not doing this anymore, I won't get attacked. It's pretty much stopped anyway. Oh. I have your ley crystals in my bedroom. I'll get it for you before you go later."

"Yeah . . . I don't know about that."

"What do you mean?"

I craned my neck to peek at her face, since she wouldn't meet my eyes again. "Just because you stopped investigating doesn't mean whoever's attacking you will stop. You know things."

"I'm not really psychic." She rolled her eyes.

"You still know things." I bit my cheek, then went for it. "You know, Erma would want you to finish this."

She jerked her head up and scowled at me. "Don't do that."

"Remember she convinced you to keep doing this?" I asked.

She sighed and averted her face.

"I'm asking for your help, too, Willa." I nudged her chin. "I need your help. All of this stopped cold when you did, and I've read the journals. Well, I tried. Some of them don't make sense, and without you . . . Honestly, without you, nothing does."

"Why is this so important to you, Rex? What're you hoping will happen at the end of this?"

I exhaled heavily through my nose and shrugged. "I'll admit I'm worried what else might come of this, and if I can get ahead of it and keep most of my professional integrity intact, that'd be great, but that's not all. I'm worried about you. I don't think that simply saying you're done is going to stop whoever's attacking you. You're a liability even if you don't know who's behind this."

"All right, fine." She pushed away from me. "I'll help you with the journals."

"Really?"

"Yeah, but only because I love you and Mimzy would want me to finish what I started."

A warm burr opened in my chest and spread through my limbs. Grinning, I cupped her jaw and kissed her. I kissed her because I'd been lonely without her, because she'd said she still loved me and I'd thought I'd lost her. And when her lips parted beneath mine and she deepened our kiss, I gathered her closer and promised to never leave her side.

Chapter Thirty-One

When the elevator opened to the tenth floor the following day, an older woman pushing a stroller loaded up with a diaper bag and a sleeping baby was waiting to board. Rex and I stepped out to let the woman in.

"So Turner was hostile with you?" I asked as we approached Nicholas Turner's apartment.

"Yep." He tapped my arm to stop me. "I figure you'll charm his pants off, and I'll just follow your lead."

I hummed in the back of my throat, remembering what Rex had said about the interaction with Nicholas. It had sounded like it'd immediately gone bad.

I shook my head. "Why don't you wait right here instead?"

"Why?"

"Because I think if he sees you, he won't cooperate, no matter how sweet I talk to him."

He nodded. "That's understandable. I'll wait right here in case you need me."

I smiled, a little impressed he didn't even try to talk his way into the apartment with me; he'd simply accepted my logic and went with it. "I don't think you'll need to jump to my rescue, but I like knowing you'll be here."

I tucked my hair back and checked my shirt, making sure there wasn't anything on it, and rubbed the shell pendant before tucking it beneath my top. I hadn't kept up with laundry or if what I wore had stains all over it. Today, I'd fished out an old crewneck sweatshirt and jeans that were slightly too tight—they pinched my gut—and brushed my hair. This was the most put together I'd been in a long while, and while I felt like a mess, I also felt like I was more productive at the same time, and it felt good. I rang the bell.

The door opened immediately to a middle-aged man with slicked back hair and running gear on. "Did you forget something, Beth? Oh!" He smiled a little, his eyes traveling along my body before glancing down the hallway toward the elevator. "I thought you were my mother-in-law."

I pasted a friendly smile on my face. "Was that adorable baby in the stroller yours?"

"Yeah. Hank's a charmer, isn't he?"

"I wish I got to meet him. All I saw were chubby cheeks."

"Is there something I can help you with?" he asked.

"There is. I was hoping I could come inside and chat with you about it."

"By all means." He stepped back and waved me in.

I stepped inside a spacious apartment. A dog dozing in a crate lifted its head and woofed hello at me but laid its head back on top of its paws. From here, I could see the gray around its muzzle. An explosion of baby toys and furniture littered the living room. Balls, blankets, plushies, bottles, one of those bouncy things, and there was even a diaper casting a malignant odor in the air.

"I see Hank has complete control of the house," I said.

"Yeah. I stay at home to take care of him, and you'd think I'd be able to keep this place clean." He chuckled and rubbed the back of his neck. "So, what did you want to talk about?"

I clasped my hands together and faced him. "Here's the thing. I'm unfortunately involved in this mess with a . . ." I touched the tip of my fingers at the base of my neck and shrugged. "I've been contracted by this couple searching for their daughter—who we've found—but there's an issue with parts of her past."

Nicholas's brows smooshed together. "I don't know how I could help with that. I was never in a search and rescue department when I was a volunteer firefighter."

"It has more to do with the unexplained money she suddenly had."

He stilled, tilting his head, but his eyes darted to the door and back to me. "Who's the girl?"

"Kendra Bruce."

His face turned red before I could even finish saying her name. "No, I can't help."

"Wait, before you say you can't help, let me explain," I said, holding my hands up. "I think she was blackmailing you—hang on, just hear me out, please."

Nicholas strode toward the door, his footsteps heavy. "I don't need to hear anything more to know I can't help."

"Her parents don't understand," I blurted. "And they want to talk to you."

He froze, a look of horror etched on his face. "Do they really want to know what their daughter did? I'm sure if you figured out this much, you'll find the tapes and can just show them what their sweet daughter was doing. Yeah, it helped me, but it also broke me."

"What're you talking about?" I asked.

"The first time I met Kendra, it was at a dive bar near the Nettles. I'll admit I knew what I was doing when I picked her up, but she promised discretion. I assumed that's why she worked from that area."

"You were seeking legal advice?" I asked slowly.

He frowned. "She's a dominatrix. Except she subbed for me because my *wife* is always in control. Always." He clenched his fist. "She's a pharmaceutical lawyer. She's got big balls and isn't afraid to treat me like an opposing party."

A lightbulb went on in my head. "So Kendra let you boss her around."

"I even called her by my wife's name. Made her do all sorts of things." He snorted. "I swear it saved our marriage."

I gave him a small smile. "Oh, that's great."

"Yeah, except Kendra recorded it all and said if I didn't pay her a grand a week, she'd tell my wife." The muscle in his jaw pulsed. "So I used her"—his voice grew rougher the more he spoke—"and the more I used her, the more she tried to gouge me. But I fucking paid her." He stepped closer to me, anger radiating off him in waves of heat. "You're that psychic, aren't you? The one who found her body. It's all over the news feeds."

"Uh, yes, I managed to locate Kendra." I took a step backward to create some space between us.

"And you decided I was a good cash cow, didn't you?" he asked.

My heartbeat quickened. "I don't know what you're implying here."

"You want to blackmail me too, don't you?"

"Sir, I'm here to investigate a murder." I lifted my hands again, only this time to show they were empty. "Did you have anything to do with her murder?"

"I just fucked her, but I recognize her type." He lunged.

I yelped and stumbled away from him. The dog lifted its head and barked, but it was in its kennel and there was nothing the old pup could do. I backed away, but I was no longer directly in front of the door.

"You're making a mistake." I said, raising my voice. "I'm just here to determine if—"

"I can't!" He backhanded me.

Pain bloomed in my cheek. I cried out.

"I can't be a part of this." He blocked my exit and shrugged, as if helpless. "If my wife finds out, there's no going back. Everything will end, and I don't want my wife to find out."

"I won't tell your wife!" I sidestepped him as fast as I could, wanting to get away.

He grabbed my shoulder in a vise-like grip. "No. You won't tell anyone."

I wrenched away, but he grabbed my hair. I cried out as he spun me around and wrapped his hands around my neck. I kicked him. Something crashed against the door. I jerked my leg up to knee him in the groin while I clawed at his hands, but he jerked his hips out of the way and squeezed. His eyes deadened, like he didn't see me as a person anymore. His lips thinned and a vein in his forehead bulged as he choked the life out of me. Someone, I hoped Rex, banged on the door.

"Help!" I croaked.

The door splintered apart with a giant gust of wind, and Rex stood at the threshold huffing like the big bad wolf before stepping into the room. He took in the scene, his face turning red, and roared, "I'll fucking kill you!"

Wind shrieked and the dog howled. Toys pelted the walls, and the rainbow xylophone trilled an airy melody before it crashed against the window with a discordant clang.

The hands around my throat clenched harder. I kicked my feet. The wind wailed until it didn't.

It all sounded muffled in my ears. Despite all the air in the room, I was having a difficult time drawing it in. A gust of air whooshed around me and my attacker, its icy currents plucking at me to no avail. Nicholas's fingers loosened at the blast. Gasping, I clawed and my nails scratched at his hands, but he snarled and redoubled his efforts.

Rex grabbed him from behind, but Nicholas wouldn't let go. My neck ached, my throat burned, and my lungs struggled for breath. Nicholas strengthened his grip.

I can't breathe.

"El Diablo!" Rex slammed his hands together, then reached down and motioned.

My vision grew tunneled. At first, I wasn't sure what I was seeing. Nicholas continued strangling me, his eyes filled with determination and fury. A phantom hand, hazy with racing eddies of oxygen, smothered Nicholas's face. Then he arched back, his hands leaving me, and we both gasped for air. I rolled away, panting. That ethereal hand had been the same one to suffocate me in the Flower Market.

Wind tore through the apartment. The dog barked and barked. Rex moved his arms like he was pulling something from Nicholas like a mime tugging on a nebulous and hazy rope from his throat. The more his breathing worsened, the more I realized Rex was stealing the air from my attacker. Nicholas's eyes rolled back, and he collapsed at my feet.

The air died down and Rex rushed to me, gently pulling my hands from my neck. I wheezed, trying to catch my breath as I gaped from Rex to the prone man on the floor.

"You killed me." Kendra's breathless accusation ricocheted against my brain.

My heart thrashed in my raw throat. I'd had visions of this during the gentle possession with Kendra. Of someone stealing the very breath from my lungs—exactly like Rex'd done to Nicholas Turner. I stared in horror at him, then slowly looked back to Rex, all the pieces clicking into place.

Black, fuzzy dots formed before my eyes as my racing heart

sped faster. I'd been such an idiot. It was there this whole time. Kendra had played Rex for a fool for years. But the last straw for him had been when she'd became engaged to Julian, his lifelong rival, without even letting Rex know their relationship was over first. And Rex had snapped.

Kendra had been telling me all along how she'd died, but I hadn't listened. Not with Rex doing whatever he could to make sure I never pointed a finger at him. And if I did . . . Well, I certainly couldn't stop him now.

"Willa!" Rex pulled me to my feet. He inspected my neck, his hands skimming over my body while he looked me over.

He continued saying things, but my ears were ringing from the realization of what he'd done. I stared at Nicholas's prone form on the floor. The dog continued to bark.

"Did you kill him?" I croaked.

He shook his head. "He's only unconscious. Are you okay?"

I rubbed my throat, frowning at him and Nicholas. "That was how Kendra died."

Rex's brows knitted together. "No, it was ley energy that caused her death, not manual strangulation."

I moved toward the broken-down door. People were coming around to see what happened. "No, not that." I motioned at Nicholas. "That was how she died."

Rex jerked as if I'd dumped a bucket of ice water over him. "No, Willa, no. Don't go there."

"It was you, wasn't it?" My heart pounded. I could tell this was rapidly getting away from me, that I'd lose control any moment, and I didn't know how to stop it. I had to leave. I needed to get out of here and far, far away.

"No." He approached me, keeping his hands up to let me know they weren't a threat. But that didn't matter for a practitioner like him, did it? "No, Willa, I see your brain's going down a rabbit hole. I promise I had nothing to do with it."

I shook my head at him. "Don't follow me."

Then I turned and pushed through the first crush of people and ran down the hallway. He called after me, but I didn't stop. I had to get out of there, but I also expected a hand formed from air to stop me from taking another step again.

How the hell had I manage to fuck my entire life up by falling in love with a murderer?

Chapter Thirty-Two

I stared at the screen, not really seeing what was in front of me. I hadn't slept well, I hadn't gone to the gym, and I was certain I was in sugar withdrawal. All I could see was yesterday playing over and over.

Hearing the struggle from the other side of the locked door. The yelling . . . and then there was no yelling. My blood had never been colder or hotter at the same time. When my first couple of shoulder checks did nothing for the deadbolt, I blew the fucking door down.

My back teeth clenched, the familiar ache returning to my jaw. I tried to take a calming breath to return my breathing to normal, but I was in the moment. Seeing Turner straddling Willa, her feet kicking between his legs as she fought for her life. The pen I'd gripped bent in my grasp. I don't think anyone could come away from that sight and not react, not be haunted by it later in their sleep.

No, the expression on Willa's face when I rendered Turner unconscious stayed with me more. Large, amber eyes regarding me with condemnation while she rubbed her throat.

The red marks left there by someone else—but me? *I* was the monster in front of her.

"It was you, wasn't it?"

I closed my eyes and swallowed down the lump lodged in my throat and threatening to gag me. I'd fucking bared myself to her. I'd given myself to her. And she threw it away. Threw me and us away. I'd felt nothing like this before, not even when I came home that one day, finding Kendra hastily packing her belongings and resembling a deer in headlights when I walked through the door. Admitting she'd gotten herself engaged to another man before leaving me. No, back then, I'd felt resignation and later relief.

I wondered if I'd ever find anyone who believed I was worth being loyal to.

My phone went off and, looking for anything to distract me from the image of Willa's horrified expression, I pulled it out.

THE BOYS
DANE MCKEE

We're booking Trixie for a tasting. Little surprised you aren't here

Riddle me this: Is the relationship over if one person accuses the other of murder?

THE BOYS
ERIC ABRAHAM

You're fucking with us

THE BOYS
DANE MCKEE

She did what?

Swallowing, I slouched in the chair and typed out a short and dirty summary of what had happened yesterday.

THE BOYS
DANE MCKEE

Do you want us to use someone else?

THE BOYS
ERIC ABRAHAM

WTF?

THE BOYS
DANE MCKEE

I don't have a problem taking our business
somewhere else. Really.

No way do I want you guys to give up the
wedding cake. This is just between me
and her

Someone knocked softly at the door before it opened. I glowered at Molly and wondered if she ever opened the door when Guy sat behind this desk, or if I was special. I straightened, ready to indulge my bad mood and get some of this hostility out of me, but I saw Detective Johnston hovering behind her.

What now?

But I knew what was going on now. Yesterday had been warning enough that I'd see the detective today. I stood and stepped around the desk. Whatever was going to happen today, I didn't want to be sitting for it.

"Mr. Slater, Detective Johnston's here," Molly said.

I met the detective's eyes and nodded to the assistant. "Close the door behind you."

Detective Johnston stepped farther into the room, and I gazed longingly at the wet bar on the far side of the office, wondering if it was too early or if she'd frown on liquid-induced steadiness.

"Detective," I said. *Should I ask if it was Nicholas Turner or Willa who pointed her to my office?* That was probably a bad idea. "How can I help you today?"

Johnston glanced toward the wet bar and back to me, a brow lifted. I supposed I was too transparent in where my thoughts went right then.

I gestured to the chair. "Feel free to sit."

"Feel free to make a drink," she countered, but didn't sit.

I shrugged. I could do this all day, beating around the bush, but I doubted she had the time for it.

"Okay, as you know, Kendra Bruce's death was ruled a homicide," she said.

I nodded.

"We are recreating the timeline, with Kendra Bruce engaged in an affair with Julian Christensen and you—"

"As the jilted boyfriend?" I strode across the office to the wet bar. "Yes, no surprise."

"Did you have any idea she and Christensen were together?" Johnston asked.

I sighed, plucking a large cube of ice and dropping it into a rocks glass. "I never put names to Kendra's lovers."

"So you knew she was having an affair?"

I peered at Johnston over my shoulder before adding ice to a shaker and measuring out whiskey, sweet vermouth, and bitters. I stirred, the ice rattling against the sides. "Of course. That's how Kendra was then, when we were young and stupid."

"She had more than one?"

I laughed as I strained the Manhattan into my glass. "She had many boyfriends, but the unspoken rule was she always came home to me."

I hadn't meant to say it like that. There were no such rules, but that was how it'd played out all those years ago. She'd get her kicks, come home to me, play sweet and loving until we had a fight, rinse and repeat.

"And you?" Johnston prompted. "I understand you weren't exclusive, either."

I glanced at the cherries and declined to add any, then wandered back to my desk. "Eh, I wasn't. No. Whenever I found out she was cheating, I paid her back with my indiscretion."

"So you both were cheating on each other." Johnston tilted her head. "How did Kendra like that?"

I sipped my drink and flashed a wolfish grin at the detective. "Half the time it put us in a vicious cycle of cheating, accusing the other of cheating, and then revenge cheating. But, in the end, we always came home to one another. We always made up."

"So you were fine with her sleeping with other people as long as she never left you." Johnston made a note in a notebook, then regarded me with calculating eyes. "I suppose when she told you she was leaving you for Julian Christensen, that was considered a rule break for you."

"It was the end of our relationship, yes," I said.

"How did you feel about your girlfriend leaving you for your rival?"

Jesus, I'm so fucking sick of this question. "A little freeing." I sipped my drink. "If Julian wanted her that bad he proposed, he could have her. I hadn't realized it at the time, but our relationship was exhausting, and when she left me for good, I could concentrate on what I wanted."

"Is that so?" Johnston smirked. "And maybe what you really wanted to do was take the very air from her lungs."

I stiffened, flashing back to Turner's wide-eyed expression when I stole the air from his lungs until he passed out. The red marks from his fingers around Willa's neck. Her fearful expression.

"No," I said harshly. "Kendra was dead to me when she left."

"Then you made sure she was dead only six months after she left you," Johnston said. "That's when you really came into your own."

"What?" I jerked toward her, startled, my fingers clenching around the glass. "No."

"Yesterday, Nicholas Turner was attacked in his home," Johnston said. "He told us all about you coming by the day prior and what you did yesterday."

"Did he also mention he was strangling my girlfriend at the time?" I slammed my glass on the desk and wanted to hurt someone all over again. I wished I hadn't used magic to contain him; I wished I'd used my own hands just like he'd used his.

Her expression remained bland, but something told me she hadn't heard about that yet. Which meant Willa hadn't gone to the police or told them she believed I was the killer.

"We'll follow up with her. Who is she?" Johnston asked.

I stared, not at Johnston but at my thoughts, a little surprised. Willa really hadn't said anything about her suspicions of me being a murderer. At least not yet. I was certain she was on the list for the detective to talk to.

"Oh. Willamina Dade." She shook her head, jotting something else down in her notebook. "The psychic. Tell me, do you put much stock in what she can see now, or is this relationship something else you're going to have to 'take care of?'"

I frowned at her. "Willa's predictions have been spot-on."

"Sure."

"What're you implying?"

"You haven't heard?" Johnston snatched the remote off my desk for the wall-mounted TV and turned it on. After a few flicks, she paused on a live streaming station, which had a large picture of Willa in her full costume with a red circle with a slash through it—the universal sign she was Muted.

My jaw dropped open. *Oh no. This is terrible.* Willa was a

damned good medium. She didn't fuck around, and she understood the way crystals and séances worked like no one else I've ever crossed paths with. I quickly went through my list to see if anyone I knew was aware of her status. I'd kept it hidden; it hadn't been my secret to tell, and honestly, I hadn't thought it important enough to declare. Dane and Eric wouldn't leak this, either. They'd encouraged me to talk to her after I'd explained what'd happened between us.

"You didn't know," Johnston said, a note of glee in her voice.

My attention snapped back to the detective, and I scowled. "I knew she's Muted."

"When did you find out?"

"I don't know." I grabbed my phone, looking for messages from her, but of course there weren't any. Though there were many from Guy and the boys. "Maybe a month or so ago."

"Is that before or after your relationship started?"

"How is this relevant?" I asked.

"I guess you could say I'm filing this away in case Willamina Dade has a mysterious disappearance just like Kendra Bruce."

"This is insulting," I said.

"So's murder, Mr. Slater." Johnston tucked her notebook in her pocket. "I need to know where you were the night of Kendra Bruce's murder."

"I was at a club, no doubt." I scowled. "This was a long time ago. I don't even know if I was in town or not."

"I'll need receipts." Johnston headed for the door and then stopped, facing me. "And if this isn't clear, Mr. Slater, don't leave town. Look into a lawyer. The next time we chat, we'll be in my office."

Something told me her office was an interrogation room.

I glared at the TV longer than I realized. The host went on and on about how she was fooling everyone and her involvement with Kendra's murder. My face came up on the screen, and then there was a somewhat blurry picture of us that night on our date at Flemming's. The flowers, the balcony, we were laughing over ice cream with my fucking quote about Muted at the bottom.

They discussed all of Slater Technologies' deals—my involvement with the charms and my work for the company, engineering weapon-grade enchantments which someone mysteriously smuggled to the criminal underground.

"Fuck." I leaned against the desk, staring at the images, no longer reading the ticker or the captions running along on the bottom of the screen.

It seemed when I wasn't paying attention, my family's company became the big bad, and I was the number one suspect for Kendra's murder.

The door to my office opened and Guy strode through. He'd slicked his hair back and dressed as if he hadn't missed a day of work in his life. He took one look at me and the hostility radiating off him diminished by fifty percent.

"Well, I see I don't need to go into detail," he said, moving to the wet bar and cleaning up.

"What?" I asked, still dazed by everything I learned.

"You've got some balls, Hendrick." Guy quickly made himself a drink. "I never thought you'd throw your own family under the bus, but here we are."

"What are you talking about?"

"You." Guy turned and lifted his Manhattan to me. "And Kendra. Let me guess. She discovered you were the one leaking all the information and threatened to tell me about it, and you did the only thing you could—you killed her."

"Don't be ridiculous," I said, straightening. "Besides, you were the one killing familiars. And . . . attacking Willa." The light went on the moment the words came out of my mouth. "You were the one, weren't you? All the water stuff stopped when the broken spirit stones came to light. It was you."

Guy waved a hand. "It was nothing serious, but I suppose to a Muted it was a huge deal."

"Nothing serious? Are you fucking around with me right now?" I strode to him and shoved his shoulder, the drink sloshing onto the back of his hand. "She was terrified!"

"And you were there to make sure she was safe." Guy flicked excess whiskey off his hand. "I know you're fucking her, even after I told you explicitly not to. Anyway. That's over. You've had your fun. Now you need to—oh, you're still going on about how you didn't kill Kendra, aren't you?"

Rage roared in my ears. I wanted to see some blood. I grabbed him by the lapel and shook him, pushing my face into his. I felt the breath stutter out of him and flutter on my face. "For the last fucking time, I. Did. Not. Kill. Kendra Bruce!"

I realized then that no matter what I said, no matter how fervently I denied it, Guy would never believe me. It'd always been like this. There was a huge age gap between us, and Guy had immediately taken on the role of an estranged father, when I didn't want or need him as that. He treated me like he needed sterile gloves before handling me, and I was done playing nice to him.

I was done rolling over to show my belly to a family that treated me as a stain first and an afterthought second.

Before Guy could react, I pushed him away from me, wiping my hands on my jacket. I strode to the desk and snatched up my phone.

"Fucking Christ, Hendrick. You need to control that temper of yours, especially now." Guy moved to block my exit. "And you're going to have to take a sabbatical from work. Shame you can't leave town, but as long as you keep your head down, we should be able to keep one of our contracts . . ."

I stared so hard at him he paused, looking me over again.

Then he cracked something like a crooked, sympathetic smile and lightly punched my shoulder. "Oh, don't be mad. You were never meant for the CEO chair here, anyway. Alexa will take it."

Alexa, his and Lynne's youngest and only ACE child. Perry had known this was the case, just as I knew I'd never belonged with the Slaters. Only Perry had enough sense not to try as hard as I had.

"Yeah . . . I never thought we were ever a good fit—all of us." I pushed him aside—I was done walking around them—and left the office.

The urge to smash something until my knuckles bled held me in a chokehold, so I went to the gym and took it out in the only way that wouldn't land me behind bars.

Chapter Thirty-Three

I always knew there'd be more to the man I fell in love with than met the eye. I simply hadn't counted on murder. Or sabotage—but at least I'd already set my website to private before Rex had outed me to the world. I used to love watching those documentaries about the women who love serial killers and marry them while they're in jail. It was entirely too unconventional and wild to me. The man literally played a scavenger hunt with body parts, and you, a woman who resembled his victims, married him?

There's only so much you can change about a person, and being a psychopath isn't one of those things.

I'd assumed, thanks to my need to have an emotional bond to catch feelings for a person, that I was safe from this. But there I was, a couple days after Turner tried to kill me, trying to discover what Rex'd done that made Kendra blackmail him. Because the man I knew had to be pushed to violence. Perhaps it really had been all her cheating that finally made him snap.

Or maybe it truly was as simple as Kendra left Rex for Julian, which only intensified their lifelong rivalry. *Maybe* Rex saw her only as a possession, and when someone else dared to play with her, he killed her.

I scrubbed a hand over my face and screwed my eyes shut against the blurry swoops and darkened lines of shorthand, a headache creeping into my temple. None of that sounded like the Rex I knew. He wasn't the jealous type—*but* he had told me to stop encouraging Julian when he knew that was not my motive with anyone. My fingers sought and found the golden shell pendant and played with it. Maybe . . . Maybe I never really knew Rex at all.

The bell over the door chimed, and I looked up from the journals I was combing through, decoding twice to make sure I knew what I was reading. Looking for something, anything, that confirmed I was right and had not, in fact, made the biggest, most colossal mistake of my life by accusing Rex of murder.

But there really hadn't been a difference, though I'd discovered Kendra sucked at spelling. And nothing about Rex. I might puke.

Dane and Eric approached the counter, and my heart nearly jolted out of my chest. I almost didn't recognize them without their pastry chef coats on, but here they were. Rex's best friends in my cousin's bakery. Oh joy.

"Oh," Eric said, his smile registering as polite, and that was as far as I'd take it. "Hi, Willa."

Dane wouldn't meet my eye, pretending he was more curious about what the special cupcake was today. It was an orange poppy with a bumblebee's butt in the air like it'd fallen in, but an enchanted edible gem was its bottom.

"Hi." I smiled and stepped away from the journals. "How're you two?"

"We're fine." Eric glanced at his fiancé, then back to me. "Is Trixie in the back? We have an appointment."

I mentally gasped. They were really considering hiring

Trixie to do their wedding cake. I knew Eric had to be over the moon about it, but Dane . . . He wouldn't even acknowledge me.

"Yeah, I'll go get her."

I pushed through the swinging door to the kitchen to find Trixie placing the finishing touches on a few cupcakes for a geode effect with the enchanted edible gems as the rock candy.

"I've got butter cake, genoise, gâteau, and that one's olive oil." She regarded me before adding a couple more. "How do they look?"

"They look great." Then I leaned in and lowered my voice. "Why didn't you tell me Rex's friends were coming in today?"

"I totally didn't even think about that when they came in yesterday to set up the appointment." Her attention darted to my neck, where I'd hidden the bruising with a thick concealer. I'd told her everything that'd happened. "Will this be difficult for you?"

At least Rex wasn't with them. I swallowed the lump forming in my throat and patted the skin under my eyes. It felt puffy, but my makeup hid most of the evidence of my tearful, sleepless nights. "I'll manage."

"I'm almost done." Trixie bent over the cupcakes, concentrating on the finishing touches.

I returned to the front of the store. Dane and Eric were examining the bee cupcakes, Eric whispering something in his ear. Dane smiled. I'd only ever seen these two while they worked, and to see them in their free time was . . . different. Dane seemed relaxed.

"She'll be right out." I grabbed my pen and returned to scanning the pages of the journal, looking for any reason to settle my conscious. How could Kendra not even mention him? And, my God, what if he was truly innocent? I gave myself whiplash from this back and forth. What I'd witnessed two days ago proved that Rex certainly had the means and the motive to kill Kendra the way she had died. But my heart adamantly insisted I was wrong.

I wanted to be wrong.

What should I say? Would it be considered poor form to ask about Rex? Do I deserve to know? Do I want to know? He was a murderer. Last night, the news mostly discussed about why he had stepped down from Slater Technologies as the temp CEO. Because he was being investigated for not only for Kendra's death, but also for selling military-grade charms through the black market in the Nettles.

They'd also discussed my Muted status with a blurry photo of our date at Flemming's. They didn't reveal who passed the information to them, merely cited "credible sources." I snorted and crossed out a mistranslation in my notes so hard the tip of my pen tore through the paper. *Sources.* If Rex wanted to shift some attention off himself, yelling to the world that I was Muted was one way to do it. But it'd failed. He'd forgotten about how many closeted ley purists there were in the world, that they'd judge him for his interest in me. Hello, sabotage, meet my friend self-sabotage.

I desperately needed to find an entry in these journals that linked Rex to finally losing his shit and killing Kendra. *Oh Willamina, you idiot.*

Eric drifted closer to me, checking out the giant peanut butter cookies, and I took a chance.

"Is Rex . . .?" *Capable of murder? In jail? Is he . . . okay?* But I couldn't ask any of those questions because I should've already known the answers.

As soon as I said his name, Dane's head snapped in my direction and his dark brows slanted angrily.

"Is Rex what?" he demanded. "In jail? Not yet. No thanks to you."

After I'd left Rex at Nicholas Turner's apartment, I'd returned home and had a major meltdown. The next evening,

Detective Johnston visited me. I answered her questions about Turner's attack truthfully. Then I pressed charges against him. Purely because she'd assumed the bruises on my neck were from Rex, and I'd set her straight. I would not be a victim of Rex Slater, especially since he was behind Kendra's murder. Wasn't he?

I shook my head, deciding not to pursue this. It shouldn't matter if Rex would be okay or if he'd recover from this. Even if he'd leaked to the entire world I was Muted, he was fine. Hurting, but fine. And what about me? I should be angry, considering he outed me. Instead, I stressed over his emotional and mental state. Jesus, I still loved him. I was no better than those women marrying serial killers.

Trixie breezed through the door, carrying a plate with the geode cupcakes on it. She took in the three of us and smiled even brighter. "Hey guys! What do you think?"

"Oh wow!" Eric said, nudging Dane and taking the plate from her. "These are amazing."

"I know you're not a fan of cupcakes," Trixie said, sending an abashed expression to Dane. "But this is the easiest way for me to let you get a good sample of the texture of the cake, the design, and the frosting."

I put my head down, refocusing on reading through Kendra's journals between serving customers. Trixie and the boys laughed a lot, jotting down ideas and even sketches. I didn't dare try to enter the conversation when I clearly wasn't welcome.

"Rex did it for you."

I jerked my head up, surprised to find Dane standing at the counter.

"Excuse me?" I stepped behind the register, using it as a barrier.

"He didn't believe that scumbag would stop fighting, so

he knocked him out." Dane lifted his brows and gestured at my neck. "For you. He did that to protect you."

Eric squinted at us, a box in his hand, before returning his attention to Trixie and the paper they were drawing on.

I rubbed my sore throat and shuddered. "I know you don't believe me when I talk about gentle possessions, but every time Kendra Bruce's spirit was near me, I had that same sensation of losing my breath. Exactly what Rex did to Turner, so I don't know what else I'm supposed to believe."

"You believe him," Dane hissed. "You believe he isn't a murderer because he isn't. Rex might come off as an asshole sometimes, but that's the worst offense he's ever committed. When Kendra left him, he was hurt, yes, but he's not the person to resort to murder over a broken heart."

"A peanut butter jar instead?" I asked, smirking.

Dane stared at me, shock and anger warring on his face. "Yeah, exactly. That you know him so well and you still chose to believe he'd hurt her baffles me."

"I wish I were wrong, but I saw what I saw, Dane." I pulled the journal over to me and flipped to the next page. A queasy sensation that'd taken place in the background pushed forward and turned over, and I took a breath to settle my stomach. It didn't help. "His entire motive is covered in these pages."

"You're going to take this too far, aren't you?" Dane narrowed his eyes. "Don't believe Kendra's lies about Rex in that damn diary of hers. She was never loyal to him."

I opened my mouth to protest, but the bell above the door jingled again, and Flo and Ro stepped inside. Dane returned to the table with Trixie and Eric.

"We heard you were attacked!" Flo hustled to the counter.

Ro was more interested in the display cases. "We had to come by and make sure you were okay . . ."

I closed the journals and set them aside. "You came here to check on me?"

"Well," Ro said, "we also wanted another go at these cakes since the ones at the funeral were really good."

Flo reached out and squeezed my hand. "It was a lovely service. Erma was always so proud of you." In a louder voice, she called, "And you too, Beatrice."

"Thank you." Trixie forced a smile; she hated being called by her full name. She returned her attention to the consultation.

"And poor Willamina," Flo continued, "being caught up in that ghastly affair with the Bruce girl and that Slater bastard."

Trixie gasped. The boys stiffened.

I jerked my hand back. "Don't call him that."

"Well, honey, what do you call a person born out of wedlock?" Ro tapped on the glass. "Gimme that peanut butter and raspberry thumbprint."

"You respect he's a person, just like you." I crossed my arms. "Honestly, that stigma of having sex *and* having a child outside of marriage is old. Real old. No one cares these days unless some old white man in a dress with a fat book tells you to."

Flo snorted. "You know, to be honest, I always thought it was weird."

I shook my head, not wanting to encourage the conversation, and set to straightening behind the counter. I could feel Dane's and Eric's gazes on me.

"What's weird?" Ro asked, unfazed by my outburst.

"Oh, that the Bruce girl suddenly left Hendrick Slater for Luther Christensen's son." Flo fiddled with the napkins.

"And why's that?"

"Oh, well, because back in our day, before those boys were

around, Luther wasn't much better than a thug, and he raised his son in his image." Flo set her purse on the counter.

"Oh yes," Ro said. "I remember there being some kind of trade war or something between Luther and the elder Slater. What's his name?"

"Alvin," Flo supplied.

Ro snapped her fingers. "Right. They were in the same business, almost. They used to sabotage each other."

Dane made significant eye contact with me. "When we were at Fulton, Rex had a presentation on the fall of the Roman empire. He even had a miniature diorama. Julian"— he curled his fingers in the air—"accidentally knocked into the table and sent it crashing to the floor. Then the jerk stepped on it."

Ro grunted. "Sounds like a Christensen. Hey, Billie. My cookie!"

"I'm sure the teacher didn't hold that against Rex." I kept my feet planted where they were. The troll ladies didn't deserve that cookie.

Dane shook his head. "They weren't there when it happened. And Rex trashed it. There was no saving it. And when it was time to present, the teacher docked him two grades for not completing the assignment, even though he told the teacher what had happened."

"That's ridiculous." Eric frowned. "Why didn't he show them the trash?"

"He did," Dane said. "And Julian swore up and down he saw Rex do it because he hadn't finished his assignment."

Trixie left the table, boxing up more treats and giving them to the boys. Then she handed me a boxed-up thumbprint cookie—the recipe I'd cobbled together for Rex weeks ago—and significantly angled her head at the troll women.

Dane held up his box. "Thanks for this, Trixie. We'll be in contact with the colors soon."

"And the display!" Eric said.

They left the bakery with one of the giant peanut butter cookies, and I knew it was meant for Rex. My heart ached and my throat throbbed. I wanted to cry, but even doing that felt overwhelming.

Instead, I rang the trolls up and forced a smile. "So what kind of war was it? Between the Christensens and Slaters?"

"Oh." Ro smacked her lips. "Somethin' about ley crystals?"

"No," Flo said. "Alvin accused Luther of stealing a prototype for a police baton. The ones that channel a person's ley energy into solid air or something, so they could render suspects immobile from a distance."

"What happened with that?" Trixie asked.

Both women frowned. I knew it couldn't have been that bad because the police used them to this day.

"You know, I think the case was dropped," Flo said. "But then Luther introduced the world to the ley baton a few years later and opened his company."

They left shortly after that.

"Hey," Trixie said, coming around the counter and wrapping an arm around my shoulders. "I'm so sorry. I should've warned you Eric and Dane were coming."

"It's okay." I rapidly blinked back tears and returned the side hug. "I'm glad they reached out to you. Rex said he was going to suggest you to them."

"That was nice of him," she said, sounding a little unsure.

"I don't understand it!" I grabbed the journal. "She's talked about her parents, her familiar, and all these men, but she never mentions Rex. She's talked about the Christensens, about their home and lifestyle, but why not Rex?"

"Maybe by the time she was writing them, she'd already

decided to leave him and was just holding out for the right time." Trixie opened the case and began consolidating the remaining baked goods together. "We can't always know who people are by their journals."

"I need to figure out why I was blind to him. How was I so fooled by him? Maybe then I can stop feeling all this guilt for leaving her that night."

Trixie straightened and observed me. "You're rarely ever blind to someone's charms, Billie, and you're not to blame for Mimzy's death. It was a stroke. It would've happened even if you were there. Please stop punishing yourself for living your life."

ANOTHER FEW DAYS LATER, TRIXIE AND ERIC SAT AT one of the small pale pink tables, scrolling through design inspirations. Dane hadn't been able to get away from Icing again, and left this to Eric since there was no longer a debate about flavors thanks to the edible charms.

While they knew what style they wanted, it was the color of the frosting and the edible charms they needed to decide on. There were discussions about favorite colors being too similar to a summer pool party, no matter what design with the edible charms they chose.

The bell over the door jingled and a sophisticated woman with silver-streaked black hair stepped in. At a glance, she appeared classy, wearing slacks with a striped sweater that hinted at bare shoulders and makeup that appeared like she wasn't wearing any. She adjusted her white and gray checkered bag, and I caught a glimpse of pastel pink lining when she hitched it higher on her shoulder.

I'd coveted that Louis Vuitton bag. It'd go with all my outfits. It was stylish and screamed money without seeming gaudy or flashy. And it'd hold my chest of crystals with room to spare for my wallet or—No. None of that mattered anymore.

I tore my gaze from the bag and smiled as she approached the counter. "Hi there! Welcome to TrixieCakes!"

She smiled, her blue eyes sweeping over me, but then frowned at my chest. I suddenly had the urge to cross my arms over my breasts, but I wasn't indecent. I never was with the girls. She paused at the counter, watching Trixie and Eric, who hadn't lifted his head, before she scanned the rest of the shop.

"Can I help you with something?" I asked.

Her eyes flicked to my chest again, a wrinkle forming between her brows. She focused on the big sign for TrixieCakes behind me, then my tits again.

Frowning, I peeked down. Just in case, you know? What if a hole appeared? Or, I don't know, sometimes the girls had a mind of their own and tried to wrestle the apron I wore. But no, that wasn't the case. My apron was sitting normally, there wasn't chocolate or custard smeared all over them, and my embroidered name tag was visible. My necklace was hidden, so I pulled the golden shell pendant out.

"I'm sorry." The woman smiled. "I'm looking for Willa. Your description matches her, but . . . Are you her sister, maybe?"

I laughed, understanding now. She'd been confused by my nametag, which read Billie.

At that moment, Eric turned toward us and beamed. "Mae! How lovely to see you." He rose and gave her a warm hug.

Mae grinned and patted Eric's cheek. "You get more handsome every day."

"And you get younger." He released her and faced me. "Willa, this is Mae Greer, Rex's mother."

Ice flooded my stomach, and my mouth worked like a fish

trying to breathe outside of water. I'd heard of her, more that she'd never get in the way of Rex's father, but I hadn't realized how young she was compared to the Slater patriarch. She appeared like she was in her early fifties, but something told me there was a lot of skin care behind that. And the math didn't add up.

I plastered a smile on my face. "Oh, it's lovely to meet you."

Trixie stared at me with wide eyes. Yeah, this was definitely going to be awkward. I wondered if Mae would berate me for believing what I'd personally witnessed. She wouldn't be the first one; by now I was wondering if what I saw was even real. Then again, spell workings were passed around. Rex surely couldn't be the only air caster who could steal air. Hadn't he mentioned a drill instructor had done something similar when he was serving?

She brushed an invisible strand of hair from her face, a friendly smile tilting her lips. "I know I'm breaking the rules, but I'm worried."

"What rules?" I peered at Eric.

His brows rose and his pleasant expression froze. "Oh, you're here for Willa?"

She nodded, patting his arm. "I'm sorry. I know I said I'd help with the cake, but I didn't think you needed my opinion. Just send me the bill."

"Mae," Eric said gravely, "you're not paying for our cake."

She made this noise in the back of her throat, something I've heard when someone craved a sticky bun and all we had were cinnamon rolls. She pursed her lips. "Let's not get into that right now." Then she faced me. "I was hoping I could have a few minutes of your time."

I nodded, not really wanting to be alone with her for many reasons that I was certain everyone in this shop except Mae was aware of. Eric gave me a tight smile and returned to the table with Trixie.

So I took the coward's way. "I can't leave the register unattended."

"That's fine, honey." She stood at the register, examining me. "I see why Rex likes you so much. You're beautiful. Definitely his type."

The heavy, tight feeling of my insides freezing abated some. She'd called him Rex, which meant she loved him. Which, you know, I'd hoped for. The rest of his family called him Hendrick and always treated him like extra baggage.

"Oh, well." I shrugged one shoulder. "My family has good genes."

Then she stared at me, examining my hair, makeup, my clothes—which weren't my best—and my hands.

I hid them. "Is there something wrong?"

"Yes." Her matter-of-fact tone spiked my heart rate. "I've been watching the news."

I gave a short laugh and threw my hands up. "Well, of course something's wrong if you're watching the news."

Mae barked out a single guffaw. "Now I get it. You're quick. Rex can only pay attention to surface-deep beauty for so long before he gets bored."

This wasn't that cute, and I wasn't that flattered, even if she'd meant it that way. Plus, she spoke as if his taste were all that mattered. I hated people like that. They loved to humble brag about how their child was the end all above all authority on whatever they were discussing. And at this moment, I was, at most, barely good enough for her son.

Who I'd accused of murderer.

Though my heart still denied it, and my brain was having a hard time reconciling fact from emotions, exactly like the feeling inside my chest. And you know, that Rex had never been mentioned in Kendra's journals. Not in either shorthand. But you know whose name *had* been mentioned? Julian's. And in both shorthand too.

"I thought you might be able to help me," Mae said, clasping her hands on the counter.

"I'm not really sure how I can help you, Ms. Greer. Rex and I are—"

"I know your relationship's new, and I know you're grieving." Mae sent me a sympathetic look. "I'm so sorry for your loss. But I'm worried about my son."

Rex'd told his mother about me, but he hadn't told her we weren't dating anymore. Honestly, I hadn't said much about that either, but I'd accused him of murder and I figured that was a deal-breaker.

"What did Rex say that has you so worried?" I asked.

"Nothing!" Mae threw her hands up in the air and shook her head. "He's ghosting me. And that's a huge sign he's in trouble or very upset about something."

"I mean, when I lived on my own, I didn't call my grandmother every day, so . . ."

Mae huffed. "It's not like that. He behaved like this when he got roped into military school, he did it when *that woman* left him, and now he's doing it again."

I blinked, not sure what to say, but accusing him of murder fit in with all those examples.

She narrowed her baby blues and leaned in. "You didn't leave him for Julian Christensen, did you?"

"What?" I leaned away from her. "No. But you should talk with Rex. I don't think—"

"That's what I'm trying to tell you, honey." The skin around her eyes grew tight. "He's not talking. It's like he fell off the face of the earth again, and I don't want to get a call from a reporter and I find out he's on a bender."

"A bender?" I tilted my head. "I've never known him to drink that much."

Mae's cheeks flushed pink. "He used to be a little bit of a slut."

I coughed, choking on air, because I hadn't expected that.

"But he said he was done with that when he told me about you." Mae waved her hands. "I don't think you need to worry about that. I just . . . His father isn't an empathetic man, and his brother's the same. Have you met them?"

"I've only met Guy." I hadn't meant for my voice to be that flat, but it came out that way.

"So you get it." Mae pursed her lips. "I'm just worried about all the bad press Slater Technologies is getting, plus *that woman's* body turning up, and the spotlight's on Rex. I can't even believe they had the gall to demand he step down after demanding he step up. Honestly, he had nothing to do with what's going on in the Nettles. He wanted to be a paramedic, for cryin' out loud."

"I'm so confused." I hadn't meant to say that, but this conversation was taking too many twists and turns for me to follow it.

"Alvin told me that the grenade from the Nettles was one of Rex's inventions."

I hadn't known that. I blinked, thinking about our past conversations and what he'd done when we'd found Kendra's body. He'd mentioned how he always tried to minimize civilian casualties when he was an airman and that he continued with that goal in his father's company.

My brain hiccupped right before my heart sped up to eighty miles an hour and my vision blurred. *Why did Rex try to preserve Kendra's body for the police when we'd found her at Crystal Lake?*

". . . it was all going well until *that woman* hooked her fingers in him, and he never put his application in because he could make better money at Alvin's company and move out of that carriage house." Mae was having a conversation that I wasn't listening to. "Joke was on her when she realized he wouldn't get special treatment from his father, the stingy bastard."

"Is that why Kendra left him for Julian?" I asked. "For money and social status?"

"Exactly." Mae shook her head, then locked gazes heavily with me. "I know you're Muted, honey. I'm going to tell you right now that no amount of money will change anything like that. My second-cousin burnt himself out, and he's a tech guy in Silicon Valley. He made that app that lets you do some kind of trading. He made millions, and it never changed anything for him."

I glared. "What're you trying to say, Ms. Greer?"

"If you're looking for money to make you happy, it'll only be temporary." She peeked at Eric. "It's why I want to pay for their cake. Spending it on others makes *me* happy."

"Magic isn't the same as money, Ms. Greer," I said coolly.

"Oh please." She waved her hand. "Call me Mae."

"Are you intentionally insulting me or just trying to make me feel better about not being able to touch ley energy, Mae?"

"A little bit of both." She smiled. "I just want to see who you are, aside from what Rex tells me. You gotta have a backbone in this world, otherwise all that'll ever happen is people wiping their feet on you." Her expression soured. "Like *that woman*. She tried to wipe her feet on a lot of people."

"Do you think that's why she got herself engaged to Julian —she was wiping her feet?"

"*That woman* had skid marks on the bottoms of her shoes that'll never come clean." Mae snorted. "It's exactly what I think. You know, it's ironic. I always thought of Luther Christensen as a wannabe gangster."

I tilted my head, showing she had my full attention. That was all I needed to do to get her to keep talking.

"Back when Alvin and I were dating, Luther wasn't privatized with his work like he is now. When things went south—like a bad charm or . . ." She frowned at the ceiling and tapped her chin. "There was something with a security company that caused a big fracas about where Luther was selling his supplies, and somehow, Julian turned it around for him." She shrugged. "I mean, he's only really recently, in the last ten years or so, become something of a family man. And now he's running for mayor."

"A security company?" I asked. "I thought he always worked with the government."

"No, private security, which is kind of like the military, depending on who it is, and these guys definitely liked to look like it. MiliSecure, I think. They protected billionaires. Took themselves too seriously, if you ask me."

"Huh." I thought of the journals. There'd been something in that unfamiliar shorthand that I'd brushed off as not translating correctly, but now that she'd said something, I wondered if there was more.

"All that to say"—Mae patted my hand—"is that I'm worried about Rex, but please don't tell him I came by to chat with you about him. I'd appreciate it."

I frowned. "I'm sorry, but what do you want me to do?"

She smiled. "Support him. I know you are. He keeps the people he trusts close, but you know." She gave me a significant look. "Let him really know that he's a valuable asset and anyone would be lucky to have him. That his father's company isn't the end all be all like I thought it was. And give him an extra hug from me. Here's my card." She slid one across the counter. "Feel free to call or text me anytime."

After I returned to my empty home, I checked the entry in the journal that I'd believed was incorrect in the translation. Mainly because it'd involved Julian, and when things were written in this shorthand, it was for blackmail. But there it was, JC, which was Julian, the symbol for air, and finally MiliSecure.

Googling MiliSecure returned the results that the business had folded, and the founder was currently serving time in prison for unauthorized weapon sales. I saw a thread about one of the people who worked in the company who had split ways and established his own security company, which was called HSI—short for Hansen Security Intelligence. I reached out to him and set up a meeting, citing my need for protection. I really wanted to see what I could learn more about Julian from him.

Tapping a pen against my lips, I sighed. I had most of the dots, but they weren't connecting in the way I thought they would. It'd certainly made sense that Rex had killed Kendra in a fit of rage—many did when love soured in such a spectacular way. Then why hadn't Nicholas Turner died when he tried to strangle me?

And in that case, why was *I* still breathing?

Chapter Thirty-Four

Serving in the military usually awarded people with lifelong friends and acquaintances. It was one of those pocket relationships that, if you were to find them anywhere, you could immediately pick up any conversation or friendship you had no matter how long it had been since you last saw them or where your service diverged.

I had an ongoing chat with a few other guys where we talked about the bases we served at, shared memes of things that happened on bases, or pictures of something you'd never see outside of duty. I'd never actually served with Casey, but he remained one of my best long-distance buddies. His time in Niagara had ended, and I'd filled his position when he moved on to RAF Croughton. He now lives in Oregon, and we meet up whenever either of us was near one another.

I'd much rather have this meeting with him.

Anyway, when I reached out to Mike, my old dorm mate from my first permanent duty station at the Elgin Air Force Base in the panhandle of Florida, it was like time hadn't passed for us. Our careers had gone vastly different in that I served my time with the Air Force, and Mike had the most unfortunate experience of being caught with illicit drugs and court-martialed. Then he'd served three years in Leavenworth, Kentucky for carrying enough of a Schedule I narcotic that they'd slapped him with an intent to distribute.

Discovering who was stealing Slater Technologies' secrets seemed to be the only way I could take my mind off Willa and her accusations of murder. From the pain in my heart each time I envisioned her expression when I'd saved her life. She wouldn't even let me defend myself. She'd—

No. I couldn't keep going over this. I saved it for later when I couldn't sleep.

When I arrived at the Filling Station, a dive bar smack dab in the center of the Nettles, I spotted Mike right away. He was the tall White dude sucking on a cigarette and staring at his phone. I climbed out of my car and strode across the half-paved parking lot to him.

"*Ah-wooo!*" he howled, grabbing my hand and tugging me forward like some kind of power play. "Wolf Man Rex!"

I didn't budge. Mike always liked to act like an alpha male, and he was the type of guy I didn't play this game with. Instead, I squeezed his hand. Hard. "Thanks for meeting me."

"No problem, man. We haven't caught up in a while." His eyes narrowed slightly as he matched my grip.

I doubled down. "You thirsty?"

"Always." He tugged his hand free and threw open the door.

It was a shitty bar. It was dimly lit, and the strands of Christmas lights stapled to the walls had a coat of dust and grease on them. A few men played pool in the back corner, but otherwise, the place remained deserted. While smoking indoors had been illegal for years and years now, it still smelled faintly like old cigarettes. The soles of my shoes stuck to the old wooden floor as we made a beeline straight for the bar top. Mike settled onto a stool, and the only one next to it had something spilled on it. I ordered two draft beers and paid cash.

"You hungry?" Mike took a swig of beer. "They got good nachos or fried tacos. Hey! Liz! Where're my nuts?"

A White woman with the side of her head shaved and gray hair spilling over half her face cracked a smile and slid a bowl filled with shelled peanuts to him. "Deeze nuts right here!"

Nudging the bowl between us, Mike grabbed a nut and shifted to face me. "So, Wolf Man! Long time no see. Shit's gettin' real for you, huh?"

I hated that nickname. Apparently I was a real asshole in the lab. At least, I had been. Maybe I still was. "Maybe a little."

"I see your ugly mug everywhere, you know?" Mike popped a peanut in his mouth and chewed. "You found a dead chick."

I rested my shoe on the runner and shrugged, taking a drink. "I did."

"Heard you used some kind of charm to help preserve the body." He leaned in. "What kind of spell working did you use to get that off the ground?"

"Oh, god. It's still shit, but I got some tips from the crime scene techs on what's important. In water like that, it wasn't necessary since the body'd been dumped there years ago."

And we talked shop for a while, about spell workings and enchanting, since Mike was similar to me with ley abilities. It was nice to trade stories over cold beer—even if it was the shitty kind. Liz even gave me a cloth to clean up the stool so I had a place to sit.

"So what's up, Rex?" Mike said, drawing his third beer closer. "We don't usually meet face-to-face."

I rubbed my beard, sighing. "I heard you work for one of the families. I was hoping—"

"Ah-ah-ah!" He lifted a hand at me, glaring darkly. "The fuck?"

"What?"

"You heard something about me and a family, and you thought it'd be a good idea to talk to me about it?" Mike scowled and took a pull from his beer.

My brows furrowed. "It's more about the charms being used out here."

He tilted his head. "How d'you mean?"

"So Sutter's Mill is . . . missing a couple stories now, and the result was found to be from one of my labs." I picked at the label on my beer.

"Oh." He leaned closer, lowering his voice. "Is this like a business deal you wanna strike up, or . . . ?"

It was amazing how quick he was to pick up on something, and he was the same dumbass who'd had a joint in his front pocket when he clocked in for duty at Elgin. Time definitely allowed for growth.

"Not really. I've been looking into this—"

"Daddy making you, huh?"

I clenched my jaw, remembering that Mike liked to bring up Alvin a lot, and wished I knew someone else who had this inside info. And it was I ignored the comment.

"The way the charm detonated—the blast—is strange. It seemed more destructive."

"Yeah it was. It took out part of the building across the street." Mike took my measure. "Are you working with the police now?"

"Right now?" I laughed. "No, I'm technically not working anywhere. What I'm trying to figure out is how someone in the Nettles got ahold of tech so long after it'd been discontinued."

Mike grinned. "So I supply a few people with tech not normally seen outside of service. Usually from guys who kept some before they left. I've got contacts all over, even some of those 'exclusive' people, you know what I mean?"

"Like Slater Technologies?"

He laughed. "God no. You guys are too far up your own asses, waxing poetically about how you only create weapons for the good of our country and your shit doesn't stink. You can't see past the military contracts to know when a better profit's sniffin' around." He glanced at me. "Sorry, but it's true. Anyway, what I get, I take to my clients and, if they have to, they can reverse engineer that shit pretty good."

"So if that's the case, then how have you or your clients gotten their hands on that grenade?"

"I said your company doesn't sell them to the public, not that I couldn't get any." He grinned. "I've got a guy."

"Who?"

"He just goes by Bandit, but sometimes what he sells are just schematics on copy paper, no less." He shook his head. "That's all I'm gonna tell you about that, though."

Everything inside me sagged straight into my stomach and drowned. "So we got a mole." I sighed and took a long pull of the beer.

"Yeah, seems like."

Then, a second thought hit me, and I decide to shoot from the hip without looking. "What about Ley Technica?"

Mike gave me this grin that said if he told me, someone would die. "That's a billion-dollar question, isn't it, Wolf Man? Not many people around from that era anymore for a reason."

"Do you know anything about it?"

"I'm still breathing, so no. I don't."

"That's an interesting way to answer that," I said.

"What can I say?" He laughed, spreading his arms wide. "I'm an interesting guy."

MY BADGE STILL WORKED, AND NO ONE STOPPED ME from entering Slater Technologies, but I caught a couple of people doing a double take when I strode past them. I supposed being a Slater afforded me some abilities when I was technically on leave, and they hadn't banned me from the building.

I walked down the hall toward my lab, Mike's words still rolling around in my head. Mostly, it was what he'd said about Xerox copies of schematics that lifted a red flag. When I was in the middle of creating grenades that needed to have a small blast area, I hung on to all my tracing paper to make the process of breaking down and recreating the spell working easier.

That meant I kept all the old prototypes in my office until we had the perfect working grenade. It could take me months, even as long as a year, to perfect the enchantment and spell working in one grenade—only because I had more than one job on my desk. Once I'd finished with a project, I sent all pertinent files up the chain and destroyed the early prototypes.

I stepped into my lab, surprising Christopher.

He lurched out of my office. "Sorry, I had to use your office. I hope you don't mind."

"It's okay, Christopher. You're lead here while I'm gone."

Christopher scurried into his alchemy lab, and I frowned after him. Had my brother approached him to take my job, and my catching him embarrassed him? He'd been doing my job since I had to fill in for Guy, so I felt like it was the natural course if they forced me to leave the family business.

I closed the door behind me and sat at my desk. There wasn't time to waste dwelling over why Christopher was being cagey. I needed to know, for my sake, what had happened with The Dome. Then I pulled up the logs.

With all the benefits of having Slater as my last name, Alvin was a stingy son of a bitch, and he ran the company that way. Yes, we spent the money where it mattered—the best ingredients, the best employees, the best equipment. Every lab had alchemy and enchanting tables, and some even had portable ones to move from desk to desk when there was a large order to fulfill.

But you needed to sign in to use the copy machine, and the company kept all activity logs. A lot of it had to do with the faxing feature and the federal contract we had. It also recorded all copied or faxed documents—no personal business on company time. And no one would get away with copying their butt cheeks and sending it off to the commander-in-chief ten years ago. We covered our asses and kept receipts.

I knew what grenade Mike'd talked about, as I'd worked on it personally. It was officially called something like DEF0-8797 on the invoices, but I'd called it The Dome.

The Dome unleashed a force shield in a circumference of about 5,000 square feet—something as big as a medium-sized office building. Once The Dome was created, the other spell working kicked off to unleash an EF0 tornado, which had wind speeds topping off at 85 mph. In a concentrated area inside The Dome, that caused more damage to that area.

But before I perfected it, The Dome sometimes broke, and if this happened, the tornado let loose some rope tornados, which we decided could potentially cause too many civilian casualties and damage. Sometimes, my spell working for the tornado was too powerful. It was amazing the level of damage an EF1 twister did compared to an EF0.

I had to scroll back a few years to the beginning of when I was creating The Dome. It was my first major project that had been sold to the military. I'd even signed an NDA and a non-compete form that would keep me from using the same spell working for the grenade for twenty years.

A couple of hours later, I had two names with logs of what they copied. One was Christopher with an old schematic of

The Dome, and the other person who'd copied another, advanced schematic of The Dome—Guy.

I printed the logs. I needed to review the spell workings to see which one matched the damage done to Sutter's Mill earlier this month. I shook my head. If my hunch was right, and Guy really had done this, then I needed to make some heavy decisions. But one thing was certain: my hardheaded brother had a lot more to be worried about than a few broken spirit stones.

Chapter Thirty-Five

When you make a mistake, you have to fix it. That'd always been a rule with Mimzy. She'd fixed her mistakes with me long ago, and I admired her ever more for it. Then she supported me when I nearly had to file for bankruptcy thanks to my desire for bolts of cloth overriding my decision to pay my car loan. And rent. That was nothing compared to now.

I'd made a colossal mistake by accusing Rex of murder. Saying sorry wouldn't be enough, and it was time my actions did the speaking for me. I'd uncover who really murdered Kendra Bruce, and if Rex never forgave me, at least I would've cleared his name.

Victor Hansen was a mildly bland man. I recognized him immediately when he stepped inside Jean's, a 24-hour diner on the corner of Second Street and Starglen Boulevard. He wore black cargo pants tucked into heavy boots, and a skintight black shirt that stretched over his shoulders and chest. He'd kept his brown hair cut short and tight to his scalp, and his mustache reminded me of a vacuum attachment.

His pale eyes sparkled when he saw me, and he sat across from me in the booth. "Willamina Dade, I presume?"

"Yes, and you must be Mr. Hansen." I reached across the table and shook his hand, but he pulled on it, like he wanted to kiss my knuckles. I pried it free. "Thank you for meeting me."

"You can call me Vic."

The nachos and margarita I ordered arrived, and he requested a beer.

"Are those nachos for everyone?" he asked.

"No, Vic, just for the people who arrived on time." I smiled sweetly. "Forty minutes is a long time to make a potential client wait."

The server set the beer down, and when she asked if he wanted anything, he waved her off.

"Well." He took a swig of his beer and smacked his lips. "I did some digging on you, you know, to get an idea of what to expect. Figured you'd"—he made bunny ears with one hand—"know I was running late."

I pulled out a round tortilla chip covered in orange cheese. "Let's just cut to the chase now. You used to work for MiliSecure and had your gear supplied by Ley Technica. Did you also provide protection for Luther Christensen?" I popped the chip into my mouth. It was okay. Nothing close to chorizo nachos, but I loved salty chips and melted cheese together.

"I've signed an NDA." Vic stared at my breasts. "I can't talk about my acquisitions with MiliSecure."

It occurred to me he was probably the one who turned on his boss, and he signed away a lot of his privileges to be free as long as he kept his mouth shut. I wonder whose lawyer did that. And why.

"Okay." I thought for a moment, wondering what questions he could answer. He didn't seem like the type of person who took women seriously, and the little jab about me "know-ing" he'd be late put me further below most women. "I'm trying to piece together information for a client of my own—"

He snorted, drinking more beer. "I'm sure you are."

"It's about Julian Christensen's involvement with—"

"Look," he snarled, "we don't need to bring him into this. Whatever you think you have or what you think you know, we can figure it out and decide what to do."

This was peculiar. I folded my hands on the table and put on my bland face, tilting my head slightly to the side. Then I placed my bet. "You don't want to upset him, Vic."

He stabbed the air with his finger. "Yeah, well, my NDA only goes so far, and you can tell Luther that no matter what he sends his little bulldog to do, I'm still holding to my end of the deal."

"I think you're confused about what this meeting's about. I've heard that Ley Technica provided you with gear and there was a problem somewhere that involved Kendra Bruce, or the law firm Kendra worked for."

His brows hiked up his forehead, and he chuckled sourly. "You know, whenever someone crossed Luther, Julian always made sure they regretted it. Lost a lot of good buddies that way."

"Julian got people fired?" I rolled my eyes. "Doesn't surprise me."

He scoffed, shaking his head. "Lady, you really don't know nothing, do you? All I'm gonna say to you, because I think you might need to hear this, is that once Luther's in power, he'll take care of me and mine because I know where he keeps his skeletons, and those can be real easy to find. Don't you think so, Miss psychic lady?"

I blinked, a little stunned the conversation turned this way.

"You know, Kendra Bruce never figured out how to shut

up and look pretty. Julian's side piece figured it out real fast. She still does, and I think you'd be pretty good at it too." His eyes deliberately dropped to my chest. "But when you try to pull a fast one over those people, you end up in *deep* water."

I'D NEVER HEARD OF JULIAN HAVING A GIRLFRIEND other than Kendra. Her journals certainly didn't mention it— just like they never mentioned Rex. But the internet remembered everything, and Google was my personal private investigator. While it kept returning Kendra's name, one popped up a few times on Facebook, of all places: Vanessa Hawkins.

While her profile was private, her profile pictures were not, so I stalked her page. Short and curvy, Vanessa loved to tan and dye her hair wild colors. I especially liked the shimmery greens and blues raven's wing-colored spiky bob she'd had a couple years ago. There were two pictures that stood out the most to me: one of her standing in front of a salon and cutting a ribbon, and the other of Julian planting a kiss to her temple while she grinned like a love-sick fool. They were dated a couple of months before Julian and Kendra's engagement.

707 Style was one of the older buildings in Old Town, tucked away in a market square that shared a wall with Patches, a quilting shop. But the salon was closed—on a Wednesday, no less. I took a step back and stared at it.

"You need somethin'?" someone said beside me.

I turned and came face to face with Vanessa Hawkins. Her hair caught my attention first: she'd changed the cut to a bob, though one side brushed her shoulder, and it reminded me of a color wheel for purple. Her makeup was smoky with natural lip gloss, and she wore a black peasant blouse with capris and flip-flops. She carried a paper sack that smelled like chicken.

I smiled. "I was looking for you."

She arched a well-plucked brow and flicked a cigarette into the street. "I'm closed on Wednesdays, but . . ." She studied my hair. "I recognize you."

Because my face was everywhere now with the Muted symbol on it. No thanks to Rex.

"Oh . . ." I straightened my shoulders, refusing to turn back into the teenager who was constantly teased for her body and lack of magic. "Well, I don't—"

"Julian said you might come by and told me to send you to him," Vanessa said.

"Oh he did, did he?" I plopped a hand on my hip.

"Yeah. We were on a date when this guy interrupts and told Julian not to trust you because you're Muted."

My head reared back. *"What?"*

"Yeah. Julian almost decked him, but he showed us your picture and told us you're Muted. And now you're on the news for finding that girl's body."

I lifted a hand to halt this odd conversation from going any further. "Who told you I was Muted?"

"Uhh." Frowning, Vanessa retrieved her phone from her bra. "It was this guy."

She pushed the screen at me, and a YouTube video showed William Barlow chatting on a podcast that'd aired yesterday. The man who'd abandoned me when I was two. Everything in my chest plummeted into my stomach and I felt sick, like I'd throw my heart right back up. I shook with cold rage and that terrible, terrible feeling that I'd really fucked everything up.

Rex had never revealed my status to the public; that worthless sack of shit who donated sperm to my mother had leaked it. Like ruining my life once wasn't enough.

I clutched the golden scallop pendant Mimzy had made for me as my brain reeled. William had asked Mimzy to watch me one night when I was two, shortly after the confirmation that the DNA switch for touching ley energy inside me was set to off. He never came back for me. I didn't remember my father. I had no blurry images of him or vague memories in my head. It'd always been me and Mimzy and Gramps, until it was just me and Mimzy. And *he* told the whole world my status? This felt worse than when I realized he hadn't wanted me. That was still true, but he also didn't want me to have a leg to stand on in this world. He wanted me pinned in my place, beneath him and everyone like him, suffering and apologizing for not having magic. For daring to be different and taking space he thought was meant for him.

Vanessa continued, oblivious to the thoughts roaring through my head and causing blunt-force trauma.

Her dark brown eyes turned glassy, and her brows crinkled. "I don't get it. I mean"—she circled her finger at me—"I get *why* he's distracted by you because he's a tits guy and you're, like, hot, but you literally don't bring anything useful to the table."

Whatever compassion I'd found for her snapped out of me, and I leaned back, curling my lip. "Excuse me?"

"You're Muted."

"And?"

"His father won't approve." She huffed and averted her face. "Honestly, when Luther forced Julian to become engaged to Kendra, I was really confused because she didn't bring much to the table, either."

I gaped at her. Luther had made Julian get engaged to Kendra? That didn't add up to what Julian or Suzana said. "Why would Luther do that?"

"I'm not going to help you, and I need you to leave." Vanessa stepped around me to the side door of the salon.

I followed her. "I'm not interested in Julian. I'm—"

She glared at me, and the words dried up on my tongue.

She didn't care about Kendra's death or that her boyfriend was sleazy. She loved him and believed everyone wanted him.

I swallowed. "The reason I'm here is because Kendra's parents hired me to find out what she did that got her killed."

Vanessa rolled her eyes. "I can't help with that. I never met her."

"I get that," I blurted. "But I talked with a guy who used to work for Julian and he said you knew how to keep your mouth shut. Vanessa, I need—"

She barked out a humorless laugh. "What makes you think I'd talk with you if I have a reputation of keeping my mouth shut?"

"Self-preservation?" I retrieved my phone and pulled up Kendra's Instagram and showed her. I flipped through all the pictures. "She didn't talk either. Her parents want closure, and you were called a side piece."

Vanessa's chin briefly wobbled. "*She* was the side piece."

"Look at her. She's happy. She's best friends with her mom." I decided to play dirty and picked a picture of Kendra and Suzana showing off their bracelets. "And Julian's trying to break me and Rex up because neither of them can get over their childhood feud."

She paled under her tan and took the phone from me, poring over the picture and zooming in on their faces and clothes. "Hendrick Slater's your boyfriend?"

"Yeah." I crossed my fingers, hoping this little white lie wouldn't turn the universe on me with a metric ton of karmic backlash.

"He was hers too, you know," Vanessa muttered. "I heard Julian thought it was funny, about . . ." She never finished her thought. The IG photo of Kendra and Suzana had her complete attention.

"Yeah, I know." I cleared my throat. "Rex and I sorted all

of that out. But we're in a fight right now, and I just need to prove to him that I'm not . . ." I didn't know how to say that I didn't believe he was a murderer when I was pretty sure Vanessa's boyfriend was.

"I get it," she whispered. When she handed back my phone, her haunted gaze met mine. "I think you should come in."

I followed her up the narrow staircase and into a small kitchen. She placed the takeout on the table and set her phone next to it.

"This is cute," I said.

It was a basic kitchen, but it had pops of color, and it turned out Vanessa was a plant mom. She had small basil, thyme, and rosemary plants on a windowsill above the sink, and air plants lining the walls. A succulent as big as a Dutch oven sat proudly in the center of the table.

"I gotta grab something to show you." She left through a beaded curtain down a hallway.

As I stood in her kitchen and looked around, I realized Vanessa was an alchemist. She had small pots of special brews on her spice rack, but what really gave it away was the portable alchemy table tucked under the counter. No wonder her hair color was amazing.

She returned a moment later carrying a jewelry box. She plopped it on the table and sighed heavily, her shoulders sagging as the breath left her body.

"Want something to drink?" She tugged open her fridge, pulled out a small box of white wine, and shook it at me.

"Sure."

After pulling down a couple stemless wineglasses, she split the box between us and sat down. "That engagement almost ended us, you know."

"I'm surprised you stayed."

"I didn't. I told him it was over." She lifted wet eyes to me and took a bracing drink.

I ran my finger over the rim of the wine glass. "What changed your mind?"

"He didn't give up on me?" She laughed sourly. "He told me his father was making him do it for political reasons because I was too . . ."

"Colorful?" I leaned in and smirked. "Not demure enough?"

"Ha." She flipped her purple locks and rolled her eyes. "Something like that."

"I think your hair's awesome, truthfully. If I had the complexion for it, I'd totally dye my hair teal or something."

"If I don't tan, I look sick." She rubbed her eyes; her makeup didn't smudge at all. Then, with another heavy exhale, she opened the box and pawed through the jewelry within until she set a thin gold chain on the table. "Julian gave me that when he said his engagement to her was over."

"How long did the engagement last?" I asked, wanting to hear what he'd told her.

"Five months and two weeks." She stared at the bracelet. "But the whole time, he was sweet-talking me and giving me random presents like this. He was always bad at giving gifts—except for the salon—but it's the thought that counts."

I hovered my hand over it. "May I?"

She nodded, taking a gulp of her wine.

The delicate chain slipped over my fingers, the infinity knot glinting in the sunlight. I'd seen a bracelet exactly like this on Suzana and in that picture I'd shown Vanessa. I lifted my head and met her tearful eyes.

"He gives me jewelry all the time, mostly to make up for things—like missing a date or spending too much time at the yard. A lot of it isn't my style, like that, but I wear them around him because he gave them to me, you know?"

I nodded. "The yard? Is that a strip club or something?"

She barked out a laugh. "No, it's a warehouse near Crystal Lake where he always has meetings. I got so fed up with him one time that he admitted he met with private security groups to supply them with their gear if no one else could."

A watery chill tripped down the knobs of my spine. Kendra's final resting place had been at the bottom of Crystal Lake. I stared at the bracelet in my hand. It was so simple and tiny, but the weight it bore being in Vanessa's jewelry box felt as heavy as having the breath stolen from my lungs.

"When did he give this to you?" I asked.

"Right after Kendra moved to Cyprus." A tear rolled down her cheek. "But that's hers, isn't it?"

"It could be. This isn't a unique bracelet."

"Bracelets get caught in clients' hair, and I don't like wearing them—I never have."

"He knew that, didn't he?"

Vanessa nodded, more tears falling off her chin and dropping on the table like a scattered rainstorm, heavy with the promise of more to come. "She was murdered. The news said she was murdered and never left the country. And he gave me that."

I dropped the bracelet on the table. "You gotta call the police."

"And end up like her? No way." Vanessa grabbed the bracelet and dropped it back in her jewelry box. "What I need to do is leave town—maybe leave California."

"But—"

She wiped her cheeks, then snatched my glass and took a gulp. "You gotta be careful about that feud he has with Hendrick Slater. It's where all this shit first started, anyway."

On the way home, sitting in the Malibu that smelled like baby powder and sweet peas, I wondered what to do with the information I'd learned. Mimzy would want me to tell the police, but all I had was juicy gossip from the woman Kendra had briefly replaced as Julian's partner. And something told me that wouldn't be enough. The exact same something that told me I'd need to go back to Crystal Lake.

I just hoped I wouldn't find my own watery grave there.

Chapter Thirty-Six

I wiped my sweaty palms on the seat, my car idling on a service road in front of the drive to the warehouse Vanessa had tipped me off to. I had to dig through public records into the late hours of the night until I found a warehouse about five miles east of where Rex and I had found Kendra's body.

A high chain-link fence, with an angled extension, surrounded the lot, and a lowered bar gate closed the entrance. There wasn't a guardhouse at the gate, only a badge reader. And there wasn't a way I'd be able to get my car in without alerting security, if there was any all the way out here in the sticks. I didn't want to bring attention to myself.

"What're you doing, Willa?" I asked myself. "You're going to get yourself killed."

Nevertheless, I pulled my car forward and parked on the side of the road. I twisted my hair back into a bun, not wanting it to get me into trouble, and pulled a black knit hat on over it. I started pulling strands down to frame my face, then shook my head, tucking them back up under the hat.

"No one's going to see you." That was more for the

universe than myself. I really didn't want any confrontations here.

But . . . Just in case, I dropped a location pin to Rex. Was I being manipulative? I bit my lip. Maybe I shouldn't have done that, but Trixie didn't have the bandwidth to deal with whatever could happen. I knew, despite our—I wouldn't say it was a fight. We'd simply went our separate ways and didn't talk. Because I'd *merely* accused him of murder and he denied it, and that was that. I hadn't informed the police what he was capable of doing to others that had been done to Kendra in my visions. He was an air caster, and every air caster with any kind of background like his could do that.

But it wouldn't stop me from giving him the location to a warehouse that I felt might have deadly information inside it. Deadly for me.

GUINEA PIG REX

What's this?

My heart hammered at the message. I hadn't expected him to text me that fast. Or at all; you know, that whole murder thing.

GUINEA PIG REX

This isn't a Slater property. Why are you there?

Willa!!

That bubble popped up with the moving dots and I winced. Okay, dropping a pin with no context apparently shook a hornets' nest.

It's a warehouse

I sent that quickly, so he'd know I was there and maybe

not drive all the way out here before I had what I needed—
whatever I was looking for.

> I got a tip about this place after speaking
> with Julian's ex

My phone rang with Rex's name on the banner. I should
send him to voicemail, but I answered anyway.

"Hey," I said, trying to sound breezy and not stressed the
hell out.

"What the fuck do you think you're doing, Willa?" he
barked. "You accused me of murder—"

"I'm sorry."

There was a slight pause before he scoffed. "Then I find
out you lied about your father being dead, and now you're
dropping location pins? I'm done with these kinds of games."

I winced. *Oh god. He's right.* "I can explain."

He snorted. "This oughta be good."

I closed my eyes tightly. "Look, the man who donated
sperm to my mother abandoned me when he discovered I
was Muted. I haven't had any contact with him since I was
two."

"Okay." His voice was all sharp edges, then softer. "Okay.
Why are you at that address?"

"I had a good tip."

"Don't do this alone. That building belongs to the
Christensens. Wait for me."

I smiled, a little more than relieved to hear the urgency in
his voice and that he didn't want me to do this alone. I
thought for sure he'd dropped me from his life. And for good
reason. I stared at the building.

"I'm not going to do anything stupid. Just find an office,
poke around, and go to the police," I said, grabbing my bag
and the charms I'd stashed inside. I began sorting them into
my zippered pockets.

"Going in there alone is dangerous," he growled. "What if someone catches you?"

"I still have some charms," I said. "But I'm just here to record." I pinned a recording charm to the outside of my black workout jacket.

"Just wait. I'll be free in a couple hours at most—"

"I'll be fine, but if I'm still here when you're done, I wouldn't mind the company."

"Willa, why're you doing this?"

I smiled a little. "I made a mistake and I'm fixing it. I gotta go. Don't worry."

I hung up. He called me right back, but I sent him to voicemail and put my phone on silent. He would not talk me out of this.

I tucked my purse under the passenger seat, like there was anyone out here to break into my car, but you know, I was doing it before I realized it. Climbing out of the car, my heart picked up speed, and my breathing grew a touch too fast. I took in a deep, calming breath. Everything would be fine.

Yet that little voice whispered to me I was being foolish. The charms I grabbed, aside from the recording one—which I activated now—were more for psychic attacks. I'd rely mostly on Rex's tie pin with a ley crystal and the gold scalloped shell Mimzy had given me. But just in case, I'd grabbed a smoky quartz that aided in making me harder to detect, and a defibrillator charm that I'd never had needed to use. I also wore all black because it's fashion law to wear black when you're breaking and entering.

Still, I didn't believe this would be enough. So I popped the trunk and grabbed my tire iron. It was one of those long skinny ones bent like an L, and the long end had a wedge. It'd do, especially if I was underestimated. Armed and charmed, I approached the barrier gate and hopped over it.

There were a couple of service vans parked in the far lot in front of a garage. A semi-trailer with no cab, and some heavy machinery. I recognized a forklift parked in front of some cargo containers, but that was about it.

The place felt deserted. There weren't any sounds of people working, there weren't any lights on in the mostly windowless two-story building. Though it was daytime, and the lot was empty aside from the vehicles I first noticed. I glanced behind me, but there was nothing there aside from the gravel lot.

I approached the side door and tried the knob. Locked. I circled around to the side, looking for another door, but there was the only one. There wasn't a plan if I couldn't get into the building, although the tire iron might *be* the plan and break a window. I frowned, wondering if that was the best idea. Maybe I should've waited for Rex. He'd know what to do in this situation.

But Rex wasn't here, and I was a resourceful woman. Hell, I'd convinced almost everyone that I was a legit enchanter and medium. The latter was true, but we all knew it didn't matter since I couldn't manipulate ley energy.

I found myself in front of the garage and knelt, grabbing the handle and heaving. It was locked. A quick check confirmed that they'd locked all the vans as well. Jeez, you'd think they were worried someone would try to break in or something.

Scowling, I craned my neck, eyed the upper story, and spotted an open window. I finished walking the perimeter, also noting that the cargo crates, when stacked as they were, reached the upper levels. They even had little service ladders on each one. How helpful.

Clutching the tire iron tight in one hand, I climbed the crates, then the next one that was atop of it. I crouched, walking along the roof of it, my soft-soled black sneakers making more noise than I'd expected as I approached the side of the building. There was a big metal box under the window. It had a vent. I didn't know what it was, maybe air conditioning or a generator. But because that was there, I could easily walk on the roof and probably climb on that to get to the window.

The issue was the gap between the building and the cargo crate. It was maybe a couple feet wide, and the building was still taller than the crate I stood on. I'd have to jump the distance and up to get there. Eh, I had long legs, and I was pretty good at long-distance jumping in high school, which was—I cringed—almost twenty years ago. And I'd have to jump up. Let's also not forget that I was heavier since school, thanks to my love of pasta, chorizo nachos, and margaritas.

Once more, I thought about waiting for Rex. But this feeling kept spurring me on, whispering that the time I had left to prove everything I suspected was coming to a close. I walked to the edge of the cargo container farthest from the building and back. This was doable. If I ran, it'd give me enough ground to build momentum and leap. But carrying the tire iron might be an issue, and I didn't want to accidentally drop it while jumping, so I chucked it across. It clanged on the roof and hit the unit.

When I first did a practice run, I stopped short and clutched my boobs. The next time I did something like this, I'd wear a sports bra. I walked back to the end and shook out my hands. I could do this. Supporting the girls with both hands, I sprinted toward the building. At the last second, I leaped into the air, flinging my hands before me. *Ohshitohshitohshit!*

My waist caught the edge of the building—*"Oof!"*—and my hands scrambled to keep me from falling. Panting, I grabbed the stout foot of the unit and pulled myself the rest of the way over. I rolled onto my back, breathing heavily and pressing my palms on my chest to calm my hammering heart.

I got to my feet, grabbed the tire iron, and climbed onto the unit. The top gave slightly under my weight. I turned to the window and cursed. What I thought meant the window was open was paint. I cupped my hand to my temple and peered into a dim office. My eyes snagged on the latch and saw that it wasn't locked, but it was painted shut and hardly budged.

"Fuck." I sat back, resting the tire iron on my thighs as I debated breaking the window or going back down to the ground and waiting for Rex.

My whole life, I'd depended on others for things, such as enchanting and recharging charms. Even protecting myself, I relied on another person. For once, I'd like to do something without help, and it felt like I was letting myself down. I know, strange, considering that I wanted to break into this building, but I also needed to fix this mistake I'd made with Rex, and I didn't want to wait for the police to do it for me.

I jammed the wedge of the tire iron under the window and heaved. There was resistance, so I put my back into it, and, with a screech, the window slammed up into the casement. And I crawled inside. *Oh crap.* I forgot gloves. Well, in for a penny, in for a pound, I supposed.

Despite the window being open, it was dark. I activated a moonstone, holding it up and casting silvery light into the room. Metal filing cabinets and plastic storage trunks lined a wall like soldiers standing from tallest to shortest, a chair pushed under a desk in front of a window to deeper into the warehouse, and a computer. I tapped the spacebar on the keyboard, and a few moments later, the screen woke up with a login prompt. I immediately abandoned that; I knew my limits.

"Let's see what I can find in here." I set my tire iron on top of one of the filing cabinets and snooped.

There were a lot of invoices: shipping, orders, returns,

inventory, and customer records. Right next to a subway sand-wich rested a bottle of whiskey and a soggy soft pack of Newport cigarettes. I moved the sandwich; the wrapper was wet and a rank stench wafted across my face, and I again cursed my lack of gloves. Gagging, I closed that drawer and wiped my hands on my leggings.

What felt like hours later—it was really twenty minutes and tons of invoices—I knelt in front of the plastic storage locker and undid the latches. But it was locked. However, rummaging through the desk turned up a keyring. I tried the short, stubby keys first, and it worked.

Inside was a broken spirit stone. I reared back, sucking in a breath. I hadn't expected that. Next to it was a milk crate filled with grenades that I suspected were enchanted or etched with spell workings. I saw a few sigils that made no sense to me, but I grabbed one anyway and pulled out my phone for a picture.

I had three texts and a voicemail from Rex. I ignored it and took a picture and returned the grenade back to where I found it.

But this was all the same as the cabinets. Files and folders of shipping invoices, but these went as far back as twelve years ago, and a lot of them had the MiliSecure listed as the receiver. Tons of weapons and other gear, which I guess wasn't odd given who Ley Technica was and what MiliSecure had done.

One invoice had a sticky note about the grenade and the request for more. It was attached to a copy of a spell working that, I noticed with a thudding heart, had the Slater Technologies symbol on it.

"What the hell?" I whispered, squinting closer at it. "How did the Christensens get a hold of you?"

Rex needed to see this too, so I folded it up and tucked it inside my inner pocket. I zipped my jacket and leaned farther into the plastic container when the office door opened.

I jerked back and spun, flashing my moonstone light on Julian Christensen's angry face.

"Willamina, Willamina." He shook his head and clucked his tongue. "Naughty girl."

I froze, my heart stalled and then pounded a sharp staccato against my ribs. "How—? I-I can explain."

He left the threshold in two strides and gripped my biceps, pulling me to my feet. He tugged me to him, making me trip over my feet. I pressed my hands to his chest to keep some space between us. His grip tightened on my arm.

"What did you find?" he asked.

I tried to break his hold on my arm. "I didn't find anything."

"You were with Vanessa." He tightened his grip. "What did she say to make you come here?"

"You're hurting me, Julian." Then his words seeped into my head. "She had to've told you what she said."

I twisted my arm and slapped at his forearm. He shifted forward, grabbed my wrist, and spun me around, torquing my arm behind me. I cried out.

He pressed his moist mouth against my ear. "I just read the tracking log of the enchantment I put on your car a long time ago when you became too friendly with Slater." His other hand groped my ass. "Didn't take you long to fuck him, I guess."

"Fuck you!"

"Yeah." He grunted, his fingers painfully gripping my hips. "You probably will if you're a good girl."

I kicked back, my heel smashing against the soft apex of his legs. Julian grunted again, the air whooshing from his mouth, and I stumbled away from him. He dropped to his knees. I darted around him toward the open door and—

He grabbed my ankle and yanked. I screamed, slamming onto the floor choked it right off as the wind punched from my lungs. I kicked backward, striking him somewhere not squishy. He released me and I scrabbled to my knees.

But his hands caught my shoulders, and he knocked me down, rolling me onto my back.

"You fucking bitch," Julian snarled, blood staining his front teeth from his cut lips. "No one screws me over and gets away with it. *No one.*"

I struggled, slapping his face with both hands as I kicked my feet. I caught him in the shins, since he was ultra-protective of his groin now. I screamed again, clawing my nails down his face. He backhanded me. My head snapped to the side as white pain blasted across my cheek and eye.

Then his hands were around my neck.

"This time, I'm gonna do it myself and feel you die," Julian grunted. "I wish I'd done this to Kendra, but this'll be the chef's kiss to the end of you and that mongrel."

I gripped his hands, clawing my throat while trying to pry his fingers from around my neck.

Chapter Thirty-Seven

I strode down the hallway at Slater Technologies, knowing that Guy was in the office today. He'd been messaging me about cleaning up my messes, which I found hysterical. He'd been the first suspect in Kendra's murder, so I didn't see where he got off.

And, funnily enough, being the number one suspect hadn't really impacted me negatively, aside from losing my girl. And even before that . . . Erma's death had blown Willa off course. However, I wasn't sure if this was something we could recover from. She lacked the same faith in me that I had in her; therefore, we were doomed from the beginning.

I pushed past Molly's desk.

She scrambled from her chair, attempting to race me to the door. "Mr. Slater isn't availab—"

I barged through and stopped short, seeing both Guy and our father. Alvin Slater sat behind the desk, wearing an oxygen tube in his nose that hooked over his ears and connected to the tank on the floor beside the chair. The nasal cannula was practically the same color as his skin: pale and slightly blue-green compared to the large brown age spots on his face and the backs of his hand.

Guy turned at the wet bar, saw me, and pulled down another glass. "Hendrick, your timing's impeccable as ever."

"Sit down," Alvin said in a gravelly voice thick with phlegm.

I swallowed, not because I was nervous but because his voice hit a spot in the back of my throat, making me want to gag.

I sat and leaned back in the chair. "Father, I didn't know you were coming in today."

He sneered, the breathing tubes making a small noise. "Apparently, I can't trust either of you to keep my legacy afloat." He coughed, the wet sound growing worse. Well, to some people. Those of us who knew him well knew he never, not once, had a throat clear of phlegm.

It'd been a few months since Alvin had last summoned me, and it took me longer than I'd liked to stop focusing on the snot and more on what was happening today. I also knew not to get too close. He didn't always cover his mouth when he coughed.

Guy set a glass in front of him. "We'll get around it, just like we did when your scandal hit."

Hi, it's me. I'm the scandal that happened to our father.

Alvin gripped the glass and slurped the drink. "We'll strategize." His beady, dark eyes landed on me. "Who's your lawyer these days?"

Guy moved back to the wet bar. "Do you know where you were when Kendra disappeared?" He returned, setting my glass on the desk. "And do you have receipts? *I* happened to be traveling to New York that day."

Father started coughing again, and I snatched my glass off the desk so fast that Guy smirked. Guy and I didn't have many "games" we played, and certainly none of them lasted long.

Except for this one. It'd started way back when I was a boy, maybe six years old, and Guy was in his mid-twenties. It was his engagement party to Lynne. Somehow, I ended up sitting next to Alvin at this fancy restaurant. Long story short, dear old dad hocked a loogie on my plate, right atop my creamed corn.

Guy thought it was the funniest thing he'd ever seen and teased me relentlessly about it. He'd get me creamed corn every time we ate together, which was a lot considering we all lived on the estate. To this day, I still can't eat creamed corn without thinking of phlegm. Anyway, we'd gotten into this game of placing the other's food or drink near our father to see if it'd catch anything from him. And, in a disgusting surprise, it'd occasionally worked.

The odds grew better once my stepmother passed away—only she dared to tell him to cover his mouth.

"Not really," I said, peering into my glass. "I can't remember what I did that day."

But I knew. Ever since talking with Detective Johnston, I'd been racking my brain for what I was prone to do and remembered getting drunk and having the worst hangover the next day. I was boxing up the last of Kendra's belongings that'd been mixed with mine and had plans to meet with her. When she blew me off and ignored my texts and calls, I eventually left the boxes with Suzana and Martin the following week. Now I know why she'd never answered me. She was dead.

"Get this sorted fast," Alvin said. "Hendrick, you're gonna take my place as an anonymous seat on the board. And when this blows over in a few years, you'll go back to managing production—What? Don't like what's happening, then don't fuck up like this and you can decide things for yourself."

It took everything I had in me not to mouth along with what he'd said. That line was a favorite of his, and he'd said it to both of us at least once in a meeting like this.

I set my drink on the corner of the desk and stood. "I'm actually here because I have some information about how the grenades are getting leaked." I retrieved the printout of the copy machine logs and shoved them in Guy's hands. "I think Christopher's our mole."

"Christopher!" Guy's eyes widened as he looked over the sheet and swore. "I can't believe it. I worked with him for a couple of years, and he was so pleased to be transferred to your neck of the woods."

I inclined my head to the paper. "Yeah."

"But Christopher's a great alchemist," Guy said, reading over it more. His face was turning red.

"Who's Christopher?" Alvin asked.

"My lab partner." I rubbed my beard and shrugged. "Aside from Guy, he's the only one who copied the schematic for the grenades around the time they started popping up outside the military. But Christopher's copy matches everything we've seen in the Nettles."

Guy crumpled the paper in his hand and jabbed a finger at me. "Don't you *dare* accuse me of corporate espionage."

I lifted my hands. "I didn't. Relax."

"Sonuvabitch!" Guy sharply kicked the leg to the desk. "I vouched for him! I said he'd be great to work with you."

Alvin coughed in surprise, which turned into a fit, and he spit into a wadded cloth from his pocket. I coughed too, just a little, because if I didn't, I'd probably throw up. He tossed it into the bin with a wet splat.

"It's a shame," I said. "I liked working with him. He never bothered me or asked inane questions. He's leading the lab now. So . . . I need you to evict him."

We left Alvin in the office and headed to my lab, Guy fuming about Christopher and disloyalty. I found his comments a little ironic, as Guy was always quick to throw me under the bus, but I decided now wasn't the time to call him out on his hypocrisy.

We stepped inside the lab to find Christopher shoulder-deep in the filing cabinets. He banged his head when he jerked out, his wide eyes bouncing between me and Guy.

"Is it true?" Guy asked, waving the crinkled paper around.

"What's going on?" Christopher asked.

Guy opened his mouth but I held a hand up, cutting him off. He was too emotional right now, too upset and shocked.

"It's come to light that you're taking schematics for The Dome." I snatched the crumpled paper from Guy and smoothed the wrinkles out. "This here—"

"Oh, fuck." Christopher sagged on his feet and expelled a giant breath of air. "I'm actually relieved."

"It's true?" Guy asked.

"I can't take it anymore. He gets so hostile, especially if there's a problem with the spell working." He sat on a stool and held his head in his hands. "And then he wants me to make them for him too, but not in his lab. Like I am *so* tired."

"Who gets hostile?" I asked. "Who're you working for?"

He sent me a sad smile. "Julian Christensen. This"—he waved around the lab—"is my second job. When I clock out here, I go to the yard and work on copying this stuff."

"The yard?" I asked sharply.

"Yeah. Over by Crystal Lake."

It was as if I'd been doused with ice water. This was too much of a coincidence for me to ignore. Julian, Kendra, our rivalry. And Christopher was a Christensen pawn. My body grew rigid and my thighs braced—for what, I didn't know. To leap at him; for him to attack me. It didn't matter.

Guy's jaw dropped open and he stared at him. "For what purpose?"

"Well, originally just to harm business, but now . . ." Christopher wouldn't look me in the eye. "Now it's just . . ."

"Just what?" I asked, my voice hard.

"When they found out you'd also put in for the armor contract, that really pissed off Julian, and he had me bury a spirit stone on your property months ago." He gave Guy an apologetic smile. "I'd told him about the broken stones."

Guy went white with rage, his entire body vibrating with it. "We agreed."

"I know, but I was paid to talk."

"That's why Julian convinced the Bruces to look for the spirit stone," I murmured, everything clicking into place. "Julian wanted the broken spirit stones to be found so we'd lose the contract."

Christopher nodded.

Guy laughed a little. "When it became public you could find spirit stones with that new spirit attunement enchantment, I immediately placed a blocker on the property to keep them from being found by accident."

"And Willa's séances just unraveled more and more," I said.

"I tried to scare her off at first." Guy snorted. "Threatened to Mute her if she kept it up." Realization dawned on his face. "Ha! No wonder she didn't stop. She was—"

I decked Guy. Rage over the fear I'd seen on her face, the torture he'd put her through, went behind that punch. I still owed him for when he first admitted to attacking her, and I hadn't known he'd threatened to Mute her, and he was *laughing?* And, honestly, years of resentment and anger too, if we're putting all our cards on the table.

He stumbled backward, shock on his face as he cradled his jaw and gaped at me. "What the fuck?"

"You're fucking laughing like it's a joke?" I growled. "You made her think she was drowning. You terrorized her because *you* had a secret."

"I didn't want to lose the contract!" Guy said, lifting his

hands to show they were empty. His chin began turning red. "They're already discussing voiding the contract and going with Ley Technica."

I paused, going over the past events of Willa being attacked and what Guy was saying. "So . . . Hang on. What about after Kendra's body was found?"

"What about it? I was cleared, thanks to my alibi," Guy said.

Christopher began edging toward the door.

I grabbed the back of his lab coat. "I'm not done with you." Then I frowned at Guy, something not adding up. "So, why did you keep attacking her?"

"No. It was just the two times. Both attempts were lost or blocked."

"But she kept getting attacked." I swallowed, pieces slowly clicking into place. "She could never breathe, and she saw images of floating bodies, and she'd always assumed it was a water caster attacking her because of that, but . . ." My heart froze. "It'd been an air caster this whole time."

And why she'd looked at me like I'd murdered someone the day Turner had strangled her.

"Look," Christopher said. "Look. I'll . . . I'll help, but you gotta help me too."

"Why would we help you?" Guy asked.

"Because Julian's crazy. If he finds out I told you what happened, he'll kill me."

I narrowed my eyes. "You want protection?"

Christopher vigorously nodded. "I've heard things. When he comes to the yard to check in with me, I've heard him talk about cleaning up messes for Luther in the Nettles. This is just one more." He gulped. "I don't want to die."

My phone pinged with Willa's notification tone. I pulled it out. She'd dropped a pin. "County Road 10 North Frontage?"

> What's this?

> This isn't a Slater property. Why are you there?

She wasn't responding. There wasn't even a bubble showing she was typing.

> Willa!!

I glared at Guy, feeling torn over this revelation, and now Willa was reaching out. I opened my mouth, but my phone buzzed.

PRINCESS HOT PSYCHIC

> It's a warehouse

> I got a tip after speaking with Julian's ex

"See? You don't really need me." Christopher edged toward the door. "You already know where the lab is."

"What?" Guy stretched his arm and blocked his exit.

I raised my phone with the pin on the map. "What's at this address?"

"That's the yard," Christopher said. "That's the second lab I work at."

A soft pain swiftly multiplied in my chest, and an icy bead of sweat slipped down my spine.

I jabbed a finger at Guy. "I need you to take care of Christopher."

The blood drained from Christopher's face, but I didn't waste time assuring him I'd meant the police. I banged out of the lab and called Willa.

"Hey," she answered, like she was trying to sound upbeat and easygoing, but a nervous edge clung to the single syllable.

"What the fuck do you think you're doing, Willa?" I barked. "You accused me of murder—"

"I'm sorry."

That unexpected apology surprised me. I shook it off. "Then I find out you lied about your father being dead, and now you're dropping location pins? I'm done with these kinds of games."

"I can explain."

I snorted. "This oughta be good."

"Look, the man who donated sperm to my mother abandoned me when he discovered I was Muted. I haven't had any contact with him since I was two."

"Okay." I had all this anger in me and damn it; her reason was a good one. But her manipulative behavior wasn't. "Okay. Why are you at that address?"

A small, sharp intake of breath. "I had a good tip."

"Don't do this alone. That building belongs to the Christensens. Wait for me."

"I'm not going to do anything stupid." Her tone warmed to a small degree, almost like she'd smiled or . . . something else. "Just find an office, poke around, and go to the police." Rustling came through the line in the background and the sound of a zipper.

"Going in there alone is dangerous," I growled. "What if someone catches you?"

"I still have some charms," she said. "But I'm just here to record."

She was insane.

"Just wait. I'll be free in a couple hours at most—"

"I'll be fine, but if I'm still here when you're done, I wouldn't mind the company."

"Willa, why're you doing this?"

"I made a mistake and I'm fixing it. I gotta go. Don't worry."

She disconnected the call. What mistake? *"Don't worry?"* Don't fucking worry when she's going into the lab where Julian reproduced stolen spell workings and charms? I jabbed the call icon on her contact to tell her exactly that.

It went to voicemail.

"God *damn* it, Willa," I mumbled when she ignored my next call. With my heart crashing in my throat, I placed a call to the police. "There's an emergency at the yard."

I gave the address, insisted someone was in danger, and hung up. I broke into a run down the hallway, passing the elevator, and bounded down the stairs two at a time. I wouldn't leave her fate to the police arriving on time. But I could trust myself.

Chapter Thirty-Eight

Julian's determined gaze bored into my eyes as his hands around my throat tightened. I sucked in a sip of air. Struggling wasn't helping. It was only causing me to lose air faster. But that didn't mean I was done. That I was giving up. I had things to do, like grovel before Rex and beg for forgiveness.

My only options now were the charms in my pockets, but that also meant partly releasing the grip I had on his hands. And losing whatever trickle of air I had, but I'd surely die if I didn't.

I wanted to live.

I let go with my left and fumbled with the zipper to my pocket. My lungs burned, my head ached, and blackness crowded the edges of my vision. If I got out of this alive, I would do anything to make things right with Rex. I'd spend my days shouting his innocence from the rooftops, and I'd devote my nights to showing him I'd always love him. That I'd always believe him.

I couldn't breathe.

I couldn't summon the effort to draw in air, regardless of

how little I'd get. Julian's mottled face grew farther and farther away as the night gradually fell upon me, only broken up by a tiny burst of stars. Their little pinpricks of light shone brightly between the folds of a black shroud falling over me.

My zipper gave and I dove into the pocket, grasping the charm. My thoughts grew muffled and scattered. It'd been one of Mimzy's, a mini defibrillator in case something happened so I could shock her heart back to beating. I knew now it wouldn't have helped. The stroke was instantly fatal.

I activated it as I pulled it out of my pocket, jabbed the charm into Julian's side, and shocked him.

My hand went numb. He grew rigid, and his grip around my neck went lax. I smacked his hands aside and rolled away onto my knees, crawling toward the door. My throat burned with each breath I sucked into my starved lungs. My heart slammed against my rib cage. With every inhalation, it still felt like I couldn't breathe, like my lungs didn't know how to operate. I didn't want to die.

"You fucking bitch!" Julian bellowed.

I looked over my shoulder, and a terrified moan slipped past my lips. He was getting back to his feet already. I clutched the doorknob and used it to shakily pull myself up to my feet. I had to get out of here; if I didn't leave soon, I'd never leave at all. Julian grabbed the back of my hat and my bun and yanked me backward. I screamed, my arms flailing behind me to grab his wrists.

He whirled me around and slammed me against the metal filing cabinet. Pain lanced into my back. I cried out and reached into my pocket again. That was when I realized I'd dropped the shocking charm. I was trapped; if he wrapped his hands around my neck one more time, I wouldn't make it. Adrenaline raced through my veins, and I stomped on his foot, then punched him in the gut. He stumbled backward as I felt my thumb bend in the wrong direction. I cried out again, cradling my hand.

Julian smirked. "Now," he said between heaving breaths, jerking me closer, "that I *finally* have you all to myself . . ."

"Get off of me!" I yelled, shoving at him, but he wouldn't budge.

He tore the hat off my head and yanked the bun out of my hair. "Not until I get what I deserve."

"You don't deserve me." I shoved him hard enough that I could get a couple of steps away from him.

He caught my arm and spun me around. "I'm sick and tired of playing this slow cat-and-mouse game with you, Willamina. I'm done with Slater and his damn company."

He unzipped my jacket and stared at my breasts, grunting low in the back of his throat. I cringed and jerked my arms, wanting to shield myself, but I couldn't break his hold. An acidic tang splashed the back of my throat, filling my mouth with sour spit.

He lifted his angry eyes to mine. "And when this is all over, he won't have any option other than to let me take charge when he's mayor—just like he promised when he made me get engaged to that skank." His fingers pinched my arms as he shoved my shoulders back. "I'm going to like this."

My legs trembled. "Fuck you."

He reached for my chest, but I knocked his hand away. My thumb throbbed from the contact. "Don't fucking touch me."

He snickered. "In any case, I won't be forced to marry you. Kendra had magic, at least."

"Why were you forced to marry her?" My desperate brain grabbed on to that comment. It was all I could do to stay coherent. I shouldn't have come here alone. I should've stayed home where I was safe—but no . . . Julian would've come for me there too.

I needed him to keep talking, to stall him so I could get out of here. I hoped Rex would arrive soon, like he said. He'd arrive, wouldn't he? I pulled my jacket shut, ensuring the recording charm could get his face while it captured his voice. Because it wasn't just my life that was on the line. Kendra's spirit needed this too, and I couldn't let her down.

"Because she saw me do something for my dear old dad and hosed us." Julian smirked. Then he leaned in, quick as a striking cobra, and sniffed my skin, running his nose along my neck. "And then she kept trying to use that to get what she wanted. Oh man, you don't hold things over Luther Christensen's head like that and expect to get away with it."

A strangled noise ripped from my ravaged throat, the sound leaving behind a burning pain as I shoved my body away from his. I stumbled into the desk—why weren't my limbs behaving like they should?—and pushed for the door. I had to get out of here; I had all I needed for the authorities to do their job.

Julian caught a hank of my hair and jerked me backward. I cried; droplets streamed down my cheeks as he tossed me against the opposite wall.

I shook my head and stared at him through blurry tears. "Please. I won't tell anyone. Please, let me go."

He laughed, knowing a lie when he heard one. "Kendra said pretty much the same thing, but she couldn't resist using secrets to get what she wanted."

"She blackmailed you?" I scanned the room, wondering how I'd get by him without getting grabbed again. "For what?"

"Eh, she saw me cleaning up an old mess from before dad's election to city council. Said if I married her, she'd keep her mouth shut. But then she wanted an allowance, and tried to used her blackmail again to get it, but dad had had enough." He laughed sourly. "You just don't get to do that to him twice, and she wasn't that much of a catch. So I got rid of her the same way I cleaned up all those messes."

"And you gave her bracelet to Vanessa," I whispered, my stomach dropping as the thin thread of hope I'd clung to snapped. I wouldn't be leaving here on my own today.

"She wasn't too happy about my surprise engagement, either." He laughed. "But it's fine. I'll visit her when I'm done with you."

My flight or fight response shifted with that last sentence. It was more than simply clearing Rex's name in Kendra's murder or giving Kendra's spirit peace. It was saving Vanessa now too. I shoved at him. "No, wait!"

He dodged, caught my wrist, and grabbed my thumb. I thought I'd broken it already, but the loud snap nearly shattered my ears. The bone breaking sent a wave of sharp fire up my wrist. I shouted, then screamed when the pain kept getting worse.

"Ooo." Julian grinned. "People don't really get a chance to scream with me. Do that again. I liked it."

I jammed my hand in my other pocket and grabbed the other charm I'd taken with me. It was a one-off enchantment for an ice arrow. A client had given it to me instead of a cash payment, and I'd never been able to sell it. I activated it, and it went off before I was ready. It sliced his ear, leaving behind a line of frozen blood, and shattered the window overlooking the lab. Glass rained below. He staggered back from me, touching the side of his head and glancing at his fingers.

"You're gonna pay for that, you little cunt." Julian lunged for me.

Rex barreled through the door, the crash thundering over the blood thrashing in my ears. He didn't even stop or yell out. But he slammed his hands together and slid one forward like he was tossing money. Electricity shot from his palm and stunned Julian.

He arched, the small electrical fingers roving over his clothes and the metal he carried. A strange growl escaped him, and electric blue threads roved over his clenched teeth.

"Run!" Rex barked. "Get out of here now!"

I sidestepped toward the door as the ropes of electricity dropped from his body.

Julian spun. "Talon!" He reached out, his fingers glowing with pale blue light.

Wind rushed through the room, tearing through my clothes and whipping my hair into my face, stinging my skin and eyes. It lifted Rex off his feet. Julian spread his legs and moved his arms, the veins in his neck bulging as if he was physically lifting and throwing him. Rex slammed against the desk, breaking it. I shouted, cradling my hand. The moment I glanced at the door, another gust of wind slammed the door shut. I reached for the doorknob, but the entire thing was covered in wind and kept pushing my hand aside.

The men traded blows, physical and magical. Wind with wind. My hair blew back, and I couldn't hear much over the howling gale. Rex had the upper hand, but then Julian jerked away. He reached for Rex, his fingers stopping well before contact, then twirled his wrist. An ethereal hand with eddies of currents shot into Rex's mouth. He gasped and clutched his throat. He gurgled, his wide blue eyes tracking the room as Julian began pulling the air directly from Rex's lungs.

An image of Kendra floating in the water passed across my mind's eye. The feeling of the air being drawn from my lungs when she'd possessed me and when I'd been attacked in the Flower Market.

I launched at Julian, but he waved a hand in the air. Rex's eyes bulged. Something invisible slammed into me, and I crashed into the cabinet one more time.

Rex's lips turned blue. His hands fell. He was suffocating.

I spotted the tire iron on the cabinet. Rex dropped to the

floor, his eyes closed. I snatched it up, not caring about my thumb, and hit Julian's back with it like I was batting for a home run.

He grunted, the wind dying instantly, and he turned on me. I swung again, the wedge cracking against his temple and knocking him off his feet. I dropped the tire iron and fell to my knees at Rex's side.

He wasn't breathing.

"No! No, no, no!" I felt at his neck, but in my panicked state, I didn't feel a pulse. "Rex! No!"

I covered his mouth with mine and breathed into him. Nothing.

"Oh please, baby." I said between breathing into his mouth. "Please."

Chapter Thirty-Nine

One moment I was up, and now I was down. My throat felt like I'd sucked in freezing air riddled with razor blades, and my lungs pinched when I took a full breath. Something patted my cheek.

"Rex? Please," Willa whispered.

I opened my eyes to see her leaning over me, light glinting on the tears slipping down her cheeks. I stared at her, somewhat unsure of what'd happened and also afraid if I moved, she'd disappear.

She smiled tentatively. "How're you feeling?"

The muffled feeling in my head dissipated. Behind her, El Diablo sat at the desk and washed his face, his spell workings glowing spirit blue on his massive body.

"I'm—"

Julian reared up behind her, blood smearing his face, as he raised a tire iron over his head.

"Look out!" I lurched forward, pressing my hand to the rune on El Diablo's body.

A dome slammed around us just as Julian brought the

weapon down. A crackle of energy reverberated off it, zapping him. He dropped to the floor, twitching. The tire iron clattered to the floor. Willa shrieked, jerking around, and gaped at Julian. The dome broke apart like wind scattering leaves.

"Oh my god, Rex." She turned to me, her face pale and drawn.

I gripped her shoulders, aching to pull her close, but, well, you know. Maybe it was best to keep my distance. "Are you hurt?" I gazed at her bruised neck and saw red.

Her amber eyes grew as round as saucers. She sucked in a deep breath and gripped my shoulders. "Just banged and bruised," she croaked. "I'll heal."

I tugged her to me, holding her close. Her arms hooked beneath mine and we huddled together, taking the moment to realize that we were fine. I stared at Julian, who still twitched every once in a while on the floor. What would it take to get him to confess to everything? What kind of deal would they need to make to find the truth, and would Luther even let any of it happen? El Diablo leaped from the desk to the filing cabinet and leaned down, his big spirit head phasing through the cabinet as he rooted around, his ringed, ley-energy-blue tail swaying in the air. There must be food in there.

Willa stirred. "Why did he yell 'Talon?'"

I smirked. "His familiar's a hawk. Original, right?"

The sound of a door banging in and a roll-up garage door engaging rumbled from downstairs.

"Police!" someone shouted. "Show yourselves!"

Boots thudded on the metal stairs, and Willa helped me to my feet. Not that I needed the help, but I also wouldn't push her away. At least not yet. She wasn't looking at me like I'd kicked her dog. Maybe I was taking advantage of the situation to have one last moment with her before reality came crashing back in.

"Rex," she whispered, pressing close. "Can we talk later? I . . ."

I glanced at her when she didn't finish her thought. Wrapping my arm around her waist, I nodded. "Yeah, we need to talk."

Uniformed police barged through the door, guns out. "Show me your hands! Show me your hands! Dismiss the familiar!"

We shot our hands up.

"El Diablo," I murmured, "it's time."

The racoon pulled his head free and chittered at me—I could imagine exactly what it sounded like—before he lumbered away from the cabinet and brushed against my hip as he left for the spirit realm. When El Diablo left, the jolts that were keeping Julian prone fizzled away. He groaned, rolling onto his back, his chest heaving with each breath.

Detective Johnston strode into the room, her gun drawn but pointed at the ground. She frowned at Willa and me, then at Julian.

"I w-want to press ch-ch-charges," Julian said, a tremor to his voice. "They both tr-tried to kill me."

Willa barked out a short laugh and pulled her jacket farther open, stretching her bruising neck. "He tried to kill me. I'm pressing charges."

I gnashed my teeth and jerked my head at Julian. I'd wrap my fingers around his throat and squeeze until he couldn't beg any longer, then I'd throw him in the lake. Later, after five years, I'd dig him back up and strangle him all over again. Willa must've sensed the direction my thoughts went because she placed a hand on my arm as she continued speaking to Johnston.

Then she unpinned a charm on her jacket and handed it to the detective. "He also spoke in detail about how he murdered Kendra Bruce."

"N-no," Julian said. "She's a con artist."

"Oh!" She sounded like she had a bull frog in her throat. Her hand plunged into an inside pocket and withdrew a folded piece of paper. "Julian was also pirating charms from Slater Technologies." She waved the paper. "Who should I give this to?"

I knew this already, but that she had grabbed the evidence during all this made me feel a certain type of way. Okay, I felt a lot of things right now, and I needed to get my thoughts sorted as soon as possible.

"We'll discuss that too." Johnston sighed, turning the charm over in her hand before she holstered her gun. "Let's all go down to the precinct, shall we?" She gestured at Julian. "Read him his rights and check him for his spirit stone."

HOURS LATER, I SAT IN AN INTERROGATION ROOM across from Detective Fowler of major crimes. He was an older Black man who looked like he ran off his stress, but it showed in the gray peppering his short dark hair. Johnston had exited the interview earlier to continue to work on Kendra's case once she had everything she needed from me since I'd been cleared of murder. Yay.

"What clued you in on Christopher Lindquist?" Fowler asked. Case files were stacked next to a legal pad, his phone counting the seconds of the recording.

I rubbed my beard and sighed. My throat still ached, but I'd declined a healing potion. Once I was done with all this talking, a Manhattan would soothe it just fine. "Nothing, really. I had a tip from . . ." I didn't want to immediately throw Mike under the bus, but I also wasn't naïve enough to believe I would be able to get away without naming him. I'd at least like to give him a heads up first. "I had a tip that the schematics that were provided were on copy paper."

Fowler frowned. "Wouldn't tracing paper be better?"

"Well, of course. But this is a proprietary spell working meant for the military. If it'd gone missing, the game would be up. So I checked the copy machine logs." I lifted a hand before he could ask about that. "You need to hang on to your receipts when you work with the government. And Alvin is a cheap bastard."

"All right." Fowler gestured at his phone. "Walk me through this."

I shifted on my chair. It felt like I'd been over this so many times, that I could recite it without thinking about it. "I watched some of the footage from Sutter's Mill collapsing and recognized it as an early prototype of my work. Because the dome wasn't containing the stray tornadoes, I knew I could figure out which spell working it was that was leaked. I compared the copied log to mine and discovered it was Christopher who copied it."

"Was there someone else who copied it? Why did you have to go through all that trouble?"

"Yeah. Guy Slater also made a copy, but it was a later prototype, and apparently he'd done that to pass it by the board for approval for production." I smirked. "It failed to pass of course."

"Why's that?"

"It wasn't stable." I huffed. "I was still working on it because I wasn't satisfied, but Guy was impatient to fulfill the order."

Fowler made a note and leaned back in the chair, tapping the ballpoint pen on paper. "What next?"

"We confronted Christopher, and he confessed to everything. He said he was employed by the Christensens to get into my company and steal schematics to recreate in their own little warehouse and supply gangsters with our weapons." I shrugged. "He's also the guy who planted Kendra Bruce's spirit stone on Guy's property. This was all a big ruse to kick Slater Technologies out of our contract with the military."

Fowler rubbed his temple and shook his head. "Luther's running for mayor of Starglen. Why would he risk his political career to spit on your company?"

"Look," I said, getting frustrated because I wanted to get out of here and talk with Willa. And I needed to empty the garden hose, so to speak. "I only have a theory, but it's mostly that Luther wants everything. He wants to supply the military and this city with everything they need from charms to gear to weapons. He wants to run this city, turn it into his empire, and sit on piles of hard cash."

Fowler huffed and dropped his pen. "I suppose that's one motive. Is there anything else you can think of right now that I need to know?"

I shook my head. "No, but give me your card. Guy should have a lot of info too."

"Oh, believe me," he said, plucking a card from his breast pocket and sliding it across the table, "I will talk with him."

I tucked the card away. "Is this it, then?"

"For now." He reached across the table and shook my hand. "I'll be in touch."

With that, he escorted me to the lobby filled with people waiting—waiting in line, waiting in chairs, waiting outside, and none of them were Willa. Apparently, she had more evidence against Julian than whatever she'd recorded with her charm, which I suppose had been quite hefty. I took one of the last available seats and waited for her.

Thirty minutes later, Johnston stepped into the lobby and came up short when she saw me. Then she approached. "Mr. Slater. Was there something else you needed to tell me?"

I glanced behind the detective, but didn't see anyone. "I'm waiting for Willa."

Johnston nodded and shrugged. "She left an hour ago."

My shoulders slumped, and I glanced at my phone. Nothing from Willa. Why had I thought she'd wait for me?

Johnston stared at me and sighed. "I called her cousin. She was really shaken after the medics cleared her for discharge. I thought you'd already left, otherwise I would've alerted you."

Something told me she wouldn't have, but it wasn't important. I nodded and stood. "Thanks. Oh, am I cleared to leave town now?"

Johnston smirked. "Yes, Mr. Slater. Thank you for your cooperation."

I nodded and pushed out into the dusk and the light sprinkle of a much-needed rain. I didn't have my car. It was still at the yard parked behind Willa's car. Unlocking my phone to order an Uber, I found myself dialing Willa's number.

"Hi, Rex, it's Trixie," she said.

I sighed. Whenever someone other than her answered the phone, it wasn't good. "Hi, Trixie. Is Willa . . .?" I let the question hang. I didn't know what to ask and if it was even worth it.

"No, I'm sorry. She's sleeping." Trixie said. "She was kinda hysterical, so I took her home with me so she wouldn't be alone, given what she's gone through recently. Then I drugged her."

Well, at least that explained why Willa hadn't reached out to him. "Uhh . . ."

"Relax, it was a sleep-tight potion," Trixie said. "She'll wake up when her body's fully rested. I'll tell her you called."

"Okay," I muttered.

"She'll call you back, don't worry." Then she clicked off.

Easier said than done. Willa was as good at ghosting as I was. I ordered the car and tilted my head back.

It was over. This bullshit with the Christensens and the mysteries surrounding the grenades and Kendra's death was over. Whatever happened from here on out about any of it was out of my hands.

I still felt like a sheet twisting in the wind.

Chapter Forty

A maid placed a bowl of hot fudge pudding cake with a dollop of vanilla ice cream in front of me on the long table that seated the entire Slater family. I inhaled the rich, creamy, and syrupy cake and sighed. This dessert looked sad compared to what I normally had. Against the crisp white tablecloth, it was brown on brown, goopy, and the ice cream was melting—which was a good thing. Since Alvin was here, it meant that not only did he get his favorite dessert, but Alexa had been called home so we could all be together for a "family" meal again. It was . . . exhausting. But at least I wasn't within coughing distance of Alvin; those seats of honor had been left to Guy and Alexa.

It also meant the conversation surrounded Alexa and her next course of studies. She'd decided on attending Starglen Enchanting University next, with a focus on chakras. The expression on Guy's face when she talked about her classes almost made his entire fucked-up situation of attacking Willa a small consolation prize to me.

It certainly wouldn't be enough for what he'd done to Willa, but it was a small start.

It'd been over twenty-four hours since I talked to Trixie, and I still had heard nothing from Willa. My texts hadn't been read. My phone didn't ring with her name on the screen. My heart ached.

Lynne, Guy's wife, leaned around the vase of purple coneflowers and lowered her voice. "Is something wrong with the cake? You've hardly touched it"

I blinked at her, then down at the dessert. It'd gotten soggier now that most of the ice cream had melted, and I simply lacked the desire to lift my spoon. "Honestly, I still have a headache from yesterday." I raised my voice so everyone could hear me. "If you don't mind, I'll find a quiet, dark room to sit in until our meeting."

Guy nodded. He'd become a little more relaxed with me since I decked him. By the looks of it, he hadn't taken a healing potion either, so his bruised and swollen jaw had made him more subdued. It was an enjoyable break from his normal personality.

Alvin grunted and waved me off. "Now Lex, you sure you want to study *chakras?*" he asked in a gravelly voice.

Lynne stood with me and touched my arm, a signal she wanted me to follow her. So I did. I didn't have a relationship with her. We were polite, but we were definitely more cogs in the clock than the face.

She stopped at an old curio cabinet and opened a drawer. "I want you to take that *Pac-Man* machine."

"I've wanted to take it this whole time," I said.

She clucked her tongue and passed me a tablet. "You'll be doing me a favor if you take it tonight."

Ah. Lynne was pissed with Guy. My soft-spoken sister-in-law was an alchemist. I'd bet my bottom dollar she hadn't helped Guy with his jaw at all outside of giving him ibuprofen. And what did she just give me for a fake headache? One of her heavy-duty pain relief concoctions that'd have me feeling like I could jump through a glass wall and come out unscathed.

"Maybe you let Perry borrow the escalade and he hangs out at my place tonight?" I said.

"That's a good idea, Hendrick." Lynne smiled. "I hope you feel better." Then she returned to the dining room.

"Mm." I pocketed the pill and curled my fingers around my spirit stone—anything to not grab my phone and look for a notification I knew wouldn't be there.

I strolled down the hallway toward Guy's study, making a stop at the wet bar for a Manhattan, not surprised at all that Perry set a second glass next to mine.

"Mom says I need to keep you company, but I have to work tomorrow," Perry said.

"What exactly do you think will happen to keep you from work?" I dropped an ice ball in our glasses.

"Oh, I just don't want to have a major hangover."

"Ah." I added some Starglen single barrel whiskey to the bottom half of a shaker filled with ice and eyed my nephew. "I thought you didn't get them."

"I'm almost thirty now." Perry rolled his eyes. "I get them, especially if I drink too much tequila."

Smirking, I added sweet vermouth and bitters before stirring. "Your mom demanded I take my *Pac-Man* game tonight, and it won't fit in my car."

"Oh, what a coincidence." He took the Manhattan from me and grinned. "Mom gave me the keys to the escalade."

Perry trailed me into Guy's study and we approached the game cabinet. It scrolled the top scores, all with Guy's initials rolling by. It felt like déjà vu; Perry and I standing here looking at the game with a couple of Manhattans. So much had changed since then. I wasn't even the same man.

"We're gonna need a hand dolly." Perry sipped the drink

before setting it on a coaster on a side table. "I'll ask Charles where it is and be back."

Alone, I unplugged the machine, and my lungs heaved. They'd stopped pinching earlier today. I took a long drink. When Julian had held my lungs hostage, I couldn't think. The sensation of drowning in open air had paralyzed me. El Diablo had been sitting on the desk, washing his hands and watching, but I couldn't reach for him; I couldn't save myself. I'd felt frozen, and I knew Julian had more than one spell interlaced with the spell working than he'd used. I'd never been so full of air and so deprived at the same time in my life.

Perry returned with a dolly, and I helped him get it loaded. Then he finished his drink, and we chatted about video games.

"So, you wanna head out now, or . . .?" Perry asked, setting his empty glass back on the coaster.

"No, I still have to meet with your dad and grandpa." I leaned back in the armchair. "Why don't you go on ahead, and I'll meet you there when I'm done?"

"Okay. I'll see you later." He grabbed the dolly and wheeled it out.

"Hey! Don't set it up without me," I called after him, thinking more about my wood floors than him having trouble with it. Perry knew the code to my penthouse, so I wasn't worried he'd get bored waiting.

In the dark quiet, I finally pulled out my phone. She still hadn't read my text. So I went to the news. There wasn't much about Julian or Luther's involvement, not yet. So far, the articles were focused on Willa and her Muted status. And William Barlow, the man who'd leaked it, turned out to be her father.

I ducked my head, my chin dropping to my chest as I squeezed my eyes closed. Maybe that was a sign about why she'd lied to me, and I understood why she'd said he was just as dead.

The man was trying to ruin her reputation as a psychic and a medium. And yeah, I'd cut him out too. But what else had she not been truthful about? Because there was still that little worm of doubt holding a big sign that read, "She's a liar, bro!"

The door opened, and Alvin shuffled in, followed by Guy, who was rolling the oxygen tank behind our father. They both held drinks and settled on the leather couch across from me.

"Here's what's gonna happen," Alvin said, the breathing tube making a sucking noise.

Alvin had already figured out my next steps, and I'd better go along with it if I knew what was best for me. A heaviness, stifling and obligatory, fell on my shoulders and chest.

"Guy has an agreement with the FCARL to work intensively with the city and raise funds for the next year," Alvin said.

I flicked my attention to Guy. He nodded, cradling his glass against his jaw. He seemed resigned to a lot of things.

"In the meantime"—Alvin jabbed a crooked finger at me—"*you're* going to fill in as CEO. I have a clause already drafted for the contract you signed earlier, and we just need to initial it, and it'll be all set."

I forgot all about breathing again. I gaped at them. I couldn't have heard them right. CEO? Me? For a fucking year?

"I don't think that's a good idea," I said.

"I don't give a good god damn what you think, Hendrick." Alvin scowled, then coughed into his drink. He made a disgusted noise that it caught something and set it on the table between us.

Guy swallowed thickly and plucked the glass up, setting it elsewhere. "I know you prefer building to managing, Hendrick, and I said so to Father, so we built in that you still need to produce two charms for grenades or a shield."

"It's good to keep your brain sharp in that," Alvin said.

"Hmm." I drained my drink and set it on the table. "But you don't really want me as CEO. Have Alexa do it so she knows what she's getting herself in to. Maybe she'll abandon that whole chakra plan of hers."

"Alexa doesn't have any experience yet. It'd be a fool's journey to give her Slater Technologies now," Guy said, producing a paper and placing it on the table in front of me before resettling on the couch once more.

"You'll resume your duties tomorrow," Alvin demanded.

I scowled, hating this idea more and more when Alvin made declarations like that. I knew I was thinking like a teenager again, but I hated it when he gave me orders expecting I do them like a good little boy. I hated I was good at it too.

"I was thinking of continuing my sabbatical." I kicked my ankle up onto my knee. "Maybe take a vacation."

Alvin opened his mouth, but Guy held up a hand. "You haven't had a real vacation in a while. Take a week. Think on this and get back to me."

Alvin muttered something about soft children, and this time we both ignored him. It felt good, for once. Guy must really want me to do this if he was being this nice. Plus, his jaw was bothering him and Lynne was icing him out. Why he wouldn't make his own remedy was beyond me—Oh. Lynne was icing him out on a lot of things.

I took the sheet of paper and folded it without reading it. "Sure. I can do that. I need to get home and set up my new game."

I laughed on my way out as I heard Guy notice my *Pac-Man* game wasn't in his study anymore.

Mom smiled and clapped her hands as I pressed a kiss to her temple. "Oh, Rex, it's so nice you could join us! I haven't had a date with just my boys in a long while."

Dane and Eric grinned as I took a seat next to Mom. This lunch date at Brew & Chew in the Flower Market had come out of the blue this morning after Perry had left and I was working on getting all the top scores on my *Pac-Man* game. I'd known she was getting worried about me from the voice notes she'd sent, so I accepted the date. Willa still hadn't contacted me, and this was better than only waiting for her.

"Well, I never say no to lunch with you, Mae," Eric said, grinning at her. "You look lovely."

She did. She'd dressed in her classic tennis sweater and slacks, like she'd go to a country club soon for mimosas. She waved a hand, grinning. "Thanks, honey. Oh. I arranged it with TrixieCakes to send me the bill for the cake."

"Mom," I said, a warning in my voice.

Dane shook his head and threw his hands in the air. "I gave up the fight. Mae really wants to do this, so why not let her, right?"

Mom beamed. "Exactly."

A bit of the emptiness inside me disappeared, and I realized, among the bustling of patrons in this bistro, that I was with my people. It felt good. I mean, I knew before that my mom, Dane, and Eric were important and I could count on them. But to feel it, especially after the last month, was better than Lynne's pain reliever pills.

I grabbed my water glass and leaned forward. "Hey, so while I've got you all here, tell me what you think of this . . ."

I told them about the contract to be CEO and the add-in of my need to produce two undisclosed spell workings for the company. I also talked about Guy's year of FCARL work, which I had no idea what it'd be, but if I knew Guy, it'd be something important. I'd barely thought about it last night.

They were asking for another year when I'd already given them a decade of service.

"Do you even want to do that?" Dane asked. "When you first took that job, it was just to get you by so you could find the perfect location to be a paramedic."

"If I'm honest," Eric murmured, "I don't see you as a medic. You have a taste for expensive things."

"I mean, it's definitely a pay cut, but he was studying for it and lining up tests right after he got out of the Air Force." Dane took a bite of his turkey sandwich. "Were you thinking of trying for that again?"

I glanced at Mom, but she merely ate and paid attention to the conversation. I stabbed a wedge of a biscuit and dragged it through some gravy. "I don't know. I think I'm past that."

Dane nodded. "I can see that. What were you thinking?"

"You talked a lot about that charm you made to preserve that scene at the lake," Eric said. "What about that?"

"Making charms for the police force?" I frowned, gazing past our table and out the window. It was a sunny day, and I wondered if she was out enjoying it. "Yeah, that was cool, but . . . I don't know. Everything eventually turns toward weapons, and if that's the case, then why leave Slater Technologies?"

"What about clean energy?" Dane asked.

"Yeah." Eric leaned on the table. "I saw a segment the other week about personal wind turbines, but the noise."

I nodded slightly. I'd heard about that too. Then I met Mom's eyes and smiled. "What do you think?"

She lifted the cloth napkin and patted her mouth. "Well, honey, it sounds like you don't know what you want to do."

I sighed and nodded.

"Maybe you sign that contract and take the year to think about it?" Mom suggested. "That way you have steady work and more savings to cushion whatever choice you make."

"That's not a bad idea," Eric said.

I pursed my lips and drummed my fingers on the table, wondering if it was a good idea. A whole year as CEO, with my brother and Alvin breathing down my neck.

"Would you want to spend a year in the chair your brother really wants back?" Dane asked.

I shrugged. "I mean, what's one more year there if I find out what I'd rather be doing? If I do leave the company, it'd also give me the chance to finish up the spell workings I've started."

"Honestly, honey," Mom said sweetly, "you've done enough already that I don't believe you should need to sign a contract, but if you're happy with it, then I support you." She reached across and patted my hand. "I'll always support you and be proud of you. I just want you to be happy."

Happiness was a simple wish to want for someone in life, and sometimes it took a lifetime to find.

Chapter Forty-One

A loud bang jolted me awake, and I stared at an unfamiliar ceiling. A murky brown water stain crowded the corner by the window, and a periodic table of elements poster hung on the wall next to a cozy picture of old apothecary bottles.

A door slammed.

"We're not done talking about this, young man!" Trixie yelled.

It all came rushing back. Detective Johnston calling my emergency contact when I finally gave in to the emotions I was feeling and broke down. Bawling to Trixie about losing Rex and my biological father coming back for one more throw down. Mimzy. Julian staring at me with dead eyes as he tried to murder me. And now I was in my niece's room.

I rolled over and nearly fell out of the top bunk bed. I grabbed the ladder quickly and caught myself in time. The door softly clicked open and Candi slinked in, keeping her steps soft as she approached her desk.

She glanced up and gasped. "Oh, I didn't mean to wake you."

The dull ache in my lower abdomen woke into a raging need to pee. "You didn't. Thanks for letting me crash here for the night."

I climbed down and used the bathroom. I scowled at my reflection. My mascara had run, shading the bags under my eyes, and I could see the beginnings of a nasty snarl in my hair when I noticed none of my toiletries were here. I washed my face and borrowed a new toothbrush from the linen closet, before following the smell of coffee and fresh yeasty bread to the kitchen.

Brandon sat at the table, scrolling on his phone with a hunk of buttery bread in front of him. "You're finally awake."

Trixie turned and set a basket of steaming bread on the table, covering it with a towel. "Hi, Billie."

I frowned. "Why aren't you at the shop?"

"It's Sunday." Trixie poured a cup of coffee and set it aside for me. "Ann's opening and closing on Sundays for me now."

"What?" I reached for my phone, but I didn't have it. "How's it Sunday?"

Her eyes grew large, and Brandon grunted, "I told you so" into his bread.

Trixie faced me and spread her hands. "Look, you weren't sleeping. All you were doing was crying over everything, so I thought I'd help you along. You weren't supposed to sleep this long."

"You *drugged* me?" I asked, stopping short of grabbing the coffee.

"I did it so you could rest." Trixie pulled my phone out of her flower-dusted apron and passed it to me. "You weren't supposed to sleep through a whole day."

I had a couple of missed calls from unknown numbers and a text from Rex checking up on me. Oh, no. Rex. We were supposed to talk, and I ghosted him for two days.

"He called, by the way," Trixie said. "I answered and told

him that you were sleeping, so he knows you weren't avoiding him . . ."

"Oh, my god." I didn't know how to react. I glared at her and shook my head. "You had no right to drug me like that."

"I'm sorry!"

"Is this coffee even safe?"

Trixie pursed her lips, snatched my cup up, and took a huge gulp. Then she swallowed and gagged, rushing to the freezer and grabbing an ice cube to suck on.

"Well, I guess it is." I took the mug to the table and unlocked my phone. "I hope he understands I wasn't ghosting him."

"Just say you're sorry and it'll be fine," Brandon said. "And definitely blame Trix."

"Hey!" Trixie said, crunching on ice.

I unlocked my phone and pulled up our text thread.

> **GUINEA PIG REX**
>
> Are you awake? Wanting to know how you're doing…
>
> I'm so sorry! I'm awake now. Can we meet?

My heart felt bruised and battered. I hadn't gotten to see him since I turned over all my evidence to Johnston and that other detective—I couldn't remember his name. And now I'd left Rex in another lurch, unanswered like I had when I was punishing myself for letting Mimzy die alone because I'd felt I hadn't deserved comfort from him. And the guilt of spending the night with Rex when she'd died. I'd almost destroyed our relationship.

And I probably, definitely, more than likely destroyed it when I accused him of killing Kendra. Julian's angry face flashed before my eyes, and a phantom pain pierced my lungs.

"What're you doing today?" Trixie asked. "I gotta take

Shawn to the shelter for his volunteer shift, and I thought about getting in some foraging in Founders' Grove. Wanna come with?"

I set my phone aside, willing him to text back, and sipped my hot coffee. "No, I need to talk with Rex."

Brandon stood. "I gotta work in the garage." He shoved the rest of his bread in his mouth and walked out.

Trixie frowned and reached into the breadbasket and retrieved a slice. "Are you sure that's a good idea?" She scraped up some softened butter from the dish and smoothed it over the slice. "He's dangerous."

"Rex is not dangerous." I thought of him electrocuting Julian. "Towards me."

She lifted a brow. "Okay, let me rephrase that. I don't think he's good for you."

I gaped at her. "What? Why?"

"I mean, his reputation isn't good, and I know you say he didn't kill Kendra Bruce but—"

"He didn't."

"—it's been nothing but awful for you." She ticked off her fingers. "You were strangled twice. Your gentle possession almost turned hostile. He has a history of not getting serious. And his family's a bag of dicks."

"Most of that isn't even his fault."

"Just most, huh?" She reached across the table and grasped my hand. "You've been nearly inconsolable over him, and you wondered why I drugged you? To give you a clear head so you can actually think if he even deserves you, Billie. You two have completely opposite worlds. Do you want that?"

I stared at her, a little disbelieving she was trying to talk me out of making up with Rex. Sure, our relationship had been rocky at first, but when he started just being a friend, it became so easy to fall in love with him. But maybe Trixie was right. Maybe I needed time to figure out how I felt about him.

Afterall, he still hadn't responded to me. Not that I should worry. He was probably at the gym.

And yet, he'd never turned away from me, not when I pushed, and not when he found out I was Muted. He *hadn't* leaked my status to the world, and he had come to my aid even though he knew I believed he'd killed someone.

"I really fucked up, Trix," I whispered. "He's exactly the type of person I want to give my heart to."

The silence in the kitchen grew as she gripped my hand and stared at me. She blinked and her features softened. "Then you better go home, shower, and reach out to him. You know, wear some clean underwear in case he decides to ravage you on the spot."

I snorted. "Ravage, really?"

"He looks like he knows how to ravage." She smiled. "Am I wrong, Billie? Does Rex not know how to ravage?"

I shook my head, not bothering to answer her.

"I support you, and I love you, Billie. But don't wait too long. He sounded desperate to talk to you."

"Okay, you're right."

"Wear the green underwear."

I chuckled. "You're as bad as Mimzy, you know that?"

THE DOORMAN AT REX'S BUILDING NARROWED HIS eyes. "I can't tell you if he's in or not. If Mr. Slater was expecting you, you'd be on the list of people to let up."

"Will you please call him and tell him Willa is here?" I asked, my stomach twisting and turning.

The man stared at me for a silent moment before he grabbed the phone and called. This was the big moment when I'd find out if he was still willing to talk, since he'd never responded to me in the last two hours since I woke up. Was it a bold move to show up at his home? I knew I couldn't let this play out on its own. If anything, I had the ball, and it was in my court.

"Come on," the doorman said, motioning me to follow him to the elevator.

With the doors opened, he leaned in, turned a key, and pressed the button for Rex's floor.

"Thank you," I said to him as the doors closed.

My heart pounded, and a giddiness I hadn't felt yet today tipped the corners of my lips up. Rex had allowed me to come in. It was a good sign. As the car slowed to a stop, I wiped my damp palms on my hips.

The doors opened, and Rex was waiting for me by an armchair, his hands tucked inside his pockets, his wavy hair tousled, and the silver lock of hair hanging over his forehead. My whole body yearned to run to him and throw my arms around him. Instead, I stepped out of the elevator and into his living room. A *Pac-Man* machine stood against the wall near the hallway.

I licked my lips. "Hi."

"Willa." His posture was stiff, like he was ready to fight.

I gestured at the game. "Looks like you finally got that back from your brother."

He turned and glanced at it, then nodded at me. "My consolation prize."

Oh shit. He was hurting, and I had just left all those wounds to fester and fester. It didn't help Trixie had drugged me. He had to sit for two days wondering what other hell I might rain down on him.

"So," I said, taking a deep breath. "I wanted to talk about a lot of things, but first I want to start with my father."

His brow reached for the gray lock of hair above his eye. "There's more?"

"It's just I'm sorry you found out he's still alive the way

that you did. I honestly didn't think he paid any attention to my existence. I think he saw my name and realized I was . . . misleading the public about my ley abilities and wanted to set the record straight."

He nodded. "Yeah. I think he's been texting me, but I blocked his number when he started talking about payments. I thought it was a scam."

I felt the blood drain from my face and gasped. "Oh, my god!"

"Yeah." He flashed me a sad smile. "I had no idea what it was about and too much other stuff to worry about. Guess he went to the news instead."

And yet there was still all this space between us, and the only way to move forward was to apologize. I didn't understand why it was so hard. I was afraid he wouldn't accept it and kick me out. Or he'd accept it, but he wouldn't want to see me again. I guessed I was prolonging the inevitable.

I ran a palm over the top of my head and released a long breath. "I'm sorry I blamed you for Kendra's death and chose to ignore everything you've said about it."

A wrinkle appeared between his brows, and he nodded. "It definitely sucked."

"Don't be light and easy with this, Rex." I licked my lips. "I accused you of something awful that I knew, deep down, you wouldn't do, but I . . . panicked."

His upper lip curled, and his eyes narrowed. "You knew I wouldn't murder someone, but you accused me anyway because you panicked?" He laughed and shook his head, taking a step back. "What the fuck?"

Ice flooded my veins, and my vision turned blurry. I rapidly blinked my eyes. I didn't want tears to enter the moment, not now. "Yeah, I panicked, Rex. I panicked because someone tried to kill me in the *exact same way*. So excuse me for jumping to conclusions."

"You wouldn't let me explain," he said tightly. "If you'd listened to me, none of this would've happened."

"I was panicking, Rex. People have been psychically attacking me, and that man tried to kill me. Then you barge in and take him out the same way I was attacked. You practically confessed."

"Because I used magic to knock him unconscious the same way you've seen someone die in a vision." He let out a long sigh and shrugged. "I see why you might make that first snap assumption, but you wouldn't listen to me after that. It hurt, Willa. I'm not gonna lie about that."

Tears welled in my eyes again. "I'm so sorry, Rex. I'm so sorry I hurt you." I took a step toward him, but the distance between us still felt like a chasm. "Everyone said I was wrong about you."

He pursed his lips, finally breaking eye contact, and peered out the giant windows overlooking the city. "Yeah, well, not everyone realizes someone can change."

I frowned, wishing he'd look at me. "Everyone said I was wrong to think you'd hurt someone, let alone kill them. But you tried to preserve her body, and that didn't make sense if you'd killed her"

His head jerked back in my direction, the sullen black expression on his face breaking like the day he'd given me the sun. He took a step toward me. "You're not talking about my past partners?"

I matched his step, wanting to eat up all the space between us but afraid to push for too much too soon. "No. After your mom came by TrixieCakes, I read over Kendra's journals again."

"Wait." He held a hand up, confused. "You met my *mom?*"

"You stopped talking to her and she was worried." I swallowed. "She didn't know that we . . . That I'd . . . blown up our relationship."

Then I launched into how things with Kendra's journals didn't line up. Mostly because he'd never been mentioned, yet Julian had, but not in the right shorthand. By the time I'd finished explaining that, we were standing close to one another again. I could reach out and touch him, but I was afraid he'd pull away.

"In the end, all I could think of was clearing your name." Then I gazed up at him, hoping he could see that I knew the truth, that I knew who he was. "I know I hurt you, and I know what I did was unforgiveable. I'm so sorry. I know who you are. You're kind, and sweet, and caring. You'll do anything to protect who you love, but I understand I blew it—"

"Hey, come on, now." He caught my chilly hands with his warm ones.

"No, let me finish. Please." I gripped his fingers tightly and swallowed. However, warmth burst in my chest, rapidly spreading tingles to my stomach. "I messed up, Rex. I just want you to know that even though what we had was temporary, it was beautiful, and I will always regret what I did to lose you."

He stared at me, beautiful blue eyes wide. I could see the wheels turning in his head. Maybe I hadn't ruined everything completely just yet. I squeezed his hands, but my heart pounded. I'd spend the rest of my days making it up to him, and I'd never make a decision about his character again without talking to him first. But if what we had really was fleeting, then I was glad that I'd had that.

He dropped my hands and closed the distance between us. "Temporary . . . You've said that before. That everything except magic was temporary. You're wrong. Even magic is fleeting,"—he cupped my jaw—"but how I feel about you is never temporary, Willamina."

"Rex?" I whispered, scanning his face. I rested my hands on his chest, my fingers curling into his shirt. I felt numb, and this moment was surreal, as if I were standing beside us watching. "You still care for me?"

"I love you," he said hoarsely. "I've loved you from the moment you made me your guinea pig, and I still love you today."

My hand slipped to the back of his neck as I rose to my toes and covered his mouth with mine. The kissed bowled me over. All I could concentrate on was Rex in my arms and our mouths moving together as if we were starved for one another.

I leaned back, my breath uneven and my heart pounding. We kissed again, slowly, more deeply. I hadn't said a word about love—I was speechless—but I hoped he tasted it, felt it in my every movement, my every breath. Then he broke the kiss slowly with small kisses until he rested his forehead against mine.

"I love you, Rex," I whispered, my voice husky as my fingertips stroked the back of his neck. My legs trembled. "I love you so damned much. If you let me, I'll spend every day for the rest of our lives making it up to you."

"Then I'll spend every day for the rest of our lives forgiving you." He stroked my cheek. "Don't live in the past so much with this, okay, princess?"

I swallowed hard, slowly shaking my head. He had to know it was eating me up I hadn't believed in him, that I wanted to punish myself for it. I was fantastic at that too. Almost better than pretending I could touch ley energy.

"How about for the next week," he said, "you do everything you need to do to make it up to me, then after that, we focus on the future?"

He smiled, and I knew right then that if I saw that smile every day, there'd be no terrible past between us.

Epilogue

ive months later . . .

Dane and Eric stood at the cake table, beaming from ear to ear. Before them sat a four-tier wedding cake with crystals resembling obsidian flowing out of it. The top of the cake had a large black lotus. The stark black and white cake was gorgeous. After they'd cut the cake, Dane grinned at his new husband, grabbed a slice, and fed Eric a bite. Then swiped frosting on his nose, much to Eric's surprise.

To mine as well, since Dane wasn't the "fun" one.

Rex laughed, his arm wrapped around my waist, and toasted the newlyweds. "To Dane and Eric, my best friends got hitched!"

Everyone cheered, and the DJ started playing music again while the staff cut the rest of the cake and set out pieces of it on plates. Trixie, Brandon, Candi, and Shawn were chatting at a table. Even though at first Trixie had declined the wedding invitation, thanks to the short-lived war Candi had tried to start with Dane, but Dane had insisted.

Now Candi used social media to advocate against those

kinds of wars. Shawn was a little harder to crack. While he seemed regretful of bullying, he also didn't enjoy apologizing for it either. Trixie grounded him for three months and made him volunteer at a pet shelter for a year.

Rex pulled me out onto the dance floor and swept me around, grinning at me. I caught sight of Mae watching us.

"Your mom's looking at us like she has plans," I said.

He grinned. "I have plans."

I lifted a brow. "For what? Your new job or me?"

"Yes." He twirled me, then pulled me close.

He'd decided to sign the contract, letting Guy know exactly how he planned to spend the year. At first, Guy tried to talk him out of it, but that chatter slowly died down. His brother also seemed to enjoy his work with the FCARL. I even saw him smile the other day.

I swayed against Rex. "Well, I have plans too."

"Do you? What're those, princess?"

"New drapes in the bedroom. The ones you hung don't block out the sun that much, especially in the summer. It's too early."

We'd been living together in his penthouse for a few months now. It was new, yet it felt natural. It'd taken that long to do the estate sale and then put the house on the market. While Mimzy had left it to me, it just wasn't viable for me to keep it.

After the arrest and the story breaking, demand for my services skyrocketed. I'd debated whether I wanted to delve into medium work again. I loved it. I loved working with crystals and looking into people's pasts and futures and giving them advice. I hadn't loved the danger, even if it had brought me to Rex. He encouraged me to keep at it as long as I agreed to no gentle possessions. I was happy with that condition, and I made the Ethereal Eye website public once more.

The song ended, and Rex had just led me out into the

hotel lobby to get some fresh air, when his phone rang. It was his brother.

"Hmm, should I ignore it?" he asked thoughtfully. "Work-life balance."

"Maybe it's about your new scanner," I said.

He rejected the call and tucked the phone away. "Not important enough. Besides, I've got to go in Monday to work on the scanner, anyway."

"What if it was about the contract?" I asked.

He frowned, then shook his head. "That's signed and taken care of. And the government already received their first order."

The military had kept the contract with Slater Technologies since they were the company with the lesser scandal. Rex glanced over my head and his eyes widened. "Oh. It's probably that."

I turned and saw on the TV that Luther Christensen was walking down the steps of the Starglen courthouse, and the banner read he'd made bail for the upcoming trial. However, Julian remained in prison. A week after evidence of corporate espionage and black-market dealings came to light, Luther withdrew from the race for mayor. During the trial, I expected Julian to point fingers at his father. Luther had been the one to force Julian to clean up his messes before going the public servant route. All that was required of me, Rex, and his family was to testify. I dreaded it, but I was also glad everything would finally be resolved.

Christopher was also awaiting trial, but last I heard he was tucked away safe and sound. Apparently, Luther still had a long reach in the Nettles even with Julian sitting behind bars. I don't know what happened to Vanessa. 707 Style closed, and her number had been disconnected. I worried about her, but I didn't know what else to do. The last time I tried to help someone find a missing person, I met the love of my life.

And I could only handle one of those.

Rex led me down a hallway tucked behind reception, then spun and pushed me against the wall. "Wanna make out?"

His laughing blue eyes and killer smile had me giggling. I tilted my face toward his. "Wild horses couldn't drag me away."

Acknowledgments

I'd like to give a huge shout out to Matt Dewar. Your comments and insights to this story has been so helpful and supportive. Your encouragement to kick things up a notch are always well thought out and welcomed. I can only go further with your words.

To my editor and friend Lori Diederich! You are wise and beautiful. There's too much to say and thank you for and we don't want to keep adding pages to this book.

Thanks so much to Auren, my secret sister who made me hug her when we first met. I was okay with waving, but she's a hugger. Your thoughts were excellent.

A special thanks to Kimberly and allowing me to pull her back in to my stories and talk about them with me. Thank you for all your help!

Thank you to Kayle Crosby for taking a chance on me. Your comments were really helpful.

An extra special thanks to my husbandface for letting me talk his ear off. And, you know, being super nice and supportive when things looked too dark. Or there's math involved.

Last but not least, to Herr Tintenfleck earnestly watching the cursor while I listened to the book, reminding me how important it is to follow along. And showing off your bum to the zoom call. They really likes your blacks and whites.

About the Author

AE McKenna is an Urban Fantasy and Paranormal Romance author who enjoys writing books with healthy relationships and interesting magic systems. She's not too shabby with fight scenes, either.
She lives in the Midwest where she drinks beer, eats cheese, and pets cats. All at the same time.

www.ingramcontent.com/pod-product-compliance
Lightning Source LLC
Chambersburg PA
CBHW020324010826
48973CB00005B/1113